EDEN

EDEN

S.T. ANDERSON

DOGMA SCHOOL OF MAGIC & FLIGHT

Published by Winters Publishing, LLC
2448 E. 81st St. Suite #4802 | Tulsa, Oklahoma 74137 USA

Book design by Christina Hicks Creative
www.christinahickscreative.com

Published in the United States of America

ISBN: 9781947426931

TABLE
OF CONTENTS

CHAPTER ONE
The Chosen One

Life is short, death eternal. What you do in life will echo thru eternity.

She checked her watch yet again: 6:56. "Come on," she murmured, as if complaining could rush time. From deep in the woods came the snap of a branch and the sound of footsteps. A wave of nervousness washed over her. Taking a deep breath, she pulled her baby tighter to her chest. Her eyes grew wide as her gaze swept the forest, searching for the source of the noise. The full moon cast long, dark shadows across the thick wooded area, while the trees danced in rhythm with the light breeze. "Probably just a squirrel," she slowly exhaled. "Only a handful of people even know this place exists, and none of them know I'm here." She threw another glance into the forest, a tense smile played on her lips. "All part of Gabriel's plan."

She looked at her watch. "Just three more minutes to go." Recalling her endless hours of training, all the strain, and secrecy, she wondered: Why so secret? Why couldn't she tell anyone? Not even her mom knew these strange circumstances. All of this for what might or might not happen in the next minute.

The baby squirmed in her arms, and then cooed, "Mmmmah."

"Don't worry, Mom's got it all under control" she lied, looking into her baby's dark brown eyes. "Mommy's got you, Jason." Jason was her whole life, and had been for what would be a full year in just minutes. Everything she had endured had been for Jason, whom Gabriel had referred to—ominously—as the "Chosen One."

She wished Jason's father could be here. He had left a few weeks after Jason was born, and never returned. If it hadn't been for Jason, the pain would have been unbearable. The training allowed her not to dwell. She had to focus for Jason's sake, but still, she missed the father of her child (especially now, when she needed him most). "Don't have time for those thoughts," she reminded herself, shaking her head as if to rid herself of a bothersome fly. "I have to stay focused." She looked again at her watch, "COME ON." Still over a minute left. The wait was taxing her patience.

What was going to happen to Jason? Why so much training?

When she thought about what she learned to do, what she could do... She had performed feats she once thought impossible, what everyone, any other human, would think impossible. She had to learn immediately that "impossible" was a forbidden word, neither to be spoken nor thought. "The only limits in life are the ones you put on yourself," she could almost hear Gabriel say—a phrase he had said to her well over a hundred times. "It is only impossible if you think it is." "All things are possible!" *Gabrielisms*, she liked to call them. All these phrases he would speak or, one might say, *drill* into her day and night.

"Where is he?" she thought, while a rope of frustration tightened within her. Almost two years of training for this moment, and Gabriel's nowhere to be seen. Any other time she couldn't have managed to get rid of him. Her routine was practice, practice, more practice, and then some more practice. "Now when we get to game time, no coach," she grumbled.

Another noise forced her to whip around. Jason let out a gasp. She starred carefully into the darkness, then gave her head a shake. "Just my imagination." Turning back around, the old cabin on top of the hill caught her eye. From this distance, she was barely able to make out the old sign Hagen nailed above the door.

She let out a small sigh, wishing she didn't have to be so far from the cabin to see the sky.

Jason stirred, reminding her of the task at hand. "Must be getting close," she thought as she glanced at her watch. "Less than a minute. It's game time Jason." Their eyes locked, and Jason seem to be studying her for a moment. She raked her hands thru his brown hair. A smile began to tug on his lips.

7, 6, 5, 4, 3… She looked up, 2, 1… A burst of light flashed across the sky—there and gone, in the flicker of a moment. She searched the sky; her gaze then swept the horizon. Her brow narrowed as she looked down at Jason. "That was it, all that work and a stupid light that is gone in like a second. That is it? GABRIEL! You have to be kidd…" and then her voice trailed off as thunder clamored from the sky. Her eyes widened in alarm as she looked up. A bright light soared from the spot where the comet had disappeared. The light shot toward them like a cannon ball from a cannon. It plowed into them forcing her to shuffle a few steps backwards.

Her gaze snapped down to Jason— She squinted as if staring into the sun. Jason was absorbed by the light. Though she could still feel him in her arms, the blinding glow forced her to finally look away. Then a small pop— and with the same suddenness that it had come upon them, the light returned to the sky.

She blinked hard, then looked back to Jason. An unnatural green glow from his hand pulled her gaze. Then it disappeared. She wasn't certain, but it looked like a ring.

Another noise from the forest made her chest tighten. She drew a ragged breath, then slowly turned away from Jason and stared into the trees.

 "Let's get back to the cabin" her voice cracked. "Gabriel, Gabriel? Come on, this isn't funny." her voice trailed off.

This wasn't Gabriel. A large, dark, cloaked figure glided toward her, like a cloud moving across the sky. She stilled her breath, then took deep breath and held it for a second. A tickle of fear ran down her spine. "Fear has no part of me!" She shook her body feeling the fear come off her like water from a dog.

The figure stretched out both its arms, and two massive Hell hounds appeared. Each fiery red dog had three enormous heads attached to a body the size of a horse. As the dogs whipped their heads around, she could see their razor-sharp teeth reflecting the moon light.

These dogs were bigger than the ones she had practiced against. In fact, these dogs made the practice dogs look like puppies. "Should be no problem," she reassured herself. Jason, too, had been part of the practices for the last year. Gabriel made it very clear that even Jason's fear could be used against them. After a year of practice, it was no surprise that Jason didn't seem to give notice to the ravenous beasts charging toward them.

The dogs, in a blaze of fire, teeth, and vicious growls, were now less than fifteen paces away. "These things are fast!" She gritted her teeth, and stretched her free hand out—

--and both Hell hounds evaporated into smoke and ashes.

"Gabriel has taught you well," came a low, dangerous voice. "Of course, he has only extended your life by a few minutes. Steals two years of your life, and in return you get just a moment to witness my great-ness." He released a laugh, the sound as sharp as a sword. "Well, maybe it was worth it."

The dark being continued to glide closer emerging from the shad-ows. He was well over six feet tall, with a square, pronounced jaw sticking out from under the hood. Under the dark folds of the cloak, two eyes glowed fiery red, with black soulless centers.

The figure stopped, some fifteen paces away, and slowly removed the hood from its head.

She let out a small gasp, as cold fear washed over her. "No! No fear!" she hissed to herself.

Her eyes narrowed as she regarded him. He wasn't human, but what looked like a burnt shadow of a man. His skin looked like black crepe paper that continued up past his long forehead and around his bald head. She could see a glow in the creases of his skin, as if a fire burned within him. On top of his head sat two goat-like horns. Where his nose should have been, two snake-sized slits moved with the rhythm of his breathing.

She stepped half a space back, and readied herself. Their gaze locked, and his lips stretched back showing his blackened teeth. He stretched out his hands. "It looks like you won't get all of your two extra minutes," his words wrapping around her like a snake around its kill. Red sparks shot from his hands striking her in the chest. Electricity cracked and snapped lighting up the air around her. Surprisingly, it tickled. She let a smile crack thru her determination. He returned a half smile and the force simply dissipated.

"Well, well. Gabriel has taught you to control your fear. This might just last all two minutes, after all." His voice then dropped to a whisper. "Of course, Danielle, if you only knew what I had in store for your baby, fear might seem like a good idea."

How did he know her name? Who was this? She looked closer at him, looked beyond the shadow of a man. And then it dawned on her. Her heart began thundering in her chest. They stared at each other in silence, she forced herself to hold his gaze. "It's you!" she said, breaking the silence like the sound of an executioner's axe.

A storm of emotion moved through her; her thoughts swept in and out of her head like a swarm of bees, each thought stinging her mind. "Your thoughts can be your greatest weapon, or your greatest enemy. Control them, or they will control you." Another Gabrielism flashed into her mind, a fraction too late.

"There we go, Danielle. Yesss, yesss, let the fear consume you." he purred. She grappled for what to say next. Then she was struck with an incredible force. It was a fire burning inside of her. The flames writhing to scorch through her flesh, desperately trying to reach outside of her body. "Noooooo!" burst a scream of agony.

"Yes, Danielle. Yes…" the figure began to move closer, the heat intensified with each step.

She wanted the pain to just end. For an instant, she welcomed death; invited it in. And then, from a far-off place, she heard a baby's cry. "Jason, no not Jason!" Anger and courage rose up inside of her. "Not my baby!"

She forced herself to picture the area in front of the cabin. It was a stretch for her, but she could do it. She had to block out the pain, block out the fear, and focus on those steps. The pain now like an anvil pulling her to the ground. But she had to: she had to make her mind envision it. And then it happened.

With a sound like a whip cracking, all the air was sucked from her lungs; everything went bright white. She seemed weightless, as if she did not exist. She felt as if she was light being shot from a flashlight. Then the light was gone; her empty lungs took an enormous breath of air. She opened her eyes— and she and Jason were on the porch.

"Danielle, now we are simply wasting my time." His words seem to slither from the bottom of the hill. She swung open the screen door, and then the huge ornate wooden door. She bolted the lock, grabbed a rocking chair from the entrance room and pushed it in front of the door. "Oh yeah, this will stop him." She let out a nervous laugh.

She turned left, went through another doorway and shut and locked this door. Danielle looked around the small dingy room, lit only by a single lamp in the corner. In the back was Jason's crib. She rushed over and laid him down. He stood up and began to fuss. "Mommy's got this. Everything is going to be all right." She wished she sounded more confident.

Danielle reached into a small grapefruit-sized sack wrapped around her waist and pulled out a golden bow as tall as she was. She glanced back at Jason, whose expression seemed to be saying, "How did you pull that out of that tiny bag?" Danielle smiled. "I know, I know, still freaks me out." She reached back in the sack and pulled out three bright red glowing arrows. She notched one of the red arrows on the string as quickly and effortlessly as if she were pointing her finger. She aimed at the door to the exact spot his heart would be once the door was gone. "Stop this!" she thought.

She heard a *fffft* sound. "There goes the front door, and that awesome barricade I put up. Never thought he could get through that." Danielle exhaled as she stared down the shaft of the arrow. She noticed a small red circle appear in the center of the door, glowing with intense heat. The circle began to expand outward, until the door shone like hot coals in a fire. Then a *fffft*, and the door burst into flames, flared and tumbled to ash.

A large shadow appeared in the doorway. As quickly as she released the first arrow, she grabbed and knocked, pulled back, and released a second, and a third. Three arrows flying toward the heart of the target, each arrow less than a foot behind the last. Right before impact, every arrow simply turned to a glowing dust, fluttering to the floor.

"NO, NO, that is impossible!" Her expression fell. She took a moment to find her voice. "Those arrows are unstoppable!" her gaze snapped to his. He let out a deep throaty laugh.

"Impossible? That seems so hypocritical. Isn't your master, Gabriel, the one who says, 'Nothing is impossible, unless you believe it is impossible'?" He did a poor imitation of Gabriel. "Were the arrows Goblin-made?"

"No, no, they were…" she took a long pause. She looked as if she were struggling to solve a complex math equation. Finally, she stuttered, "Forest… elves, enchanted…, they can't…, they are indestructible."

"Ah, just like Gabriel to give you false hope. Where is the winged wisdom-giver anyway?" he asked, searching the room with a mocking air. "Danielle, did you really think you had a chance against, me? Lord Brone, the most powerful being heaven and earth has ever seen? The greatest Angel of all time?" His unpleasant smile widened.

She forced herself to hold his gaze as he began to brush his index finger across a rocking chair. Disappointment was now galloping thru her. Then a hateful smile snaked across his face. "The simple mention of my name brings all to their knees. What I can do would surely impresses even the Almighty. And now," his speech slowed, "I will take both your lives." The chair shot from his hand, shattering like broken glass against the wall. He took a step towards her. "I will return to Eden, retake my world, and then, with my army, come back here and destroy this sad, pathetic world." The poison of his words slid thru her.

He stretched his hands out again. Danielle, in a last-ditch effort, focused on the massive refrigerator in the kitchen. The appliance ripped from the wall and soared toward Brone. On impact, it merely dissipated into a glowing dust. He seemed amused, like a kitten had just showed its claws. "Still you have hope? I must admit, I admire that, Danielle." Brone paused, his gaze sweeping her body. His eyes narrowed, impatience washed across his face. They stood in deafening silence, he then hissed out a breath. "Let us not waste any more time."

Once again, the pain hit her like a ton of bricks. The fire consumed her from the inside out. Time to let go. But then, why all the training? Why did Gabriel waste two years of her life? Was it like Brone said: for two extra minutes? Why the secrecy if she was just going to be discovered? Where was Gabriel? Why be chosen if it was only for a few minutes? Questions raced through her mind. Why have a second hidden place, a place no one knew about, even Gabriel did not know where this place was? Gabriel had been very specific about this. Each night he had made her focus and see it.

The place came from the summer of her fourteenth birthday. Her family vacationed in Falmouth, Cape Cod, right on Carriage Shop Road. She and her mother had a huge argument one morning. Danielle stormed out of the house determined to teach her mother a lesson. She walked four miles down to the pier, and bought a ticket on *Highline Cruises* to Oaks Bluff on Martha's Vineyard. After a one-hour ferry ride and few hours touring the town, she ended up at the Ginger Bread cottages at the old Methodist campgrounds. She went from house to house to house. She must have walked around and studied each house a dozen times. They were beautiful, each one in their own way. She found herself lying in the grass, looking up at the heavens thinking what it would be like to grow up in one of those houses. No more screaming and yelling, no more drunken father out of control. What a life that would be: a life she wanted for her son. Later that evening, she boarded the ferry and went home, never telling anyone of that day

That place was where she wished she were right now. She wished Jason could see it, could grow up there. And then it hit her. "What if? No, it's impossible!" she told herself. "But nothing is impossible," a louder voice echoed in her mind. But she could barely appearate up the old road, let alone two-thousand miles away. "But I have to try, for Jason," Danielle argued with herself. "No! Not try. I will."

She fought to gain a sense of consciousness and found herself on the floor. She reached back to where she thought the crib was. The burning intensified, and she realized that Brone was losing patience, that her time was drawing close, and that if she didn't act now, she never would.

Danielle threw her arm up onto the crib. Jason seemed to latch onto her shaking hand. Danielle took a moment to feel his touch for the last time. She gave his hand a squeeze, then she began to picture the spot in the grass by the largest of the cottages. She heard a thunderous roar come from Brone as the pain escalated unbearably. "No, come on, for Jason," she screamed to herself. She could see it now; she forced herself to picture Jason amidst the cottages. Now she had to know he was there. It had to be a fact in her mind. The pain was drowning her. She couldn't breathe. It suddenly went beyond her threshold, and then— it was over. The pain vanished, but she was still there. She hadn't left. "It...it didn't work," the words escaped her. Her body felt light... as if she were weightless. She had never experienced anything like this before: it was happiness so intense that she felt like screaming with joy. She had no fear. She had no worries. She was just— happy.

Danielle hovered above the whole scene, looking down. Then the realization hit her.

She had died.

But if this was how death felt, she was not upset, nor worried about Jason.

"Aaaggghhh!!!" She heard a dark scream of rage come from below. She stared at her body, lying on the floor. She dared to look into the crib. The child, the Chosen One—Jason—was gone. Brone, in a heat of rage, was destroying everything in sight.

Danielle began to rise like a balloon that had just been set free. She drifted higher, and higher her speed increasing with every moment. Then came a blinding flash, and she stopped in an unreal light. It was as if Danielle *was* light.

Then she heard a deep calming voice say, "Well done, Danielle, well done."

"Gabriel, is that you? Get where I can see you!" she spat through gritted teeth. "Why didn't you tell me I would have to appearate Jason there?" Frustration echoed in her voice. Then with a small pop, Gabriel was standing before her. He was enormous, at least two feet taller than Brone, with long gray hair and a flowing beard that hung to his white cloak. He had piercing blue eyes and a masculine nose.

"Because it is impossible," Gabriel's deep calming voice seem to hang in the air. He offered her a grin.

"What do you mean impossible? I just did it." a smile tugging at her lips.

"Oh, yes," Gabriel's smile grew, "proving yet again that what is impossible and possible is determined by your beliefs, not by the circumstances, or certain laws of physics."

"Why not practice it? Why not tell me that I would need to do it? Why burden me with so much anxiety!" she said, her words clipped.

"Had I told you that it would have to be done, it would have given you time to come up with all the reasons why you couldn't do it. You would have failed before you ever tried," His blue eyes widened. "You didn't have time to doubt, didn't have time to come up with all the reasons why you couldn't do it. You simply had to do it, and failing was not an option. You believed it could be done, and your faith made it so." Gabriel paused for a moment, "It's time for you to go on ahead. There is still much left for you to do. I will see you soon." And just like that he was gone, and Danielle found herself once again traveling at light speed.

CHAPTER TWO
Boy Named Boy

“But, you…” There was long pause as her expression changed from surprise to anger and then finally settled on warmth. “You were dead?” her voice cracked. “This is the second time you died and came back to me.” A smile played on her mouth.

He regarded her for a moment. “Last time, it was my twin that died.” He cast her a dark look. “What I didn't tell you was…” The dramatic music from the small television now echoed loudly in the tiny kitchen. “I have a triplet.”

“Bababa” the television blared. “Join us tomorrow to find out if this really is Elwardo, does he love Lorretta, or…”

“Uugghh!” She hit the off button on the television a little harder than she planned. Slumping back into her wooden chair, her gaze blanked and her expression washed with frustration. She let out a heavy breath as she closed her eyes tight. She didn't expect Elwardo to come back. He was dead. Now Lorretta, who just moved on. “Oh, my gosh!” Her eyes popped wide open. “What about Dingo, the Aussie oil tycoon she has fallen in love with? She let out a heavy sigh.

She sat in silence for a few moments until a thought wandered into her head. “Where is that boy? Never around when you need him, and when he is around, nothing but bad luck.” She felt guilty right after she said it, but she couldn't deny the truth. “Twelve years of bad luck.”

On the night of the comet, Carla and Jack finished a 12-pack and took a stroll through the cool night air to the old tent hall. That was when Carla heard a faint cry. She rushed over to where the noise came from and lying there was not one, but two babies. A boy and a girl.

"Leave 'em be," Jack burped, then threw the last empty can of beer into the bushes.

Carla studied him for a moment her brow narrowed. "We can't just leave them out here." Her voice seemed small and uncertain.

"They ain't my problem," Jack burped.

"Least we can do is find the parents," she said, her arms on her hips. "Fine! But you carry them." Jack spat into the bushes.

They searched around the area for the parents, yet none could be found. Going door to door that night, no one had any information. She called CPS, who came and picked up the two babies. In the conversation with the officer, Jack found out that the state paid if you took foster children into your home. Jack said that he and Carla would be happy to watch the babies until the parents were found. The next day, social services placed the babies in their care temporarily while they searched for the parents. Days turned into weeks, which turned into months, and now twelve years had passed.

Three weeks after the children were in their home, Jack lost his job after 22 years at the factory. For the next six months and dozens of job interviews, he was told he was too old, not qualified, not educated enough.

"This whole house changed when those brats came into our lives!" he bellowed one night during an argument with Carla.

Over the next few unemployed years, Jack's drinking intensified, as did his mood swings. He would lash out for no reason, going into fits of rage.

Three years after the children arrived, the couple lost the cute little gingerbread cottage that had been in Carla's family for two generations.

"Thanks to you worthless brats, we lost the house!" Jack snapped at the kids as he threw an old chair into the back of the beat-up Nissan truck.

They moved to the outskirts of town, into a one-room shack. Carla took work where she could find it. Jack used most of the grocery money for booze.

"Boy!" she yelled. Where is he? She heard footsteps come up from the basement. Out from the stairway came the boy, wearing clothes three times too big for him—old clothes Jack no longer cared for. The pants bunched up around the waist; safety pinned to keep from falling off his slight frame. The shirt looked like an enormous robe. If not for the oversized clothes, one would have noticed a very skinny boy who was quite small for his age. He had brown unruly hair, and piercing, bright brown eyes.

"Yes," he said, tossing his head to the side to get the hair out of his eyes.

Carla's gray eyes glared down her crooked nose at him. Then she pursed her tiny bird mouth for a moment. "Did you hear me calling you for the last hour?" she asked, her eyes wide with frustration.

Laken held her gaze for a moment, his expression pinched. "I couldn't hear you over the washing machine." His lips tightened. Their eyes remained locked in the silence until finally he looked away and began examining a small spot on the doorway.

"Excuses, excuses. It's all I ever get from you." Exasperation seeped through her tone. "Lawn done?" Her voice was sharp.

"Yes!" Laken looked up and answered proudly.

"Mowed, trimmed, and the bushes watered!"

"Yes."

"Clean out wood shed?"

"Yes."

"Dogs bathed?"

"Yes!"

"Floors washed and waxed?"

"Yes."

"Back wall painted?"

"Yes."

"Toilet scrubbed?"

"Yes."

"Fence fixed?"

"Yes."

Carla paused, her eyes narrowed with suspicion. "Laundry done?"

Laken looked back towards the stairs where the sound of the washing machine rattled its way up. "Almost."

"Almost? Almost?!" Carla's hands waved through the air. "Do you do anything around here? Do I have to do it all!"

"Sorry," the boy murmured, his jaw tense.

"Get the laundry done!" Carla snapped. "And keep it quiet down there tonight, so Jack and I can enjoy our dinner."

The boy paused and looked as if he were contemplating something. He leveled his gaze, his eyes widened. Then, the boy then spoke softly. "Will there be dinner for me and Sum...rr," he hesitated and finished, "the girl?" Right when he said it, he wished he could reel the words back into his mouth like a fish on the end of a pole. The color from Carla's cheeks drained away. Anger filled her eyes as she began to shake her finger in his face.

"I have enough to worry about in this house without trying to figure out what you and that... that *girl* have to eat!" Carla spit the words out.

His expression fell as he turned towards the steps. "Sorry," he mumbled as he stomped down the basement stairs to the words tossed behind him.

"Ungrateful!"

"Moochers!"

"Brats!"

The boy clambered down the rickety wooden steps into the dingy basement. The smell of rotting wood and empty beer cans filled the thick, warm air. Light leaked in thru the one outside window leading to the ground level. One small bulb hanging from the ceiling blinked on and off, casting eerie shadows on the cinderblock walls.

Absently, he began to rub the spot where the invisible object wrapped around his finger. It had been there his whole life. Any time he was frustrated or bored he would twirl the item as if it were an actual ring.

Once, he pressed it into some mud, to see the indentation. He could tell it had a large stone on top, and five smaller stones surrounding it. No matter how hard he tried, he could not remove the ring. He used Vaseline, soap; he even hit it with large rock. His sister looked on in amazement as the rock shattered into a million pieces, not leaving a mark on his finger. The boy never told Jack or Carla. He assumed that Jack would most likely cut off his finger to try and sell the ring for a bottle of the "good stuff."

The boy hopped over the spot that was missing a step. He had fallen through that step a few years back, and earned a good beating for having broken the stair, and for getting blood on the floor. "Who is going to clean up all this blood?" Carla spat.

"Ohhh food, do you remember what it was like?" a voice in his head asked sarcastically. His stomach let out a growl. The boy looked over to his right shoulder where his little friend sat eating a huge turkey leg, a juicy piece hanging off his upper lip. The six-inch blue monster looked the boy in the eye and held up the imaginary turkey leg. "Like a bite?" he asked, as turkey spit splattered out of his big mouth.

"Nah, think I will just gnaw on some…" he paused and hunted through his oversized pockets. He could in fact have fit a whole turkey in those huge pockets. The boy rummaged for a second, then pulled out part of a Dorito he had found on the kitchen floor a few days ago. "This should hold me over for a couple of days," a smile curling the corners of his mouth. The little blue monster chuckled.

The creature had been part of the boy's life for as long as he could remember. Around age four, he'd begun to refer to the monster as "Dave." Even more fascinating—the boy could see everyone else's little monsters, yet as far as he knew, no one could see his, or even their own.

Everyone's monster was different. Each monster's appearance usually took after their person, like how some owners, after many years, begin to look like their dog. Most fascinating was the monsters' color, which seemed to represent what type of person they were. His sister's was blue, like his, but much brighter, while Jack's was black and withered. Carla's was sickly looking, emaciated, and gray. Mrs. Maureen, the woman across the street who often times would sneak them a meal, had a bright blue monster, much like his sister's.

Dave's color changed in response to the boy's actions. The time the boy stole a package of Zingers from Tony's Market, Dave turned a shade darker and dingier. Dave made him feel guilty for days. The next time at the market, the boy stole some doughnuts and a drink. Dave grew a little darker still, and made him feel less guilty. One month and a lot of stealing later, Dave was dark, and obsessed with thievery. Dave began to beg the boy to steal something, anything, everywhere they went. He was like a drug addict striving to get a "theft fix."

The boy didn't like the change in Dave. The monster went from being fun and sarcastic to perpetually moody and angry. One day, Dave got the boy to yell at his sister. To the boy, that was unacceptable. His sister was the only good thing in his life. He vowed to never steal again. Though it only took a month to turn Dave dark blue, it took nearly three months until he was back to his normal, sarcastic, fun self.

The boy hopped over the last three steps and landed on the cold, cracked concrete floor. The basement was the size of a very small bedroom, yet it housed him, his sister, an old washer and dryer, a furnace, and a large collection of Jack's whiskey bottles.

The boy had used some old cinder blocks to elevate the plywood they slept on, which was important during the rainy season, since the basement usually flooded.

His sister sat on the makeshift bed with a smile, her bright blue monster smiling as well. They always seemed to smile when he was around. Most of the time, that made the boy feel good. Sometimes, it grew tiresome and annoying.

The brother and sister weren't given the luxuries that most children get, like food, clothes that fit, a birthday, or even a name.

Six years earlier, they chose names for when Jack and Carla weren't around. The boy went by the name Laken. His sister had found a picture of a boy on a lake that she carried with her everywhere she went. She said looking at it made her feel good, and Laken made her feel good.

Laken called his sister Summer. Summertime made him smile. No more cold, wet, freezing nights in the basement. All the summer tourists provided extra income for Carla, and that meant a meal every day, sometimes two meals. Summertime made him feel good, and his sister was the only person who did the same.

Summer just sat on the plywood offering him a grin. She began to pull her long blonde hair together, then took a bread bag tie from her pocket wrapping it around, completing the pony tail. Her big blue eyes were wide with anticipation.

"Me and Jack want to have a quiet evening," Laken did his best Carla impression, shaking his hips. The siblings both burst out laughing.

"Why isn't the laundry done?" Summer asked in a very poor attempt at a Carla impression, which made things even funnier. "How about the dog, what about the floor, what about my big nose that needs to be picked?" She blurted out, barely able to contain the laughter.

"KEEP IT DOWN!" Carla's voice carried down the steps. "Don't make me come down there!" Laken and Summer looked at each other and burst into a muffled fit of giggles.

Dong! Dong! The old grandfather clock boomed through the house, carrying a rumble down to the basement. The fourth-generation grandfather clock was the only thing Carla would not allow Jack to sell. *Dong... Dong... Dong... Dong.*

"Jack should be home anytime between now and morning," Summer giggled.

"Can hardly wait," mumbled Laken.

When Jack was home, everything was always worse. For the most part, Carla left the kids alone. Jack, on the other hand, liked to torment the two. "I don't think Jack can sleep unless he's given you a good beating," was Dave's favorite joke.

Laken cringed every night when he heard the old Nissan truck pull up to the house. Wasn't fear. Laken stopped being afraid years ago. It was not knowing what to expect. Would it be screaming night, or would he knock Laken around a little? Maybe Laken would be lucky and Jack would just say hurtful things. As long as he left Summer alone, Laken could manage the abuse.

Jack steered away from hurting Summer, knowing it was the one thing Laken would not tolerate. In a sense, no one touched Summer.

When she was ten years old, Jack grabbed Summer and yanked her off the floor for spilling her milk. Laken didn't think—he just attacked. Kicking, hitting, screaming, biting, and throwing. The neighbors called the police because of the noise coming from the shack. It took three cops, Carla, and the injection of a sedative to calm Laken down. The police report suggested mental problems, and recommended Laken be put on some drug and see a psychologist immediately. Of course, all that would have cost money, which would be better spent on booze for Jack. So instead, Jack gave Laken the worst beating of his life. But Jack never touched Summer again, which made the ordeal worthwhile for Laken.

The same year, a sixth-grader named Wade knocked Summer's books out of her hands. Once again, it took three teachers to pull the small, younger-by-three-years Laken off the bloody and bruised Wade. Kids at school knew you did not touch, insult, or hurt Summer.

Because all the bullying was directed towards Laken, he and Dave had decided that fear was a waste of time. What did he have to fear? A beating from a bully only hurt for a few minutes, while fear was a constant pain. What could Jack do to him that was worse than that rotting feeling of fear? "Fear is a waste of time," Dave kept saying until, one day, Laken and Dave vowed never to fear again. In some weird way, Laken felt like he had learned this before. It seemed to come natural and easy, as if he had already accomplished this feat.

Everything in Laken's life changed the moment he stopped being afraid. The very next day, Laken stood up to the big Miller brothers. He took a beating, got a black eye and a bloody lip. Didn't seem to hurt that bad. Definitely didn't hurt as bad as that sickening feeling of fear he had lived with. The following day, he stood up to them again and the same thing happened. Another quick and relatively painless beating. On the third day, he stood up again, and this time they just walked away and left him alone. "He's crazy. I'm done wasting my time on him!" the oldest Miller brother swore.

From that moment on, Laken wasn't picked on again. Laken started ignoring Jack's words, and his beatings didn't hurt that bad. Life became better all around, now that fear was out of his life.

"Come, sit, and tell me again what we will do when we get out of this place." Summer's smile grew.

"...97, 98, I'm thinking bag lady, 99, 100," said Dave, who was doing pushups on Laken's shoulder.

"Shut it!" Laken snapped.

"What?" Summer's expression turned to puzzled.

"Nothing, not talking to you... didn't say anything," he stuttered.

"You talking to Dave?" Summer's eyes bright again, looking at Laken's wrong shoulder.

"Over here! Over here!" Dave screamed, jumping up and down. "Yes, and he is being annoying." a smirk washed across his face.

"Okay, so we have a huge house." Laken sat on the plywood, which let out a groan of cracks and pops from his added weight. "With a massive back yard, and a tire swing on our big oak tree." Laken looked over at Summer who was now lying back on the plywood bed, her eyes closed and a huge smile on her face. "We'll eat Happy Meals seven times a day, have a freezer full of ice cream sandwiches, Nerd pushups, and frozen bananas."

"We'll have Jell-O, cherry Jell-O, butterscotch candy, and lots and lots of warm blankets," Summer added as she opened her eyes and sat up. "We'll eat, and eat, and eat. We'll be warm and full every day. Can we have a dog?" Her words were like a light breeze.

"Seven of them," Laken said. "We will love six of them, and have one named Jack that we will kick for no reason, and give it just enough food to keep it alive," Laken snickered. Dave was pretending to kick an imaginary dog.

"Absolutely not!" Summer sat up, her gaze hot. Laken and Dave both hung their heads in shame. Summer had a way of keeping them in line. "We will never treat anything the way that Jack treats us. We are not like that." She paused letting the words sink in, then her expression softened. "Make me a promise!"

"Come on, Summer, not another promise."

"No, Laken, you make me a promise. You, too, Dave," she looked at his shoulder. She of course was looking way over Dave's head.

Dave jumped up and down again screaming, "Down here, down here!"

"Fine, we promise." he said, his jaw tense.

Dave had one hand in the air. "I, Dave, do solemnly swear not to kick a dog named Jack. I further promise not to ever fart in the presence of a lady." *Fffthlp*, Dave ripped a fart out. "Well... I do promise... not to kick the dog." Dave tried to squeeze the words out between fits of laughter. This made Laken let out a ruffled laugh.

"Stop it! Be serious!" cried Summer. She grabbed Laken's arm, dragged him backwards so they were both lying down looking up. The old board let out a loud crack as if it was about to break. "When do you think we can leave?" Summer's wistful voice filled the basement.

"As soon as we have $500. You know that."

"Let's count our money," Summer urged as she hopped off the bed. "Come on. Let's see how close we are," Summer grabbed Laken's arm pulling him up. She then dragged him over to the old furnace in the corner of the basement.

"What if Jack comes down here? You know we'll lose it all."

"Oh, he's not home. Besides we can hear him from a block away. Come on, please, please, please," she was pulling his arm toward the hiding spot. Her monster was also on her knees, begging, "Pleeeeeeze!"

"Fine," Laken's brow narrowed. "But if Jack finds out, it's your fault."

"Yay!" screamed Summer, clapping her hands.

"KEEP IT DOWN!" came a screech from upstairs. Laken and Summer looked at each other, put a finger up to each of their mouths and quietly mocked, "Shhhh." This caused another small giggle fit.

Laken squeezed behind the old furnace, reached as far as his arms would stretch, grabbed the last cinderblock, and pulled it free from the others. He set the block down, and then reached in the newly formed hole and pulled out a makeshift pouch that had a piece of yellow ribbon wrapped around its mouth.

Summer's eyes screamed with excitement as she and Laken kneeled beside the old furnace and opened the pouch.

Laken glanced over at Summer who looked like she was going to burst with anticipation. As soon as the yellow ribbon was untied, the contents of the pouch spilled out onto the floor. Coins of every denomination clanged onto the pavement. In the center of the pouch was a large wad of bills. Laken slowly began to separate the bills, and sort them out. Summer was organizing the coins by making piles of pennies, nickels, dimes, and even a few quarters.

For the next forty-five minutes, they found themselves in a dream world, free from problems. They were counting their dreams, and with every penny, they were closer and closer to that dream.

"Ninety-two dollars and seventy-nine cents. Ninety-two dollars and eighty cents." Laken counted out loud. "Ninety- two dollars and—" Bam! Something smashed into Laken's head sending him crashing to the floor. Laken's head spun. Noises from so many directions seemed to be attacking him. He was drowning in a fury of sound and commotion. He lifted his face off the concrete floor, shaking the cobwebs out of his head.

"What the..?" He looked up to see a shoe coming for him. It hit Laken square in the face and knocked him skidding across the floor into the pile of whiskey bottles. There boomed the loud sound of glass and concrete grinding together.

"You hide money from me boy?" a dark voice growled. Laken could hear the burning anger in his voice as it escalated to a high pitch crack with every syllable. "I slave! I slave my life away for you two brats! Two good-for-nothing brats!"

Dave shouted, "Where's Summer? Where's Summer?" Laken whipped his head left and right, searching for her. He could hear her scream from across the room but the weight of the bottles had him pinned to the floor. Laken twisted his body trying to free himself from the pile of bottles. Dave kept reminding him that he had to protect his sister. Another scream from Summer, and Laken, fueled by pure adrenalin and with a lash of strength and effort, finally broke free and shot to his feet.

Laken frantically searched the dimly lit basement, until his eye caught Summer, who was huddled in the corner of the room, tears splashing her cheeks.

"Leave him alone!" Summer wiped her face.

"Shut that worthless girl up!" Jack barked. "Jack, calm down." Carla was rushing down the old steps. Laken looked at Summer, and then his gaze snapped to Jack.

"DON'T YOU TALK ABOUT HER LIKE THAT!" Laken's face flushed a deep crimson. Jack eyes narrowed, regarding him with distaste. The boy was quite a bit bigger than that ten-year-old who had attacked him a few years earlier. But no child was going to intimidate him.

"What did you say to me, boy?" Jack moved towards Laken.

"I said DON'T… TALK… ABOUT… HER… LIKE… THAT!" pausing after each word.

"I'll talk about the girl-no-one-wants any way I choose," Jack's gaze shifted to Summer, crying in the corner.

"Laken, don't worry about it." Summer's voice broke. "Let it go, it's no big deal!"

"Yes, boy. No one else worries about her, why should you?" His words were edged in poison. There was a pause; the air seemed to be draining from the basement. Laken's heart thundered in his chest.

"Come on, no one has ever wanted her." A hurtful laugh leaked out. "Her parents didn't want her. We don't want her. It looks like no one wants her." A sob gushed from Summer.

Laken looked over at Summer, the pain in her eyes reached into his heart and squeezed. His gaze snapped back to Jack's. Laken began to slowly walk toward Jack. He couldn't care less what beating was in store. All he cared about was that Jack leave Summer alone.

"I said LEAVE HER ALONE!" An even lower growl of confidence came out of Laken. Jack's eyes widened, a thin smile on his face. "What are you going to do, boy? Bring me more bad luck?" Jack spat on the floor. "Between you and that stupid…ugly…worthless….girl who…" Jack trailed off as he noticed Laken's eyes. They began to glow. The red light danced along Laken's features.

All the years of abuse (*Dong*) all the hurtful words, years of freezing cold, years of no food, and nights of fear crashed through Laken's mind. Each memory, (*Dong*), each thought was like a hot iron searing the pain in his mind. A beast in him seemed to stir. Rage began to pulse through his veins. He felt like he no longer had blood coursing through him. Rather, it was hate, it was anger. It was vengeance. HE WOULD NEVER LET JACK HURT SUMMER AGAIN! (*Dong*) Laken's head felt like a boiling teapot screaming from the steam trying to escape. He took another step.

"Jack has to pay. He has to pay for all he has done!" Dave growled. (*Dong*) Laken could feel the fire in him growing hotter and hotter. The fire was too much. He was going to explode. He had to release it.

And then he felt like a balloon that had sprung a hole. Strands of blue electrical lights shot from Laken's hands, hitting Jack square in the chest, and sending the drunk crashing into the wall behind him.

"I...SAID...LEAVE...HER...ALONE!" With each syllable Laken released another burst of electrical current into Jack. Jack's screams filled the basement. "YOU WILL NEVER HURT HER AGAIN!" Laken screamed as a continuous current of electricity shot from his hands, consuming Jack's body and sending it into convulsions. Blood gushed from Jack's eyes, ears, nose and mouth. With each thought of hate, a surge of intense blue light shot from Laken to Jack, and Jack's screams became more extreme. (*Dong*) Jack's body began to pulse to the rhythm as each of Laken's painful memories surfaced.

"Stop it, Laken, stop it!" Carla screamed as she ran and grabbed Laken's arm. Laken felt something release where she touched him, and with the sound of breaking glass, she shot across the room and crashed into the wall. (Dong) Laken was done hurting; he was done with the pain, and he was done with Jack abusing Summer.

"Burn! Burn!" Dave yelled.

Then a familiar voice bawled, "You promised, Laken, you promised!"

Laken pushed those thoughts aside, "Sorry, Summer, I can't keep that promise," Laken whispered. And with one last push from the depths of Laken's scarred soul…

(Dong)

CHAPTER THREE
A Ring, an Angel, and
a few Hellhounds

Bam! A loud snap—

Laken's body felt torn apart, then slowly reassembled, piece-by-piece. His chest constricted, as if being squeezed by a large snake. He gasped helplessly. His surroundings gradually evaporated into a mere shadow of the present world. Laken could see Carla, blood trickling from her lip, cradling Jack, who lay on the floor. Summer was screaming, "Laken, Laken," frantically searching the room. Jack lifted his head and opened his eyes. Suddenly— the world vanished.

Bam! Another snap and Laken's chest heaved, the serpent uncoiling its grip. He drew in a ragged breath as everything around him began to rearrange. Venerable buildings constructed themselves in front of his eyes. With broad brush strokes, the scene became complete as cottages, store fronts, sidewalk cafes, two story buildings with eaves and gables came into view. There were ivy-covered stone walls and quaint window boxes filled with flowers of every color of the rainbow. Streets of Old World cobblestone began to form. Mature trees and flowering bushes erupted around him. Birds materialized mid-flight in the air above. Laken's eyes went wide with amazement. People began to appear. First one person, then another, then another, until an entirely new world had come to fruition in a matter of seconds.

Laken's heart fluttered, his gaze snapping from one new thing to another. "Excuse me," a plump man in a red and blue robe said as he bustled past Laken.

"What in the world are you doing in the middle of the street?" squealed something behind him. Laken turned around to see the top of a green straw hat on an Elf.

"Oh, sorry." Laken blinked hard. Then looked again.

"Yep, a green hat on an Elf. You roll in Jack's whiskey bottles or drink from them." Dave let out a hic-up.

"Out of my way! Get out of my WAY!" Laken whipped around to see what looked like the back of a lion attached to a human torso. Laken shook his head, as if jarring water from his ear.

"Yep, we be drunk." Dave rubbed his eyes.

Laken took a few hesitant steps, almost crushing two small Fairies in a heated discussion.

"Watch it!" screeched the taller of the two.

"So sorry!" Laken apologized. He stopped and drew in large breath. The smell of baked bread and flowers filling his nostrils. Laken's gaze slowly swept the scene, searching for normality; something to which his mind could anchor.

Two old ladies were in mid-conversation with a lion. An Elf in a green robe argued with a couple of centaurs some twenty paces away. Another Elf with orange skin and bright blue hair was playing cards with a few Goblins over at a bistro table across the courtyard.

"Get out of the middle of the street!" someone shouted from behind him. He turned and saw a creature he could only have imagined, with a human top half and the bottom half of a goat. Beside him was a huge rabbit with a horn on top of his head. Laken stared in disbelief. "You would think he has never seen a Satyr and a Jackalope before!" gasped the goat-man to the rabbit, as the two rushed past.

Boom, boom, boom. Laken steadied himself as the earth shook. He looked over his right shoulder to see a Giant over fifteen feet tall, carefully treading along the street in a concerted effort not to step on pedestrians.

Dave rubbed his eyes; then rubbed them again. For the first time in thirteen years, the blue monster was speechless.

Out in the distance, people flew through the sky, but not by plane or balloon. They had wings, and soared at an incredible speed.

Laken absently started to twirl the invisible ring around his finger. Out of the corner of his eye he saw a bright light coming from below. His gaze shifted to his hand. The ring was no longer invisible. There it was on his finger: the center stone green, the size of a marble. The color faded from dark to light, as if it were breathing. The outer five stones glowed with different colors, as if alive; each stone beating to a different rhythm. The ring band looked like gold, but unlike any gold Laken had ever seen. It was transparent, like a golden piece of glass.

Immersed in his inspection of the ring, Laken failed to spot five huge Minotaur guards heading his way. Each guard had a massive axe slung over his shoulder, leather breast plates, golden war bracelets, and a huge golden ring in its bull nose. "Boy! Boy! What are you doing in the middle of the street!" A high-pitched squeak of a voice came from the largest of the guards. Laken turned, looking down to try and find the mouse who was speaking to him, only to find himself staring at a massive boot. Laken slowly forced his gaze to move upward until finally he was looking nearly straight up into the black eyes of a bull. "I said, get out of the way, Boy!" the high-pitched voice squeaked again.

"Best loosen those pants of yours, big boy," Dave tugging at his own waist.

Laken tried to speak, but the words stuck in his throat. One of the guards nudged Laken from behind, "We said get a move on," he said in an even higher pitched squeak.

"Uh, ok," Laken said, now completely puzzled. He began to step towards the buildings when the largest guard grabbed his left hand.

"What is this!" As soon as he saw the ring, he dropped Laken's hand and shrieked in an ear-piercing high pitched note, "The CHOSEN ONE!"

Everyone and everything froze, as if time had suddenly stopped. Every eye was on him. A small boy let out a gasp and hid behind his mother. The table housing the cards from the Elf and Goblins tipped over. A fairy flew into a building, and then fluttered to the ground. The Centaurs galloped out of the courtyard. Even the giant stood still, staring down at Laken with a shocked expression.

Then, as quickly as motion had stopped, activity began again. But rather than the normal hustle and bustle of the courtyard, with people coming in and going out, everyone began to exit. A few moments later the town was quiet, with only a handful of people and creatures left.

Coming from the farthest gate, fifty paces away, Laken noticed an old woman hobbling towards him. On Laken's left, some thirty paces away, a couple of Elves leaned up against an old oak tree, feigning disinterest. Laken could hear the breathing of the huge Giant behind him. He turned to see the Giant pretending to examine a spiked club the size of a tree. Laken turned back around to see the guards were still in sight, though they had shuffled a few paces back from him.

"You must be the Chosen One?" a very old, coarse voice said from right behind him. Laken jumped, a gasp escaping him. He whipped around, his heart thundering. Standing beside him was the old woman, hunched over and held up only by the sure will of her cane. The old woman's gray hair was thin, and large spots of her scalp were visible. Her skin was wrinkled, and spotted from age. On her shoulder sat a bright blue monster, smiling at Laken. "You must be the Chosen One?" her voice cracked.

"Oh, sorry, I, I… How did you get over here so fast?"

"My tired old bones worked very hard to hurry to you, that they did." She smiled to show her two black crooked teeth. "Are you the Chosen One?"

"Don't think they have a good dental plan in this crazy place," Dave whispered.

"I...I...don't know...what you are talking about," Laken said, the words leaking out. "I was at home, got really angry, then Summer... Oh, my God, where is Summer? I've got to help her!" Laken's body twisting left and right, searching franticly.

"I will help you with Summer." Her voice seemed certain and encouraging. "But first, let me see your ring." She pointed at his hand, a slight grin resurrected from within the wrinkles.

Laken drew a long shaky breathe. His expression tensed. "I really need to find my sister."

The old lady regarded him for a moment. "I promise; I will help you find her." She eyed him with apparent concern. "First, let me see the ring."

Relief rose in him at her words. "This?" Laken held up the ring, the light pulsing from the gem. The green glow reflected off the old woman's eyes, leaving awkward shadows of myrtle and teal across her wrinkled face.

Her monster, a tiny beast even more shriveled than she, began to scream, "It is, it's the ring!"

There was a short pause. Then the woman snapped out of the trance and croaked, "Follow me."

Laken's eyes narrowed as he stood his ground. The monster on her shoulder screeched. "Follow, come on, follow," sending a chill across his skin.

"We better decide fast. She looks like she'll keel over at any moment," Dave's voice interrupted.

Should we? Can we trust her? Laken thought.

"Better her than Mickey and Minnie over there with the axes." Dave motioning to the Minotaurs. "Besides, her monster is bright blue."

"Come, boy, come, follow me," cracked the old voice. "You have to be hungry. I have stew boiling on the stove." Laken could feel his stomach nudge him towards her.

Laken began to follow the old woman towards the alley she pointed towards. "He's coming, he's coming," her monster bellowed, the excitement growing in her voice. The Elves' gaze fixed on them. Every time Laken turned back towards the Giant, the large creature shifted its head away from Laken, feigning interest in something far off in the distance.

Laken and the old woman reached the gate leading to the alley. Barrels and broken boxes lay wasted on the ground up ahead. The only light source in the alley came from what little sun seeped through the gate. The darkness had a sickening feeling to it. "Just inside the alley, boy, is my home, with stew, and we can discuss how to help that Summer of yours." Her voice cracked. "You go ahead, I will follow." Laken hesitated as he tried to adjust his eyes to the darkness.

"Come on, come on. Go!" Her monster gestured. "Our reward is so close!"

"What reward?" Laken's eyes went wide with alarm.

Suddenly, the old woman grabbed Laken's arm, her grip much stronger than he would have guessed. A sizzling sound like bacon hitting a hot pan echoed through the alley. The old woman shrieked in pain as she ripped her blistered hands away from Laken's arm. In the instant of the scream, Laken noticed a change in the monster on her shoulder, going from bright blue to a dark, withered black. Then it returned to bright blue.

Laken jumped and with a focused effort, retreated a few paces back.

"Sorry, sorry. Come on, boy. Let's go get some stew," begged the woman.

"No, I'm fine. I have a friend coming anytime now to pick me up. Big fellow, he is."

"Good one. I think we pretty safe now!" A nervous laugh escaped Dave.

She let out a weary breath, any remaining friendliness fading from her face. "Well, if you won't come on your own, I guess you will come by force!" The old woman's voice went deeper with each word.

Like a snake shedding its skin, a creature began to work its way out of the old woman's flesh, until finally, a huge figure stood before Laken. His eyes looked like they were on fire and his skin was a blistered red. "Then let's do this the hard way." He held out his hands, materializing two massive winged fiery beasts. Each deformed head sported enormous razor-like teeth. Huge wings flapped against the cobblestone, creating a fog of dust around them. Each had a body the size of horse. In unison, their heads flailed towards the sky as they both let out a screech. Then they charged. Sparks lit up the cobblestones as the beasts accelerated towards Laken, claws scuffing the stone floor. In an instant, they leapt onto Laken, gnashing and tearing at him. But each bite felt like raindrops brushing his skin. "Stop, come on stop it," Laken cried out in laughter. Then the beasts disappeared.

The red figure's expression pinched. "I guess we will have to do this the *very* hard way." Reaching into a small, grapefruit-sized sack attached to his waist, the figure brandished a massive sword far too huge to have fit inside the sack. In the blink of an eye, the red figure stood directly in front of Laken, swinging the sword, the blade plummeting down toward Laken's head!

Laken flinched as the sword struck his head, instantaneously evaporating to ash. The gust of air from the swing merely flipped Laken's hair this way and that. The dark figure's expression changed from rage to amazement, as he nearly toppled over himself from the lack of solid impact.

An ear-pounding thunderclap boomed overhead. A force of wind, companion to the noise, drove Laken and the red man to their knees. Laken looked up to see wings spreading more than twenty feet across, attached to a massive figure in a glowing white robe. A violent blue light shot from the figure's eyes, directed wherever they gazed. His long gray hair and beard danced in the wind that his wings kicked up. Everything shook as his feet hit the ground. Even the monster on his shoulder was massive, barking a report of the forces that surrounded them. "Archers to the left, Giant behind, Radkus to the front, five Minotaurs to the right."

Out of the corner of his eye, Laken saw the Elves release an arrow each, and in a flash, a second arrow, and a third. Laken tried to shout a warning, but the words got stuck in his throat. Just before striking the Angel, each arrow transformed into a butterfly. The millisecond before, Laken heard the monster on the Angel's shoulder say, "Butterfly."

The monster on the Angel's shoulder then bellowed, "Sword, Elves!" Suddenly— the Angel vanished, but in the same instant materialized before the first Elf, and then vanishing again only to appear instantly be-hind the second Elf, and then finally back to the middle of the courtyard. Laken saw both Elves collapse in a pool of blood—the same blood that stained the massive gold sword the Angel now held out in front of him.

Whoosh came the sound of a giant club swinging towards the Angel. Simultaneously, five Minotaurs rushed the Angel from all different sides. "Dissipate," cried the monster on the Angel's shoulder. The club, just like the red figure's sword, disappeared, and the Giant stumbled from the lack of impact. The Minotaurs hurled their axes towards the Angel, but his wings, as if each were a separate entity, reacted swiftly, wrapping around the Angel to form a protective shield. On impact, the axes bounced off, clanging onto the cobblestone. The wings then recoiled, knocking the Minotaurs into the surrounding buildings.

The Giant rose, and Radkus—the red figure that had so recently been an old woman—picked up two of the axes. The Angel pushed out with his hands, sending Radkus hurtling across the courtyard. Radkus crashed through the wall of the *Mantor's Café*. With a flurry of movement, the Angel disappeared and reappeared, landing in a different position around the Giant with each movement, and then finally next to Laken. The Giant crumbled to the ground, each of his appendages lying beside his quivering torso. With another stretch of his right arm, Radkus came soaring through the hole his body had made in the Café wall and skidded to a stop in front of them. Golden ropes appeared and began to weave in, out, and around Radkus until he looked like a butterfly cocoon with a red human head.

The massive Angel looked down at Laken whose mouth was agape with amazement, and with a warm smile said, "You must be Jason. I'm Gabriel."

CHAPTER FOUR
The Whisperer Gets
Some Soowoodoo

❝ You... you... and the sword... and the arrows— then the *butter-flies*," Laken twisted and pointed all over the courtyard, "and the wings with the— but they were arrows, and your monster... and he said butterflies— they *became butterflies!*" Laken's mind was spinning at an uncontrollable rate, trying to process wonders he could hardly believe. Dave was acting out each scene in tandem with Laken's diz-zied recapitulation.

Gabriel's warm expression set on Laken as he listened intently to the boy's babbling. "Then the bulls... but you— and the wings. Jason— who is Jason?" Laken's heart thundering in his chest. "The old lady be-came Radcan or something... and he had winged beasts. They tickled, *why tickled?* But then— and you came... and the giant. Oh my gosh, I forgot about the *giant.* He's over there— look at him!" Laken now wav-ing his hands in a wild gesture towards the Giant's dismembered torso and limbs.

A smile played on Gabriel's mouth as he placed his hand on Laken's shoulder. "Yes, the giant is not doing so well." A warm sensation washed across Laken's skin. "Take a deep breath." Gabriel's blue eyes widened a fraction.

"Calm, I'm calm, why wouldn't I be calm? Just because a Giant, some Elves, an old lady with huge fire butterflies, and five bulls tried to kill me, why wouldn't I be calm?"

"Breathe, Jason, breathe." The warmth now pulsating down Lak-en's back.

"Big breath, okay." Laken drew in a deep breath, then coughed the air out suddenly. "Jason! Who is this Jason? I'm not Jason." Gabriel searched the boy's face, then a smile cracked thru his beard.

Laken's brow narrowed as he took in another breath and then slowly exhaled.

"Yes, of course you would have a new name," Gabriel said, stroking his beard. "Age sometimes causes me to forget the obvious." A smile crept back up his face. "So, what is your name?" Laken watched in awe as Gabriel slid the massive sword into a tiny pouch that hung neatly around his waist, seemingly far too small to ever house the blade. Gabriel's wings then folded up into his back and disappeared.

"Uh, it's Laken."

"Do not forget, we need to take care of Radkus," said the monster on Gabriel's shoulder.

"Oh, of course," Gabriel said aloud. "Please let Argus know we will be returning to Eden in a moment, and that I have a small mess for him to clean up here in Helsware."

The small creature split into another identical monster, which flew off in a flash of light.

Laken and Dave's eyes bulged. *Dave, how come you've never done that?*

"Why haven't you ever killed two Elves, a Giant, five bulls, and one really creepy looking dude before?" countered Dave.

"Fair enough." Laken shifted his gaze back to Gabriel. "Who are you, and why do you think my name is Jason?"

"Oh, we will get to that in a bit." A Minotaur behind them began to stir.

"It is very dangerous. We need to get the boy out of here," the monster on Gabriel's shoulder whispered.

"Dangerous? I thought you took care of all the danger?" Laken's brow narrowed again.

Gabriel's gaze snapped to Laken, staring for a moment. "How did you hear the word *dangerous?*"

"From your mons- Ah, never mind," Laken's voice trailed off.

"Did you hear my numa speak?" Gabriel looked around suspiciously.

"Your what? If by Nemo, you mean that monster on your shoulder, then yes." Laken watched him carefully.

"No, not Nemo, numa."

"Nemo, numa, whatever. You can hear and see mine, right?" Laken's eyes widened.

"See? Of course. Here we can all see each other's numas. But hear? No." Gabriel paused for a moment. "Only two others in the last 6000 years were able to do so." Gabriel stared off in the distance.

"A *whisperer*," claimed Gabriel's numa.

"What's a whisperer?" Laken asked. Gabriel looked over at his numa, mumbled a few words, and the creature was no longer audible. Laken could see the monster's lips move, but he couldn't hear a word. "Hey, what did you do? How did you do that? Why did you put it on mute?"

"Remis has a way of saying things that your ears should never have to hear." Something mysterious slid behind Gabriel's eyes, and he seemed more distant somehow.

"What's a whisperer?" Laken eyed the Angel with curiosity.

There was a long pause as if Gabriel was calculating something. Gabriel gave Laken's shoulder a slight squeeze, intensifying the warmth now pulsating down his back. "Simply put, it is one who can hear others' numas." Gabriel paused. "And *that* is a very powerful ability." The Angel looked around the empty courtyard, leaned close to Laken, and whispered, "Laken, it is very important that you never tell anyone of your gift." Gabriel looked around again, then leaned even closer in. "Unknown, it will be your greatest weapon. If discovered, it will be your greatest enemy."

"I've kept it a secret my whole life; it should be fairly easy," Laken said, shrugging his shoulders.

"Good, then let's take care of a few simple things, and be on our way." Gabriel reached back into his small pouch and pulled out a golden flask. He popped the lid, like opening the cover of a teapot, and lifted it up to Remis, who ceremoniously spat in the flask.

"Disgusting little fellow, that Remis is," whispered Dave.

"Alright, now we need a testimony from Dave," Gabriel said as he brought the golden flask down toward Dave. The events of the battle were being replayed three dimensionally on a holograph that appeared above the flask.

"What, the..." Laken's eye brows seem to be standing at attention.

"It's a numanator," Gabriel smiled. "It allows others to view what your numa saw during a specific event. I simply need Dave to spit in the numanator." Dave looked at Laken, who nodded his head. Dave let out huge snort as he inhaled air and the grime accumulated in his nostril, hacked a substance into his huge mouth, and then spit an enormous wad of phlegm into the flask. Immediately, the flask began to project the events, but started at the old lady's introduction to Laken.

"Great, we can be on our way." Gabriel wedged the flask into the golden ropes that bound Radkus. With a wave of his arms, Radkus disappeared. "Argus will know what to do with him," Gabriel said confidently. "We have a small journey ahead of us. Please grab my arm, Laken." Gabriel held out a long arm and smiled at Laken. Laken hesitated as the memory of old lady replayed through his mind. "It's okay," Gabriel smiled. Laken, looked to Dave, then back to Gabriel, hesitated then Dave shrugged his shoulders and Laken reached up and put his arm through the massive arm of Gabriel.

"Close your eyes and relax." Gabriel's voice was warm. With a loud snap the air was once more sucked out of Laken's lungs. His body felt like it was gone, and all that was left was his mind flying through space and time. Laken opened his eyes to see nothing but a blur of lights blowing past him. Then another snap, and Laken's feet seemed to land on solid ground, and air rushed into his lungs as his eyes slowly focused to the world around him.

Beauty unfolded before him. Rolling green hills dotted with flowers of every color. Barge trees heavy with pink and gold blossoms hung over the path they stood on. The bright crystal blue horizon weighed majestically on the vibrant hills. Birds, fairies with wings of every imaginable color, and small forest creatures danced all along the knolls. Directly in front of them were two ornate golden gates filled with huge basketball-sized rubies and sapphires, glowing as if they were alive. There were two massive Angels on either side of the gates. Their size made Gabriel look like a small boy. Each angel wore a golden robe that looked as if it were not just for beauty but for protection as well. Where their eyes should have been, bright lights lit up their stone-shaped faces. In their arms, each held an enormous flaming sword as tall as Gabriel. The weapons undulated like a pendulum, forming a half ring of fire in front of each.

"Those are some big Angels!" Laken exhaled a big breath.

"They're small for being Qwerubs, but they make up for their size with strength," Gabriel smiled.

Laken's gaze moved from the Qwerubs to what they guarded. The Gate behind the Qwerubs was connected to a golden brick wall over twenty feet high, stretching to their left as far as the eye could see. To the right, it extended for a few hundred yards. Laken's eyes flickered left, then right, up then down, trying to drink in this whole new world.

The boy whipped his body around, stepping on Gabriel's sandaled feet. "Oh, sorry," apologized Laken, as his eye caught a glimpse of what was behind them. Two deep-banked rivers ran parallel to each other. Laken had to rub his eyes a few times to make sure he was seeing right—mermaids and mermen swimming, playing, and sunning themselves in the river. A group of young merpeople played a game using their tridents, two enchanted goals, and a golden orb the size of a beach ball. A mermaid dove under water, flipped her huge tail out and hit the ball straight into the goal. Many of the onlookers roared at what had just happened.

"Beautiful, isn't it?" Gabriel's voice sounded a mile away. Laken shook his head, trying to extract himself from his dream-like state.

"More beautiful than anything I have ever seen," Laken purred. Dave couldn't' take his eye off a couple of the mermaids sunning themselves on some rocks, his tongue hanging out his big blue mouth, panting like an oversized dog.

"Let get going. We have much to do." Gabriel's voice snapped them out of the trance.

"Uugghh, what? Of course, yes. I was looking at the birds over there, not the river. I love birds." Laken's face flushed bright red. The angel offered Laken a smile, then turned and headed towards the gate. Laken followed in Gabriel's wake.

"Good afternoon, Zot and Ferk," Gabriel said as they approached the two Qwerubs. Neither one gave him notice. The warm air from the flaming swords, swinging back and forth, swept Gabriel's long hair and beard. "This is Gabriel, High Archangel and Headmaster of Dogma, and his new student, Laken." Gabriel gave Laken a half smile. "We wish to enter Outer Eden." There was a loud clang, and then the gates slowly creaked open.

Gabriel strode through the gates with Laken following closely behind him. Once again, Laken's head moved about in amazement. At first, his eye was drawn to the grand, old-style buildings that lined the street. He saw large shuttered windows, most of which were open, wood shingles, and fireplaces bellowing smoke into the cool breeze. Each building was vibrant with colors, and no two were the same. *Qwoogle's Market* was blue with white trim, while *Draugr's Battle Supplies* was eye-piercing green and red. *Nooner's Barber Shop* was red, white, and blue.

Laken's gaze shifted to the street they were now on. "They're gold!" Dave realized in astonishment. Laken took a moment to study the streets. They were indeed gold, but an unreal gold, like the ring on his finger. The material was so pure you could see through it, as if you were walking on ice. Laken blinked his eyes a few times, then allowed his gaze to drift upwards towards the large patches of grass that lined the outskirts of the courtyard. A massive tree, some forty feet tall and nearly the same width, was the central point of the town, as if the whole town had been built around it. The tree had an ominous glow; lit up from the inside. Purple fruit the size of basketballs hung sporadically along the canopy of the tree, surrounded by what looked like golden pinecones. Children climbed and ran around its substantial trunk. There were about a dozen gnomes up in the branches of the tree, tossing the golden pinecones playfully at the children, in the midst of what looked like some sort of game. The air was scented with chimney smoke, cinnamon, and baked bread.

The courtyard was busy. People came and went, talking, and doing business. Everyone wore gowns and cloaks of various colors. The range of people's sizes was so dramatic and irregular that it was difficult to focus on any one group of people. Some were over seven feet tall, while others were only knee high. Some skinny as a pole, while others as wide as tall. You could see gnomes, dwarves, even a few centaurs, conducting business on the outskirts of the courtyard. Small fairies were whizzing to and fro, like bees gathering pollen.

"Good day, Empera," Gabriel smiled at an old plump woman wearing a bright green gown, pushing a rickety wooden cart full of fruit.

"Like some fruit, Gabriel?" She smiled politely. Laken's gaze stopped at the cart full of fruit, his eyes wide in amazement. The cart held purple fruit, orange fruit, pink fruit; one particular fruit changed colors six or seven times. Each piece of fruit was a different shape and size. The smallest was the size of a marble, but cube-shaped, and the largest was as big as a pear-shaped watermelon.

"No, thank you. Thought I would take the boy to get some Soowoodoo's."

"Ooohhh, my favorite," Empera's face lit up.

"Get out of the way, boy!" a plump Dwarf bumped into Laken, and whisked by, dressed in a bright blue robe, green knee high boots, and an orange hat. He had an old sack over his shoulder overflowing with golden treasures, cups, goblets, a small chest, daggers, and many other objects that looked as if they struggled not spill out.

A group of children dressed in cloaks of all different colors were throwing a ball to one another, or so it seemed at first glance. But when Laken took a better look, the ball went from child to child yet never touched their hands. It simply floated from one player to another.

Gabriel leaned over with a wink and a whisper, "What do you say we get some Soowoodoo's?"

"Sowo who?" Laken stumbled as he snapped out of his trance.

"Soowoodoo's!" Gabriel said enthusiastically. "Best treats in the universe. At least, that is my opinion," Laken looked up, Gabriel's eyes glowed with excitement.

"Sounds good," Laken agreed as a group of gnomes ran between his legs.

"Follow me," smiled Gabriel. As Laken took a step, his legs tangled and he toppled onto the street almost squishing a gnome who screamed and took off running. "Those gnomes make life so interesting." Gabriel let out a small chuckle. Laken glanced at his shoes to see that they had been tied together.

"I like those gnomes," laughed Dave.

Laken untied the knots, rose, and caught up to Gabriel, who was still smiling. They passed *Quoogle's, Nooner's,* and *Draugr's,* then with the grin of a six-year-old on Christmas morning, Gabriel said, "Welcome to heaven," as he turned into the little red and white shop with a big sign hanging over the door announcing, "Soowoodoo."

The warm smell of what could only be described as *delicious* hit them as they stepped into the shop. The room was bright and intense. The colors of the wall were piercing red, yellow, green, blue, and changed hue every few seconds. Large bottles and candy danced weightlessly all along the top of the walls to the rhythm of a fun, fast jingle played by a golden harp and two orange flutes that flew carelessly about the room. Immense glass cases lined the color changing walls, each case filled with treats. Small dancing placards named each of the goodies: Gubdubbers, Harguhlas, Narples, Wirples, Nirbs, and Rockdees. The glass counters were stacked three feet high with bottles of Nirple and Scblappa.

Laken went over and picked up a bottle filled with a blue, yellow, and red liquid stacked one color on top of the other. Where Laken's hand pressed against the bottle, the liquid glowed radiantly.

"Say a flavor, any flavor," Gabriel encouraged, as if asking him to open a present.

Laken, unable to take his eye off the glow, whispered, "Strawberry." Instantly, the liquid swirled and turned a bright red. "Orange," Laken said and the liquid swirled and turned orange. "Blueberry!" Laken blurted out. Liquid once again swirled, and turned a bright blue. Laken set the bottle down and noticed that where his hand had been covering, the label now read, "Blueberry."

"Gabriel, my friend, a Serub smiles, but usually only once." The high-pitched voice came from a little gnome wearing a bright orange apron, his large ears poking out of his white chef's hat, and long gray hair draping out past his shoulders.

"Soowoo, you look good," Gabriel said as he bent over and gave the gnome a warm smile and a handshake.

"Thank you, my friend, thank you," Soowoo blushed. "An imp was given the gift of flight, proves two things," and then Soowoo trailed off into a trance for an uncomfortable moment. Laken, unsure of what was going on, shot a glance at Gabriel, who responded with a *Soowoo-is-not-*

all-there grin. They both turned their attention back to Soowoo, who was still staring off into space. Then, with a shutter of his eyes and a small shake of his head, Soowoo said, "I suppose you want a bag of Nirbs, my old friend?"

"Make it two bags, please. One for me and one for Laken here." Gabriel made a small glance towards Laken. Soowoo turned his gaze to Laken. His eyes instantly locked onto the ring on Laken's hand.

"Oooooh, a Chosen One." Soowoo's ears went back and his face became closed as his gaze met Laken's. "A Dipsa may strike, but a Golem with only one shoe can be heard coming," Soowoo whispered, and then continued to stare at Laken. The boy turned his head toward Gabriel as if to ask for help, but Gabriel merely smiled back. Laken stared into the gaze of Soowoo, who didn't so much as blink.

After a long silence, Gabriel said, "Very wise, Soowoo. You need to write these things down."

Soowoo shook his head, and turned his attention back to Gabriel. "A centaur may make a mark in a tree, but why not just let a Dweeder make a song?"

A confused expression washed over Gabriel's face. A smile then tugged on his lips. "Please excuse my rudeness, but we have pressing matters that we must tend to before the big celebration."

"Of course, of course. A Troll and Pixie will never bury the other, but a dragon won't either." Soowoo grabbed some large orange bags out of his apron and then filling both sacks to the top with golden, acorn-shaped Nirbs. He handed one to Gabriel, and then held out the other to Laken. Soowoo's expression stiffened. Laken tried to accept the bag, but Soowoo held on. "The dark of night may come, but the light of day will also come." Soowoo glared at Laken, and then his face faded into a smile.

"Uhhh, thank you."

"Thank *you*, my good friend." Gabriel wore a pained smile. "A snurb and a dragon never make good company. Please come along, Laken, we have much to do. "

"You are so right, you are so right." Soowoo shook his bowed head as he made his way to the back room.

Laken quickly caught up to Gabriel and the two of them exited Soowoodoo's. Laken had to blink a few times to regain his focus in the bright sunlight. The hustle and bustle of the courtyard still played full force. Laken eyed a group of gnomes who were looking at him and whispering.

"Look, next to Gabriel, it's the CHOSEN ONE!" a very plump man in a tall green hat cried out. Everyone stopped what they were doing, and stared fixedly at Laken. A lump formed in his throat, and his face turned red.

"Yes, yes, it is the Chosen One, but let us not make our guest feel uncomfortable. Instead, welcome him graciously when your opportunity presents itself." Gabriel's soothing voice resonated across the entire courtyard.

Then, in an instant, the courtyard resumed its busy pace. But now, people peered out of the corner of their eyes, trying to catch a glimpse of Laken surreptitiously. If there had been only a handful of clandestine onlookers, Laken would not have noticed. But there were hundreds of pairs of eyes, each trying to steal a glimpse of the boy and his ring.

"Try one. A Nirb, that is," Gabriel suggested in an attempt to take Laken's attention off of the curious onlookers. Laken looked up into Gabriel's anxious face, then looked at the bag, reached in and reluctantly grabbed a golden acorn-shaped nirb. He held up the strange candy, allowing the sunlight to shimmer upon it. The tiny nirb glittered in the light. Laken looked back to Gabriel who nodded his head quickly nudging him to try one. Laken looked back to the nirb, then lightly pressed it to his lips, paused, and then slowly touched his tongue to the candy.

"Come on, put it into your mouth!" Gabriel's excitement was obvious. Laken paused, looked up at Gabriel, and then put it in his mouth.

Suddenly, Gabriel said, "Fudge," and the candy instantly tasted like fudge. "Carmel," Gabriel cried out. And in the flash of an eye, it was Carmel. "Peanut butter!" and the nirb became peanut butter. "Whatever you think, it becomes that flavor," Gabriel blurted, as if he had been holding in this timeless secret for years. "Try another and think of something." Gabriel's smile stretched across his face.

Laken grabbed another Nirb, popped the candy into his mouth, thought, and then Dave said, "Pot roast," and instantly a warm pot roast flavor filled Laken's taste buds. He thought again, and Dave concurred. "Mashed potatoes and gravy." Once again, the flavor changed to mashed potatoes and gravy.

"Old shoe," Laken heard Gabriel say, and Laken began to gag and spit out the Nirb, which tasted like the inside of a shoe. Gabriel and his numa looked like they were going to fall over laughing.

"That's disgusting," Laken croaked as he continued to spit.

Gabriel's expression became serious. "Your first lesson, Laken: before you allow what others say to change what you are thinking, make sure it does not change what you want out of life." Gabriel then offered him a smile.

"I'll try to remember that," Laken said, rubbing his tongue up and down his sleeve.

Just then, a withered and blackened numa whizzed through the air and landed on Gabriel's shoulder. His high-pitched whisper announced, "I am back, my lord. As foreseen, her grandparents Bach and Nelvia are dead. We have evidence that the Chosen One is behind this..."

CHAPTER FIVE
Grog, Zog, and a Couple of Bullies

Gabriel shook his head. His expression turned grave, and then washed away. Remis whispered a few words to the blackened numa. "Very well, my lord," said the numa before flying away. "Please follow me, Laken, I have some urgent business I must attend to." Gabriel turned and rushed down a path leading away from the buildings towards another set of large golden gates identical to the ones through which they had entered the city. Laken jogged to keep up with Gabriel's pace. There were carts, and small makeshift tables along the path, creatures and people conducting business and trade. Golden Park benches were positioned along the road. A light breeze brushed against Laken's face, and the smell of flowers filled his lungs.

The area closest to the gates were surrounded by picnic tables and sitting areas. Nearly every table was occupied by people or creatures who talked, laughed, or just relaxed. As they reached the Gate, Laken noticed two Qwerub's at the gate who were considerably larger than the ones at the outer gate. These Angels, too, each had a massive flaming sword, swinging back and forth in a hypnotic rhythm.

Laken shook his head as if freeing himself from the rhythmic trance. His attention was drawn by an overhanging sign, spanning the entire width of the gate. The sign was engraved with letters as tall as Laken, forming the word "Dogma." Under that word, in a smaller font, was written *Angelic School of Magic and Flight*. Laken's heart pounded as he continued to read. Along the bottom of the sign there were six symbols, their meanings etched into the gold. First, a Yellow Unicorn (Charm and Beauty), then a Brown Owl (Wisdom and Knowledge), then a Red Serpent (Cunning and Shrewd), a Blue Lion (Courage and Strength), and a White Lamb (Love and Kindness). Last was a Green Dragon but the words ascribing its meaning looked like they had been scratched out.

"Weird," Dave whispered.

Laken didn't disagree. His view encompassed the totality of the gates, noticing that the golden brick walls extended the length of the courtyard and attached to the outer walls.

"Grog and Zog," Gabriel said, his voice urgent. "I need you to keep an eye on Laken for me, as I have some dire business to attend to."

"Of course, my lord," the deep voiced Qwerub on the left responded. "He will be safer than a…" but he was cut off by the Qwerub on the right.

"Grog!" a thunderous voice growled. "We do not utter in audible tones! Thousand years of training, and this one simple vow you can't manage! His numa heard me say yes. It's that simple!"

"And what if I *did* speak audibly? Who cares? Who does it hurt?" Grog snapped.

"Grog, by the power of the Almighty, I will cut your tongue out myself!"

"Hey, *you* talked. Why don't *you* have to observe the code?" Grog's eyes narrowed.

"Grog and Zog, I must go. *Please take care of Laken.*" Gabriel looked at Laken. "I will be back by dusk. Please stay here." And before Laken could reply, he turned and with the same purposeful pace, strode off, his robes whipping along the golden path.

"Don't tell me not to talk when you talk," muttered Grog. "I will not talk in my head. I'm going to talk out loud. You don't tell me what to do. If you can talk, I can talk. Tell me what to do." Grog let out a heavy breath. "I've taking your orders for five hundred boring years. Now you can listen to *me*." Grog's expression pinched.

Laken leaned up against the golden wall, which seemed to warm his back. "Where do you think we are?" Laken thought.

"Don't know, but it sure is peaceful," answered Dave. Laken's eye caught three fairies darting in and out among the leaves on the massive tree. Laken let out a big, relaxing sigh and, without so much as a thought, reached down, grabbed a Nirb and popped it into his mouth.

"Oh, turkey and cranberries," said Dave. The flavor burst into his mouth! Laken savored every second of that Nirb.

Out across the court, Laken spotted a group of kids his age sitting around a bench. Upon closer inspection, Laken noticed one boy surrounded by six girls, all seemingly in a school-girl trance, mesmerized. Laken couldn't blame them: the boy had to be one of the handsomest beings he had ever seen. Long, flowing blonde hair complimented his strong square jaw and perfect nose. Laken could see the boy's bright blue eyes nearly twenty feet away.

"Whatever, does he have a cool ring like us?" Dave asked. He didn't sound sure.

Laken reached down for another Nirb, and just as it touched his tongue, Dave said, "Warm apple pie, with vanilla ice cream." *Ohhh*. The taste gave Laken goose bumps.

To the left of the golden boy with blue eyes was a small group that looked like a motley gang. Four boys and a girl had black cloaks and all wore scowls across their faces. All of them had midnight black hair hanging shoulder length, except the very tall boy, who had brown curly hair cut mid-ear level.

"I think he is a giant." Dave said.

The second tallest of the group barely reached his massive chest.

"I don't think you even come up to his waist," Dave continued.

Next to the giant were two hefty kids. Their pale skin oozed with red-colored blotches.

"Looks like they've had way too many Nirbs," Dave interjected. The fourth boy was skinny and, if possible, a little paler than the rest. He seemed to be the ring leader of the gang. Laken could barely make out each of their numas, all very dark blue, similar to the color Dave had turned during their stealing spree.

Laken noticed that when kids passed by the group, they would seemingly trip over nothing, as if an invisible force had picked the boy up and slammed him on the ground. One poor kid had his cloak raised up in the air over his head, exposing his heavenly *fruit of the looms* for all to see. Each time, the gang broke into hysterical laughter, and the victims rushed off, bursting into tears. Laken couldn't help but notice that the giant seemed disinterested in these antics. Instead, he played with what looked like a large butterfly.

Laken reached down, grabbed another Nirb, placed it into his mouth. Grog's voice bellowed, "Centaur poop!" Laken coughed, hacked, and spit out the entire Nirb. His stomach lurched upward, stopping at the top of his throat, adding another nasty flavor to Laken's mouth. A roar of laughter burst out beside him.

"Grog! That is absolutely unacceptable. I will be putting that in my report."

"Oh, they can punish me for a hundred years," Grog laughed. "The look on the Chosen One's face when I said, *poop*, was worth it."

"A talking Cherub, or is it Qwerub? No, definitely Cherub. How delightful," a voice slithered. "I will have to let mother know. She is part of the Senate. The senate doesn't have a lot of patience with unintelligent creatures, but of course you wouldn't know that, being one yourself."

Laken looked up to see where the voice was coming from. Strolling towards him was the motley gang.

"You must be the Chosen One," the skinny boy said in a droll voice. His face held a cold smirk. "Chosen for what, no one knows. Maybe chosen to be in charge of these two idiots." The boy motioned to Grog and Zog.

"Good one, Daeth," the two hefty kids said in unison looking to their leader. Laken noticed Grog's knuckles turn white around the massive sword. "Maybe we'll luck out and the real Chosen One will finish you." Daeth had moved within inches of Laken, his glare like broken glass. Laken held his gaze, his eyes narrowed.

"Maybe I was chosen to rid this place of ugly, and you're my first assignment." A smirk stretched across Laken's face. The giant boy pushed his way past Daeth and grabbed Laken by the arm. The giant screamed out in pain, accompanied by the sound of sizzling bacon. He wrenched away his blistered hand. Out of the corner of his eye, Laken noticed the giant's numa flicker like that of the old woman's, but this numa went bright blue then back to pale blue.

"Daeth, Baylor, Grap, Scorpious, Ravana; just get a move on. Leave Laken alone." Grog's voice was edged in caution.

Daeth whipped his head towards Grog. "Keep your mouth shut, you stupid cherub." Then he paused taking a deep breath. "You know, there's a reason why they have the code of silence for cherubs like you." Hate spread across his features. "It's so the rest of us don't have to listen to all the dumb things you have to say."

Out of the corner of his eye, Laken noticed that the strange ball the children in the courtyard were playing with made an awkward U-turn, and began to sail at an incredible rate towards himself and the others. Daeth's brows narrowed as he held Grog's gaze.

"You big, stupid, dumb moro—" *Whammm!* The ball slammed into Daeth's head with such force that the boy did a complete flip before crashing to the ground. Everyone jumped back in terror. Ravana let out a scream. Grap and Scorpious each cursed a different set of words. Baylor's face lost its color.

"Grog!" Zog said.

The gang surrounded Daeth, each trying to help him up. "Daeth, are you alright?"

The giant grabbed Daeth by the hand, and pulled. Daeth wrenched his arm away. "Get your Ogre hands off me! I'm fine!"

Daeth stumbled to his feet. He took a ragged breath as he dusted off his cloak. His face flushed to a deep crimson, and a vein in his neck throbbed as if ready to burst. Daeth's eyes focused on his dirty cloak. He began to make threats, his words following the cadence to which he struck the dust from his cloak. "My... mother... will...report... you... to... Euphoram!" Daeth's eyes wide with anger, his gaze snapped to Grog's. "She *knows* him. Knows him well. I promise you, you will be stripped of that sword, and will find yourself guarding a, a..." He paused, searching for a thought. "...an outhouse out at Dung's Troll Manure plant before the end of the week!" His breath was heavy, as if he'd just run a mile.

Grog's expression tightened. "You don't scare me, little boy." Venom coated his words. "Your mom sure doesn't scare me." A fresh smile snaked across his face. "You know she's Fallen, don't you? We all know it. She will find herself soon enough in Outer Darkness. Much like your father."

"Grog, stop, now!" Zog interrupted. But Grog's words had already struck a nerve with Daeth. He began to walk towards Grog, his face turning past crimson to purple. "Please, please put your hands on me, you little son of a Fallen," Grog goaded Daeth.

"Not very wise, Daeth," came the calm, familiar voice of Gabriel. "Taunting the most powerful creature in our world? Not wise, not wise at all." Daeth turned to see Gabriel's warm smile beaming at him. Daeth looked back to Grog, then to his gang, and finally back to Gabriel. Daeth looked like he'd taken a fist to the stomach. He gave his cloak one last pat, inhaled deeply and held it. He stared at Gabriel; pain washed across his expression. The sounds of the courtyard filled the void as they waited. Finally, he exhaled his frustration, and began to stutter as his voice cracked. " Sor...sorry, Headmaster."

Gabriel offered Daeth a smile, then looked around at each of the students. "Good to see you all have had a chance to meet one another. We'll have an exciting year together. Daeth, Ravana, Grap, Scorpious, could you please excuse Baylor and me for a moment?"

"Yes, Headmaster," the gang muttered in unison, slinking off like a pack of dogs with their tails tucked behind their legs.

Gabriel turned a concerned gaze on Baylor. "Baylor, you become the company you keep. You can't roll around in mud and not get dirty."

"They are my friends." Baylor looked down to his massive feet.

"Friends? No." Gabriel's hand now on Baylor's shoulder. "An influence in your life? Most definitely." Gabriel pulled Baylor closer. "They are not your true friends. Baylor. You need to open your eyes. Friendship is a gift that you give to another. It comes from a desire for what is best for the other. Neither the gift nor the desire is evident in any of their actions." Gabriel's voice softened. "Sadly, your supposed friends don't know what friendship is." Gabriel paused and looked at Baylor, who kicked the ground with his sandal.

"Baylor, I see your real numa. There is nothing wrong with you letting the rest of the world see who you really are." Gabriel raised his hand slightly and Baylor's numa changed from dark blue to bright blue, the shade of Summer's. "A true friend would accept and admire the gifts that you possess." Gabriel paused again as Baylor let out a sigh. "Baylor, I believe that in this year, you will be choosing a side. The side you choose will determine your destiny." Gabriel shifted his body to look Baylor in the eyes. "Your destiny was foreseen long, long ago, as a fork in the road." Baylor's eyes widened. "Yes, the prophecy concerns you. You will be a key instrument in what is to come." A smile curled at the corners of Gabriel's mouth. "You must choose which side your gifts will be used for." There was a moment of silence and then Gabriel, shifting tones, pleasantly dismissed him. "Looking forward to seeing you tomorrow."

"You, too, Headmaster," Baylor said somberly, lumbering away, his head hung down.

"Thank you, Grog and Zog," Gabriel offered them a smile.

"Your welcome, Headmaster!" Grog's jaw tensed as he looked to Zog. Gabriel then turned his attention to Laken, "Tomorrow is the first day of school. What do you say we get you a sword?"

CHAPTER SIX
Laken Gets a Sword

"A sword. I'm getting a sword," Laken announced, following eagerly on Gabriel's heels. Dave slashed this way and that, slaying invisible creatures one after the other. Laken and Dave were still discussing the sword when they arrived at Draugr's Armor and Battle Shop. The door creaked as Gabriel opened it for Laken, ushering the boy through. A small bell went off on the other side of the huge, stable-sized door, wide open against the farthest wall. Laken winced at the strong smell of pasture.

Laken's eye was drawn to a fire pit just right of the door. The blue and orange smoke danced up to a chimney above; the hot coal fire was the greatest source of light in the room, casting long shadows all about. There were displays of armor, boots, vests, daggers and swords strewn around the room; as if an epic battle had taken place, the weapons and armor abandoned on the field once the fighting had ended. A large conveyer belt served as a barrier running through the middle of the room.

An enormous oil painting of a handsome Centaur hung on the wall to the left. The Centaur had long flowing blonde hair, a proud chin, and large green eyes. His body a massive, strong black horse, the torso in full armor, and a white tennis ball-sized gemstone glowing vibrantly from the center of the armor.

"Yas, yas, what da wown't?" asked a deep, scratchy voice. *Clank, clank, clank.* From beyond the stable door came the sound of hooves. A centaur filled the doorway. Laken stared at the Centaur for a moment, then glanced at the painting, then back to the Centaur. "I think that's him." Dave said. "Time has not been kind to the old horse."

Laken's eyes went wide. The Centaur looked much older. His face, now unshaven and unkempt, looked old and weathered. His hair was long, gray and matted. A long scar stretched from his left shoulder down to his navel.

"Ah, Gabe, it has been a lung, lung time." A thin smile tried to break free from the Centaur.

"Yes, my old friend, Draugr, it has. Seventy-five years to the day," Draugr's gaze turned toward Laken. The Centaur's lip curled and his eyes narrowed as he regarded Laken. Draugr then turned his gaze back to Gabriel.

"Well, let us hope ya do better with this lad than ya did with the last." The Centaur slowly shook his head.

"Yes, I learned a great deal." Gabriel's lips thinned. "And I see much promise in Laken here," he finished proudly, giving Laken a warm smile.

"Yas, yas, you can't run ferwurd if yar always looking back," Draugr eyed Laken yet again. He strode up to the conveyer. He considered the boy head to toe, even more carefully than before. A wary smile curled up his mouth as he turned his attention to Gabriel.

"The boy looks a little scrawny. Yur sure this is the promised one?" he asked, ignoring Laken's presence. Laken's gaze snapped to Gabriel who held up his hand, anticipating a prompt defense from the boy.

"I seem to remember a scrawny Centaur who was called *Pony Boy* most of his childhood." A smirk played across Gabriel's face. "And he turned out to be one of the greatest warriors Eden has ever seen." Draugr winced at the mention of his old nickname.

"Ya have a good point there, my old friend," Draugr shook his head. "I take we need to get the young lad ready fur battle," Draugr winked at Gabriel. "Blark! Blark! Ya lazy rodent, get yur green backside out here!" Draugr turned towards the stable door. "Blark! You pointy-eared-durt-bag, let's go!"

Through the huge door scampered a Dwarf wearing blue pants, blue boots, a green vest, and a green hat, through which his long, pointed ears poked out. "It's about time, ya little squirrel. Now get the boy's cloak of arms, ya pint-sized dunkey." The Dwarf ignored the insults as he hopped over the conveyer and rushed over to Laken. Blark reached into a small marble-sized sack tied to his waist and pulled out a measuring stick much too large to have fit in the bag.

"I know. *I know.* That is weird," Dave said, shaking his head.

Blark let the stick go and it floated in the air for a moment— and then whizzed over to Laken. The stick began to worm its way all over Laken's body bending and shaping itself like a rope around his waist, then up his leg, all the while calling out measurements in a high, screeching voice. "...36 inches, 17 inches, 13 inches..." Finally, the stick flew back to Blark who shoved it into his sack. The conveyer belt began to move clockwise. A few seconds later, a sparkling white cloak appeared hovering over the conveyer. Laken was about to walk towards the cloak when the cloak began to move on its own. It floated over to where Laken stood, and dressed itself to his frame, draping down to a perfect length just brushing the ground. Laken felt the cloak begin to shake, then there was a heat burst, and suddenly he could no longer feel his old clothes hugging his body. He ran his hands up down where his pants and shirt had been to feel nothing underneath the cloak.

"All right there, ya sure will be the prettiest girl at the dance. Where did that little fur ball go?" Draugr now looking about the room.

"Here, sir," piped Blark, directly behind him. Draugr jumped a little in surprise, his expression tightened. *Blththth!* Draugr ripped a fart. Blark was thrown backwards a few feet and rolled to the ground—Blart now a shade greener than he already was.

"That's what ya get fur standing there in the line of fire. I hope it burnt that little smirk off yur ugly face. Let's get the boy his Hallow sac."

Laken bit his lip to keep from laughing, Dave fell over laughing. "Hahaha I can't breathe, I can't breathe!" Dave kept crying out between each laughing fit.

Blark got up, shook himself off and scampered into the back room. A few moments later, he returned with a small sack, seemingly identical to the one around his waist.

"Let's go, let's go, dunkey, we don't have all day," Blark shot Draugr a contemptuous look, and made his way over to Laken.

"Here is your Hallow sac. It will hold all your weapons, school supplies and everything else you want to keep with you," Blark squeaked. Laken grabbed the bag, barely the size of his hand. He held it up into the light, his eyes narrowed. He then looked over at Gabriel, confusion sliding across his face.

"The swords must be a couple inches long, I'm figuring." Dave's brows stood at attention. Gabriel gave a slight smirk and then, in a demonstration, grabbed his identical Hallow sac. He reached into it pulling out the huge golden sword they had seen earlier that day. He then pulled out a chest the size of a golf bag and placed it on the floor. Then he pulled out a barrel that was overflowing with Nirbs.

"Oops, didn't mean to pull that out. Meant to get this." Another much smaller barrel full of fruits, vegetables, and what looked like a type of beef jerky. "The Sac is quite handy, I would say." Gabriel wore an amused expression.

"Love to stay up all night and watch yur magic show, but me and the little weasel have to close up shop here soon," Draugr spat in Blark's direction. "What are ya waiting fur, a written invitation, ya mindless goat? Make the bag his!"

Blark let out a weary breath, then leveled his gaze at Laken. "We must first make it yours and yours alone," Gabriel motioned back to Blark who began to explain. "That way someone can't steal your Hallow. If they try, it simply disappears, and reappears where you left it." Laken looked to the sac, then back to Blark. Laken sat in silence, grappling with what to say next.

"Hurry, ya long winded turd. I don't have all day. Be done with the great speech already," barked Draugr. Blark's ears shot back.

"If your numa could please spit in the bag," Blark said, his voice cracking. Dave and Laken looked at each other, and Dave leaned over and spat in the bag, which let off a faint golden glow, lifted off Laken's hand, hovered for a moment, and floated over and attached itself to Laken's side. Laken's eyes looked as if they were about to burst from their sockets.

"Holy craaa–" Dave burst out.

"Yas, yas, very mystical. I was hoping to be done befur Christmas, Chosen Boy." Draugr interrupted. "Blark, let's get the weapons claim done, while I'm still alive!"

"Weapons claim?" Dave inquired. Laken shrugged his shoulders.

Blark rushed over to a large red box connected to the conveyer belt, opened it up, and pulled out a black cylinder. The cylinder had a long hose attached to it, feeding into the conveyer box. Blark walked over to Laken and said, "Spit in this." Laken shrugged his shoulders, hacked up the contents of his throat, leaned over, and spat in the cylinder.

SSSSREEEEEE-an ear-piercing whistle rang through the shop. The conveyer belt went haywire—the belt jolted back and forth, then back again, so fast its motion was a blur. The box smoked and spat out orange and green sparks. Blark ran around the room as if on fire, while Draugr barked out orders randomly.

"Ya dumb monkey, shut it down, *shut it down!* Get to the power button. Hit the button, ya lazy turdsicle, shut it down!" Gabriel held out a hand and the machine suddenly stopped. Blark sat, panting in place. Draugr had turned a deep red, his narrowed eyes fixed on Laken.

"Not you, genius, yur numa there!" Draugr said. "Blark, every seventy-five years—the same thing. The boy don't live here. He don't know the difference between a rhema and a blogsette. Ya dumb furball."

Blark picked up the cylinder again and walked over to Laken. "Have your numa spit into it," his voice shook. Laken and Dave looked at each other; Dave coughed up another loogey, and spat in the cylinder.

The conveyer belt began to move slowly, counter clockwise this time. Every few feet a weapon hovered over the conveyer belt. A golden sword covered with blue jewels passed by.

"Wish that was ours," Dave said dreamily.

A massive sword the size of Laken whooshed by. The next ten weapons were swords of various sizes and colors, followed by a golden bow, a few small daggers, a spear made of diamonds, and a couple of swords. Finally, the conveyer slowed. Another six-foot tall sword passed by, letting off an eerie green glow. Then a small golden dagger with a blue pearl on the end passed by.

And then Laken saw it. It was gorgeous, and it was coming out of the wall. The sword's handle was that of pure gold, with two large, red emeralds placed in the handle. The blade looked like glass, and the red light emanating from the blade lit up the room. Laken rushed over as the sword was still moving. He followed the enchanted weapon until the conveyer belt stopped. Laken felt like he couldn't have dreamt a better or greater sword. Laken reached out for the sword.

"What are doing there, Chosen Boy? That there ain't yur sword. *This* one is," Draugr said, a chuckle leaking out. Laken looked over at what Draugr was pointing to. Laken shook his head, as if tossing the image from his sight. It had to be the oldest sword in this world. Made before they had gold, or even metal. It was a tarnished, worn, gray-looking object. The blade was long and dark, as if blackened in a fire. The dull bluish hilt of the sword had five nickel-sized colorless stones embedded, one above the other, along the length. Each stone went all the way through the hilt to the other side.

Laken jaw tensed, looking over to Gabriel, then to Draugr. They each nodded their heads in unison as if giving permission for Laken to pick it up. Disappointment galloped through him.

"Get yur hands on it boy! Come on, we ain't got all day!"

Laken shook his head, stared at the sword for a moment, and then reached out to grasp the sword by its handle. When his hand came into contact with the sword, Laken felt a jolt of electricity travel through his body, and the sword let out a slight purr.

Laken lifted up the sword and spun it around, staring uncomfortably at the weapon. Laken slashed back and forth as if blocking an attack.

"For da luv of all dat is good and 'oly, can we finish up sometime today!" Laken could barely make out what Draugr was saying, he was in such a trance-like state. Laken lifted the sword even higher so the hilt was eye level, and he looked through the top stone at the fire across the room. Etched in the clear stone was something he couldn't quite make out.

"Looks like an animal, or maybe a bug," Dave suggested. Laken then gazed through the other four stones one at a time. Each had a different shape, and as with the first, he had no clue what that shape was. Laken then flipped the sword upside down to examine the large stone embedded in the base of the hilt. It too, had no color. Once again there was a slight outline of something etched inside the stone. Laken squinted, held it up to the light, but couldn't make out this image either.

Finally, Laken looked up to Gabriel. Gabriel was in deep thought. Laken thought he saw triumph slide behind the headmaster's eyes.

"You're sure, Draugr? You're *sure* this is the sword?" Gabriel's eyes widened.

"Da claim box never been wrong befur, ya know dat. Dis one is da one. Dis sword hadn't had an owner in over six-thousand years, da legend has it." Draugr scratched his head.

"Ask him if we can just have an old stick instead," Dave spat. The sword gave out a small violent shake.

"Yes, you are correct. It has been six-thousand years since the Bathsheda has claimed an owner," Gabriel whispered.

"Bathsheda? How 'bout turdsheda, oldsheda, or piece of sh-" But Laken was interrupted by the sudden jerk of the sword in his hand, and a burst of heat so hot that he almost dropped the sword. Laken quickly looked to Gabriel.

"Laken, there is no better sword in this place, nor in this world as far as I know." Gabriel's gaze swept the length of him. "Please remember, Draugr assessed you based on your outward appearance, and how wrong was he? Don't make the same mistake. You will do great things with this sword." A smile crept thru his beard.

Laken took a moment to digest what Gabriel had said. "But it is so, so—" Laken tried to declare, but Gabriel held up his hand, interrupting Laken. His expression filled with concern.

"Be careful of what you say. Your every word has the power of life and death. Your sword hears your voice, and what it becomes to you is contingent on how you speak about it."

"Dat der sword saved da wurld before. Sur it will do it again." Draugr was now staring off in the distance.

CHAPTER SEVEN
Blegs & Qwesters, Gabriel & Secrets

B
ack out on the street, Gabriel and Laken walked along in comfortable silence. The sun was low in the sky, the shadows long and dark. Laken inhaled an immense breath of the cool night air, smelling of orange blossoms. As he exhaled, Laken noticed how his new cloak sparkled in the light and swirled along the ground. He put his hand to his new sac, assuring himself that it was still there. Even now, Laken remained amazed as to how he was able to store his sword into this tiny sac. Though the weapon was quite heavy, once in the bag, it was weightless.

As they walked down the quieting street, Dave struggled to understand the impossibilities of the bag. "Magic, must be magic. Tow barrels, and chest in there?" Dave continued to mutter under his breath.

Gabriel's voice interrupted Dave, "Let's turn in here and get the last of your supplies." Laken had been so lost in thought, he hadn't noticed that most of the street's bustle had abated. Just a few stragglers walked down the street. Gabriel held the door open for Laken as he passed under the sign "Blegs & Qwesters Angelic Supplies."

A large golden chandelier hung in the center of the room, giving off a radiant glow that lit the entire store. The smell of paper and new books filled Laken's nostrils. Unlike Draugr's, this place was quite organized. Books were nicely arranged on shelves against the wall. There were a few dozen robes and cloaks floating as if on a clothes rack. Gabriel walked over to a pyramid shaped pile of golden sandals sitting under the chandelier. Carefully ducking under the ornamental lamp, he grabbed an enormous pair of sandals. "Here, Laken, put these on." Gabriel handed him the shoes.

"These are way too big," Laken protested as he waved the tennis racquet-sized sandals at Gabriel.

Gabriel tilted his head and studied them for a moment. "No, I believe they are your exact fit. Please give them try." Laken shook his head, bent over and put the Sasquatch sandals on. The instant his foot was in the shoe, it began to sparkle, there was a burst of heat and light, and then the sandal shrunk around his foot, until it was an exact fit.

"What do you know? It is your size." Gabriel seemed amused. "We can't always believe what we see. Instead, believe, and then you will see." Gabriel rubbed his hands together. Laken put on the other shoe, which shrink to fit, as did the first. "Okay, Laken, you will need some dress robes." Gabriel handed him a robe the size of a tent.

Laken shrugged his shoulders and replied, "Just my size. Extra-extra-extra huge."

Gabriel let out a small laugh. "Now you are getting it. Place the robe in your Hallow."

Laken looked around with caution and whispered, "We're not paying for these?"

"Steal them. Yeah! Grab them. Grab a bunch!" Dave's urge to steal returned, like the rush of a river.

"Oh, I am so sorry, of course not. I, too, forget you are not from Eden," Gabriel apologized. "We have streets of Gold, walls filled with precious gems, so of course currency in Eden is of no use. Everything is free," he explained with a smile.

Dave looked like he was going to explode with excitement. "Grab some more robes. Get your hands on those books. Let's take the chandelier!" Dave was screaming.

"But then why would anyone work, or make anything?" Laken's expression filled with curiosity.

"Oh, it is that mindset that holds the world back," sighed Gabriel."-So much of this type of thinking makes life difficult. If only you could grasp that it is much better to give than to receive." Gabriel brushed his hand across some robes. "Of course, we could sit around and do nothing, taking from others. But true joy comes from working for the good of others, with no expectation of return." Gabriel paused to smile at some students passing by the window.

"The outside world has greed, envy, anger, unhappiness, all which stem from selfish desires. If everyone uses their skills and talents for the good of others, no one goes without, and all gain." Triumph dotted his eyes.

Laken nodded as Dave screamed, "It's all mine. *Mine.* I will have it all!" Laken shot a look at Dave, who put his head down in shame and said, "I know, I know, the greater good. Love others, blah blah blah."

"Alright, follow me and let's get your school book," Gabriel said, striding over to the bookshelves.

"School book? Don't you mean books?" Laken's eyes narrowed. Gabriel ignored this question, reached up and grabbed a blue book that had the word "Rhema" along its spine. As Laken took a closer look he noticed that all the books said Rhema. Gabriel brought the book down to Laken, who grabbed and opened it. The first page was blank, so he turned the page to find out the next page was blank, and the next and the next.

"I got a misprint. This book is full of blank paper," Laken's brows shot up.

"Laken, close the book," Gabriel instructed. Laken looked up at Gabriel with a puzzled expression. A smile tugged on Gabriel's lips. Laken closed the book. "Now think of something you want to read about, and then open it," Gabriel's smile grew.

Laken thought for a moment; then Dave said, "Bathsheda Sword." Laken opened the book and, to Laken and Dave's surprise, there was an enormous picture of a glorious sword; above it was written, "Bathsheda

Sword." Laken presumed that the sword pictured in the book had to be the complete opposite of his own sword. This sword was spinning weightlessly on the page. Its blade was hewn of that mysterious transparent gold, and its handle looked as if carved out of a giant blue pearl. Even on the page, it gave out a glorious glow. It had a large green emerald on its hilt with five emerald cut stones embedded in it. Each stone was a different color—yellow, blue, brown, red, and white. Each one's glow was beating separately.

"I think you could compare this book to the Internet of your world," said Gabriel.

Laken looked at Gabriel in a surprise and said, "This is not the sword in my sac. Draugr ripped us off." His brows creased deeply. "Well, I guess it was free, but even at the price of free, I think we got ripped off!" Suddenly, Laken felt the Hallow shake on his side.

"Laken, *it hears you*, and from what you say, *it will become*," Gabriel's voice firm. "I promise you Laken, that the sword in your Hallow and the one you see in the Rhema are one and the same."

Laken looked back down and began to read:

Bathsheda Blade Created: Year Unknown. Creator: The Most High (Legend has it) Made of: Unicorn Horn (A unicorn's horn also is known as the "bane of evil" in that it has the ability to dispel anything malignant in water and can also kill most truly evil creatures it comes into contact with. For more information on Unicorns think, "Unicorn.") Known Master: ...

Laken could not believe what he read next. He looked up at Gabriel who, despite his usually cool demeanor, was actually smirking. "You? It was your sword?" Laken's awestruck expression washed across his face.

"Laken, read on."

Last Known Master: Gabriel (for more information think, "Gabriel"). Accomplishments: Legend has that this is the sword Gabriel used during the first Great Fall to defeat Belzatat and Drxore in a legendary battle lasting over 27 hours. Gabriel was said to retire the sword after the battle stating, "This sword will once again be of use when great evil attempts to rise again to ill-gained power."

Laken closed the book. His heart jumped with a newfound love for the sword in the Hallow. "I love my sword," Laken declared. He felt his Hallow purr like a cat.

"The celebration is about to begin. Let us go out and get a good spot," smiled Gabriel.

As Gabriel turned towards the door, Dave said, "Gabriel," and Laken opened the book. There stood Gabriel, the wings Laken had seen earlier spanned both pages, his large golden sword swinging left and right. The picture looked alive, in some ways like a video of Gabriel moving.

Gabriel Born: Unknown-present Birthplace: Unknown About Gabriel: Gabriel is an Archangel who stands over eight feet tall, and whose wings are said to be those created by the Most High. Gabriel's wing span is speculated to be over twenty feet (some say more). Original master of the Bathsheda Blade (think Bathsheda for more information). Gabriel used this blade to defeat Belzatat and Drxore in a legendary battle lasting over 27 hours. He has been awarded the Jehova Medal of Valor (for more information, think, "Jehova Medal of Valor"), the highest medal of honor given, three times. The first for his part in defeating the original Fallen, second for his part in defeating the Fallen of the Dark Ages, and third for his part in the defeat of the Fallen of the 19th century. Gabriel is the only Angel to receive the Jehova Medal more than a single time. Gabriel was given the Shalom Medal of Peace when he orchestrated the Treaty of Shadowmore in 1230 A.D. This treaty is still in force today. (Think, "Shadowmore," for more information.) Gabriel is responsible for giving the blessing to Jacob thus creating the Chosen One (think Chosen One for more information). Gabriel is father to (this area had been blacked out) Gabriel is husband to (this area had been blacked out also). Gabriel is currently the Headmaster at Dogma, Chancellor of Archangels, has been nominated thirty-seven times to the Supreme Angelic Court, currently is the presiding Lord of the Angelic Judicial Committee and is on the board of directors of "Nirbs" treats. Gabriel is currently standing in Blegs and Qwesters behind Laken wondering what is taking so long…

Laken looked up in surprise.

"Now that you have read my secrets, are you ready?" Gabriel, amusedly, peered down on Laken a smile playing on his face.

"Ah, yes, of course," Laken stuttered, as if caught stealing from a cookie jar.

"Follow me, then." Gabriel strode out of the shop and into the dark, very crowded street.

Laken, hard on Gabriel's heels, looked around in surprise. It seemed as if moments ago, it was light out and the streets were empty. Now it was dark and wall-to-wall with people. Laken grabbed onto Gabriel's cloak and followed in his wake, as Gabriel made his way through the crowd. Finally, they stopped in front of Grog and Zog's Gate. Gabriel turned to the mass and spoke.

"We celebrate tonight what we have celebrated for the last twelve years: the end of darkness, and the beginning of light." Gabriel's voice boomed throughout the courtyard as if he were talking into a microphone. "It has been twelve years without the oppression, the fear and, for some of you, the constant threat of death." Gabriel's gaze swept the crowd as he drew a large breath. "Tonight, we celebrate love. We celebrate the opportunity of peace, joy, and happiness that come from the giving of ourselves. WE CELEBRATE LIFE AND LIVE MORE ABUNDANTLY!"

The crowd erupted into cheers, clapping, and screams of excitement. "LET US CELEBRATE THE GREAT LIFE THAT IS AHEAD OF US!"

Gabriel lifted his hands, blasting fireworks just feet above the crowd. Then, throughout the gathering, everyone shot fireworks out of their own hands, in explosions of red, green, purple, and orange; then in a cacophony of colors. The explosions overhead gave a warm thrust of air with each explosion, slicing through the cold breeze. To Laken, it was as if he were inside the firework display. Suddenly, there were explosions just above ground level. Laken noticed that small children were attempting to produce fireworks. Some made a small pop, here and there, while others summoned merely a little poof of light and smoke.

"Out of the way!" Daeth's familiar drawl rang out from the crowd. Laken turned to see the gang pushing their way through the crowd, knocking over smaller children. The giant was the only one without a scowl—he looked as if he were, in fact, enjoying the show.

"Revel now, it'll all end when the *real* Chosen One returns," Daeth whispered in Laken's ear, and then shoved his way past, as Grap and Scorpious shot Laken a scowl.

"Glad we made some friends so quickly," Dave sneered

"It's a gift. It is a true gift I possess," Laken thought with a smile, and then turned his attention back to the fireworks. The show lasted some thirty minutes and then, as quickly as the fireworks had started, it was over, and the crowd began to disperse.

Without hesitation, Gabriel grabbed Laken's hand and led him back towards the buildings, wading their way through the crowd.

Laken could hear murmurings of, "Look, the Chosen One," "That's him there," "Kind of scrawny, don't you think?" and "Let's hope he isn't like the last one."

"It's been a long day. Let's go get settled in," Gabriel said. Laken blocked out what the crowd was saying by replaying the day in his mind.

He saw Gabriel's battle. Then, he recalled the sword and Hallow experience in his mind. His thoughts finally settled on Gabriel, and what the Rhema had said about him.

"Here we are." Gabriel's voice startled Laken back to reality. Laken looked up to see a large wood sign that read, "Twine's Inn." The building was quite a bit larger than any other on the block, made of huge logs stacked one on top of another. A large rock fireplace billowed smoke into the night air. Laken could see silhouettes of people as they strode by the large windows, making their way around the cabin.

They walked up the ancient stone steps and entered the inn through a massive wooden door that groaned as Gabriel opened it. A muddle of light conversations filled the air as they entered. Laken took note of the large stone fireplace in the middle of the room that gave off a tremendous glare from a roaring fire. Chairs were strewn throughout, with Gnomes, Dwarves and people sitting in them carrying on conversations, some reading, others just staring at the fire. In the corner of the room a golden harp played a soothing melody.

"Gabriel! And the Chosen One!" A very plump dwarf's voice boomed, as everyone in the room fell silent at once. The only remaining sound was the harp, still plucking lightly. Laken drew near to Gabriel as all eyes were on him. Gabriel's right arm wrapped around Laken drawing him in. An unnatural warming pulse washed across Laken's skin.

Gabriel allowed his smile to sweep across the room before speaking. "Good to see all of you. Laken and I will be heading up to our room. We have a big day ahead of us." Gabriel gave the group a nod, grabbed Laken's hand and led him through the room with all the normal pleasantries going on:

"Hi, Gabriel," "Hello, Headmaster," and "Good evening, Gabriel." Gabriel returned each pleasantry with one of his own. One by one, all those in the room went back to what they had been doing before Laken had entered. As Laken and Gabriel made their way through the room,

Laken could hear the whispers that seemed to follow in his wake. "The Chosen One," "Did you see him?" and "Boy he sure is small!"

Laken and Gabriel headed up the old rickety staircase, which creaked with each step. Finally, they reached the second floor, out of earshot of all the gossiping patrons. Gabriel turned left down the small hall, ducking the whole way to keep from hitting the low ceiling. The third door on the right swung open, and Laken and Gabriel entered. There was a single bed that filled most of the small room. A floating fireball over a small nightstand was the only source of light. There were a half-dozen pictures of elves, performing various tasks, hung at all different awkward heights.

Gabriel sat on the bed, his head still just below the ceiling. He smiled, and motioned for Laken to sit next to him. "Before we go to sleep, I owe it to you to answer some of your questions." Gabriel's voice cracked with sincerity. "Now I may not be able to answer all of them, or I may choose not to, but you have to trust me that I will always have your best interest at heart." A warm smile showed thru his beard.

Laken stared at the fireball for a few moments, "Where are we, I, I mean not at Twine's, but what world, what place?"

"Ah yes, that's usually the first question," Gabriel said as he raised a finger. "We are in Outer Eden, or I should say, the town of Outer Eden." Gabriel rubbed his hands together. "As far as the world is concerned, we are on what you call Earth, but in another dimension. I guess you could say we coexist on this planet."

They sat in silence as Laken processed this information. Laken began to absently turn the ring on his hand. Laken looked away from the light, and gazed into Gabriel's face. Gabriel's expression was warm, with long shadows cast upon it.

"How did I get here?"

"That ring on your finger is what brought you here," Gabriel paused his eyes widened. "We call the ring *the blessing*. On your thirteenth birthday, it brings you here. You will remain here for the next sixty-three years until the ring is given to the next Chosen One."

Laken's gaze dropped to the floor. "Sixty-three years? That's a long time. I mean, what will summer do without me?" His own words pinned him in place. The memory of what had happened flooded through him. How in the world had he forgotten about the most important person in his life? A rope of frustration tightened within him. His eyes wide in horror. "What about Summer? OMG! I forgot!" Laken shot off the bed, grabbing the door handle. Gabriel's hand held the door closed as Laken kept pulling. Laken's gaze locked to Gabriel's. His face flushed in frustration. "I have to get back!" He gave the door a huge pull. The door handle broke off, sending him tumbling to the ground. Laken jumped to his feet, now wedging the door handle back into the door. Gabriel's hand began to pull Laken's shoulder back to the center of the room. Laken's horror-struck gaze settled on Gabriel. "I have to protect Summer!" Tears splashed Laken's cheeks. Gabriel drew him into his arms, Laken's face brushed Gabriel's robe. "She is all alone." Laken's voice cracked in agony.

"She is quite alright." Gabriel cupped Laken's face, forcing their gazes to lock. "I don't believe there is anything to worry about. I have things in place to secure her safety."

Laken rubbed the tears from his eyes with the sleeve of his garment. "You sure?" Laken's brown eyes blinked hard splashing a few last tears on his face.

"I am positive!" Gabriel's voice was strong. "Summer is of our highest concerns, and the DAA is doing all he can right now to get another guardian to her."

"Guardian? What guardian? Another one? Where has the first one been? D-A- what?"

Gabriel held a hand up, cutting Laken off. "Slow down. The DAA is the Director of Angelic Affairs, and he is assigning a Guardian as we speak." Gabriel held up his hand again as Laken opened his mouth to speak. "Trust me, Laken, she is being looked after. She will be safe." Gabriel smiled. "When will she will be part of your life again?" Gabriel's jaw tensed. "Sadly, I don't know when. But I do know, that she will be in your life again" Triumph dotted his eyes.

"Laken?" Gabriel paused. "I need you to trust me." Laken gave Gabriel a slight nod of acceptance. "If you could please answer a question for me?" Gabriel asked, his eyes wide.

"Uugghh, of course," Laken stuttered in surprise. "What is Summer like?" Gabriel smiled.

This threw Laken off for a few seconds. Then he gathered himself and replied, "She is all the good things in life. Her smile can make a dark day bright. Her voice is, well, it is beautiful. She is my best friend and the one person I would be willing to die for. She has been my hope for a better life for the last twelve years." Laken got up off the bed and walked over to the window where he stared out at a couple of fairies fluttering by, having a tug-o-war over what looked like a blue apple. Laken turned back to Gabriel to catch a large smile stretching across Gabriel's face.

"Of course. That is exactly how I pictured her," Gabriel said, pride sliding across his face. There was a long, pause in the conversation.

"Did you know my father and mother?"

"Your father? That I cannot say. Your mother?" Gabriel paused as if he was stuck in a great memory. "Yes, I did get to have that extraordinary young woman in my life for nearly two years." Gabriel walked over and stood next to Laken, gazing out into the night. "She was one of the bravest people I have ever known, and I have known a lot of people. Gabriel looked into Laken's eyes. "She died so that you could live. She stood up to the most powerful Fallen Angel we have seen in over six thousand years." Gabriel turned his water-filled eyes back outside. "And she *won*," Gabriel whispered.

"Won? How? Where is she? I want to see her." Laken's questions and demands ricocheted around the room, his head turning this way and that as if he expected to see her appear at any moment.

"By won, I meant she saved you, and I believe she saved our future." A grin stretched across his face. "To do this, she had to give her life." A tear dripped down Gabriel's cheek, catching itself in his grey beard.

"Who? Who killed her?" Laken had to squeeze the words around the knot in his throat.

"Killed? No, he did not kill her. She was a rare one in that you could not take her life. She had to *give* it. She protected you from Rick." Gabriel's water filled eyes turned back to Laken, searching for a reaction.

"Rick? The evilest dude ever is named *Rick*?" Laken flopped back onto the bed.

Gabriel pondered for a moment and posed the next question with great anticipation. "You did not hear the name *Brone*?"

"Now, *Brone*. That seems right, but *Rick*? Not so scary."

Gabriel sank again into deep thought.

"So where Rick?" Laken's lips thinned.

"Laken, do you feel anything when you hear the name Rick?"

Laken looked puzzled, then shrugged. "I feel anger, like I want to hurt him."

"No, that is not what I mean. Do you feel fear? Deep, dark, painful, uncontrollable fear?" Gabriel, kneeling down in front of Laken, his blues eyes wide.

"No, nothing."

"Interesting, very interesting. The name does nothing, but how?" Gabriel was now muttering to himself. He stood up to pace the small room, but in two long strides he was across it and back again. "Laken, let me explain something, and this will clear up why I am acting the way I am. Rick, many years back, using Dark, Dark Fallen Magic, enchanted his name, so that now anytime anyone who is not Fallen hears the name, it comes out *Lord Brone*. This enchanted name attaches to your worst fears and nightmares, and consumes your soul for a few agonizing moments of torment. This is why no one says the name except the Fallen. They speak it to produce fear, which greatly increases their power."

Laken thought for a moment then replied, "But you say the name and nothing happens, and you say *Rick* sometimes and *Brone* others."

"Each time I speak, I say the name *Brone*. But the enchantment does not work on your ears, so you hear what I am actually saying. When I say *Rick*, everyone else hears *Brone* but you? When I say *Brone*, you hear *Brone*. Do you understand?"

Laken looked up muttering, "You say Rick, it is Brone, you say Brone it is Brone. I hear Rick, others hear Brone." Laken paused with a shrug, clarity entering his expression.

"I think I've got it, but why doesn't the name affect you, Gabriel?"

"Oh, fear has had no part of me for a long time. His name has nothing to attach to, and I believe that same quality resides in you," Gabriel smirked. "The question is why you can say the name Rick, and I hear the name Rick, not Brone. Very interesting."

"What will happen to Radkus, the old lady who tried to kill me today?" Laken interrupted Gabriel's thoughts.

"Radkus will be judged, and then thrown into Outer Darkness," Gabriel replied.

"Judged by who? And what is Outer Darkness?"

"Whom," Gabriel corrected. "He will be judged by our court system, and if found guilty, then judged by the Almighty. Outer Darkness is—"

But Laken interrupted, "Who is the Almighty?"

Gabriel smiled as he sat next to Laken again, "He is the Alpha and Omega, the Beginning and the End. He is the Great I Am."

"You are?" Laken got a little excited.

"No, no, not me, but he is 'I Am', meaning what do you need? You need joy? Then I am joy. You need peace? Then I am peace. He is 'I

Am,' or whatever you need." Laken shook his head as if this puzzle of a thought was attacking his mind.

"What is Outer Darkness?" said Laken, changing the subject.

"Oh, good question," smiled Gabriel, warming to the topic. "The Most High is the Creator of all, and it is His energy that holds it all together. Outer Darkness is simply a place where the Most High does not exist. It is a place of nothing, like a black hole for your soul. You are there, but nothing is there, and nor are you. Your soul feels torn apart, and fights to come together. It is this war of the soul that burns like fire for all of eternity. This is why some call it the Lake of Fire," Gabriel finished, his expression flushed with sadness.

There was another long pause until Laken asked, "Why did his hand burn when he touched me? I mean Radkus…and that big kid."

"Angels were created to enhance human life, make it better. In our very makeup as a being is the inability to ever harm a human." Gabriel stood up. "When someone touches you with harm in mind, it will sear. A sword swung by an Angel meant to hurt, will disintegrate upon impact. This makes the Chosen One a very powerful being in our world, and of course in yours."

"So, I'm invincible in this place?"

"Angels can't hurt you, but most other creatures can," Gabriel's smile retreated.

"Those big ol' dogs tickled me. They didn't hurt me," Laken's brows stood at attention.

"Oh, yes. Those are not real, but conjured up by the Fallen. They can only feed on fear, and their main purpose is to produce more fear, making them—and the Fallen—stronger yet." There was a long pause, where Laken stared out the window, listening to the crickets and bullfrogs sing from somewhere out in the darkness.

Finally, Laken looked up at Gabriel and asked, "Why am I here?"

Gabriel rose, walked over to the door, smiled at Laken, and said, "To save the world, of course." He closed the door, and Laken could hear his footsteps fade down the hall.

CHAPTER EIGHT
Summertime Dreams

Tat, tat, tat. Laken rolled over to look at the moonlit window. "Stupid birds," muttered Dave.

Laken had been lying in bed for a couple of hours, reliving the day with Dave, from the battle with the old lady and Gabriel's wings, to the Nirbs and Daeth. They finally settled on his mother—what she had done—and Laken reminded himself to ask Gabriel about the fight between her and Ricky. Calling Brone "Ricky" made Laken smile—it was like an insult hurled at Ricky every time he thought it.

What was his mother like? At times, an image of a beautiful woman with long brown hair forming perfectly around her petite face played in his mind. Her eyes were brown like Laken's, but her exotic-colored skin was a few shades darker than his. Her big bright smile sent a warmth through him. Was this her? She was beautiful in every way. Her image was so vivid, it had to be her.

Laken lay for quite some time with the image of his mom transfixed in his mind. Finally, he realized that his face hurt from smiling—a set of muscles he hadn't worked on much.

"Summer!" Dave blurted out. A wave of guilt rushed through Laken. How could he be so happy, while she was off alone? His heart felt like a heavy weight. "She is alright! She is alright!" Laken reminded himself. "Gabriel did say she has the best protection!" Dave said.

"I know, I know. But I miss her." Laken wiped the wetness from his eyes.

Dave blew into a large white handkerchief. "Me too." Dave turned so Laken couldn't see his face.

Laken's thoughts turned back to Summer. She had been his only reason worth living for the last twelve years. They spent nearly every waking second together. This was the first night they had ever been apart. What was she doing now? Who was taking care of her?

"That Jack!" Laken cursed. How could he be afraid of little ol' Ricky, when Jack had been tormenting his life for the last dozen years?

Laken's thoughts seemed to wander in and out of his mind, until he found himself in a field with his new sword. Not the one in his Hallow, but the one from the book. A couple of bulls swung an axe at him, and with great ease, Laken blocked the attackers and sent them sailing the way Gabriel had done. The old lady was swinging a green cat at him, using it as her weapon. Her feet were made of Nirbs, and Laken wanted them. With a slice, and a whish of the sword, Laken now had the Nirbs in his hand. As he was about to take a bite of the leg, he heard a familiar voice—the voice he longed to hear.

"Laken, I need you. Laken, please come back, please come back." It was Summer. She was crying and begging.

"I'm coming!" Laken's jaw tensed. He had to get to her. He began to run aimlessly through the fields. Then an unseen energy stopped him dead in his tracks. Suddenly, with the force of a life-sized vacuum, something stronger began to pull him. It wasn't wrenching him up or down or left or right, but rather, it pulled him inward. His muscles and flesh felt as if his whole body was being torn from the inside out. At the point he thought he was going to burst, there was a release and a loud *whsssshh*.

Everything around him began slowly to disintegrate, as if existence itself was crumbling apart. His view went black, and then the world began to reassemble, piece by piece, until Laken was in the basement of the old shack. He was there, but not in reality. He was like a shadow, unable to cast itself. He hovered over the place where Summer lay. She was sniffling and coughing. Her face was wet and red from crying. Her numa sat crumpled in a ball on her shoulder. Laken had never seen her like this before. The sight weighed heavily on him, like a boulder crushing his chest. He had trouble catching his breath. Laken floated to Summer, and tried to touch her, to shake her and tell her he was there, but his hand passed right through her.

"Laken, you are the best brother ever. I don't know what I will do without you." Tears splashed her cheeks. "Please come back."

"Why are we here? Who is punishing us?" Dave's anger colored his voice.

"SUMMER, I'm right here!" Laken cried. "Come on, Summer!" Laken put his head into his hands. "Please Summer, please hear me." Laken struggled to hold back his grief, and then let out a snort of a cry.

"Laken?" Summer sat up. "Is that you?"

Laken took his face from his hands. "Summer can you hear me? Summer, answer me!"

Summer rose, and tracked through the wet concrete floor. "Laken, is that you?" She looked up the steps, and then proceeded to the old furnace to check behind it.

"Summer, I am here. Can you hear me?" He was shouting now. Summer stopped in her tracks, looked slowly around the room, let out a small smile, and then said, "I knew you would never leave me." She made her way back to the old plywood bed. The plywood let out a creak as she climbed up and laid down. Summer rested her head on the pillow, closed her eyes. Laken went over to the spot where he used to sleep, laid down, and attempted to hug Summer. His hands went through her again, but he felt a slight warmth at point of contact.

"Laken," Summer whispered. "Please stay with me until I fall asleep." Laken was glued beside her. Nothing could move him. Slowly, her breathing slowed down, and Summer fell fast asleep. Laken quickly followed suite.

"Laken, Laken, time to get up." Gabriel's voice distant. It sounded as if he was calling from a few houses away. "Laken, time to get up." Laken opened his eyes. He was still in the basement, still hugging Summer. Laken felt the strange vacuum sucking him inside out again. The basement began to fade away, like his room had done earlier.

Then everything went black—but nothing appeared this time. There were no buildings, no images. Nothing. Laken tried to focus but there was no light. He stretched out his hands and felt around. Above him swam a mysterious creature, and under him hundreds of something scurried, biting and scratching at his flesh. Then something wrapped itself around his body, constricted, and began to squeeze the very life from him.

"It must be a snake!" Dave screamed. "Kill it! Gouge its eyes out! Strangle it!" At every struggle and pull, the snake's grip tightened. Laken's heart thundered in his chest. The small creatures beneath began to overwhelm him. He gasped, hardly able to breathe. He could feel his consciousness fading out. He needed Gabriel, needed to scream to Gabriel.

"Gabblththht!" he barely had enough air to whisper. He let out one last scream for Gabriel, but the words died in his throat. He could feel his eyes growing heavy. "This is it," he thought. "I'm going to die."

CHAPTER NINE
Laken goes to Paradise

In a last-ditch effort, Laken put all of his will power, determination, and soul into one last stand. He screamed, hit, and kicked, until he felt a snap and a sudden release, sending him tumbling out of the closet and into his room. He was tangled in his cloak, both hands choking a sandal.

Gabriel bent over him, a smile stretched across his face. "Good morning. If I had known you wanted to sleep in the closet, I would have provided you with a much smaller room."

"How did I get in there?" Laken gave a sidelong look. "Where is Summer? I was with Summer. I was there."

"Calm down. It is normal to dream of the old world," Gabriel said. "Let us wash up, and go down and have some breakfast. Today is the first day of school." He backed out of the room, closing the door behind him.

"But I was there," Laken protested to the closed door. He untangled the cloak from himself, shook out the wrinkles, but discovered that there were none. The cloak looked as if it had just been washed and pressed. Laken grabbed a handful of the cloak, twisted it, and knotted it up. Then he straightened it out, and once again, not a wrinkle.

"Pretty cool," Dave observed.

Laken washed up, put on his cloak, and tied his Hallow around his waist. He reached in to see if his sword was still there, and underneath his book, he felt the hilt of the sword. Laken put his sandals on, and strode downstairs.

Gabriel was mid-conversation with a bald, heavy-set man in a green cloak and a Dwarf, whose face was puckered, as if he had just swallowed a lemon.

"I'm telling you, those kids need discipline," the dwarf implored. "Never hurt in my day. Had you given that old Chosen One a few good licks, things might have been different."

"Laken," Gabriel said warmly as he gestured to his two companions. "This is Campee," motioning to the ursine fellow, "and Eli. Campee and Eli, this is Laken." They exchanged the expected pleasantries.

"Please excuse us, we have much to do...First day of school you know," Gabriel said as he motioned Laken to follow him to the door. You could still hear Eli spouting something about discipline, and how it wouldn't hurt Laken to get a good beating today, as their sandaled feet hit the street.

"Busy day ahead, so I thought we could eat while we walk," Gabriel said as he reached into his Hallow, pulling out two bright purple nut-looking foods. "It's a Swig. Try it." His expression flushed with amusement. Laken stared at the tiny purple edible for a moment, his eyes wide with curiosity.

"There is more to breakfast right? Not to be ungrateful, but even Carla gave me more than this."

Gabriel laughed, "Laken, you are so hung up on the outside appearance of things. Try it, and if you're still hungry, I will give you as many as you can eat." Laken's eyes narrowed as he stared at the little Swig.

"Gabriel knows his food. Let's try it," Dave advised.

Laken grabbed the Swig, which was soft, like a plum. He examined it closely, then looked over at Gabriel who gave a nod. Laken offered a half smile then put the whole thing in his mouth. Instantly Laken's taste buds danced. The Swig was fruity, but unlike any fruit he had ever eaten. It swished through his mouth on its own accord, as if alive. Laken's tongue struggled to grasp the Swig when, suddenly the treat shot down his throat by its own will, followed by a warm sensation growing in his stomach. Laken shook his whole body, trying to shrug off the chill that ran up his spine. A burst of energy hit him. He wanted to run, or jump, or do some sit-ups. He took off running, only to have his arm grabbed and held in place as his feet continued to move.

"Hold on, Laken, hold on. Give it a second. Your body is not used to it." Gabriel's grin widened. "It's like drinking six espressos in your world." Laken forced himself to sit still as his legs shook uncontrollably. A few moments later, Laken experienced a calming release, and then felt normal.

"That was awesome!" Dave cheered. Surprisingly, Laken was full. Not just full—he was stuffed.

"Alright, here is another one, Laken. Eat up," Gabriel grinned as he held out another Swig.

"Aaagh, no, that's alright. I don't want to eat yours. You eat it."

"I'm fine, Laken, really," Gabriel insisted. "Eat another. I have plenty here." He pushed the Swig into Laken's face.

"I think I can make it until lunch on that little snack you gave me," Laken conceded with a smile. Gabriel let out a small chuckle, and popped the Swig into his mouth. Gabriel gave a slight shiver of his body, and then a warm smile spread across his face. "Follow me."

The bright sunlight warmed the cool air as they took the path toward the large gates. The courtyard was bustling once again. People and creatures greeted Gabriel over and over with, "Good day, Gabriel," and, "Make it a good year, Headmaster." Most of them tried to grab a glance at Laken's ring.

"The Chosen One," whispered a small chubby man dressed in a white cloak and green hat as he walked by.

"That is the thirty-ninth time today," Dave complained, his expression pinched.

As they approached Grog and Zog's gate, families stood huddled together. They were hugging, kissing, crying, and smiling. There were grins and tears coming from each of the groups, some of who wore the same white cloak Laken had received the previous night.

"Why the different color cloaks?" Laken asked.

Gabriel looked at Laken as they continued their brisk pace. "White is for first year students, gray second, light green third, green fourth, and numa-blue is for fifth year students."

"Give them heaven, there, son," one dad encouraged as he patted his boy on the back.

"You send me a numa every day, you hear me?" A plump lady lovingly demanded as she squeezed the air out of her third-year daughter.

"Mom! We talked about this. I don't want to be the only one." The girl stood, her hands on her hips.

"Brista, at least make it twice a week for your mother," boomed a large bald man wearing a rainbow colored robe.

Laken could see the nervousness on the faces of the first-year students, who seemed to stay close to their parents. The older kids looked a little annoyed at the long goodbyes, and acted as if it were all one big plan to embarrass them in front of their friends.

"Stop it, mom, you already kissed me like a hundred times."

"Well, this makes it a hundred and one. No one, not even a third year, will tell me how many times I can kiss my son!"

"Heath and Peyton, you knock it off this instant." Laken looked over to see a young, pretty lady talking to a couple of large sunflowers. "Fine, then I will just kiss you until your petals fall off," she said to the flowers, as she began to kiss them one after the other. The flowers began to giggle and squirm. Laken had to blink hard twice, to know if his eyes deceived him. The two flowers turned into two first year boys. The mom wrapped them up in her arms and kissed them over and over. "Alright, boys, no funny business, no shapeshifting. Do you hear me?"

"Gotcha, Mom," they promised in unison.

"Best sons in the world," the mom said, her smile stretching across her face.

"Best mom in the world!" the boys called out as they trotted off, suddenly turning into butterflies, soaring past the crowd to the front of the gate.

"I said no shapeshifting!" she cried, her now shaking back and forth. "Those two will put me in an old folks home before I turn three hundred."

Gabriel and Laken made their way to the gates. "Good morning Grog. Good morning Zog," Gabriel greeted with a smile.

"Good morning…" Grog looked guilty as he trailed off. Gabriel turned and faced the crowd of families, his expression bright.

"Good Morning!" Gabriel's salutation commanded everyone's attention.

The crowd boomed, "Good Morning!" back to Gabriel.

"This year will be the best year ever, here at Dogma." Gabriel's blue eyes widened. "Moms and Dads, please give your children one last hug and one last kiss. Children, remember that valuing your parents is the key to a long healthy life." The kids let out a groan in unison. Gabriel's smile widened. "In other words, put a smile on, and let them embarrass you with some big hugs and kisses." There was a small ruckus in the crowd, as parents grabbed, kissed and hugged their kids one last time.

"All first years?" Gabriel's voice seemed to calm the commotion.

"Mom! Stop!" bellowed through the crowd, to the snickers of all those present. Gabriel smiled, and then continued.

"First year students, please make sure your numa spits into the enrollment jar." Laken looked down to see a large blue jar in Gabriel's hand. "When your numa spits in the jar, this is an angelic contract, enrolling you in this school. As long as you are a student of Dogma, the garden offers you protection." Gabriel's gaze swept the crowd a smile played on his face.

Gabriel turned to the gates and announced, "This is Gabriel High Archangel and Headmaster of Dogma and three hundred and seven students. We wish to enter Eden."

"Of course," said Grog, tightening his lips. The gates slowly creaked open. Gabriel and Laken stood at the gates as each child walked past, receiving a "Welcome" and a handshake from Gabriel. Then their numas spit in the jar.

Laken heard some loud giggles, and as he turned his head, he was almost run over by a large group of girls. Their arms draped over the handsome kid from the day before.

"STOP!" boomed Zog's voice as the group passed the gate. The girls all let out a screech, and the Adonis-like boy jumped. Everyone else froze in their place.

Zog held out his hand toward Eden, and in the distance, something semi-invisible from past the gates fluttered and flew to Zog's massive hands. With a thud, it hit Zog's palm and a man appeared. Zog's massive fingers wrapped completely around his torso. The man had a black cloak, with the hood pulled over his head. His red eyes glared out into the crowd. Sparks began to fly from Zog's fingers, and with a poof, the man simply turned to dust, that sprinkled the ground. The crowd sat in an eerie silence—the breeze brushing the trees the only audible noise.

"Continue on!" boomed Zog, breaking the silence.

Gabriel shook his head in dismay. "Every few years, someone tries. An imperceptible charm, Sithius. You know better," Gabriel mumbled, and then looked to the students, "Qwerubs don't just see, they feel. They have senses beyond anything imaginable." Gabriel gazed across the crowd of frightened students and parents. "They become one with whatever they are guarding and can detect even the slightest change in the molecular structure of their protectorate. They were created to guard and protect. In over six thousand years, no one has ever made it past them." Gabriel paused, a crooked smile on his face as he leaned over and whispered to Laken, "Well, maybe one Angel made it past. At least that is what legend says."

Gabriel turned back to the students and urged them, "Continue on, continue on."

By this time, the handsome boy and his gang of admirers had moved way off in the distance. The other children were quite hesitant to step forward. "You are fine. Only those who are not welcomed will be stopped by the Qwerubs," Gabriel assured the students. Three hundred and six students later, Gabriel put his arm around Laken.

"Dave, if you would?" Gabriel put the jar up to Dave. Dave let out a shrug, and spit into the vase. Laken felt a warmth travel up his spine, then down to his feet; then it was gone. Gabriel smiled and then led him into Eden. Behind them, Laken could hear the gate creak shut to a world they were leaving.

In front of him was... Paradise.

CHAPTER TEN
Laken Goes to Dogma

Beautiful was far too inadequate a word to describe what lay before Laken. It was as if he needed another word entirely. "I guess *Eden* would be that word," he thought.

Flocks of birds soared across the pure blue sky. A cool, gentle breeze carried the clouds effortlessly. Laken looked down and could see through the golden bridge, as if walking on glass. Merfolk, dolphins, whales, and what looked like a huge squid were all waving in their own way, either with a tentacle, an arm, or a slap of the tail.

The smell of blooming flowers prompted Laken to take a big deep breath. Laken looked up and Dave let out a "Wowww."

Unlike the square, this place had no streets. It was a verdant kaleidoscope of flowers, massive trees, hills, and grass for as far as the eye could see.

The view was surreal, like looking into a painting that could have only been dreamt. Deer, antelope, rabbits, dogs, cats, bears, tigers, lions, elephants, giraffes—the world's entire menagerie lay ahead.

Laken noticed that the animals didn't act normal. In the shade of a beautiful old tree, a group of lions lay in the grass with sheep nestled up against them. Tigers and deer appeared to be playing tag. At first glance, a tiger seemed to pounce on a deer, but the tiger merely tapped it and then turned and took off. The deer whipped around and took chase after the tiger. Laken rubbed his eyes, blinked a few times, and refocused. His sight did not deceive him—a bear was giving four bunnies a ride on its back. A group of squirrels mischievously tossed nuts out of a tree at a group of dogs, who wagged their tails and barked playfully.

Eventually, Laken's eyes began to focus on the non-animal creatures. He saw large groups of gnomes running through the grass, prompting Laken to look down at his feet.

"I like the sandals. They're gnome-proof," joked Dave. He saw six or seven different groups of centaurs strolling through the grass and flowers. He saw a unicorn being chased by some gnomes, who were trying to climb on his back. Thousands of fairies of all colors of the rainbow flittered through the garden. They zoomed in and out of trees, from flower to flower, around animals, and many just flying above. Eden was an orchestra of color and beauty.

Laken let out a gasp as his eye caught hold of a blue dragon, sleeping under a massive oak tree. Squirrels were scurrying up and down his spiny back and into a huge hole in the tree.

"Here we are," Gabriel's voice interrupted. Gabriel stood next to a golden doorway, though it had no door, and was connected to nothing. The entryway simply stood there, by itself, in the middle of the grassy paradise.

"This is called the Portal of Reflection. If you—a Gabriel cut himself off as a young student curiously walked into the doorway and vanished. All the first-years let out a huge gasp. A few of the girls screamed.

Laken could see what lay through the open door way, but the boy wasn't anywhere in sight. Gabriel turned to his numa. "Remis, go fetch me Argus." Remis split into two, and the twin took off. "As I was saying!" Gabriel's gaze swept over the student's shocked faces. His eyes widened, while a smile tugged at his lips. "Yes, he will be fine. We will find him. This happens every year." Gabriel's smile grew. "Last year we didn't find the boy for two days, isn't that right, Flever?" Gabriel gaze snapped down to a blushing boy in a gray cloak. "This Portal is what takes you to and from every area in Dogma. You will find a similar portal in every room. Well, as far as I know." He paused, his brow narrowing. "Since there are infinite rooms, and I've only explored a small portion, I cannot be sure." Amusement washed across Gabriel's expression.

"We are currently in Eden. If you ever need to get back here, or if you get lost, just think Eden, and walk into the Portal." Gabriel paused to take note of the students. "Whatever you think, if it is in Dogma, the portal will take you there. If you are not thinking anything, then the Portal, who is a little jokester, will randomly take you to some fun, crazy room within Dogma." He chuckled and patted the door frame. "That is where little Sift is now." Gabriel looked up as if he were trying to catch a memory.

"Once, it put me in the recurring floor-less room, as I would call it. You simply fell through the floor and then came through the ceiling in the same room. This would continue forever, until you glide through the portal. This little trickster has taken me to more bizarre places than I can remember." Gabriel patted the doorway again. He sounded as if he were talking to an old high school buddy who had played countless pranks on him back in his youthful days.

"Now, if you are holding someone's hand, then the thoughts that are the strongest will decide your destination. So, everyone hold hands, and follow me. We are going to enter the Great Hall."

Just then, someone enormous came out of the Portal. He was the same height as Gabriel, but he had a chest like a massive tree trunk connecting to his huge bear-like arms and hands. Three Gabriel's could fit into the bearskin shirt that covered his torso and draped down to his knees. His skin was dark purple, and his long hair was a light orange. He had bold, pronounced features. But what grabbed Laken's attention were his bright silver eyes.

"Oh, good. Argus!" Gabriel greeted the new arrival. "Students, I would like you to meet Argus." Argus bowed his gigantic head. "Argus is a Night Elf." Laken heard a few gasps from the students and a murmur spread through the crowd. "Calm down, calm down." Gabriel motioned with his hands. "I don't know what you've heard about Night Elves, but the first lesson of Dogma is: Don't believe everything you've heard. Second, we never judge a person based on color, size, or race." Laken noticed Daeth whisper to his gang, and they all let out a snicker. "Instead we look to the character of their heart. Not what they look like on the outside, but who they are on the inside." Gabriel's bright blue eyes scanned the students slowly. "Argus is my most trusted friend and confidant. I would, and have many times, put my life in his hands. You will always treat him with the same respect you afford to me." Gabriel gave the group a warm smile and turned to Argus. "Sift went into the Portal. Could you see if you can find him before he gets into too much trouble?"

"Of course!" Argus's coarse voice was like gravel in a tin can. Argus then stepped into the Portal and vanished.

"Alright, everyone, grab a hand and follow me." One by one, the students disappeared into the Portal. As Laken went in, he felt a warmth tingle his skin. Suddenly, they were stepping out into a massive Hall lined with golden tables.

The Hall was about the same size as his school gymnasium, but that was the only similarity to anything he'd seen before. The floors were that same transparent gold he'd seen on the bridge. Boulder-sized fireballs floated over each of the tables giving an omniscient glow to the room. Laken looked up along the wall, stretching his neck to see past its incredible height, finding no ceiling, just blue sky. Five large transparent clouds covered the span of the ceiling. Each one took the shape of the animals Laken had seen on the gate. There was a lion, owl, unicorn, lamb, and a snake. Each cloud had a single star glowing brightly in is center. Hundreds of small cherub angels flew throughout the hall. They looked like a large swarm of bees looking for a flower to rest upon.

Massive golden-framed portraits of Angels lined the walls. The largest of the portraits, centered on the far end of the room, was one of Gabriel, with the title "Headmaster" engraved on a plaque below it. Statues of dragons, lions, elves, centaurs and various creatures Laken had never seen before were strewn throughout the Hall. A massive twenty-foot tall Green Dragon stood out among all of the statues.

"If you will all find a seat, we can begin." Gabriel's voice echoed throughout the hall. Everyone scattered in an attempt to find a seat. Laken, who tried to ignore the clamor whispering about the Chosen One, waded through the crowd as if upstream, finding a quiet spot in which to sit.

"Sit with us," Laken heard from behind him. Laken turned around to see the handsome boy he had watched in the courtyard the day before. "Name is Cirque." The boy's bright white teeth smiled through his perfectly formed mouth. "Grab a seat with us," Cirque motioned to a spot beside himself. Laken went to sit in the chair, when a girl wedged herself between him and the seat.

"I'm sitting here," said the girl with long blonde hair and a scowl.

"Oh, sorry." Laken's jaw tightened.

"Ephra, scoot over for our guest," Cirque said. Ephra shot Laken a hot glance, and then wrenched herself into the next chair. "Please, please take a seat." Cirque's blue eyes widened a fraction. Laken looked around to see if any other over-zealous girls were racing to take the seat. Then he sat down.

"Like I said, the name is Cirque. You must be the Chosen One." He offered Laken a smile.

Laken hesitated, then returned the smile "Yes, I'm Laken."

"Stick with me. I will show you all the ropes." Cirque's expression washed with confidence. "Plus, I can introduce you to some of the ladies here at Dogma." Laken turned red, while the girls let out a dreamy sigh. "Laken, what do you think so far?" Cirque draped an arm over the girl next to him.

Laken, still red in the face, tried to assume an air of nonchalance. "Aughhh, I would say it was pretty alright." A girl across the table cast a glare at him like broken glass.

"I guess you're stealing their precious *Cirque time*," mumbled Dave.

"So, you think you will be serpent? A lion?" Cirque whispered. "Definitely not a lamb. That is for the ladies. I'm sure to be a unicorn: charm and beauty." A couple of girls let out another heavy sigh.

"Den? What den? A lion? How did you become a unicorn?" Laken questioned, looking confused.

"Your den," smiled Cirque, "Serpent is cunning and crafty, a Lion is strength and courage, Lamb is love, kindness and all that girly stuff, an Owl is wisdom and knowledge, and a Unicorn is, well, look at me." Laken tried to ignore the Cirque groupies' sigh-in-stereo as he recalled the Dogma sign he had seen yesterday.

"Well, I really haven't given it any thought," Laken shrugged slightly, acting as if he knew what was going on.

"No thought? I've been thinking about it since I was six," huffed the sour-faced, redheaded girl. "I'm going to be a unicorn, too," she said dreamily.

"Looks more like toad to me," Cirque whispered. Laken almost hurt himself trying to hold back the laugh.

"Students, hands in the air," Gabriel boomed. Everyone raised their hands, and golden plates piled with Nirbs appeared. "A treat, for your first day." An excited ruckus filled the hall, as kids popped Nirbs into their mouth and their numas cried out their flavor.

"Pot roast."

"Peach Cobbler."

"Spaghetti and meatballs."

"Roast duck."

"Mom's beef surprise."

"Rhubarb pie."

Laken thought for a moment and popped a nirb in. As soon as Dave said the single word, "Swig," that addictive flavor hit his mouth and continued down to his stomach.

"Wow, the single nirb actually filled you up. It must have become a swig," observed Dave Laken looked around, and then tucked his remaining Nirbs in his Hallow.

"Now, I need all first years up to the front," Gabriel instructed over the children's voices. There was quite a commotion as students got up and walked to the front.

Cirque touched Laken's shoulder "That's us. Let's get up there. Let's hope you get Unicorn with me."

Laken rose and followed Cirque to the front. "Hey, watch where you're going," came a voice from below. Laken looked down to see two squirrels. "Sorry, just having a go at you," the smaller of the two said. They transformed into the boys he had seen at the gate.

"Hey, you're the flower and butterfly boys I saw this morning," Laken said.

"I'm Heath, and this here is my twin brother, Peyton. We're shapeshifters." They both had an ear-to-ear grin.

"We're the first shapeshifters in seven hundred and fifty years," Peyton amended, his smile transformed into a smirk. The two blonde boys, each with bright blue eyes, held out their hands. They were quite a bit shorter than Laken, who was already short for a first year. Heath was slightly taller than his brother, and his hair was short. Peyton's hair was unruly, hanging past his brow. Peyton had a determined look about him, while Heath had an air of confidence.

"I'm Laken." But as Laken went to grab Peyton's hand it suddenly transformed into a snake. Laken jumped back, almost knocking over the redheaded girl.

"Watch it!" She shoved Laken back into Heath and Peyton, who were laughing hysterically.

"Sorry, one more time," Peyton said, as he put his hand out.

"Let's skip the handshake," Laken suggested, ushering them forward.

"You should have seen your face!" Peyton cried out. "You would have thought you saw a snake." There was a pause, and they all burst out laughing.

When they reached the front, they lined up, shoulder-to-shoulder and turned to face Gabriel, who was now joined by a group of people. Gabriel stood silent for a moment, until a smile slowly peeled back his lips. "First years? Today you will join a group of disciples. We will be placing you each in a den. Each den has a den master." Gabriel motioned to the group around him. "Though you will be instructed by many teachers, your den master will be responsible for your overall experience here at Dogma." Gabriel took a moment to sweep his gaze across all the students. "Please look up!" The students looked towards the ceiling of transparent clouds. "You will see each of the dens represented above. In the middle, you see a single star." Murmurs of the students washed thru the hall. "The stars represent points for your den. You earn points for your den by doing things above the norm. In the same manner, you can lose points for your den for any actions that are below Dogma's expectations." Gabriel's blue eyes widened. "At the end of each month, the den with the most points is awarded a trip to outer Eden."

At this, the place erupted in excitement. Gabriel paused a moment, until the noise died down. His smile widened. "At the end of the year, the den with the most points becomes *Lord of Dens*." Another commotion of mumbles and excitement broke out. "What do you say each den starts with 25 stars!" Gabriel's hands shot in the air with a theatric style motion. Everyone's eyes followed Gabriel's hands then shot to the ceiling as stars filled each of the den's clouds. Another eruption of excitement from the students followed. Gabriel paused and looked down the line of teachers, and began to speak over the noise. "With that, I would like to introduce my staff." The hall became silent. "Argus, you have met," he said as he motioned to the huge Night Elf. The students let out a small nervous clap. "Zeetle is Eden's grounds keeper." Laken had to search to find Zeetle. Finally, his eye caught a little gnome that came up to Argus's calf. Zeetle was slightly chunkier than most gnomes Laken had seen, and had splotches of grey hair on his head. His dark green cloak was weathered, and dingy. The students let out a thunderous clap, as a few choruses of "WE LOVE YOU ZEETLE!" echoed through the hall.

"Next to Zeetle is Professor Davide." Laken glanced up at a strikingly beautiful female Centaur. Her long blonde hair hung down past her light blue blouse. Her green eyes gave off a radiant light. She had no smile, or expression of any emotion. A courteous clap issued from the students. "And next to Professor Davide is Professor Alona." Laken tore his eyes from the Centaur to the towering creature next to her. She was another Night Elf, but a female one. Her skin was blue, and her hair bright red. Though she was still massive in size, next to Argus she was comparatively petite. The polite clapping was even lighter than it was for Argus. "Next to Professor Alona, is Professor Rivka." A tall, hardened-faced woman pursed her lips toward the crowd. In a weird way, she was beautiful. The students let out a clap, while a few whistles shot through the hall.

"Wooo, that is one scary lady," Dave whistled as he jumped back.

"Now, let's get to the head of dens." Gabriel's hands motioned for quiet. "Next to Rivka is Professor Malgor. This is his first year teaching here at Dogma." Malgor was a dark, malevolent looking man. His skin was murky red color, covered with blackened splotches. His eyes, while small, glowed ominously red. He had a large hooked nose, and a small mouth that took a sinister curve. Laken noticed that two small horns protruded through his greasy long black hair. Malgor's eye caught Laken's, and a look of disgust crawled across his face. Malgor's gaze flitted out toward the distance, while his numa stared intently at Laken.

Then Laken heard something.

Malgor's withered and black numa wheezed, "I think he is the one we must kill." The numa was interrupted by the applause of the students, but his words shot a shiver down Laken's spine.

Laken's horror was interrupted by Gabriel's voice, "Malgor's disciples will be in the Serpents den." A group of students seated in the Hall let out a *hissssss*.

"Next to Malgor is Gideon. His disciples will be in the Lion's den." Another group of students let out a roar. Laken looked over to see an actual lion. Gideon was considerably larger than most lions he had seen in Eden. Laken was even more surprised to see a bright blue numa on Gideon's shoulder.

"That's a first—an animal with a numa?" Dave blurted. "The teacher of the lions is a lion, huh? Weird." Laken shrugged.

"Next to Gideon is Miss Luvly. Her disciples will be in the Lambs den." *Baaahhhh* boomed forth from the students. Laken was surprised to discover the oldest woman he had ever seen. Miss Luvly looked like she was dead, and had started the decaying process. Her skin was a continuous wrinkle, barely holding onto to her skinny skeleton. Two lumps of weathered flesh made up her cheeks, seeming to hang over where her mouth should have been. What looked like five strands of hair were pulled up into a bun on her balding head. She had a torn, grayish blue, old robe on. One sandal was orange, and the other one was purple. Miss Luvly, cane in hand, turned around and began to walk away. Rivka walked over and gently grabbed her arm and led her back around to face the students as the old lady hit her in the leg repeatedly with her cane. "Next to Professor Luvly is Professor Orion, whose disciples will be in the Owl's den." A massive male Centaur, with shoulder length curly blonde hair, and a small pointed chin, waved to the audience. Calls of "Hoo! Hooo!" came from yet another group of students. "And finally, we have Cronus. His disciples will be in the Unicorn Den."

"CRONUS! CRONUS!" chanted a group of students. Cronus, who was bowing to the crowd as if receiving an award, looked like an older version of Cirque. Long, blonde, curly hair wrapped around his perfectly proportioned face. Laken looked out across the Hall to see many girls sighing each time he bowed. Laken noticed that even Cronus' handsome numa was bowing and shaking his clenched hands over his head as having won some great victory.

"Alright, let us begin the discipleship process. Jamieus, if you would please come forward." Gabriel motioned to a small black-haired boy, who nervously looked around and then stumbled forward. "First years, listen closely. I will ask you the name of your den." Gabriel rubbed his palms together. "Your numa will let you know, and you will tell me what the numa said. It's very important that you tell me the truth." Gabriel's brows narrowed. "As in life, there are always *consequences* to a lie." Gabriel emphasized the word consequences. "Okay, Jamieus, what den?" A smile peeked thru Gabriel's beard.

Laken heard Jamieus' numa say, "Lion."

In a squeak of a voice, Jamieus relayed, "Lion's den." A roar came from the crowd.

"Jamieus, if you would, please get behind professor Gideon, your den master." Gabriel motioned to the massive lion. Jamieus cautiously strode over to where Gideon stood proud and tall, and then very obviously walked nervously around Gideon keeping a safe distance from the lion. Laken caught a fleeting smile appear on Gideon's face. "Patilda, what den?"

"Serpent," she announced. A hiss came from the students as she made her way over to Malgor.

"What den you hoping for?" asked Heath.

"Don't know," responded Laken.

"We know that my brother Peyton here will be in Lion's den." Heath motioned to Peyton. "No one around more stupid—I mean courageous—than him."

"And we also know that my brother Heath here will be in Serpent. His long, snake-like tongue is a dead giveaway." A green snake tongue hissed out of Heath's mouth, and then retracted. "No, seriously, Heath will be in Owl. I've never met anyone smarter than Heath," Peyton bragged. "Bet there isn't another student here as smart as him, probably not a teacher, either!"

"Daeth, if you would please come forward." At this, Laken turned his head toward the front a little faster than he may have wanted. Laken looked around to see if anyone had noticed. Daeth strolled up, his expression pinched.

"Wonder if they have a Jackass den," cracked Peyton.

"I'm thinking more of a Turd's den for him," laughed Heath.

"Serpent," Daeth's numa oozed. Daeth repeated, "Serpent," in that same sickening, droll tone.

Laken looked at Heath and Peyton, who mocked in unison. "And that is no surprise." Heath and Peyton looked at each other and then Heath said, "Yes, nearly all Fallen come out of the serpent. Sure, the rest of the dens have some Fallens, but not near as many as Serpent."

Heath leaned over and whispered, "My dad says it has to do with thinking too highly of themselves It's what caused the first fall you know."

"That sounds like him alright," Laken blurted, to the "Shhhh!" of the tiresome red-head. Laken continued to watch as, one after another, the remaining students, now *disciples*, were placed in their respective dens. Grap, Scorpious, and Ravana each went into Serpent.

"Who would have guessed? Cirque is Unicorn," Dave smirked after the sounds of students making horse noises died down. A group of girls went into Lamb. A few more kids went into Lion, while a small boy went into owl. Laken took a keen interest in the next boy's den.

"And, Baylor, which den?" Gabriel asked. Laken couldn't believe what he heard.

Baylor's numa said, "Lamb." Baylor looked to his numa and shook his head hard like a dog shirking water off his back. The numa repeated, "*Lamb*," more forcefully this time.

"Serpent!" Baylor said.

"Take your place behind Malgor, Gabriel said, his eyes narrowed as he stared at the large boy. Baylor barely took three steps when he suddenly began to cough, then gasp.

"Mmmmbl tung, mmmmm tung!" Baylor mumbled Baylor's face swung around to where Laken could see his expression. Out of Baylor's mouth flowed a huge tongue that seemed to be slithering like a large endless snake.

"Aaaaagghhhh, aaaagh!" Baylor's screams were muffled by the massive tongue.

"Baylor, Baylor, you are so concerned of what others think that you can't be yourself?" Gabriel shook his head as he walked over to Baylor. Gabriel held up his right hand and instantly Baylor's tongue slithered back into his mouth. Gabriel's placed his hand on Baylor's shoulder, "Baylor would you like to try again? Remember, I said the truth was important."

Baylor looked over at Daeth, Grap, and Scorpious for support, then softer than a whisper, he surrendered. "Lamb." The hall erupted into laughter. Baylor pulled his shoulder from Gabriel, and stomped over behind all the girls in Lamb. A huge sheep sound erupted from the crowd.

The laughter died down, with a few snickers popping up sporadically. "May we continue?" Gabriel asked. The place quieted down, "Okay, Sandur, you're next."

For the next twenty minutes, student after student went up. Some went to Unicorn, some Serpent, others went to Lion. Every time a girl chose Lamb, the students would chant, "Baylor, Baylor, Baylor." Baylor's bright red face looked as if he were going to explode. This always put a small smile on Laken's face.

"Heath, which den?" Laken snapped out of his daydream trance and looked up towards Heath and Gabriel.

Before Heath's numa could answer, Heath called out confidently, "Owl." Then his blue numa said, "Owl."

"Take your place, behind Professor Orion. Peyton, you are next." Gabriel motioned to Peyton.

Peyton, unlike his brother, waited for his light blue numa, then said, "Lion." A large roar ensued.

"And finally, Laken. It is your turn," Gabriel announced. The room fell deathly quiet. You could hear students fidget all throughout the Hall as they leaned over to whisper, "The Chosen One" or "Which house do you think?"

Laken blocked out all the whispers, walked up, and asked Dave, "Which den?"

"Dragon," answered Dave, very excited.

Laken shook his head. "What?" Laken's voice cracked.

"Dragon," Dave responded.

"Knock it off. Stop fooling around. Which den?" Blood rushed into Laken's face.

"I didn't stutter. I said *DRAGON*!" Dave's jaw tensed.

"What do you mean *Dragon*? This is not pick-a-creature. Our choices are Lion, Serpent, Owl, or Unicorn—that's it!" Laken's heart now pounded in his chest.

"Laken, which den?" Gabriel asked.

"For the love of all that is good and holy, what den, you little blue turd?" A rope of frustration tightened within him.

"I'm not talking to you anymore." Dave folded his arms and turned away.

"Laken!" came Gabriel's distant voice.

"Uugghh, I don't know. Dave won't tell me." A surprised expression washed across the students, who began to mumble.

"Your numa said nothing?" Gabriel prodded. Laken's expression tightened.

"Well, he said something, but it isn't an option."

"Laken, let us hear it." Clarity entered Gabriel's expression.

Laken looked nervously around the room at all the students who crouched on the edge of their seats in anticipation. "Well, he said, *Dragon*." Laken let the word slowly drain from his mouth. The entire room let out a collective gasp. Then voices erupted into pure chaos.

"Quiet now!" Argus's booming command forced everyone in the room, even the teachers, to jump. Then utter silence fell.

Gabriel had a large smile on his face as if to say *I knew it.* "Laken, and to all you students, the Dragon's den has not been chosen in over six thousand years. Not since the first Great Fall, has this den been used." Gabriel's blue eyes beamed across the surprised students' faces. "This den will be made up of Laken and one student from each of the other dens—students who Laken's numa will choose." Gabriel looked Laken in the eyes. "I will be your den master, as it has always been the Headmaster's responsibility to disciple those in the Dragon's den." His eyes widened. A murmur rippled through the student body.

Gabriel's voice carried throughout the hall. "Den masters, please take your disciples to your place in the room. This will help in the selection process." It took a few minutes of disruption, like herding cattle, for the students to finally get to their spots by their respective den masters. During this time, nearly every student who passed by Laken let him know that they should be picked. "Move along to your places, please," Gabriel instructed.

As soon as everyone settled into their places, Gabriel turned to Laken and said, "Your numa will choose five others to be my disciples. Please choose one from each house."

Laken could hear students cry out, "Pick me, pick me."

"I suppose it makes sense," Dave said over his turned shoulder to Laken. "Who wouldn't want to be discipled by Gabriel?"

"Who will it be?" Gabriel interrupted.

Before Dave could respond, Laken's eye caught Cirque. "Cirque" Laken said a little too enthusiastically. "Uhhh, Cirque," Laken repeated, this time more calmly.

"Cirque, please take your place behind me," invited Gabriel.

"You're supposed to wait for me!" Dave protested.

"Like last time, with your made-up choice?" Laken scoffed. "Maybe I'm scared you will just make up some students' names." Laken looked over to the Owl's den. "Heath," Laken said before Dave could respond. Ignoring his protests, Laken turned his attention to the Lion's den. "Peyton," Laken announced before Dave could pick.

Next, Laken turned to the corner of the room where the Lambs were gathered. *Maybe we can get a real pretty girl*, Laken thought. Laken's eye caught a gorgeous third year with long, blonde hair, but before Laken could say a name, he heard Dave say, "Baylor."

"What? No! Don't try to get even because I won't let you pick!"

"Pick someone else and see what happens. I'd love to see you with a six-foot tongue," Dave retorted.

"I'm not picking him. Pick someone else now, you little blue—"

"It's Baylor, Baylor, Baylor, Baylor!" Dave insisted, jumping up and down.

"No, I am not picking Baylor." Not thinking, Laken spoke out loud.

"Baylor it is," Gabriel announced to the students who let out a strong, "Baaaaahhlor." Baylor looked half-angry and half-relieved that he was no longer a Lamb.

"No, I didn't say…I didn't mean—" Laken tried to amend. Shouts of "Baaaaaaahhhlor!" from the students drowned out Laken's protest.

"And now, choose one from Serpent," Gabriel interrupted. Laken glanced over the group. Daeth wouldn't make eye contact, while Grap and Scorpious gave Laken a heated glare.

Laken turned to Dave, "So who is it? You want to complete the group by picking Daeth?" Laken snapped sarcastically. Dave stuck his tongue out at Laken and then glanced over the group.

After an uncomfortable amount of time, and Dave seemingly going through each individual and noting, "No, no, no, not you, no," Dave turned to Laken and announced, "No one here."

"You annoying blue piece of garbage, that is not an option!" Laken lashed out.

"Who is your choice?" Gabriel interrupted.

"Ugh, Dave said they are not here?" Laken said with hesitancy in his voice. A sound of surprise erupted from the students.

"This is quite possible," Gabriel said as he held up his hands silencing the students. "In the next few years, the student that is to take the place of Serpent will start school here in Dogma. For now, it is just the four of you, and Laken," Gabriel said then turned to the students and announced. "First years? Follow your teachers to your dens. The rest of you are dismissed. Laken, Heath, Baylor, Peyton, and Cirque? Please see me."

The commotion of the room was jarring to Laken, who had just been stuck with one of his enemies for the whole first year. "You little two-faced, dumb, stupid thing!" Laken was so mad he couldn't think of what to call Dave.

"Oh, I forgot. I'm not talking to you," Dave said, and went back to pouting on the corner of Laken's shoulder.

"Be nice to have some quiet for a change, not having to listen to that annoying rambling of nonsense." Frustration welled inside Laken, swirling like lava.

Dave just plugged his ears and sang, "Lolalalalala, I can't hear you."

"Laken, could you please join us?" Laken jumped at the sound of Gabriel's voice. Laken looked over to see Gabriel and his den waiting on him. Laken hesitated, then muttered, "Whatever," under his breath and slowly walked to the group.

"Boys, this will be a very exciting year for all of us." Gabriel's enthusiasm was unnerving to Laken. "It has been many years since I have discipled a den, but what I used to say still holds true." Gabriel slowly looked to each of them until his gaze settled on Baylor, who immediately looked down. "What you put in, you will get out. I expect excellence, dedication, and heart. I want each of you to realize and think about this." Gabriel took a moment, and then his gaze became intense. "I am not as concerned about what you learn, as I am about who you become." Gabriel pointed to his chest. "Who you become will determine what you do. What you do will create your life experiences. Your experiences will dictate the destiny you live and the lives you touch." Gabriel paused as if he wanted this to sink in. Then his expression changed to a more casual one. "I need you to wait here. I need to see what kind of shape the old den is in. There is a good chance it is still on fire!" At that Gabriel turned, and strode through the Portal.

CHAPTER ELEVEN
The Oath of the Furies

"Still on fire? That's awesome," Peyton cried out.

"According to *Blathardt's History of the Fallen,*" Heath said, a finger placed in his opened Rhema, "the Den of the Dragons has only been used one other time. Six Angels were chosen. Their names were Remiel, Uriel, Jahphael, Adkiel, Regudiel…and Gabriel," Heath paused. Each boy looked at one another in awe.

"What else?" Peyton whispered.

"It says that Regudiel, Jahphael, and Adkiel were killed in battle, while the others went on to become Archangels."

Each of the boys, wide-eyed, mouthed, "Killed!"

"It also says that the Den of the Dragons was instrumental in the defeat of the Original Fall. The Den of Dragons was then removed from the list of Dens until such a time when Dark Evil was on the rise again." Heath's eyes narrowed as he closed his Rhema. Laken shook his whole body, trying to calm the goose bumps climbing up his back.

"Baaahhhh," a taunting sheep noise resounded from behind them. "The sheep boy has joined the Chosen, how cute." The boys turned to see Daeth, Grap, and Scorpious strolling towards them. Each member on the gang wore a smirk. "So BaBah… Baylor, you have a new group of friends," Daeth bleated. Grap and Scorpious stood snickering behind him. Baylor's face flushed a deep crimson.

"N-n-no. I didn't want to be in this stupid den. You know that," Baylor stared at his feet.

"I didn't want you in this den to start with," Laken said. "You can get out anytime you want!"

Baylor's eyes found Laken's. "You're the idiot who picked me."

"No. Gabriel picked you!" Laken stepped up to Baylor, his face belly-button height. "I said I don't want a stupid sheep boy in my den." Laken strained his neck to look Baylor in the eye. Nearly thirty students had gathered around by this time. "Go ahead, sheep boy, you can baaaaaaack out," Laken mocked, bleating like a sheep. The crowd let out a nervous laugh. At that, Baylor's face turned a deeper violet. Suddenly, his hand swung out towards Laken's throat. The crowd gasped.

Peyton called, "Watch out!" but it was too late. The massive fingers wrapped around Laken's neck. Suddenly, there was a loud sizzling sound. Baylor roared with a blood-curdling scream as he retracted his enormous blistered hand to his chest. Baylor's moan was the only sound in the room. A smile played across Laken's face.

"Can't hurt the Chosen One. How inconvenient for the rest of us," Daeth hissed.

"Did the little sheep burn his hoof?" Laken's smile grew. At this Baylor reached into his Hallow and pulled out a massive sword well over six feet long. Gasps and screams came from the crowd. Dave erupted with a string of curses.

A large, fourth-year boy jumped between Baylor and Laken, attempting to hold the giant back. With one hand, Baylor hurled the boy aside as easily as if he were tossing a blanket. The boy crashed into Cirque, and the two flew across the room, smashing into a large statue of three elves battling a dragon. Seeing their hero hurt, six girls screamed in anguish and rushed to Cirque's aid. Baylor raised the massive sword into the air. Peyton lunged towards Baylor. To everyone's surprise, Peyton turned into a massive rope, weaving himself around and around Baylor's arms and body. Likewise, Heath transformed into a black slippery liquid, and forced himself under Baylor's feet. Baylor's began to kick to keep balance, and then slid out from underneath himself, sending the massive sword flying across the room. Baylor fell backwards onto Scorpious, obliterating the table and four chairs onto which they fell. Students not already engaged with the spectacle were quickly and cautiously making their way over to the clamor. Underneath the rising dust and debris Baylor, struggled to free himself from the ropes. His face flushed in anger.

Scorpious, buried under Baylor's massive figure, screamed in pain every time Baylor made the slightest movement.

Peyton released Baylor, and he and Heath transformed back into their smirking selves. "That will teach the big bully!" They gave each other a high-five. Baylor wrenched himself up, causing Scorpious to let out one last scream of agony. "This is not over!" Baylor grumbled through clenched teeth as he went over, grabbed the massive sword and then slid it back into his Hallow.

"Best to put that away," Heath warned. Baylor shoved three kids aside as he got back into Laken's face.

"You will pay. You will pay." There was an edge of caution in is his voice.

"Pay for what?" An all too familiar voice asked, as Gabriel stepped onto the scene. The group all looked up in shame to see the Headmaster's friendly gaze shifting from child to child, then to the smashed table, then back to Baylor. "Pay for what?" Gabriel asked again, now eyeing him with varying expression.

"Uugghh, nothing, nothing at all," Baylor murmured.

"Well, then. Laken, Heath, Baylor, Peyton, and Cirque?" Gabriel held out a hand, pointing. "Please follow me to the Portal. Let's head to our den." All five of them, heads hung low, followed in Gabriel's wake to the Portal.

"Please take a hand and follow me," Gabriel announced. The boys looked to Baylor, who was slowly shuffling his way to the portal. When Baylor finally arrived at the portal, he wedged himself in between Peyton and Heath, demonstrating that he would not be holding Laken's hand. "Dragon's Den," Gabriel announced as he led the boys into the Portal.

Once again, a warm tingle hit Laken's skin, and suddenly, they stepped out of the Portal.

It took a moment for Laken's eyes to focus on the room he had just entered. The Portal from which they exited seemed to be located on one end of the theatre-sized room. The massive circular marble table in the center of the chamber caught Laken's eye. The table had six marble chairs attached to it. Each chair had an entry point to its right. At first, they looked like six high-backed chairs, but as Laken drew closer, he noticed that each chair had a specific design. The first chair was a dragon, second a lion, third an owl, fourth a lamb, fifth a unicorn, and the last chair was a serpent. Each structure had jewels for eyes, respective of the dens' colors. Laken's gaze then swept across the room to see six large beds, one for each of the students. As with the chairs, each bed had a unique, ornately designed den creature on the enormous headboards to signify whose bed it was. On each of the three other walls protruded two gigantic sculptures of the dens' mascots hanging over the proper beds. Laken estimated that each was at least twenty feet tall. A massive lion emerged from the wall to his right. Next to it, on the same wall, was an owl. On the wall, directly ahead of him was a huge lamb, then a unicorn. A serpent hung on the wall to Laken's left. Finally, the closest bed on the same wall held a dragon. On each side of the sculptures, large floating fire-balls illuminated the entire room.

"Holy craaa—"

Peyton's amazement was interrupted by Gabriel, who agreed, "It is quite a place." Gabriel offered Peyton a smile. There was a pause of silence as the boys took in the room. The boys slowly wandered around, drinking in everything the room had to offer.

Boys, please have a seat at your respective positions around the table." Gabriel made a grand motion to the marble table.

As Laken sat down in the dragon shaped chair, he noticed a large rectangular-sized indent in the center of the table. It looked as if a thick piece of paper would fit flush inside it. In front of each seat was an indent, the size of which could hold some stone or similar object. It took all of Laken's self-control not to put the stone from his ring in the indentation. To him, it looked like a perfect match.

Some snickering from around the table made Laken look up to see Baylor trying to force his massive frame into the petite Lamb's chair. Laken smiled as Dave reminded him how he would squeeze himself into the child swing at the park to make Summer laugh.

"I'll be more amazed at you squeezing in that seat than I was to see you pull that massive sword out of your little Hallow," Heath ribbed him.

"Yeah, it's like shoving a dragon into a small sock," Peyton chimed in, barely able to control his laughter.

"Shut up, just shut up!" Baylor grunted, now wedged in so tightly that, it seemed, he would never be able to get out.

"Baylor, learning to laugh at yourself and with others is an important key to happiness." A grin peeked through Gabriel's beard. Then the seat magically stretched out, and Baylor relieved a huge breath of air as his body plopped into the seat. Baylor shook his head as his red face began to regain its color.

"Boys, I can say with all honesty," Gabriel's voice turned serious, "I wish that the amount of responsibility that is about to be thrust upon you is something I could take on myself." His brow narrowed. "No amount of warning I can give you will prepare you for what is ahead." Gabriel paused to look at each of them. "You will deal with life and death situations that, in order to overcome, will require an ability that only a handful of people possess. You will fight creatures, and things, evil things that I will not even tell you about today, because I fear it will do as much damage as when you actually face them." Gabriel paused, drawing a deep breath. "I apologize for what is ahead, and so I offer you an out." His expression turned grave. "If you choose to leave, no one outside of this room will ever know, nor will anyone in this room blame you." Gabriel began to stroke his beard. "You are not old enough, nor mature enough for what lies ahead. That is a *fact*."

Gabriel paused again before continuing. "I know that there are qualities and characteristics in you that the Almighty has seen, and it is these character traits which have brought you to this room. I must have faith that He knows more than I. But if you wish to leave, now is the time. If you choose to stay, leaving at a later time will *not* be an option." His eyes widened in alarm. "We will be taking a vow tonight—an unbreakable vow. The *Oath of Furies*." Gabriel paused as Baylor, Heath, and Peyton let out a gasp.

"If you break this vow, this oath, a part of your soul will die, a consequence that is irreversible. Most transgressors do not survive, and they themselves die within moments of the break." Gabriel stared at Laken. "I do not want you to go into this situation blind. I want you to know what is in store, though even I myself don't fully know. What I *do* know is that you will be fighting against the most powerful evil force this universe has ever seen."

Gabriel looked towards the large Dragon on the wall. "I wish I could guarantee you victory, or promise that all of you will survive." Gabriel's eyes flitted to the Lion, the Owl, and finally settled on the Lamb. "I cannot."

Laken thought he saw, for a moment, the Angel's eyes water. "Anyone who knows what I know, would probably warn you that you will face imminent death—and the end could come very soon." Gabriel sighed. "But remember, there are far worse things than death. To die is to gain, if you live a life of character, as a wise man once said," His blue eyes held concern.

There was a long moment of silence. "If you have questions, now is the time to ask." Gabriel looked first to Laken, a look full of such compassion, the likes of which Laken had never seen before. Gabriel's eyes were still tear-filled. "Laken? Do you have any questions?" Laken glanced around to the other boys, noticing that each was in a state of shock from Gabriel's speech.

"Is this evil force Ricky?" Every boy's head snapped quickly toward Laken as if he had suddenly stripped completely naked.

"What did you say?" all the boys asked in horrified unison.

Laken, puzzled by everyone's reaction, slowly repeated, "Is this evil force Ricky?"

"That's what I thought you said," said Heath. "How in the world were you able to say that?"

Gabriel interrupted, "Boys, the enchantment does not affect Laken, he can say Ricky's name…" But before he could finish, each boy let out a terrified scream.

"GET THEM OFF OF ME. GET THEM OFF OF ME!" Peyton shrieked, brushing his hands violently up and down his body. "THEY'RE BITING ME, AGHHHHHH!"

"I DON'T KNOW! I DON'T KNOW THE ANSWER!" Heath clutched his head with both hands.

"NO, GET AWAY, I DON'T WANT A BALLOON!!!" Baylor flung himself from the chair.

"I'm bald, nooo. I'm bald!" Cirque bellowed. Then, as quickly as the attack started, it stopped. Each boy shook his head violently, as if to get water out of his ears. Then they sighed collectively, as if having just escaped death.

"Why in the heck would you say that?" Heath demanded, unable to control the anger in his voice.

"I do apologize to each of you. But understand this. That is just his name. Imagine actually battling Ric—" but then Gabriel caught himself.

"Hey, how come when Laken says the name, we hear the name. When Gabriel said it, it came out Lord B-R-O-N-E, but when Laken said it was R-I-C-K-Y?" Heath inquired, spelling the names.

"That I do not know. I can only speculate," Gabriel said, putting a finger to his cheek. "I believe that Laken, not being of our world, just in it, is not affected by the enchantment. There are many things about Laken that I believe will play a huge part in R-I-C-K-Y's defeat."

"Aaagh, get them off me! I don't want to ride the PONIES!" Baylor started to scream again.

"What the...?" Laken started.

"If you even think the letters together and let them form the word in your mind, enchantment strikes you," Heath informed him.

"This is stupid. How in the world can we fight something we can't even talk about?" asked Laken, annoyed. "Why say his name at all? Why not call him something totally different, something so opposite of what he wants us to feel?" Everyone looked at Laken with an expression of interest and surprise. "Seriously, what is the least scary thing you can think of?" asked Laken.

The boys looked to each other in contemplation, then Peyton slowly proffered, "A clown?"

"NO!" Baylor shrieked. And then, trying to control his embarrassment, he resolved himself and said, noticeably softer, "No, not a clown, maybe something else."

"Well, what about a bunny?" said Heath, more as a question than as a statement.

"How about a pink bunny? We can call him Lord Pink Bunny," Peyton suggested excitedly as he motioned with his hands, as if holding a small bunny rabbit.

The boys let out a roar of laughter. Laken thought he even saw Gabriel chuckle. "Lord Pink Bunny it is!" Laken announced. Turning to Gabriel, he rephrased his question: "Is the evil force Lord Pink Bunny?"

Gabriel, holding back a laugh, answered, "Yes, Lord Pink Bunny is the evil force. He and his Fallen comrades, and those from the last six thousand years who have been cast into Outer Darkness. He will no doubt attempt to free them."

"We will call them the Pink Bunny Gang," Laken guffawed. The other boys nearly fell out of their chairs laughing. It took Gabriel a while to get the boys' attention back to the matters at hand. "What does Lord Pink Bunny want?" asked Laken, snorting derisively.

"He wants power, of course. But ultimately, he wants to destroy the lineage of Adam, or humans, as you know them." Gabriel's expression turned grave.

"Humans? But he is human!" Laken blurted.

"Yes, you are right, I believe that the Pink Bunny hates himself, or the human part of himself. He can't destroy himself, so he takes that out on other humans. He has a deep-seated hatred for the human race." Gabriel shook his head.

"But he's in the human world now. Why not just destroy it? From what I have seen you do, it should be quite easy." Laken's eyes widened.

"Powerful he is, but by himself he wouldn't last a day." Gabriel clasped his hands together. "Maybe a few thousand years ago, but with today's technology, and weapons, humans are quite powerful. The Bunny needs his Fallen, and he needs to bring them into your world," he explained, gesturing to Laken. "With a massive army of fallen angels and creatures, destroying mankind will be quite simple." Gabriel's jaw tensed. "Okay, boys, if you want out, now is the time. If you have any other questions, now is the time. Laken, once again, to you." Gabriel's voice was soft.

"I'm not afraid of any little pink bunny. I'm in!" Laken assured.

"And what about you, Peyton?" Gabriel turned his focus towards the Lion chair.

"I could go for some rabbit stew. I'm in," Peyton smirked.

"I assume if Peyton is in, then, Heath, you are in?" Gabriel's gaze turned to Heath.

"You were part of the Dragon's Den six thousand years ago. If you had to do it again, would you?" Heath's brows raised.

Gabriel stared off into the distance for a moment then turned back to the boys. "It was the most difficult and most terrifying time of my life. But what came out of it, what we were able to do, and overcome? I would have to say that without a doubt I would take the *Fury Oath* all over again." Gabriel offered Heath a smile.

"Well, I can't let my little brother take all the glory now can I? I'm in."

"Little brother by what, thirty seconds?" Peyton's expression amused.

Gabriel seemed to ignore this banter and turned his attention to Baylor, who was deep in thought. "And, Baylor, what about you? Remember no one will blame you if you leave," Gabriel's tone low.

Laken heard Baylor's numa almost demanding "Let's get out, get out now. But...we don't want to be a sheep either. Our choices are death or years of embarrassment. What a great choice." Baylor shook his head as if a war raged in his mind.

"I don't...I don't belong here," Baylor stuttered.

"Baylor, there is a war in you." Gabriel's gaze was soft. "Whoever wins the battle will shape your future. I don't say that to convince you to stay. You may remain or leave. Either way, you must win the war of good and evil in your mind. I see such greatness in you, and maybe that is why the Fallen seem to be after your talents." Gabriel's hand found Baylor's shoulder again. "Baylor, you were chosen, not because Laken likes you, but because it is your destiny. Don't worry about whether you fit in or not. That will come. You do what seems right, or should I say, *feels* right." Baylor looked to each of the other boys, purposefully skipping over Laken.

"No, no, get out! Don't do it," Baylor's numa pleaded. "But wait! I don't want to be a LAMB!" Then Baylor blurted, "I'm in!" He said it hesitantly but convincingly enough, as his numa let out a scream of agony and then a sigh of relief.

"Good, and what about you, Cirque?" Gabriel smiled.

"I'm in!" Cirque said without thought.

"Well, on behalf of all Angels, and creatures in our world, I say thank you." Gabriel looked proud. "There is no greater act of love than to lay down one's life. I believe that is what each of you is doing here today." Laken thought he saw tears glistening right at the edge of Gabriel's eyes again. "Please hold out your right hands, with your palms facing up. The *Furies Oath* is a blood covenant." The boys looked cautiously to each other, settling their gazes finally on Gabriel. Gabriel made eye contact with each as they held out their palms. When Gabriel made a small motion with his right hand, a small trickle of blood formed in each of their palms. Gabriel then pulled out a piece of parchment from his Hallow and began to read it out loud.

"By placing our blood onto this parchment, we understand that we are entering into the *Oath of the Furies*. This oath is a blood covenant, a covenant that can only be broken by death. In this oath, we accept the responsibilities entailed for the Dragon's den. We give our lives to the fight against the Fallen, and the forces of evil, to have the heart and attitude of doing what is right and of good character. We promise to look after one another as if each other's life were more important than our own. To these things, we take the *Furies Oath*." Gabriel ceased to read and handed the parchment to Laken. "Place your palm on the parchment, but only if you are sure you can live up to this oath." Laken looked around at each of the other boys, and then finally, his eyes caught Baylor's.

"If we break covenant it will be because of him," Dave sighed.

Laken took a deep breath and placed his palm on the parchment. When his blood touched the contract, a light flashed between his palm and the parchment, and that familiar warmth went up his spine, then down to his feet. Each boy then repeated the process, until finally Cirque had completed the ritual. Gabriel then slid the parchment onto the rectangular slot on top of the table. There was a quick burst of light, and the parchment disappeared, the table letting off a light glow as if it had just come alive. Then the eyes on each statue illuminated, in the order in which the boys had signed the oath with their blood. Each eye except for the Serpent's.

"Am I the only one who is a little freaked out?" Peyton asked nervously.

"The oath is complete, boys! I suggest each of you get right to bed. Tomorrow, you will begin the most rigorous and difficult training program this school has ever known." Gabriel's warm smile settled on Laken. "For in the not-too-distant future, you will enter Golem's Cave." Laken heard the gasp escape from the other boys at the mention of the cave. Gabriel paused then continued, "You will enter Golem's Cave, and you will retrieve the Yachid Relic."

"What!" Heath gaped.

"The Yachid Relic," Gabriel repeated. "In the last six thousand years, not a single being has been able to get close enough to even see, nor live to tell, of its existence."

"Yeah, I know!" Heath said with a sarcastic tone. Gabriel gave Heath a smile. "Most of those who know what is happening would say you probably will not live through the experience. You agree Heath?" Gabriel winked. "I, of course, have seen things in each of you tonight that bring me to expect that we will get the Yachid Relic, and we will be one step closer to defeating Lord Pink Bunny." Gabriel raised his fist in a triumphant gesture.

"I wish you each a good night." At that, Gabriel turned and disappeared through the Portal.

CHAPTER TWELVE
a Numa to Die For

Although each of the boys intended to follow Gabriele's instruction to go sleep straight away, the tension and excitement was too much. Laken, Heath, Peyton, and Cirque sat around the table for the next few hours talking, wondering, discussing all the events of the day. Baylor immediately left the group and slipped into his Lamb bed. The boys once again had a laugh at the fact that the Lamb's bed was fitted to a child's size, and with Baylor's massive frame, nearly half his body hung over the end of the bed.

"That is how I would look trying to sleep in my sister's doll bed." Peyton let out a whoop of laughter, and everyone joined in—all but Baylor, who whipped himself onto his side, causing the bed to squeal as if about to collapse. Baylor muttered something about a stupid lamb and dumb fury, and Laken thought he heard a grumble or two about clowns.

As the night wore on and the boys continued to discuss what all this meant, Baylor, every twenty minutes or so, would sharply suggest that they "shut up and go to bed."

"Sure, Baylor, as soon as you're more than half in bed yourself, we'll be sure to do that," Peyton replied after the third time. The boys let out a laugh as Baylor rolled over and slammed his body into the mattress.

After a few hours, each made it to his respective bed. Laken could not keep his mind from racing. What was Golem's Cave, and what was a Yachid Relic, and what kind of training? Why is Baylor in our group (stupid Dave); why pick Baylor?

"Hey, who had the bunny idea?" Dave boasted.

"That doesn't make up for it. But that *was* a cool idea," Laken smiled.

"Man, that Elf was huge, and what about that evil guy who wants me dead? And what about Heath and Peyton, turned into rope and liquid? That was cool." Question after question sped through Laken's brain until faintly, in the distance, he could hear his name.

Summer was calling for him, drawing him to her. Then, just as the night before, he found himself in the basement, as close to holding her as he was able to do the previous time. Once again, she settled and went to sleep soon after he held her.

"Laken! Laken! Where in the world did he go? You think he went to breakfast without us?" Laken could hear the voices, but they seemed distant. Suddenly, his body was sucked out of the basement and back into the Dragon's den.

"What in the heavens?" Heath screamed, as he and Cirque jumped back.

"What? What is the problem?" Laken struggled as he rose. The problem was that he wasn't in his bed. He was lying in the middle of the room! "Who took me out of bed and put me on the floor?" Laken demanded, glaring at Baylor.

"What's the *problem*? The problem is you weren't there, and then you just appeared!" Heath's eyes wide. "Do you know how to appearate?" Heath's expression puzzled. "That is quite impressive. That is a third-year ability," Heath's brows were at attention.

"Ummm, yeah, sure, must be one of those gifts or talents Gabriel was talking about," Laken blinked hard.

"Well, don't do that again. I nearly laid a load in my shorts here," Peyton let out a raspberry as each boy chuckled.

"You have to show us how. That is way cool." Heath said. "Anyways, we need to hurry and get ready so we can all go down to breakfast together."

"Breakfast, where? How do you know about breakfast?" Laken's regarded him.

"Your schedule. It's in your Rhema," Heath said as he shoved his Rhema in his Hallow. "Better take a look at it. I know mine and Peyton's schedules are horrendous," Heath winced.

Laken walked over to his bed and pulled his Rhema from his Hallow.

"Stupid bed!" Laken heard Baylor announce from across the room. Laken looked up and saw Baylor rubbing his back and cringing in pain. "If Gabriel doesn't fix that bed, I'm sleeping on the floor tonight."

"From what I saw, half of you was sleeping on the floor last night anyway," Peyton said, and all the boys, even Baylor, began to laugh.

"So how do I get my schedule?" Laken inquired, flipping through the blank pages of his Rhema.

The other boys looked at each other as if Laken had asked how to move his arm, or how to open his mouth. Finally, Heath advised, "Close the book, think Dogma schedule, and then open it up."

Laken, now turning a slight red from the 'duhhh' looks of his den members, closed the book. "Dogma schedule," Dave pronounced. When Laken opened the book, he saw a page full of events.

Monday:

7-7:30 Breakfast in the Great Hall

8-9 Numa training year I: Prof Malgor

9:30-11:30 Introduction to Magic year I: Headmaster Gabriel

11:30-1 Lunch in the Great Hall

1—2 Angelic History I In the Beginning: Prof Luvly

2:30-3:30 Intro to Wings: Prof Cronus

4-6 Art of War: Argus

6-7 Discipleship: Headmaster Gabriel

7:30-8 Dinner in the Great Hall

8-10 Homework

10 Lights out

"Mine seems to be missing something. Can't quite put my finger on what's missing. Oh, yeah! A break! What the heck?" Laken's expression pinched.

"I know. Welcome to the Dragon's den," Peyton agreed. "I went down to the Great Hall earlier and talked to some other students, and their schedules are not even half as filled as ours. Study time and free time in the day, an hour for lunch and literally half as long on Magic and Art of War. They have Saturday and Sunday completely free," Peyton went on.

Laken looked through the schedule for the rest of the week. Monday, Wednesday, and Friday were the same. Tuesday and Thursday substituted Numa Training and Angelic History for Creature Studies taught by Professor Zeetle, and Study of the Chosen One taught by Professor Gideon.

"What in the world? Are you telling me we don't even get Saturday and Sunday off?" Laken's jaw tensed. "We have Art of War and Magic over the weekend? You have to be kidding me."

"Hey, on the upside, we may not last that long." Peyton smiled. All the boys let out nervous laughter.

The five stepped out of the Portal into the busy Great Hall. Cherubs were zooming throughout, delivering eggs, pancakes, bacon and hash browns to every student, nearly as quickly as they sat down. Laken noticed that many second year and older students had multiple numas on their shoulders.

Laken overheard the closest one say, "Your mother and I love you so much and miss you. Stay out of trouble, and make sure you study."

"Weird," Dave muttered.

"Baylor, sit over here!" a familiar a voice interrupted Laken's thoughts. He looked over to see Daeth and his gang sitting about six tables down. Scorpious and Grap shoveled food into their mouths, spilling large portions onto the table and their robes. Baylor looked torn. He hesitated, shook his head, and made his way over to Daeth's table. "Don't forget who your real friends are," said Daeth, glaring at Laken. Laken heard Grap and Scorpious blast a couple of sheep noises as scrambled eggs flew out of their mouth.

Laken, Heath, Baylor, and Cirque found a seat and sat down. As soon as they were seated, a cherub in a red cloth dropped breakfast in front of them. "There you boys go!" squeaked the tiny voice. The boys did not hesitate. They each tore into their breakfast like a school of piranhas swarming a hippo. Not a word was said until Laken sopped up the last of his egg yolks with some bread.

"That Baylor is really going to hold us back," Peyton's expression tensed.

"He's an idiot and will probably get us killed!" Cirque said as he smiled at a couple of first year girls walking by. One of the girls dropped her Rhema in flustered excitement. "We need to find a way to get him out of the den. He's trouble. And if you ask me, he'll take Laken out the first chance he gets." He winked at another couple girls sitting at the next table over. CRASH! One of the girls knocked her plate off the table.

"Can you let the ladies have a few minutes break from the three ring Circus!" Heath moaned.

"I guess I can lay off for a moment!" As he nearly made a third-year girl faint from a quick smile thrown her way.

"For the love of all that is good and holy, stop it. I'm having trouble keeping my food down as it is." Peyton made a gagging noise.

"Alright, alright. Like I was saying, Laken better watch his back." Cirque leaned in and began to whisper. "I overheard Baylor talking in his sleep, and it sounded like he's going to try to do you in." Cirque made a slicing motion with his fork across his throat, staring straight at Laken.

"I'd like to see him try!" Laken said.

"Well, anyway you dice it, he needs to be off the team." Cirque sat back as his tone returned to normal. "If he is going to hang out with the Fallen, then we need to let Gabriel know he has to be out of the den,"

Cirque gave a wave at a group of first year girls. "Hi, ladies. Next meal, do me the honor and sit by me." Another large crash as one of the girls fell backwards, knocking three plates out of a cherub's hand.

"O.M.G.! I'm getting out of here."

"Same here!"

"I'm with you!" Laken, Heath and Peyton got up and headed towards the Portal.

"Hey, wait up, I'm coming, too. Hey, what's your name?" Cirque was jogging to keep up while still trying to flirt with a girl walking by.

Once they all arrived at the Portal, Laken asked, "So how do we get to our classroom? There's no room listed on my Rhema."

"I read up on that this morning," Heath said. "It seems we just say the name of the class and, based on the time of day, the portal knows which room and takes us there."

"Numa Training I," said each of their numas as they entered the Portal.

One by one they stepped into a dingy room that smelled of wet socks. "Smells like Baylor's sandals," Peyton said, plugging his nose. The boys chuckled while their heads moved around in curiosity, taking in the room. Laken swept his hands through the chilled fog that lay dormant from their knees down.

"That's pretty creepy," Dave shuddered. Laken's eyes swept the classroom, if that is what the room could even be called. If desks hadn't been placed throughout, Laken would have sworn that the room was a dungeon. Through the mist, small puddles of water lying on the dingy stone floor could barely be seen.

"Watch your step!" Heath exclaimed as he hopped over a large crack that ran the length of the room, then up the far wall, splitting into the massive sculpture of a snake. The inlaid stonewalls were scarred with huge claw marks, as if a massive creature had tried to scratch its way out.

"Probably from students trying to escape the smell," Dave chuckled as he plugged his nose.

Large chain links were anchored to the right wall. The chains looked like they were used to restrain something massive. Laken noticed small tally marks engraved on the same wall, as if someone or something was counting or keeping track of who-knows-what.

"I guess we just grab a seat," Heath shrugged. "Come on, let's sit together." But it was too late. Cirque was already sitting by three girls in the front, all of whom dissolved into a fit of giggles as he introduced himself. "Whatever. Let Casanova sit with them. Let's all sit back here."

Laken had just grabbed the seat next to Peyton when—

"Laken, you will be sitting up here where I can keep an eye on you!" A cold dark voice carried through the room. Laken squinted in the dim light to see the two small red eyes of Malgor right outside the portal fixed on him. Laken looked over at Heath and Peyton. "You don't need Dumb or Dumber's approval. Let's deduct one star from the Dragons Den!" A smile snaked across Malgor's face.

"What the heaven?" Laken mumbled, as he got up and stammered towards the front.

"Heaven has nothing to do with it, but since you obviously don't understand, let's take one star," Malgor's lip curled. Laken heard Peyton let out a huge sigh.

"Fine by me! Why don't we just make it an even five stars!" The words escaped Laken before he knew what happened. Peyton let out a muffled shriek.

"I like that! And let's add a Saturday's detention?" Malgor sounded even more vindictive, his red gums now showing thru his grin. Laken was silent as he threw himself into the chair next to the one Malgor had motioned for him to sit in. "Actually let's make it *all weekend*. That way we have time to work out the correct seat for you to sit in!" Malgor hissed, his eyes shifting to the seat he had pointed to moments before. Laken ripped himself out of his seat, and threw himself into the designated chair. Laken's face boiled in anger, his heart thundered in his chest.

"I hate him…I hate him…I hate him!" Dave growled.

"Daeth and Baylor, please find a seat and we will begin," Malgor's tone turned pleasant.

"Oh, goody. The Laken fan club is now complete," snarled Dave.

"Class, open your Rhemas up to Numa Training I." Malgor's voice incensed Laken as he turned a deep crimson. Laken slammed his Rhema onto the desk a little louder than he had meant to do. Everyone's eyes quickly turned to him. "It seems the Chosen One wants to be the center of attention. Good. Laken, please tell us the purpose of the numa." Malgor's eyes narrowed.

"Professor Malgor, allow me," Heath asked from the back.

"Dumb, or is it Dumber?" Malgor paused. "One star from Dragons Den." Malgor's cold gaze turned to Heath. "If I want to hear from you, I will call on you! Laken, please let us know the purpose of the numa." Malgor's voice was like a magnifying glass scorching the sunlight into Laken's skin. "Laken, can you share some of that Chosen One wisdom with us?" Bile rose in Laken's throat.

"I don't know," Laken whispered.

"I'm sorry. We couldn't hear you. Please share your wisdom, but this time loud enough for the class to hear."

"I DON'T KNOW!" Laken let each syllable out slowly.

Malgor starred at him incredulously for a moment, then smile tugged at the corners of his mouth. "Of course you don't. Just because you have been chosen does not make you smart. Alright, Dumber, please let the class know the purpose of the numa." Malgor turned his red glare back to Heath.

"According to Glindenhert's findings of 1403, the numa is the soul of an individual, made up of the mind, will, and emotions." Heath's gaze swept over the other students. "Glindenhert argues that this is where the subconscious lies and is there to help direct your decision making. Glindenhert's theory suggests that what an angel hears, then believes, becomes the guiding voice of the numa. The numa is what he refers to as the 'moral warehouse' that stores all of your thoughts and beliefs." Heath drew in a big breath. "According to Glindenhert, when a circumstance arises, your numa looks into the warehouse to search for what you believe should be done. It then suggests the course of action. If you follow the numa's instructions, the numa makes you feel good. If you go against the recommendation, then guilt sets in. Glindenhert compares this to how you train a house gnome. Do good, get a reward. Do bad, get discipline. Glindenhert discovered that if you continue to go against the numa in the same circumstance, the numa will change the belief to line up with the action."

Laken was amazed at how Heath spouted this out like he was actually reading it from a book.

"Glindenhert claims that numas' uses are limitless, and we have just scratched the surface on what we know about them. The main uses today are aids in decision making, sensing danger, key parts of the battle process, and sending messages to others—they are an intricate part in knowing what gifts, talents, and character traits you possess, as we witnessed in the weapon choosing, in the den choosing, and in literally all major choices made in our world."

Heath drew in another large breath through a big smile before continuing. "For centuries, we have used them as a witness tool. They see three hundred and sixty degrees, and take in every detail of a situation. While angels perceive something which is usually far from the truth, a numa sees the truth of what *really* happened." Heath finished, and the whole class was bug-eyed in amazement.

"One star from Dragons Den for boring us all." Malgor yawned.

"What? Why?" Peyton blurted, as if holding the words in any longer would cause his head to explode. Malgor shot Peyton a cautionary glance as Daeth and his gang let out a small laugh. "But somewhere in there is what I was looking for." Malgor shook his head impatiently.

"Today we will begin working on messaging one another with our numas. As most of you have had your parents send you a numa message, you have a basic understanding of how it works." Malgor's gaze snapped to Laken as if to say, *Not you— your mother is dead*. It took every bit of self-control Laken could muster not to attack Malgor.

"Turn to page thirty-four, and then get into groups of three and work on messaging each other."

Laken nearly leapt out of his desk, to get back to Heath and Peyton. He was almost as fast as the half dozen girls racing to Cirque.

"Ladies, ladies, no fighting. If you're not in my group today, next time I will make sure you get Cirque time." Cirque had his arms around two girls.

"Us three." Laken cut across a taller blonde-haired boy, as he reached Heath and Peyton.

"We would have it no other way!" Peyton smiled. Peyton then tipped his head towards Malgor and whispered "This should be one fun semester. Bet we finish the year with zero stars."

"Alright, according to Glindenhert's three F's, we must—"

Heath, who was not even looking at the book, interrupted. "Number one, focus your thoughts on who you want the message to go to. Number two, focus what you want said. Number three, focus on seeing it done." Heath's voice made it clear that he regarded the steps as common knowledge.

"I will go first," Heath announced. Laken looked over at Heath whose eyes were squinted, a small crease forming between his eyebrows, and face puckered, as if he had just eaten a lemon. Laken watched as Heath's numa split into a pair of twin numas. The replica raced over to Dave.

"Heath wants to know what you are doing this weekend," Dave relayed to Laken.

"Holy crud! That was awesome!" Laken blurted out a little too loudly, as other groups turned and glared at him. "O.M.G.! That is too cool," Laken whispered. "It's like a text message from a phone!"

"A text what?" asked Peyton.

"Never mind, never mind. Let me try," Laken said, shaking his hands. Laken scrunched up his face, focused on Peyton, and said to Dave, "Your brother is a dork!"

Dave just sat there, and finally said, "So what's your point?"

"What do you mean what's my point? Go let Peyton know what I said," Laken lashed out.

"He's right there, why don't you let him know yourself?" Dave shot back, folding his arms defiantly.

"You have to be kidding me. Are you not paying attention? Split into two, and tell Peyton's numa what I said." Laken's face flushed red.

Dave put his hand to his mouth and yelled, "Hey Peyton's numa, tell Peyton his brother is a dork." Dave laughed. Laken narrowed his eyes, and bit his lip.

"My stupid numa is useless," Laken said, turning to Heath, flailing his right arm about. "He won't message. He refuses!" Laken's complaint prompted an annoyed, "Shhh!" from the groups around them.

"You shhh!" Laken snapped.

"It's not the numa's fault. It's you," Heath said shaking his head. "It says it right there on page thirty-four. If your numa is confused, don't blame the numa. Keep trying. It then says that most angels make the mistake on part three, focusing on seeing it done," Heath pointed to a page in his Rhema.

"It's your fault! Not mine, yours! *You! You!*" Dave shouted, cupping his hands around his mouth. Laken slouched back and drew a ragged breath.

For the next hour, Peyton and Heath took turns sending numas to Laken, while Laken grew more and more frustrated. Finally, the bell rang.

"Class, read chapters one through four by Wednesday!" Malgor shouted over the ruckus of the students leaving.

As Laken shoved his Rhema into his Hallow, Dave sounded truly concerned when he relayed another message, "A numa, who would not tell me who he was, just warned me," Dave paused and looked around suspiciously. "Someone is planning on killing you with fire…by week's end!"

CHAPTER THIRTEEN
In Between a Rock and a Pessimist

"What? Are you sure?" Peyton seemed flushed with confusion as the boys exited the Portal into the Great Hall, busy with students coming, going, talking and fooling around. Cherubs flew about with harps in their hands, playing a simple but light-hearted melody, which brought a sense of calm over the room.

"Yes, Dave said someone, I think Baylor or Malgor, will try and kill me by week's end," Laken responded, looking up to see from where the music came.

"And you don't know who sent the numa?" Peyton questioned, his gaze following Laken's.

Laken's glance shot back to Peyton. "No, Dave said it was an unknown numa. Can you do that? Disguise your numa?" Laken inquired, his eyes wide in horror.

"Well, it says here," Heath had his Rhema open and was fingering through the pages, "that a numa's source can be concealed, but that it is not an easy task to master. You have to be skilled in numalistics, that is: the art of numa, for those of you who have not read your homework, yet." Heath smiled as he shut his rhema.

"Well, my fault." Peyton threw his hands up into the air. "I've been out of class almost two minutes now. How did I not get the thirty plus pages of reading done? I am an oaf, a big lazy oaf."

"Guys, stop." Laken shook his head. "Baylor wants me dead. We have to let Gabriel know."

"Dave said Baylor is going to kill you?" Heath asked, his brows raised.

"No, for the third time, I said *someone*," clarified Dave.

"Well, not exactly."

"Well, then what, exactly?" Heath asked as the twins each starred at him. Laken regarded them for a moment, then conceded "Dave said *someone*, but we know that means Baylor or Malgor, or who else?"

"Maybe it's me. Maybe your snoring last night and sleep-talking about summer time was annoying, and now I want you dead." A smile played along Peyton's lips.

"Be serious. We know it's not you two. Cirque wouldn't take time away from the ladies to try and knock me off. Baylor hates me and hangs out with a gang of Fallen. It's pretty simple reasoning," Laken shrugged.

"Don't you have Gabriel alone today after *Wings*?" Heath said.

"I have discipleship, but I assumed that we would all be there." Laken's eyes widened.

"No, it's you alone. I think that's when you need to let Gabriel know what happened—"

Heath was interrupted by an eruption of giggles. "Hey, boys, time for our next class," came Cirque's voice from behind them. Laken turned to see Cirque, a girl under each arm, and three others grouped around him. "Ladies, it's time for me to have some bonding time with the guys. I'll meet up with you later," said Cirque.

"Ohhh, we can't wait. Numa me, please," a very pretty blonde girl pleaded, as if her life depended on it.

"Numa me, too!"

"Cirque, numa me."

"Don't forget me."

Peyton slid his finger down his throat and made a gagging sound. "I think I just puked a little in my mouth."

"Alright, guys, let's head off to Magic." Cirque said 'Magic' with an off-putting French accent as he flung his arms around Peyton and Heath. The three boys stared at Cirque for a moment, then shook their heads in disbelief as Peyton and Heath ducked under Cirque's grasp.

They each walked into the Portal, numas saying, *Introduction to Magic*. To Laken's surprise, they exited the Portal, not into a classroom, but outside in Eden. The perfect mix of warm sunshine and cool breeze permeated the grove. Laken took in a huge breath of the flower-scented air.

"Welcome, boys. Come join Baylor and me." On some rocks by a small pond sat Gabriel and Baylor. The light breeze stroked the angel's long beard and hair, making them dance. "Please take a seat," Gabriel invited, once the boys had reached the pond.

"Today we begin what I would say is your most important training." Gabriel's striking blue eyes sweeping to each boy. "I believe that if you give your heart to training and learning magic, that it will be the main ingredient in the defeat of the little pink bunny." Gabriel smiled at the last part. "Can anyone tell me what magic is?" he asked, his gaze traveling from boy to boy.

"I'm sure Heath can," Peyton blurted out.

"Of course he can." Gabriel shot Heath a warm smile. "Heath scored an 1883 on his SAT's, his Scholastic Angelic Test, for those of you who don't know." Gabriel looked over to Laken, who shrugged as if he had known the meaning of the acronym. "The highest score we have seen in a few thousand years. I believe Plato was the last to score over 1800. Even Da Vinci only scored a 1789," Gabriel stroked his beard.

"Da Vinci? Plato? Are these the same people I have heard of?" Laken asked, his eyes wide.

"I believe so, but you will learn more about them and others in your *Study of the Chosen One*," Gabriel said, turning then to Heath. "Please explain Magic."

"According to the Blasslet letters," Heath began, looking as serious as if he were presenting the State of the Union, "Magic is taking dominion over our environment. According to the ancient writings, 'The Almighty gave them dominion over all things on this earth.' Dominion is something each angelic being and human possesses, though very few humans even know it exists. Dominion is the ability to control things around them in an unnatural manner, or supernaturally. Dominion is what we call Magic, the ability to control things around us." Heath paused as if to give everyone time to take in his vast wisdom. Gabriel nodded to Heath, as if to say "continue."

"The Blasslet letters go on to describe the powers of Magic. It is important to note that many more powers and abilities have been discovered since, and the Blasslet letters do say that the abilities of Magic are limitless. Abilities include moving, controlling, or pushing objects without touching them; producing an invisible shield of protection; and changing the form of most objects, including one's self. It has not yet been possible to change other living beings, which is why many Goblin-made and Dwarf-made weapons cannot be changed, as these specialty weapons actually come alive." Laken's eyes widened.

"Magic can also produce a blinding light, open and unlock objects, make things appear and disappear, control the mind of the weak-willed, dissappearate—" Heath spoke, again, as if reading directly from a book.

"Good. I think you covered more than our below- 1800-minds can handle, one star to Dragon's Den" Gabriel interrupted with a smile. "Thank thee Almighty!" Peyton blurted out. Gabriel glanced at Peyton and then continued. "I think the important thing to draw from what Heath said was that nothing is impossible." Gabriel paused. "I said nothing is impossible. This will be a phrase you will hear me say over and over." Gabriel paused as he regarded the boys. "What makes something impossible is when you believe it is impossible. Whether it is possible or impossible is contingent on the beliefs of the individual, not the laws of nature." A smiled tugged on Gabriel's lips.

"Is this magic like witches and wizards use?" Laken asked, expression curious.

"Ahhh, terms the other boys probably have never heard, terms from your world." Gabriel paused in thought, and then continued. "Yes I believe in many ways it is the same, except this is not make-believe." Gabriel wore a crooked smile. "I believe that some witches and wizard stories may have some truth contained in them, the truth of what you can do." Gabriel placed a finger alongside his mouth, his gaze was looking up. There was a slight pause as the boys sat in silence staring at the headmaster.

"Yes, yes, they would be quite similar, except we won't be using wands, or saying certain spells out loud. We will need simply to think it, and then believe it." Gabriel drew in a long breath as he looked back down at the boys.

"So, Peyton, what is the source of power in Magic?" Gabriel looked over to Peyton who was transforming his hand into a rabbit and playing with some other rabbits that had gathered around him.

"Uugghh…what? Sorry." Peyton, caught by surprise, allowed his hand to return back to normal, prompting the rabbits to scamper off.

"What is the source of power in Magic?" Gabriel asked again, his grin widened.

"Please excuse my 1602 mind, but my mother said it has to do with faith, or what you believe."

"Not as long-winded as Heath, but just the same, a right answer," Gabriel smiled, while Heath turned a shade of scarlet. "Faith is the power behind Magic. Cirque, would you like to explain what faith is?"

Cirque's eyes rolled up into his head as if he were staring into his brain for the answer. "Got it. Faith is the substance of what you expect and the evidence of the unseen," Cirque said proudly.

"Very good, one star to Dragons Den. Faith, simply put, is the result of what you believe." Gabriel paused when he saw Laken shake his head as if his mind were trying to rid itself of painful thoughts. "Laken, you have a question?" Gabriel inquired.

"Aaagh, yeah, I guess," Laken said slowly, words now caught in his throat. "So you are saying faith is the evidence of what I don't see? How is that possible? If I don't see it, I have no evidence of it being there." Gabriel's smile grew as he regarded him.

"Laken, please understand that Magic will take you longer because you come from a backwards belief world. Your world believes and teaches their young to *believe it when they see it*," explained Gabriel. "Well, if you wait to see it but you don't believe it first, it will never come. That is *backwards*. When you believe it, then you will see it. Belief comes before you see. It is the belief that brings its existence. It is faith." Gabriel paused, looking around until his eye caught a small rock twenty feet away. "You see that rock?" Gabriel motioned to the rock, and each of the boys' gazes fell upon it. "If I wait to see it move and then I believe it will move, guess what? It will never move." Gabriel shrugged in mock frustration. "Instead, if I believe I can move it, then when I believe it, it moves and I see it." The rock began to rise off the ground and then, suddenly, shot over, hitting Peyton's hand which was, once again, a rabbit playing with the other rabbits.

"Owww!" Peyton shouted, shaking his rabbit hand. The other boys let out a laugh.

"Laken, are you starting to understand? I know it will take you some time to forget the ways of your backwards world." Gabriel looked to the other boys and then asked, "Can anyone let Laken know how you build your faith, or build the power of your magic?"

"Faith comes and grows from hearing your desired belief over and over and over again," Heath blurted out.

"Very good, another star to Dragon's Den" Gabriel turned his gaze back to Laken. "To build up your faith you have to say over and over again what you want to believe. If you want to move a rock, you say, 'I can move a rock, I can move a rock.' You then see yourself doing it and doing it. You see it in your mind long enough until Dave believes it, and then it will actually happen."

"Wait. Is this another Dave thing? Because he seems to be a little slow." Laken shook his head.

"Hey, who's slow, mister? How can I believe if I don't see it?" Dave shot back.

"Yes, Laken, your numa is your belief system. When Dave believes it, it will happen," Gabriel explained as Laken shook his head even harder. "Laken, give it time, give Dave some time. You will be amazed at what you can do!" Gabriel smiled.

"Okay, finally, before we get to some applications, what is the dark side of magic?" Gabriel asked, clasping his hands together.

"Fear!" Before anyone could answer. "Fear is the reciprocal of Faith. It is the opposite, yet produces in the same manner. Fear is a belief that something negative will happen. Because you believe it, it happens," Heath explained, matter-of-factly, before Gabriel could call on anyone else.

"Yes, very good. Fear is what the Fallen use. The Fallen use fear to destroy, while we use faith to build." Gabriel's hands and expressions emphasized each phrase. "Fear is about bringing out the worst in others, while faith is about bringing out the best in you. Fear is the bully side of Magic, or the taking side, while faith is the helper side, or giving side of Magic." Gabriel paused, his brows narrowed.

"I must warn all of you that fear is much easier to learn, and can become quite powerful very quickly." Gabriel's gaze settled on Laken, who could feel his face flush red. "Faith takes much more work, and a lot more time to become powerful. Of course, ultimately, faith is more powerful than fear. Just like darkness cannot hold back the light, so fear cannot hold back faith. Fear will bring death, while faith brings life." Gabriel's glance now fell on Baylor, who was looking down, pretending to focus on a group of ants carrying a green glowing fruit.

"I want each of you to practice with these rocks." With that, a rock fell into each of the boys' laps. "I want you to practice moving the rocks in your mind. Remember, you have to believe you can do it first. Then it will move." Gabriel paused, looking at Baylor once again. "Baylor, may I have a quick word with you?" Baylor rose, his head hung low. Gabriel placed his arm around the giant-boy's shoulders, and the two walked to the other side of the pond, Gabriel speaking into Baylor's ear.

"Hey, look! It's moving!" Peyton shouted, startling Laken with his excitement. Laken looked over to see Peyton's rock shaking ever so slightly.

"That's nothing. Watch mine," boasted Heath, his rock almost rolling over, but then falling back down.

"Watch mine," Cirque said as his rock did a complete flip and then shot across the pond, skipping five times before coming to a rest next to Gabriel, who retorted with a warning look.

"WOW! Don't know my own magical strength," Cirque announced to the shocked expressions on the faces of his den members.

Laken looked down at his rock, and said to himself, "Move."

"You can't move a rock with your mind," Dave protested.

"Yes, we can. They can do it. We can do it!" Laken blasted back to Dave. "Now move the stupid rock, you blue worthless turd."

"Hey, if you talk to me like that, then you can move it yourself." Dave folded his arms and turned away from Laken.

"Aaaagghhhh!" Laken screamed out loud.

"What's wrong?" asked Heath as his rock flipped over. "I did it!" Heath exclaimed, without giving Laken a chance to reply.

"Nothing, nothing is wrong. Except I have a useless numa." Laken crossed his arms and shifted his head away from Dave.

He sat there mad at Dave for the remainder of the lesson. By the time the bell rang, Peyton could move his rock a few inches, while Heath could float his rock a full foot off the ground. Even Baylor, who was talking to Gabriel most of the time, could get his rock to shake.

When the bell sounded, Laken picked up his rock and threw it, nearly hitting a group of squirrels playfully stacking themselves into a pyramid.

Laken, without thinking, stomped into the Portal only to find himself exiting then into a small room chest high in water.

"Ohhh, another person coming here to get my hopes up, and then just leave," sighed a dejected voice. Laken looked to where the voice was coming from and, to his surprise, saw a very plump, blue-skinned cherub floating in the corner of the room. Her body was as wide as it was tall. She looked like a blue beach ball.

"What? Where am I?" Laken demanded as he continued to look around the room, raising his soaked arms up out of the water. The small chamber glowed bright yellow and had a large portrait of a unicorn hung on the wall to his right.

"Of course, come in here and scream at me, why wouldn't you? Why not scream at Pezamist? Everyone else does." She sounded even more forlorn.

"No, sorry, I didn't mean to scream. It's just that… you do realize this room is, like, half full of water?" Laken said in a gentler voice.

"No, actually, it is half-empty. It's because of my parents, you know. They never let me do anything fun. That is why I'm stuck here. Why I've been stuck in this room for fifty years now. Nobody cares about me," she finished, tears splashed on her big blue cheeks.

"Wish I could stay, but I have to get to class," said Laken, wading his way to the Portal.

"Of course, leave! Leave like the rest." She began splashing water violently at Laken. "Let… Pezamist… Be… by… *herself*." Pezamist enunciated each word as she hit the water. "It's not like anyone even notices I'm gone…"

The last words of her tirade trailed off as Laken entered the Portal saying, as fast as his mouth could move, "The Great Hall, please the Great Hall."

Laken entered the Great Hall to a room full of laughter as water poured from his drenched robes.

"Hey, the Chosen One is all wet!" laughed a third year.

"How was your underwater basket weaving class?" roared a second-year girl.

Laken shook himself like a wet dog and then, squishing with every step, made his way over to a table by himself. As a cherub flew by to drop off Laken's meal, Laken batted at the cherub.

"Get away! Stupid cherub. I'm not hungry." The cherub made a rude hand gesture and flew away.

"Hey, you alright?" asked Peyton and Heath as they brought their plates over and sat next to Laken. They were barely audible over the commotion of all the students eating and talking.

"I'm fine. Just leave me alone," Laken mumbled.

"Nah, we are fury brothers, and we stick together." Heath sat right next to Laken. "You don't have to talk to us, but we'll sit next to you even if you are dripping all over us," he said with a mouth full of food, bringing a small smile to Laken's face.

"Come on, tell us what happened," Peyton's cheeks looked ready to burst with food.

"I have no idea," Laken threw his hands in the air, spraying water all over the table. "I was mad about Dave not moving the rock, and so I went into the stupid Portal," Laken motioned to the Portal, water flying onto a table of girls who screamed out in anger, "and it took me to this room that was half full off water," Laken ignored the scowls and words from the girls, "with this sour-faced blueberry-looking cherub. Her name was Pezamist or something, and she has to be the most depressing cherub ever. 'Poor me, nobody likes me, the room is half empty.'" Laken did a poor impression of Pezamist.

"That is quite funny and ironic—a depressing cherub whose name is Pezamist," Heath laughed. At that moment, it hit Laken: the humor in the name, and the room, and what she said.

The rest of the hour brought Laken's spirits back up, as they laughed about the day and the Pezamist Room, as they now called it. They even laughed at the fact that the cherub would not bring Laken a plate. Instead, the cherub would fly by at full speed and chuck food at Laken.

"Looks like you made yourself another friend," Peyton handed Laken half of his BLT sandwich.

"Mind if I sit here?" a quiet yet familiar voice interrupted. Laken turned to see Baylor's massive head looking at his own feet. "Sorry for not sitting with you this morning," Baylor apologized.

"Sure, you big sheep. You are always welcome to sit with us," Peyton offered magnanimously as he scooted a considerable distance to make sure Baylor had enough room to sit down.

As Baylor took his seat, Laken overheard Baylor's numa mutter: "None of this will matter once Laken is dead!"

CHAPTER FOURTEEN
Butterfly Wings on an Elephant

The entire Dragon's den sat together in the Angelic History classroom. Laken couldn't help but notice that the room was decorated oddly. Paintings were either upside down, or hung sideways. One portrait was actually mounted with the picture facing the wall. The walls were painted every color you could imagine, but with no plan or order. It looked like someone had started painting with one color, stopped, and then began painting with another.

"Baylor, over here," Daeth's called from across the room. Baylor pretended to study an upside-down painting of an Angel with large pepperoni pizzas for legs. "Baylor, over..."

Daeth's summons was interrupted by an old crackly voice. "Quiet now, everyone quiet." Laken looked up to see the ancient Professor Luvly slowly making her way to the front of the classroom with the aid of a cane. "I am Professor Luvly, and today we begin *Angelic History I: The Beginning.*"

"From the looks of her, I'll bet she was there in the beginning," Peyton whispered, prompting the boys to giggle quietly. "In the beginning, I was there and here is what I saw," Peyton imitated Professor Luvly's old voice. The boys snorted, trying to hold back their laughter.

"We will be starting with Creation and work our way to the Great Fall. Please open your Rhemas to page ten of Angelic History I," Professor Luvly crackled. Laken pulled out his Rhema along with the rest of the class, opened to page ten, and then turned his attention back to the Professor.

There was a long uncomfortable pause, during which Professor Luvly simply stood in silence, staring out over the students with a glazed look in her eyes.

Laken looked to Peyton, then to Heath. "What is she doing?" he whispered.

"Don't know," Heath shrugged.

"Professor Luvly, are you alright?" cried out a blonde-haired boy in the second row. The sound of the boy's voice shook Professor Luvly, who shuddered as if waking suddenly from a daydream.

The old woman simply turned and walked out of the room, into what looked like her office. The class erupted into a cacophony of voices.

"What the…?"

"Is she nuts?"

"I heard she was crazy."

"She's so old, she's lost her marbles."

Student after student shared an opinion.

Then: "Quiet now, everyone quiet," came the same elderly voice.

Laken looked over to see Professor Luvly coming in the exact way she had gone a few minutes earlier.

"Can you say déjà vu?" Peyton's eyes widened.

"I am Professor Luvly, and today we begin *Angelic History I: The Beginning*. We will be starting with Creation and work our way to the Great Fall. Please open your Rhemas to page ten." Professor Luvly looked around the room, waiting for the class to turn to the required page.

"Well, it seems as if you are already there. Good, I like a class that is prepared," Professor Luvly said over the snickers in the room. "You, in the back. You, the only one without a book open." Everyone looked to where the professor was pointing.

"Is she talking to that plant?" asked Heath as he made a hand motion signaling that she must be insane.

"You!" Professor Luvly shook her finger like an incensed nanny. "Don't make me ask you again, or it will be detention. Open your book." The professor narrowed her brow. "Don't ignore me. Open your book now!"

"Uh, let me help Pete with his book," Heath said as he took his Rhema and rested it in the plant.

"Good, thank you, little girl, for your help," said the professor. The class let out a snort of laughter.

"Hurry and sit down, little girl," Peyton mocked his brother.

"Funny, very funny," Heath said, attempting a feminine wiggle.

"Ummm, where was I?" the professor inquired with a dazed look.

"The bell just rang and you were releasing us from class," Peyton suggested over the giggles in the room.

"Ah, yes, a very good class we had today. Make sure you read pages one through twenty-two for homework. You are dismissed, except for Pete in the back. I would like to have a word with you."

The students rushed into the Portal as if her mind could change at any moment. As Laken entered the Portal, he could still hear Professor Luvly demanding that Pete come to the front immediately.

Laken stepped into the Great Hall behind his den members.

"That is my favorite class, hands down," laughed Peyton.

"You're going to get yourself thrown out of Dogma pulling a stunt like that," Heath warned as he shook his head at Peyton.

"Hey, don't worry about me getting thrown out. It's Pete who probably won't make it through the semester." At that, the boys laughed.

"Let's get a head start on our homework," Heath advised. Each boy sat down and they began to go through their Rhemas.

When the bell rang, the boys rose and entered the Portal saying, "Intro to Wings." Out of the Portal the boys stepped into what— Laken did not know.

"Wow!" Baylor whispered.

"Unbelievable!" Laken agreed.

The room was the size of a professional football arena. There were thousands and thousands of wings attached to the walls rising a hundred feet up or so. The wings were displayed much the same way a hunter mounts an animal's head on his wall. There were wings of every color, shape and size. Each seemed to be alive with movement. Some were flapping while others rubbed themselves together. There were a number of wings snoring overhead. Laken noticed wings flying by themselves hundreds of feet above them. Upon closer examination, he saw a few pairs of wings remove themselves from the wall and fly off, while others would reattach themselves to the wall, much like a bird perching itself on a tree limb.

"This place wins the coolest room award." Peyton's eyes were wide. "Well, not counting Laken's Pezamist room," he amended.

"Alright, class, make your way over to me. I'm the tall handsome one over here." The deep, calming voice belonged to Professor Cronus. Laken looked to see the Professor's blonde hair perfectly combed, and his strong jaw jutting out as if he were posing for a statue. He wore a deep purple robe that one might wear to a formal party or ball.

"Over here, over here, but, please, not too close. We don't want to wrinkle this Venwa robe." Cronus preened with an air of superiority. Laken and the other students made their way to where their professor was posing.

"Today will be a memorable day in your life, and not just because you met me." Cronus paused to let out a small, vain laugh, waiting for a group laugh that never came, then cleared his throat and continued. "But because you will be receiving your match. In other words, the wings you will have for the rest of your life will be choosing you today."

"Doesn't he mean I choose?" Laken asked Heath.

"No, the wings choose you." Heath leaned close to Laken to whisper in his ear. "Some say the wings knew at the moment of your birth that they were to be your wings. They have been anticipating this day ever since then. That's why so many of the wings are excited." Heath motioned overhead to the wings flying above and displaying tricks.

"Now, you won't get wings as glorious as mine." Cronus posed again. "Please, step back. Step Back!" he said sharply. Students leapt back as Cronus's wings emerged out of his back and then, like a convertible car, expanded outward. Cronus's wings were massive, alive, and to Laken, beautiful. They seemed to be breathing with life as they fluttered and flapped gently with the breeze. Then, Cronus's wings folded up and disappeared.

"Like I said, don't expect anything that nice, but you're not me! Right?" He let out a pompous laugh. "Anyone care to tell me where the wings come from?" Cronus looked around the room. "Yes, you with your hand up. What is your name?"

"Name is Heath. Wings come from Dragons, Unicorns, a Pegasus, Imps, Griffins, Hippogriffs, Phoenixes, Fairies, and Angels who have passed on, or in some cases, have been thrown into Outer Darkness. The list of creatures our wings come from seems to be infinite."

"Yes, very good. Mine, of course, might have come from the Almighty Himself." Cronus let out that same braggart's laugh. He looked around to find no one impressed. "Listen! I do not have time to go over everything about wings today," his brow narrowed as he changed the subject. "You will need to read about that on your own. Today is simply about getting you your wings." Cronus moved to the side and a small, older man, in a blue cloak stepped forward. Everyone had been so focused on Cronus that they had overlooked him.

"This is Elkan. He is Dogma's *Wingerd* and is in charge of the distribution and care of all wings here at the school. He will be overseeing the process." Cronus motioned to the small frail looking man wearing a small brown hat which covered his wiry grey hair. Elkan had one huge eye, one very small eye, thick grey eyebrows and a large handle bar mustache that looked as if it were being held up by his massive crooked nose.

"Uuuuckhum!" Elkan cleared his throat. "I will need a volunteer," his voice sounded like broken glass. A small blonde girl near the front threw her hand up and rushed beside Elkan. The girl had a dreamy look in her eyes, seeming to stare through Elkan to Cronus's perfect face.

"Very good, you will do nicely," Elkan said as he patted her on the head. "Everyone, please stand back." Elkan waved his hands motioning for everyone to move away. His gaze then intensified on the girl. "Young lady, if you would please stand perfectly still with your arms stretched out." Elkan raised his stick-thin arms to motion the instructions. "Now, speak loudly and clearly, and say *I am ready for my match.*" The girl, with her arms outstretched, repeated the phrase.

Everyone's gaze shot towards the sky until, finally, one girl shouted, "There, there they are. They're headed right to her." Sure enough, a pair of bright white wings six feet long were soaring towards the girl. The wings circled around her a few times, then slowly dropped behind her. Her body jerked awkwardly, and by that Laken knew they had attached. The young girl was awestruck. She looked at each wing, and Laken could tell she was trying to move both separately, like a baby testing each finger when he discovers his hands.

"Enough. You have a lifetime to play with your wings. Elkan, show her how to put them away," Cronus said impatiently.

"Yes, of course. First, young lady, your wings are from a Brokst Unicorn." Elkan's gaze turned serious once again. "They have a wing span of six feet, three inches. They are first-generation, meaning you are their first match." The girl broke into an ear-to-ear smile as if she had just received a new pony.

Elkan turned to the students. "This is very important. You must know that your wings are a very proud and sensitive creature and require respect if they are to function properly." Elkan turned to the girl. "Think to yourself, *Wings, please take a rest.* Make sure you are polite!" Elkan interrupted before she had a chance to think. The girl looked like she was in deep concentration, Laken heard her numa say, "Wings, please take a rest." Then the wings folded up and vanished. Elkan motioned to a blonde-haired boy who sat behind Laken in Numa Studies. "You will be next."

One after another, students received their wings. Some wings were white, others brown, one pair was even a bright red. They were all different shapes and sizes. Most were first-generation, but there were some second and third-generation wings, even a seventh-generation pair. Laken was not surprised that Daeth's ten-foot wings were black, third-generation Fallen from a Skeletor Imp.

Heath received a bizarre pair of color-changing wings. One moment they were the color of the sky, then a greenish brown that looked like camouflage material. No one could even see them until they were attached and flapping on Heath's back.

"Ohhh, third-generation wings from the extinct Shrouded Griffin. At least we think they are extinct, but you couldn't find the creatures even if you wanted to." Elkan shook his head. "They are chameleons, blending into their surroundings, changing colors. They become invisible. Quite amazing creatures." A smile tugged on Elkan's lips.

Peyton's wings were small and fast. They reminded Laken of a hummingbird's. They flapped so quickly that you could barely see them. "A wing span of five foot, nine inches. They are first-generation wings from a wooded Fairy. Hmmm, that is a first." Elkan put his finger to his face.

Cirque's wings were nearly an identical match to those of Cronus. Huge, glorious, and white. Laken thought he saw a few girls nearly fall over and faint when Cirque gave the wings a good flap.

"Alright, big boy, it is your turn," Elkan motioned to Baylor, whose massive frame filled the open area. Laken looked around trying to guess which would be Baylor's.

"Those." Dave pointed at two massive wings. They must have been twenty feet across.

"I think you're right," Laken smiled.

"I am ready for my match," Baylor's voice boomed. Everyone's attention was on the massive wings as they continued to soar overhead. But the wings made no change in direction. They did not fly down towards Baylor.

"I am ready for my match!" Baylor announced more clearly and forcefully. Still nothing.

"I see them. They are coming!" There was a huge gasp of surprise from the students as they took sight of what floated down toward Baylor. Then they began to laugh, and point.

The wings were by far the smallest wings given out that day—not even the size of Peyton's tiny pair. Baylor attempted to shoo them away as if they were a pesky little fly. The wings whipped around him and, with a jerk of Baylor's body, attached themselves to him. The entire place erupted with laughter. Laken laughed so hard he fell on top of Heath who was already rolling on the ground with huge tears of bemusement in his eyes. Even Elkan had a hard time not toppling over.

The pair looked like butterfly wings pinned to an elephant.

"First-generation wings from a mountain Sprite, with a wing span of five feet, ten inches." Elkan could barely get the last words out. He burst into contagious laughter, ranging through the entire group.

Baylor knocked over several kids as he trampled to the Portal, disappearing.

"I couldn't tell, did he put them away?" Peyton induced another fit of laughter.

When the laughter died down, Elkan proceeded. Student after student received their wings until only Laken was left. "As we do every seventy or so years, we get the honor of witnessing the wings of the Chosen One," Elkan remarked reverently, a small pathetic clap ringing through the students, mainly egged on by Peyton and Heath. "Hold your arms out, and call your wings," Elkan instructed eagerly as Laken stepped towards the center area.

Laken held his arms out and said confidently, "I am ready for my match." The whole group looked up in extreme anticipation. At first, nothing unusual happened. And then Laken saw them. They were, in fact, the wings he had spotted from the beginning. He hadn't wanted to raise his hopes too high, but they were the ones he wanted. They were big—at least twelve feet, and bright white like Gabriel's. There was an opalescent glow to them unlike any other set of wings he had seen. Down, down, down the wings soared gracefully towards Laken. They hovered just above him, settled in place behind, and slowly descended.

Suddenly there was a loud scream from a group of girls, and then BAMMMM—a large crash sent Laken flying to the ground. Laken could hear screaming and shouting. His mind reeled from the impact. As he shook the cobwebs from his head, he looked up to see a fight between his wings and a set of onyx-black wings. They flapped and rammed into each other like two cocks in a hen house. Laken's wings dodged and swept down towards Laken in what looked like an attempt to attach themselves to him. The ebony wings, which seemed to be faster and much larger, rammed into the top of the white pair, sending them both spiraling downward, nearly smashing into a group of screaming students who barely dove out of the way. With a massive thud of dust and debris, they crashed into the ground. The black wings shook off the dust and soared upwards. Laken's white wings did the same, but just a fraction of a second behind the black pair. The black wings were now headed towards Laken, with the white wings following close behind. As the black pair reached Laken, they stopped and did a quick one hundred and eighty-degree spin, catching the white wings off guard. The black pair, with a massive flap of its right wing, sent the white pair crashing into the wall, knocking five other wings to the ground. Before Laken had time to react, the black wings had whipped around him and, with a jerk of Laken's body, attached themselves.

Laken looked over at his massive wing span. The wings were a deep, dark shiny pearl black. They exuded a mysterious strength. Merely having them attached felt dangerous and exciting.

"With a wing span of fourteen feet, nine inches, they come from Faldon, one of the Mares of Diomedes. They are a second-generation wing. The original match was Lord Dagon who is now in Outer Darkness." The heaviness in Elkan's voice was tempered only by the loud gasps and small screams that came from the terrified students and teachers.

CHAPTER FIFTEEN
Laken Picks Cherries
for a Night Elf

"Dagon's wings? You have to be kidding me." Heath exhaled slowly, his eyes wide open. "He killed what? Ten, eleven DAS officers and the DAA at the time? I think her name was Dzblen." Heath spoke faster than normal as his hands moved about as if he were in the midst of the battle. "It was front page news of the Angelic Times for well over a month. I heard Gabriel finally brought him in, after a huge battle." Heath sounded impressed as he, Laken, and Peyton entered the Great Hall.

"DAS, DA- what? Who or what are you talking about?" Laken asked as he closed his eyes and shook his head.

"DAS is the *Department of Angelic Safety*," Heath replied, rolling his eyes. "The DAA is the *Director of Angelic Affairs*. Her name, I am sure of it, was Dzblen." Heath's eyes widened. "Real hard nose, as my uncle always said. Some say she was in with some Fallen. Rumors, mom said," Heath's voice rang with excitement, "but to take on that many officers, he was one bad ol' Fallen Angel,"

As Heath went on, Laken's mind drifted and Dave's voice was all Laken could hear. "Why him? Why did he get the evil wings? Was he to go down the same path as the last Chosen One? Why couldn't he get the good wings, the white ones? It was just like his whole life. Couldn't get the good parents—got Jack and Carla. Couldn't get a nice house, he had to sleep in the basement. Got the old, beat-up sword, the evil wings." Dave went on and on in Laken's ear.

"Hey, let's get going to the *Art of War*," Heath interrupted Dave's tirade.

"Huh? Oh yeah, right. Let's go." Laken tried to act as if he had been listening to Heath the whole time.

The three boys entered the Portal and walked out into what looked like an old gladiators' battle arena. The boys all paused and stared at what lay before them.

"Wow!" Peyton said in a loud whisper. "I've heard of this place. This is where the WWC is held."

"The what?" asked Laken as he observed a group of six men with weapons attacking a small elf armed with only a couple of daggers. The elf blocked, ducked, jumped, and hit all six men in the blink of an eye. Within seconds the six men where lying on the ground moaning.

"The *World Warrior Championships*—just the biggest thing this side of Heaven," Peyton said with the grin of a six-year-old who'd just tasted his first nirb. "Every five years, thousands of warriors from around the world come to battle, trying to win the Crown. For the last three, Gorgus has been unbeatable. In his last battle for the Crown, he took on the second, third, and fourth ranked warriors all at once. The battle lasted just under a minute." Peyton spoke with pride, as if he were the one who had done it.

As Peyton went on and on about Gorgus, Laken's gaze swept the arena looking at battle upon battle. There must have been a hundred different battles going on at once, using hundreds of different weapons. A large group of Angels and various creatures fired arrows at some targets at the far end. At the other end lay a massive obstacle course with swinging axes, and large spiked balls weaving back and forth. Arrows fired out of holes at a couple of Angels trying to make their way through.

"Oh my God!" cried Laken as an arrow pierced one of the angels, throwing him to the ground.

"What, what happened?" asked Peyton and Heath in unison. But just then the angel got up, dusted himself off and continued on through the maze of death.

"That angel got hit with and arrow. I saw it, but he seems fine." Laken couldn't rattle the words out fast enough.

"Ohhh, this is all practice. Those arrows are RI's, or *Real Illusions*," Heath said dismissively as his eyes darted from one thing to another. "Everything in here, the swords, arrows, axes, look real, hit for real, but leave no permanent damage. It allows us to really train, yet not die, which is a good thing, I guess." Heath gave Laken a small smirk.

"It's the Butterfly Lamb, or is it Lamb Butterfly?" a voice cried out from the distance. Laken looked over to see Baylor with his head hung low, entering the arena through the Portal.

"Hey! You better watch your mouth!" Peyton cried out, his fists clinched, to Laken's and Baylor's surprise.

"Or what?" the large second-year boy yelled back.

"Or this!"

Each of the boys looked aghast at Peyton, who turned into a massive eight-foot spider and ran at the boy. The boy let out a high-pitched scream and took off running.

"That's enough!" a voice boomed throughout the arena. Laken looked up to see Argus's massive silhouette walking towards them, his long orange hair dancing in the wind, his silver eyes piercing through the shadows cast by the low sun behind him. "Students! Let's go, over here!" growled the deep voice of Argus. The large spider stopped dead in its tracks and turned back into Peyton's usual impish self. The other boy, who was hiding behind a group of girls, peeked out and let out a sigh of relief.

"Let's go. I ain't got all day!" Argus's voice boomed impatiently. Students ran over to where he stood.

As Laken, who was now jogging, made his way over to Argus, Peyton grabbed his arm. "That's HIM! That's HIM! That's Gorgus, the Champion!" Peyton pointed, sounding like a girl at a rock concert. Laken looked over to see a Night Elf that towered over Argus.

"A creature bigger than Argus, wow!" Dave let out gasp, standing at attention. Gorgus must have been 10 feet tall. His skin was dark, dark green, and had an old leathery look to it. His long hair was flaming red, which was an identical match to his pupils. Each of his arms looked to be the size of Argus himself, as if two huge oak trees had attached to his body. There was a sword sheath strapped to his back that even Baylor could have climbed into and had room to spare.

"No wonder he is the champion!" Dave sighed dreamily.

"Students and spiders!" Argus shot Peyton a glance. "Let me introduce you to my staff who will be training you in the art of war," Argus said as he motioned to his left and right. "My tiny friend here," Argus looked up at Gorgus with a smirk, "is Gorgus. He is the reigning WWC Crown holder, and the only member of my staff who can almost beat me." Argus gave another tiny smirk. The members of his staff let out a small laugh, as Gorgus' massive hand covered Argus's shoulder and gave him a shake.

"Almost you say." Gorgus' voice sounded like the rumble of thunder. "You still will not fight me, my old friend," Gorgus emphasizing the word old.

"If you remember, I beat you twenty years ago when you were a student of mine. I retire champion." Argus returned the smirk, and they both laughed at the memory.

"Gorgus will be training those of you who have a great sword," Argus motioned to Gorgus' nine-foot sword that he was now wielding in demonstration. Laken shook his head from the speed in which Gorgus had drawn the sword from its sheath. "That's a great, great, great sword!" Peyton whispered to Laken. Gorgus swung the massive sword around like it was an extension of his arm. There were times it moved so fast, Laken lost sight of it, only to see it reappear in a totally different spot. Then the sword seemed to lunge towards Argus, slice and move at a lightning speed along his chest, then the sword was back in its sheath, before Laken could blink. There was a slight pause, and a small square-shape piece of Argus's bearskin shirt seemed to peel away from the rest of the outfit and flutter to the ground.

"Son of a Mkunish!" Argus roared playfully as he looked down at his now exposed hairy chest. "Brand new outfit! That will be coming out of your hide!" Argus shoved Gorgus, and the class let out a nervous laugh.

"Looked old to me!" laughed Gorgus as he took a small step backwards from the push, and the class' laugh became louder and more confident as they applauded appreciatively.

"Next to Gorgus," Argus directed his smile to an Angel, "is Skar, who has been on my staff for over twenty years, and is one of the best swordsmen you will ever meet." Argus motioned to the black-cloaked Angel who had his long gray hair tied back in a ponytail and a patch over his right eye.

"Kind of looks like a pirate," Dave commented. Skar brought his sword out and the two became one as partners on a stage. The sword danced to the rhythm of a beautiful song that only Skar and sword could hear.

"Wow!" echoed the whisper among the students as the sword show went on for nearly a minute. Finally, with the same Gorgus lunge, another patch fell from Argus's outfit, just below the first.

"For the love of the Almighty!" Argus sounded playfully annoyed, his silver gaze following the piece of garment floating to the ground. The class let out a roar of laughter. "What are you laughing at?" Argus glared at the students, and the place got deathly quiet.

After an uncomfortable pause, Gorgus cried, "He's kidding!" Argus shot them a smile, and the class gave out another nervous laugh.

"Next to him is Jez." Argus'ss voice boomed over the dying laughter. "She is the greatest archer Eden has ever known." At that, Argus threw a pebble-sized object well over the students' heads some fifty yards out of sight. Before Laken could blink, the long blonde- haired elf's bow had been pulled from her Hallow, arrow knocked and released. The arrow soared overhead at deafening speed, hit something, but as it fell to the ground another arrow caught it on the side, sending it spinning to the ground. Peyton ran out, grabbed the two arrows and brought them back. Argus held up the two arrows that had stuck into the target at a perfect ninety-degree angle. The kids cheered.

Laken's gaze went back to Jez who, for an Elf, was quite attractive. She was dressed in a dark green blouse that hung to her knees, with light green tights. She had pointy ears behind which her long blonde hair had been pulled up and tucked back.

"Elniz will be teaching the cloaked." Argus's voice snapped Laken out of the trance. "See if you can find him," Argus challenged as he looked around mysteriously. The students, not knowing who or what to look for, muttered amongst themselves. Then as if he had walked out of Argus, a small Dwarf appeared out of thin air.

"What the-!" Dave cried in unison with most of the class. Then, as quickly as he appeared, he vanished back into Argus. Laken looked closely and there, just in front of Argus, was the faint outline of the dwarf, though if you didn't look closely, you never would have seen him.

"Alright, enough, Elniz. Make yourself known," Argus laughed deeply. Once again Elniz appeared magically in front of them.

Elniz was small, four feet tall at most, and very skinny, wearing a green and brown cloak pulled over his head that seemed to blend in with whatever was behind him. The students applauded again.

"Finally we have Blanquo!" Argus motioned to a small, bald Elf wearing a gray pair of pants, no shirt, and a large golden medallion hanging around his neck. "Here!" Argus yelled as he threw a huge log at Blanquo. Right before impact, Blanguo's arms flared faster than sight, and the log fell to his feet cut into hundreds of small toothpick sized pieces. "There is no one faster with a dagger, nor with his mouth, than Blanquo," Argus boasted. Laken realized this was the Elf he had seen earlier taking on six men.

"In four weeks on Friday night is the D.C. Make sure you are ready," Argus warned, his gaze sharp.

"D-what?" Laken turned to Heath.

"D.C., it is the *Den's Championship*," Heath explained.

"Heath, please say it louder so all the new students can hear," Argus interrupted.

"Yes, sir," his face turning a shade of violet. "D.C. stands for Den's Championship. It is where each of the dens competes with each other for the ultimate title of Den Champion, crowned at the end of the year" a huge smile played across his expression. "The winning den also receives twenty-five stars." Heath ignited the excited jitters of the other students.

"Very good. The Serpents have won it four years straight, and look to win it again." Argus smiled over at the Serpent's den. Daeth shot Laken a pale smirk. Dave stuck his tongue out at Daeth, Daeth's numa returned a rude hand gesture. "Every den will nominate someone in each of the categories, and then one person to compete in flight." Argus paused to look around. "There are two DC events, the den with the most points at the end of the year is crowned Den Champion!" Argus said enthusiastically.

"Everyone join the teacher who specializes in the weapon given to you at Draugr's. Then train with heart and with honor!" Argus cried as he hit his bare chest with his fists on the words *heart* and *honor,* clumsily catching his fist in the top hole. He good naturedly shook his fist free of his torn garment, and Argus then turned to Laken.

"You're with me," Argus motioned to Laken. Working his way through all the students crowding their way to their teachers, he strolled over to a large tree. "Let's go. We're burning daylight!" Laken hurried over to where Argus was, a little taken aback at the turn of events.

"Why am I with you and not with the class?" Laken asked.

"We don't have time to waste on questions. Every second we aren't training is a moment of advantage for the enemy." Argus looked Laken up and down. "You are a little small to be a swordsman, but your numa knows something I don't, so let's maximize what we have." Argus thought out loud as if Laken couldn't hear him. "We will work on your speed and quickness. This should compensate for your lack of size and strength."

"The boy doesn't have a chance in Outer Darkness at beating Brone!" Argus's numa said with a heavy sigh.

"This guy is a real motivator," Dave moaned as Laken began to remove his sword from his Hallow.

"What do you think you are doing?" Argus's brow narrowed.

"Getting my sword out for training?" Laken said more as a question than a statement.

"Put it back. We won't be needing that for some time." Argus regarded him coldly.

"Sword training with no sword? Great plan!" Dave muttered.

"Come, stand here, underneath this tree." Argus motioned to where he wanted Laken to stand. Laken walked over, stood in the place Argus had pointed to, and then looked up into Argus's silver eyes. "We need some cherries before we begin!" Argus said, as Laken's expression went from questioning to absolute bewilderment. Argus held up his hand. His huge, dark blue numa called out the word *cherries*, and thousands of cherries appeared in the tree. "Alright, get into a good battle stance, feet shoulder length apart, left leg forward, shoulders back, hands at a ninety degree angle," Argus said as he pulled, pushed, and prodded Laken's body into place. "Good, now as quickly as you can, I want you to snatch a cherry out of the tree with your sword hand." Argus demonstrated what he meant with such speed, Laken barely saw his hand move, cherry gone, hand back in place.

"What is, what, why…" Laken stammered when Argus said in a more forceful tone:

"Pick a cherry!"

Laken gave a shrug and a hopeless glance into Argus's eyes, then looked up into the tree. Laken's eye focused on a cherry and then he reached up and grabbed it, and brought the cherry back down and held it up for Argus to see.

"My 300-year-old grandmother is faster than that! Let's see some speed," Argus mocked. Laken's red face now showed determined anger. Laken focused on another cherry, then he reached up, but this time the cherry disappeared before he could grab it.

"Too slow, grandma. Your tired old bones bothering you?" Argus said in an old crackly voice. Laken shot Argus a glare, then Laken reached up faster this time but still missed the cherry.

"How about we train you with a cane instead of sword? Seems to be more your speed," Argus continued. Laken's ears turned red as he reached for another, still no cherry. An old woman's shawl appeared on Laken's shoulders.

"If you're going to act old, might as well dress old!" Argus laughed. Laken threw the shawl onto the ground and with everything in him sprang his hand towards the cherry, this time touching it right before it disappeared.

"Good! Now let's see you catch one!" Argus disparaged as he sat down under the tree and began to play what looked like an old flute.

For the next two hours Laken snatched at the cherries. Every time he missed Argus would stop playing the flute to mutter some old person remark aimed at him. When Laken missed five times in a row, a cane appeared in his right hand, which he threw out from the tree, almost hitting a couple of Elves sparring some twenty feet away.

"Sorry, slipped out of his hand," apologized Argus. He turned back to Laken. "Don't punish them for your slow reflexes." Laken paused to give Argus a frustrated glance. His attention turned to the two numas on Argus's shoulder.

"You know you are wasting your time. I will kill him long before he is ready to fight Lord Brone," sneered the blackened numa.

CHAPTER SIXTEEN
Laken's on Fire!

For the next ten minutes Laken did not catch a single cherry, and Argus didn't make a comment. What the withered numa said seemed to have a greater effect on Argus than it did on Laken. Argus's expression became weighted and flushed with anguish. His mind seemed to be somewhere else.

When the bell rang, Laken's arm was numb, except for the throbbing that felt as if his heart was beating from inside his arm.

"See you tomorrow!" Argus looked grim as he strolled off, his massive head hung low.

Baylor came running over, his face bruised and battered, but with a smile like a six-year-old kid who just saw Santa Claus.

"What happened to you?" Laken asked, his eyes widening. Baylor wiped the sweat and blood from his face onto his sleeve. "Battling with some third-years and then with Gorgus himself. He hit me so hard, I flew nearly 30 feet into those targets over there." Laken looked, but there were no targets, just a pile of rubble and debris. "Well, they used to be targets!" A smile danced across his bruised face.

"Laken, how did it go?"

Laken turned toward the voice but could see no one. "Right here, behind you." Laken whirled around but no one was there. "Here! Boo!" Heath jumped out of thin air causing Laken to step back and let out a small scream.

"HOLY crud! You nearly gave me a heart attack!" Laken grabbed his chest.

"Cool trick! Learning to be invisible. Well, not really invisible, but invisible in a sense that you can't see me because I blend into the environment," A grin stretched across Heath's face.

"Well, for your first day, I would say you're pretty dang good," Laken returned the smile.

"Check this out, guys!" Peyton shouted from across the way. Laken looked over to see Peyton's two daggers cutting and slicing at a piece of wood at lighting speed. Then as Peyton stepped back it was a wooden statue of Laken holding a cherry.

"Very funny. Ha. Ha." Laken tightened his lips.

"Anyone see Cirque?" Baylor asked, looking around.

"I saw him leave with a couple girls when I was scaring Laken here," replied Heath. "From what I saw, archery is not his thing. He sent a half dozen arrows flying up into the stands. One ricocheted, almost hitting another kid." Heaths brows narrowed. He directed his gaze to Laken. "We need to let you get to your Gabriel time. See you in a bit." At that, the three other boys exited through the Portal.

Laken couldn't help being aggravated. Dave reminded him of all the things the other boys did, and how he was stuck picking fruit. Laken stomped into the Portal thinking, *Discipleship*, and he exited out of the Portal into Eden.

By now Laken was annoyed at the entire day. Malgor gave him detention, he couldn't message with his numa, he couldn't move a rock, his clothes were still damp from Pezamist's room, cherry picking, and half this place wanted him dead. Oh, and he almost forgot, he had evil wings. As he thought about his wings, something flinched in his body.

"Think that was the wings?" Dave's voice was uneasy.

"Laken, please come, come and sit down." Gabriel's voice interrupted his musings as it echoed over the sound of the birds and wind whistling through the trees.

Laken looked up and saw Gabriel sitting over on the same rocks as this morning. His hair and beard had a reddish glow from the setting sun and were dancing in the cool breeze. A herd of unicorns rushed between them, almost hitting Laken who jumped back slightly but just in time to be out of the way. Laken looked both ways to see if it was safe to continue and then slowly made his way over to Gabriel and took a seat.

"By the looks of it, not a good day?" Gabriel offered a weary smile.

Like a balloon with a hole in it, Laken lost control and let it all out. "No! Not a good day? Baylor wants to kill me! Malgor hates me and probably wants to kill me too. Someone else wants me dead, maybe Argus, who knows? I have Dave, who won't do anything, and seems to be helping both of them kill me!"

"Hey!" Dave interrupted.

"Yes, you are trying to kill me!" Laken shot back. "I can't move a rock, can't message anyone, I have devil wings…" Laken stopped his tirade only because his body was flung onto the ground from that same force that shook moments earlier. Gabriel leaned over and picked Laken up.

"Be careful how you speak about your wings. They are very proud," Gabriel said with an edge of caution in his voice.

"I know, I know. What I say about them is important. Yeah, I got it. Give me all the junk, and tell me it's great, and I have to just take it and be happy with it. All the while, I have to fight great evil with bloody useless equipment!" The Hallow and his body jerked in unison sending him again to the ground.

"Sit down, Laken," Gabriel said quietly as he helped Laken up again. Laken gave his dusty cloak a pat with both hands and just stood there staring down, his lip clenched and brow narrowed. There was a long pause as the sound of the stream seemed to be the only noise. Laken took a ragged breath and then slowly exhaled. He regarded Gabriel for a moment before he went over and sat down. Laken ran his hand thru his hair as he turned his body slightly away from Gabriel. A few more moments passed and then Gabriel put his hand on Laken's shoulder. The all too familiar warmth slid down his back. Laken was pretending to be interested in a beetle making its way towards the water, while he mindlessly rubbed his sore arm.

"Laken, by the looks of you, there is no way that what is being asked of you is possible." Laken looked up into Gabriel blue eyes, but could not hold his gaze. "But inside you, reside gifts and qualities that could make anything possible. I know the same to be true about your sword, and I assume the same for your wings." A smile tugged at the corners of his mouth. "It will take time for you to develop into all you can be, and the same is true for the sword and for your wings. What would happen if I had cast you aside when I first saw you? Based just on what I saw," Gabriel gave Laken's shoulder a slight squeeze.

"I know, I know," Laken conceded feeling the unnatural warmth of Gabriel's grip still pulsating down his back.

"Give it time, and as I am doing with you, accept these gifts as the chosen ones in *your* life. You choose to accept them the way they are, in that they will become what you desire," Gabriel's voice was as calming as the stream behind them.

Laken thought for a moment, and then he felt all the anger and frustration seep away from him.

"I love my sword, and I love my wings," Laken said with a forced effort, and a warmth rang through his body, and purr came from his Hallow.

"See, much better," Gabriel offered Laken a smile. "Tell me about your wings."

Laken went through the entire story, starting first with Peyton's camo wings and then Baylor's wings. Gabriel laughed at the story of Baylor's butterfly wings. Laken then went into the battle between the first set of wings and his current wings.

"I have never heard of such a thing," Gabriel mused, but more to himself than to Laken.

"Elkan said they came from Faldon of the Mares of Diomedes, and they were from a Fallen Angel by the name of Dagon." At those words

Laken noticed a look of surprise flit across Gabriel's face, and then a look of despair settled in.

"Dagon? Are you sure he said Dagon?" Gabriel asked, a heaviness in his voice.

"Yes, positive. And that he was in Outer Darkness." Laken rubbed the sore spot on his arm.

Gabriel looked like someone had just told him a loved one had died. He turned towards the red and purple horizon as the sun was just about to set. The sky unnaturally turned dark and gray, and Laken thought he saw Gabriel's eyes tear up just before he turned his head. A slight drizzle of rain began pour. "Dagon's wings, or should I say *your wings*, have greatness in them," Gabriel's voice cracked. "Do not let rumors and lies about Dagon and those wings take hold of you. Dagon was a great Angel." There was another pause. "No greater love is there than when one lays his life down for another," Gabriel finished softly. A soft thunder boomed across the sky in the distance.

Laken didn't know how long they sat there in silence, but it was long enough for a group of Gnomes, squirrels, and a large bear to play three rounds of what looked like hide and go seek. To no surprise the bear lost every round.

"Did you know Dagon?" Laken finally broke the silence.

"Ahhh, yes, very well I must say. He was a student here at Dogma. He lost his way early, but after Dogma, he found his way back to what was right," Gabriel said, still staring off into the distance. "His reputation for wrong could not be overcome by his new ways. In the end, it was accusations, rumors, and…." Gabriel trailed off.

"And what?" Laken could tell by Gabriel's expression he had asked a little too enthusiastically. "And what?" Laken asked again.

"And…that will be for another time. Did I hear correctly that Baylor and Malgor are trying to kill you?" Gabriel changed the subject.

Laken told Gabriel the story of Malgor, the numa at the end of class, and the numa at the end of Art of War. Gabriel had his hand on his chin with a single finger curved around his mouth nodding as Laken told the tale.

"I don't think Baylor has it in him to kill a bug, much less you. And as for Malgor, well he has issues of his own, but kill you? Never," Gabriel added when Laken had finished.

"But you should have been there. He hates me. I got a month's detention for nothing." Laken's voice cracked in anger.

"Malgor just wants to spend time with you," smiled Gabriel.

"Well, I don't want to spend time with him. And what about his withered numa? That has to say something about him," Laken added.

"Oh, the choices of our past—how they haunt our future. Malgor has done some very bad things in his past, but he is doing even more to right the wrongs he has made," Gabriel now beaming down at Laken. "Let's talk Magic, since that is one of the most important areas you need to master," Gabriel suggested.

"I can't do it." As the words left Laken's lips, Gabriel was already speaking.

"Whether you can or can't both are true. It depends on which you believe," Gabriel talked over Laken. "Let's practice some more on this rock." A massive boulder appeared out of nowhere in front of Laken.

"What? I can't move a small rock. How can I do this one?" Laken said shaking his head still rubbing his sore arm.

"Size of rock means nothing. The size of your faith means everything. For the rest of the hour, every time you say you can't, you lose a Nirb," Gabriel said as a plate of Nirbs appeared beside them. "I believe I get three Nirbs." Gabriel grabbed his Nirbs.

"Hey, you can't take them, yet," but as soon as Laken said it—

"Ohhh, you said can't again. That makes four!" Gabriel grabbed another. The sky brightened up and a light cool breeze began to blow.

For the remainder of the hour, Laken tried and tried to move the boulder. Once, a small amount of dust bellowed from the top of the boulder, but that was it. As Gabriel dismissed Laken with a hug and the two Nirbs that were left, Gabriel smiled and said, "At this rate, I'll probably gain 50 pounds by month's end." And at that, Gabriel disappeared into the Portal his cloak whisking behind him from the cool night's air.

"Another thing we can't do," Dave reminded Laken. "I don't think we belong. Nothing has gone right. Actually, nothing *ever* goes right." Dave was going on. Laken could feel Dave's words burning into him. Each syllable seemed to stoke the fire hotter.

"I'll move that stupid rock," Laken said through gritted teeth. Laken concentrated on the rock, but it still wouldn't move.

"Chalk it up to another thing we aren't good at," Dave said, and Laken felt the beast in him get hotter. "Jack was right, we are useless." As Dave said, this Laken could feel the beast in him scream. "Summer is much better with you not around, screwing her life up…"

That was it. Laken felt that familiar release of the anger; the beast was loose. Fire and energy shot from Laken into the rock, the two were connected for an instant and then the rock exploded into a million smoldering pieces.

Laken was knocked back into a group of frightened Gnomes who took off running. Animals and creatures scampered all around. Laken shook the cob webs from his head and checked to see that his body was still intact.

He then turned to Dave and said triumphantly, "I guess I can move that rock!"

CHAPTER SEVENTEEN
No Really, Laken is on Fire!

Laken exited the Portal into the Great Hall with a small skip in his step. His shoulders were back, and for the first time, he felt confident. He had power. He could do something for a change.

"Let's blow something up!" Dave threw his hands in the air as he made an explosion noise. "Baylor! Let's blow him up!"

"Stop it. We have plenty of time to show off our powers!" Laken responded, a smile creeping onto his face.

The Great Hall was full of students studying, eating, and talking. Cherubs flew around the room delivering food and picking up plates.

"Oof!" Laken gasped as a drum stick hit him in the head. The cherub he had been mean to earlier in the day gave him another hand gesture and zoomed off.

"How'd it go?" Heath asked as Laken rubbed the spot where the drumstick had hit.

"You got some chicken skin on your shoulder," Peyton said as he snatched the skin off and flipped it in his mouth.

"That's disgusting!" Heath shuddered, and then gazed at Laken. "So, what happened? How was discipleship?"

Laken paused for a second, debating whether or not to tell them about his new found power. At the last second, he decided to hold off for now until he could really develop it.

"You know, *Never say can't... You can do anything you put your mind to.* Same ol' Gabriel stuff." Laken grabbed a chicken breast off the plate Peyton was offering him.

"Bbrbbththth is thbrrrth," Peyton, who had just forced a shovel sized helping of potatoes in his mouth, now was spitting potatoes out inadvertently as he was trying to say something.

"No one can understand you with that sack of potatoes in your mouth, you cherub," Heath said as he wiped the potatoes off his own face.

Peyton swallowed hard, "Who you calling a cherub, jackalope?" At that, Peyton turned into a rabbit with horns and then began to imitate Heath. "The square root of sixty trillion can be found using the Pythagorean Theorem and my super-sized mind."

Heath turned into a small bug. "I'm Peyton. I'm small and helpless. Mommy, did I wet the bed again?"

Peyton turned into a massive flyswatter and flew down to smash Heath.

"I'll teach you," Peyton cried. The flyswatter was grabbed by an enormous hand and stopped inches from Heath, who turned back to himself with a look of utter surprise. Peyton, too, turned back to himself, but now he was being held up by Baylor.

"We are a team. Let's act like it!" Baylor's brow narrowed and then he set Peyton down.

"Uugghh, sure," the brothers said in unison.

Then Peyton looked over at his brother. "Let me apologize. I'm sorry you are a jackalope."

"I, too, am sorry you are a bedwetting cherub," Heath responded. They both laughed uproariously.

For the next couple of hours, everyone did homework. Laken couldn't remember reading so much in his life. But to him, this wasn't like real homework. Reading was interesting and quite fun. All the things the numa could do fascinated him, but those same things annoyed him, given how little Dave could to do.

"Hey, it says there on page twenty-two, it is your fault, not mine." Dave made sure to call pertinent information to Laken's attention.

The Angelic History, on the other hand, was amazing. They learned about the creation of Angels, Heavens, earth, humans and all the creatures.

"Sunday School didn't do the story justice," Dave decided as they read about the battle with Lucifer and the Fallen Angels. "Don't eat the fruit, Eve!" he cried out in the middle of another story.

Finally, it was time to study wings. As Laken closed the book, Dave had a thought. "Let's look up Dagon."

"Good idea," thought Laken as he opened the book and Dave said, "Dagon!" Laken felt the wings give him a gentle warm flutter down his spine.

Laken looked down into the Rhema to see a large picture on the left-hand page. A massive Angel wielding two swords was battling what looked like a dozen other Angels. The caption under the picture read, "An actual numa documentation of Dagon taking on eight DAS officers and DAA Dzblen." Laken looked again at Dagon, who was equal to Gabriel's height but much stockier. He wore what looked like a white sleeping garment, and by the look of his messed-up jet black hair, and bare feet, it looked as if the officers had attacked while he was sleeping. Laken stared in awe as Dagon spun, blocked, and flew around the room, battling the officers. He was reminded of Gabriel against the gang a few days earlier.

Then, a lady with a small caption, *Dzblen* over her image, threw a massive axe towards the back of Dagon's head. And there they were! Laken's wings sprung out, blocked the axe, then expanded and hit Dzblen, throwing her against a wall. The wings seemed to be acting on their own, blocking punches, knocking officer after officer down and sending a few of them crashing through walls. The battle was over, and Dagon was the only one left standing. He walked over and grabbed Dzblen, who had been badly cut across the face and had a large amount of blood coming from her abdomen. Dagon pulled her to just inches from his face, said something inaudible, and then with a wrench of his arms, Dzblen fell limp to the floor. Laken shuddered at the sight of what just happened.

"He's a murderer!" Dave's voice cracked.

They kept watching the Rhema to see Dagon go into the next room, and to Laken's surprise he came out with a baby. Behind him came a beautiful woman with long blonde hair clutching at him. The woman was screaming something.

"How do you turn up the volume on this thing?" Dave wondered.

As he said it, Laken could hear the woman and the child's screams. "NO! NO! Not my baby. Leave my baby! Leave my baby!" Laken, surprised by the increased volume, covered the book as all those around him turn their heads in curiosity to see what the muffled noise was.

"Sorry, sorry," Laken apologized. *Turn down!* Laken thought. The volume dropped to a whisper, and Laken's attention went back to the woman who was now clawing and grabbing Dagon. With one hand, Dagon threw her to the side, jumped through the glass window, and took off in flight with the baby in hand.

"Seems like a nice fellow," mocked Dave.

"Wow, that is one evil dude," Laken said in surprise, and then began to read the text on the right hand page. *Dagon: Born 1968 to Father: Unknown… Mother: Davorah (deceased, think Davorah for more information) Married to Aliya (deceased, think Aliya for more information) Children: Alona (deceased, too young for any records). Headboy at Dogma 1987 and Dogma Warrior champion 1986-1987. Best known for his slaying of nine DAS officers and DAA Dzblen when they attempted to arrest him for conspiracy to commit treason, and working for Lord Pink Bunny. Captured by Gabriel (think Gabriel for more information). He was accused and convicted for a total of 28 murders and thrown into Outer Darkness more than ten years ago. His wings are the current match to Laken (think Laken for more information).*

Laken closed the book, and shook his head trying to sort his thoughts. "Our wings came from a murderer," Dave said. Laken's body shook angrily.

"You ready to head up to the den?" Laken heard a voice in the distance. "You ready, Laken? Are you ready?" Heath's voice now boomed in his ear.

Laken shook his head as he snapped back to reality. "Aaagh, yeah sure," Laken answered.

"Cirque, give it a rest. Let's go!" Heath called out. Cirque was having his hair combed by three girls. You could hear the sigh and moan of the girls as Cirque said, "Can't wait to see you ladies tomorrow, especially you." The tall blonde third-year girl Cirque pointed to fell limp onto the floor.

"Baylor, did you tell them?" Cirque asked as he approached the boys. Baylor shook his head. "Thought you should know I caught Malgor up in our den. Probably no big deal, but a little freaky. He acted like he was up to something," Cirque said with a shrug.

"What the heck? Is he allowed to just come and go in our den?" Laken growled.

"As a professor, I guess so, but even so, from what you said, I think we need to let Gabriel know in the morning," Heath replied.

"If he doesn't come and kill me in the night, I think that will be my first order of business." Laken frowned so deeply that creases formed on his brow.

The four boys entered the Portal, each one's numa saying, "Dragon's den," and they exited into their den looking at the back of some large cloaked figure. Malgor spun around, a look of both surprise and dismay flittering across his face.

"What the heck you doing in my room?" demanded Laken. Malgor looked taken aback by the situation for a brief moment. He then gathered himself and straightened up to his full height.

"As a Professor, what I do is none of your business." Malgor strolled toward the Portal, but Laken stepped into his way.

"You don't leave until you tell me what you are doing in my room!" Laken said through gritted teeth.

Malgor let out a mocking laugh. "You are choice, aren't you? Or is it chosen? Let's add another weekend of detentions. That is, if you are still alive by then," Malgor hissed. Malgor then grabbed Laken by the arms.

"Shouldn't do that," warned Dave. Laken waited for the burning of Malgor's hands, but nothing. Malgor threw Laken to the side like a rag doll. Laken rolled to the floor crashing into a statue of a lamb and a lion. The statue toppled over smashing into a million pieces.

"What, why, how…" Laken asked from the floor. Malgor raised his arm, the statue pieces rose from the ground, formed together, recreating the statue as if it had never been smashed.

"Your Chosen One abilities have no effect on me, boy," Malgor sneered as he whisked himself through the Portal and out of the room.

"That son of a Banshee. He can't just come in our room, throw us around!" thundered Peyton. "Next time I will take care of him, you can bet on that!"

"What do you think he was doing up here?" asked Cirque as he and Baylor were searching the room.

"Don't know, but he wasn't up here to tuck me in, that is for sure." Laken got up, brushing off his cloak, his face hot from anger.

The boys searched the room for the next hour, finding only a small golden goblet with the words *Angel of Light Award for Excellence in Music* inscribed on it. Wedged into the goblet was a cracked locket that would not open, and could not be removed from the goblet.

The boys climbed into bed. Laken was exhausted. He peered over at Baylor, whose bed had been magically enlarged so it was twice as big as the rest of their beds. Laken couldn't remember ever being so tired. He heard the other boys say goodnight before he was somewhere else, picking cherries and throwing them at Malgor, but Malgor just caught them in his mouth while laughing. Argus was dressed like a clown, playing hide and go seek with the bear. Then he heard Summer's voice again, and he found himself lying in the basement.

"I know you are here every night with me, watching over me," Summer said with a muffled sob.

"I am here. I'm right here!" Laken cried out. Knowing that Summer couldn't hear him, he laid back down beside her and went to sleep.

"FIRE! LAKEN'S ON FIRE!"

The words rang in Laken's head as he looked around the dingy basement. "LAKEN! GET OUT OF THERE! SOMEONE GET HELP! LAKEN IS ON FIRE!" It was Heath screaming at him, but Heath was nowhere around. Then Laken felt himself being sucked out of the basement, and once again he opened his eyes to see Heath, Peyton, Cirque gathered around him.

They were frantic, grabbing him and hoisting him up. Laken turned his head towards a hissing sound coming from his right to see his bed completely on fire. The fire went from the ground to the ceiling.

"Laken, you alright?" the three boys yelled in unison.

"Yes, yes. What happened?" Laken's eyes went wide with horror.

"What happened is, your bed is on fire, and we thought you were a goner. And then you just appeared again in the middle of the room." Peyton spoke faster than usual, his arms flailing about.

Laken walked towards his bed, surprised that no heat was coming from the fire. A blaze that big should be scorching his skin this close. As Laken reached out to touch the flame something hit him and sent him to the floor.

"Are you mental? That's how you lose a hand!" Heath's voice echoed through the den.

"What are you talking about, it's not even hot!" Laken winced as he got up.

"It's Goblin fire!" Heath noticed this meant nothing to Laken, so he went into teacher mode. "Goblin fire only burns living beings. Nothing else is affected. Notice how the bed and sheets are just sitting there in the fire, not a mark on them." Heath bent over and picked up a small orange beetle. He threw the beetle into the fire and at the moment of contact the beetle was engulfed in the flames, and then disintegrated.

"Holy heavens! That is freaky!" Laken recoiled like a snake had just struck.

"I know. Imagine if you had been in your bed? You'd be one crispy little critter." Peyton made a pop motion with his hands.

"So what do we do?" asked Laken, still visibly shaken.

"Baylor went to get help, but that won't put out the fire. Goblin fire is impossible to put out. You have to let it burn till it goes out on its own, usually twenty-four hours," Heath shrugged his shoulders.

Just then, Gabriel came through the portal his blue eyes glowing with anger. He held up his hand and the flames instantly went away. He walked over to Laken, grabbed him with both hands, and Laken felt that unnatural warmth hit his skin again.

"Are you alright?" Laken could see tears welling up in Gabriel's eyes.

"Yeah. I'm fine. Thought we would have a late-night bonfire. Got any marshmallows?"

CHAPTER EIGHTEEN
Dr. Seuss Has a Riddle for Laken

"Malgor! It was Malgor who was in our room. He is the one who tried to burn me alive!" Laken's face flushed to a deep crimson.

"Yes!" the other boys said in near unison. "Actually, Malgor was in here twice," Heath continued.

"Malgor didn't—" Gabriel tried to get something out, but the boys immediately spoke over him.

"Malgor! We promise it was him!"

"Boys, boys! Quiet, please!" Gabriel did not raise his voice, yet he brought silence to the room. "One, Malgor has already explained himself to me." Gabriel paused as his gaze moved across each of the boys. "Two, it is impossible for any teacher here at Dogma to do a student harm. Code of Dogma!" Gabriel's eyes held deep concern.

"Oh yeah, I totally forgot about the Code of Dogma!" Laken threw his hands in the air. "Guess the Ogre fire just got in here on its own, the exact same time Malgor was in the room!" Laken raked his fingers through his hair.

"Goblin fire," Heath corrected. Laken shot Heath a glare.

"Laken, please calm down." Gabriel's voice was calm. "Before the fire even happened, Malgor told me about being in your den, and—"

"So, that makes it okay? He covers his tracks and so he's innocent?" Laken interrupted.

"Laken, let me finish." Gabriel held Laken's gaze. "Malgor had a very good reason for being here." Gabriel offered a weary smile.

"Yes, doing me in!"

"Why was he here then?" Heath's brow narrowed.

Gabriel's eyes stared off somewhere distant, where his thoughts seemed to go for a moment. Then his gaze slowly came back to Heath.

"There will be a time he will share this, but I will allow him to decide the proper moment. It will be his answer, not mine," Gabriel's blue eyes widened a fraction.

Gabriel's gaze settled back on Laken, who seemed to be interested in a freckle on top of his left foot. "Why were you out of your bed?" Gabriel asked, adding, "Not that I mind. On the contrary, I'm quite happy about it" Laken pondered telling Gabriel about Summer, but then Dave brought up a good point.

"He keeps secrets, why shouldn't we have secrets? Let Malgor tell him why I was out of bed," Dave said, his expression flushed.

"Agggh, I was..." Laken stalled as he tried to come up with a good reason.

"He got up to go to the bathroom. Got up half a dozen times. That chicken leg gave him the cra—" but Peyton was cut off.

"I got it. I got the idea." Gabriel shook his head. "Any way you look at it, Laken being out of bed was a good thing." Gabriel smiled as he shook his hand towards the beds. "Let's get back to bed. We have a big day tomorrow."

"What if there is more Goblin fire?" Laken's eyes widened.

"I have put a detection charm on the room. Should have done it earlier." Gabriel let out a sigh. "I have become somewhat careless in my old age. Please forgive me. If someone so much as puts a gnome trap in this room, we will know it." Gabriel allowed a big smile to play across his face. "Good night boys. Please, no playing with fire." Gabriel whisked his way into the Portal and out of the room.

"Laken! Laken! Get up. Class starts in five minutes!" Heath shook Laken, who could barely open his eyes. They had stayed up talking till nearly dawn. The topic of choice was Malgor, and how he tried to kill Laken. Over and over, they tried to figure out what excuse Malgor could have, and why in the world Gabriel would believe him. Sometime around 4:30 a.m., they decided Laken would do some investigating during his detentions to see what Malgor was up to.

Laken rubbed the crust from his eyes, jumped out of bed and rushed to get ready. He ran into the Portal, popping a Nirb into his mouth just as the bell rang. His body shook with energy as Dave said "Swig"," then that familiar feeling of traveling through the Portal.

"Nooo!" Laken screamed as realization grabbed him. Where the Portal was taking him, Laken had no clue, but one thing he did know, it wasn't to class.

Laken stepped out of the Portal and into what looked like pure light. Laken had to shield his eyes and look down. It felt like he was looking into the sun. Laken quickly turned around to go back into the Portal, but it was gone.

"A riddle I have to give,
A riddle I have for you,
Answer me correctly
And two answers I have for you.
Go you won't, stay you will,
Portal you will see,
When an answer is given to me."
The high-pitched voice echoed these words through the room.

"What?" Laken called out, still shielding his eyes.

"*How far will a blind dog walk into a forest?*" the high-pitched voice asked. Laken, whose eyes were now squinting towards the light, shook his head.

"What? What dog?"

"*Staying you will be, until an answer is given to me,*" the voice called out.

"This is crazy! I have class right now. I need the Portal." Laken looked frantically around him for the Portal that was still not there.

"*Portal you will see, when an answer is given to me.*" The high-pitched voice sounded like nails on a chalk board.

"Please turn down the light!" Laken screamed, and at that, the light seemed to dim. As Laken's eyes focused on the room. The walls, the floor, ceiling, were a bright white. In the center of the room was a brain. There was no other way to describe it. A brain, the size of a person sat on the floor. Laken walked over to it and slowly put his finger out to try and touch it. His hand went into it, but he felt nothing, as if it wasn't really there.

"Please show me the Portal!" Laken yelled again. As Laken looked back, he saw nothing but white walls.

"*A riddle one I can give again, since no answer came in.*" To Laken's surprise, the sound seemed to come from the brain.

"Sure, give me your stupid riddle." Laken's fists clenched.

"*How far will a blind dog walk into a forest?*" The brain asked again.

"How in the world would I know?" Laken said as he walked completely into the brain. "I have a riddle for you. How do I get out of this stupid room?" Laken's face flushed red.

"*In you stay, out you cannot go, until an answer you show,*" the brain sang out.

"Listen, Dr. Seuss, you have three seconds to open the door, or your brain I will scatter on the floor!" The room got silent. "Did you hear me?" Laken shouted. "Fine, let's do it the hard way." Laken began to kick and punch the brain. "Take that, and that!" This went on until finally he fell on the ground exhausted, out of breath, his heart feeling like it was going to pound out of his chest.

"*Hit you may, hit you might, go somewhere, not tonight!*"

"It's... not... night, you... stupid...BRAIN!" Laken was barely able to get the words out between his heavy breaths. "Fine, let's just stay here. No homework, no one can kill me here. Though right now, I would probably welcome it."

Laken lay flat on the floor and stared through the brain at the ceiling. This was it, where he was going to spend his life, in a psycho brain room. A life time of riddles.

"It's not fun, it hurts like a knife, but it fits the pattern of our life," Dave let out a laugh.

"Sad, but true," Laken licked his dry lips.

"What are you doing? And what is with the big brain?" A familiar voice startled Laken.

A riddle I have to give,
A riddle I have for you,
Answer me correctly
And two answers I have for you.
Go you won't, stay you will,
Portal you will see,
When an answer is given to me..."

"Give it a rest!" Laken cried out as he sat up and saw Heath standing in front of him. "How did you—I mean, where did you come from?" Laken stammered. "How did you know I was here?"

"How far will a blind dog walk into a forest?" interrupted the voice.

"I promise you, if you do not shut-uu–" Laken began.

"Half-way. Then the blind dog will be walking out of the forest," Heath answered matter-of-factly.

"Right you are, right you be, ask two questions and correct answers you will get from me." As the voice said this the Portal appeared.

Laken grabbed Heath's hand and began to pull him towards the portal. "We need to get out of this place before Dr. Seuss here comes up with another riddle."

"Is one plus one always two?" Heath stopped and asked as Laken pulled on his arm.

"The answer to question one of two is 'No'," the high voice responded.

Laken stopped at this, and said "What? Of course it is. How can you be so big and so dumb?"

"*What is one drop of water plus one drop of water?*" the voice interrupted.

"One drop of water," Heath said with a curious smile. "Question two is, what is the name of this room?" Heath asked. "I may want to come back here," Heath leaned closed to Laken and whispered.

"Room of Conundrum," the voice rang out.

"Great, let's take your one and my one and get one way out of this crazy room," Laken said as he dragged Heath into the Portal.

"Creature Studies," Dave said as they entered the Portal. The rush of cool air from Eden hit them as they walked out of the Portal.

"I wanted to find out the secrets of life," Heath whined.

"The secret is not to ever go to that crazy place again," Laken said as they headed toward the group of students gathered under a large oak tree.

Laken turned to face Professor Zeetle and the class up ahead. An explosion of sound and a crash happened so fast that Laken didn't have time to scream. A massive purple dragon collided with the ground just feet from the professor, the ground shook, students screamed, and many of them were thrown backwards from the force, dust bellowing high into the air. Then the massive head whipped down upon Professor Zeetle, mouth open, razor sharp teeth glaring in the sun. The Professor disappeared into the dragon's mouth.

CHAPTER NINETEEN
"Peaches and Dreams"

Laken let out a huge gasp. Heath grabbed Laken's arm and pulled him back toward the portal. Students scattered in all directions. Most were screaming.

"Smmop! Smmop!" Laken looked around to hear where the muffled scream was coming from.

"Calm down! It's alright. I'm alright." Laken heard Professor Zeetle's high-pitched voice. Laken looked on in utter surprise. The professor was standing in the dragon's mouth. "You big goof! Put me down!" Zeettle demanded. His arms were raised, holding the dragons mouth open. "I ought to have you stuffed! Or better yet, skinned for some new boots, you idget!" The dragon's head swept down, and then rested on the ground. The professor stepped out onto the grass, his small green robe and brown hat dripping with dragon spit.

The dragon's head stayed low and steady, but the rest of the dragon looked like it had swigs running through its veins. His feet stomped, and his tail wagged like a humming bird's wings. The dragon looked like a golden retriever, waiting to play fetch.

"Get out of here with ya now! Come on. I've got a class to teach. Get going!" The professor shooed the dragon off. But the huge 20-foot purple wanna-be-dog, stayed low and playful.

"Oh, alright!" conceded the professor, as he pushed his arms out. An orange ball the size of Laken appeared. The dragon went into a frenzy, whipping around in circles, his tail nearly crushing three girls who jumped out of the way just in time. The dragon shook large blue fruit from the surrounding trees. "You want the ball, you want the ball!" The professor said in a very playful tone. Just when Laken thought the dragon couldn't get any more excited, he was proven wrong yet again. The dragon jumped up on his hind legs like a poodle. The constant smashing of the ground sent earthquake-sized tremors roiling across the garden. Students tumbled over one another. Laken and Heath had to hold onto to each other just to keep themselves up.

"That big dragon-dog is going to kill someone if Zeetle doesn't throw the ball," Heath said, his voice cracking with each tremor. Finally, the professor made a quick motion upwards with his hands and the ball flew toward the center of the garden. The dragon whipped around, its tail hitting a large boulder, sending it soaring 30 feet, smashing into a small open pasture, sinking half way into the ground. The dragon tore after the ball, knocking over trees, animals, and anything else in its destructive path.

The students stood silent for nearly a minute, waiting to see what would happen next.

"Class, gather around again. Peaches won't be back for some time," the professor assured them as he made his way back under the massive tree.

"Peaches? Peaches? Where in the world do you get Peaches from that?" Heath half-demanded, half-joked to Laken.

"Hurry, class, hurry. Peaches took up quite a bit of our time." The professor clapped his hands three times.

As Laken settled down next to the Heath, Peyton and Baylor, each asked him in a whisper where he ended up in the Portal.

"Tell you later," Laken had to say over and over. "It will freak you out!" A huge smile lit Peyton's face.

"Where is Cirque?" Laken asked as he looked around.

"Over there protecting the ladies." Heath pointed to the outskirts of the group. Laken looked over to see Cirque consoling five or six emotion-struck girls.

"It figures!" Laken whispered.

"Laken?" Professor's voice rang out, grabbing Laken's attention.

"Yes, professor?"

"Question is, what type of dragon is Peaches?" The professor's voice tensed.

"Ummmm, a big ol' purple one." The class broke out in laughter.

"Yes, you could say that. I was looking for a little more than that. Yes, young man next to him. Heath, is it?"

"Yes, sir." Heath stood up, a smile tugging at the corners of his mouth. "From the size, skin color, and the smaller legs, I would have to it is a Brazter Dragon."

"Close… Yes, you in the front. Your name is Autumn, I believe." The Professor pointed to a fully extended hand that was shaking vigorously in the air.

The class let out a sigh of shock that sounded like the air being released from a balloon. All heads turned to Heath, who looked like he had just learned of a loved one's death. Peyton fell over in a mock faint.

"Wrong. I was *wrong*," Heath muttered under his breath, as if he were being told the world is flat, and the moon is made of cheese.

"Where Heath went WRONG," the words emphasized by the most beautiful voice Laken had ever heard, "is he over looked the three small horns on top of the dragon's head, and the clockwise curve of the tail. It has to be a Bollgoden Dragon, or as some call it, a Bolla Dragon." Autumn shot Heath a smirk, and then continued. "This name came from Bollgoden Hensten, the man who discovered and—"

"I think they got the point, Autumn," the professor interrupted. "Impressive! Very, very impressive! You are the first student in fifty years to get that correct. *Five stars to the Owl's Den.*"

"Heath, if you ask real nice, maybe she will help you with your homework," Peyton said as the boys fought to control their laughter.

"Shut it!" Heath growled as he gave Peyton a shove.

"Heath, if you ask her maybe she will—

"Are they dangerous, Peyton?" The professor's voice interrupted the boys.

Peyton's gaze shot towards the professor, and then Peyton gave a slow shake of his head. "Show them a ball, and I would definitely say so," Peyton said, as the group let out a good laugh.

"Yes, very true. But a Bolla found in the wild, are they dangerous?" The professor's brow narrowed. Heath's hand shot up as if he wanted nothing more than to restore his reign as smartest kid in the class.

"Yes, Autumn?" The professor looked at Heath, then Autumn, paused and asked with a warm smile.

"Why waste time on Heath's wrong answer when you get the right one so much faster," Peyton said as he fell to the ground in laughter.

"I am going to... I'm going... I will knock you out!" Heath's face was now two shades redder.

"I will have to check with Autumn, but I don't think that was a proper sentence." Peyton could barely get the words out between fits of laughter.

Suddenly, Heath jumped on Peyton, who was laughing uncontrollably on the ground. Peyton suddenly turned into a mud puddle that splashed everywhere. Baylor grabbed Heath by the back of his mud-soaked cloak. Kids around them jumped back in surprise letting out squeals of shock. Heath turned into a huge rock, freeing himself from Baylor's grip smashing onto the mud that sprayed everyone nearby.

"SNAP!" At the sound, the boys were back in their regular forms, floating a few feet in the air. "I think Saturday detention should help you two control yourselves," the professor bellowed. Laken turned to see the professor's arms raised up as if he were controlling their flight with his arms. The professor lowered his arms and the boys collapsed on the ground.

"Autumn, you may continue," the professor said.

"The Bolla, like most creatures, if in the wild can be dangerous." That beautiful voice sounded again, and now Laken had to see whose voice it was. As Autumn continued, Laken slipped between students, trying to get a glimpse of the girl. "They do not go looking for trouble, but if they feel threatened, they have been known to attack, and even kill." She finished, and then her head turned, and her eyes caught Laken's. Long black hair that was so shiny it looked like onyx, a small perfect nose, rosy cheeks, red amazing lips surrounded by a beautiful shade of brown skin.

Laken and Autumn's eyes seemed to share a very brief moment, and she gave Laken a smile that made Dave nearly fall over. Then she turned back to the professor.

"Very good, Autumn," the professor said.

"Peaches was given to me some fifty years ago when she was just an egg. I raised and nurtured her like my own child, and today look at her. Wouldn't hurt a fly, unless of course the fly tried to hurt me." The professor offered a crooked smile.

"For homework, think up 2000 words for me describing the 68 different types of dragons, where they can be found, what they eat, what they are used for, and how dangerous they are to Angels. You have the rest of the hour to work on it."

The sound of students pulling their Rhemas out of their Hallows overcame the whistle of the wind and chirp of the birds in the trees above.

"Think what for him? What? What, is he talking about?" Laken questioned as his gaze went to and from each member of his den.

The three boys looked at each other, a little puzzled, until finally Heath spoke for the group. "Think up 2000 words. I'm surprised Gabriel didn't show you this on the Rhema." Heath pulled out his Rhema. His numa said, "Write," as he opened it up. A blank page stared at him. Then Heath's numa began to speak.

"The Bolla dragon, much like Laken, is very playful, but a tad bit on the slow side." As his numa said this, those exact words appeared in the book. The boys laughed as they read it.

"Funny, very funny," Laken said with a smile. "So we then turn the Rhema into him, but how do I do my other homework?"

"No, no. Haven't you read ahead in the numa book yet?" Heath asked, shaking his head.

"Yeah, right after the barbeque last night and before the big brain kidnapping today." Laken's expression tensed.

"Big brain what?" Peyton's eyes widened.

"I was held ransom for an answer to a riddle by some big brain in the Portal of fun there." Laken pointed off towards the Portal.

"Boys get to work!" A voice came from the front.

"Sorry, Professor. Heath was asking if Autumn could answer a couple dragon questions for him," Peyton said to the laughter of the class. Peyton quickly shifted his body, barely missing the leg from Heath meant to kick him.

"I'm sure Heath can ask Autumn for her help after the class, and I'm sure she would be glad to give it," the professor said, as Peyton fell to the ground in a newfound fit of laughter. "Peyton, let's make it two Saturday's detention."

"Gladly...sir...I...can...honestly...say...it...was...worth...it," Peyton finally gasped between laughs.

"I hate you!" Heath turned his attention to his Rhema and his numa began to speak about dragons.

For the rest of the class Laken, Baylor, and Peyton pretended to be working, while Laken told the whole brain story.

"That is crazy!" Peyton looked like he would burst from excitement.

"I know! Thought I was there for good," Laken said. He turned to Heath, who was now pretending not to be listening. "I still don't know how to turn in my homework."

"Oh, yeah." Heath turned towards Laken purposefully making sure his eyes avoided Peyton. "When we get to class, the professor will have your numa spit in his numanator. What you wrote, or *thought* I should say, will be stored in there for him to go over and grade."

"That is tooooo cool," Laken said a little louder than he wanted, judging by the "shhhhh!" from students around them. "Wow," whispered Laken.

Just then, the bell rang, and the students headed towards the Portal with Professor Zeetle yelling, "Make sure you do 2000 words by Thursday."

Laken shoved his Rhema into his sac and was off, trying to get close to Autumn. If only he could see her, maybe talk to her.

"What in the world would we say?" Dave reminded Laken.

"I don't kno—" Laken was saying, but then was interrupted.

"Hi." Autumn stood directly in front of Laken, her smile the most beautiful Laken had ever seen. Dave seemed to short circuit and began to spin in place, mumbling to himself. Laken just stared at her for what seemed like forever. "Hi," Autumn said again with a more puzzled look.

"Aaagh, aaagh, thbthbth…"

"Laken, you took the words right out of my mouth, you smooth talking devil. My name is Cirque. How about I walk you to lunch?" Cirque offered Autumn a smile.

"Ah, sure," Autumn hesitated. "Bye." She smiled at Laken and turned away with Cirque, whose arm was now draped comfortably over her shoulder. Three other girls followed them with disappointed scowls on their faces.

"Bbbbb, bthb…aaagh, bye," Laken finally said when she was out of ear shot.

Dave stopped spinning and mumbling long enough to say, "Man, you sure blew that one!"

CHAPTER TWENTY
An Elephant Flies

"Nice job, Romeo!"

"You're quite the lady killer there, Laken!"

"Cirque has finally met his match!"

All fun little phrases Laken had to endure during Magic class, adding to the frustration Laken felt from not being able to move the rock. Everyone else had their rocks floating or flipping. Heath even sent his rock flying hard enough to knock a squirrel off the back of a rabbit. The squirrel returned a hand gesture and took off as all the boys laughed, except Laken whose rock hadn't even shaken yet.

"Can anyone tell me who I am, aaagh, aaagh, blthhththt! If you said Chosen One, you are right," Peyton said as the other boys laughed.

"Shut it!" Laken focused even harder on his rock. "I'll give them the Chosen One!" Laken thought of Cirque with his arm around Autumn, and BAM! The rock exploded into ashes. The others stopped what they were doing. Baylor's rock fell to the ground. Heath's rock went soaring into the water.

"What in the world happened?" Heath asked with a shocked expression, mirrored by the other den members.

"Don't know. It just… exploded?" Laken lied. Just then the bell rang.

"Continue to practice! Every moment of practice is a seed sown towards the harvest of victory." Gabriel's voice rang from behind the boys as they entered the Portal.

The boys exited the Portal into the busy Great Hall. They grabbed a table, but Laken sat at the table right next to theirs.

"Sit with us, Romeo," Baylor said, his giant smile stretched across his face.

"I have a lot of homework I want to get done. I'm just going to sit over here," Laken said as food was delivered to all the boys except Laken. A crash sounded as Laken's plate smashed to pieces right next to him. Laken looked up to see the hateful cherub zoom off.

"You can have some of mine," Peyton offered, but Laken huffed, shaking his head and rolling his eyes.

"I've got a lot of homework." Laken flipped himself away from the den members He sat by himself the entire lunch hour, pretending to do homework, if for no other reason than to get away from all the Romeo comments. Laken could tell Heath was relieved not to be the target of the jokes and comments now thrown Laken's way.

"They're just having fun. Don't let it bother you," Dave kept reminding him.

"I'm fine!"

"I can tell," Dave said, shaking his head.

Laken wanted to study, but his mind kept wandering to Autumn's smile, and something warm in him stirred. Then he thought of Cirque, and Laken could feel a caged monster in him trying to get out. Then back to Autumn; then back to Cirque.

"He has enough girls, why can't he leave her alone?" Laken muttered.

"With those smooth words of yours, how could he compete with you?" Dave smiled, and they both let out a little laugh.

Just then, an ear of corn came whizzing toward Laken for the third time, and Laken ducked just in time as it grazed the top of his head. Laken looked up to see that stupid cherub making an obscene gesture towards him.

"Man, he has it in for you!" Heath said.

"Too bad it's not a female cherub. You could woo her with those sweet words of yours," Peyton chided, and the boys nearly fell out of their seats laughing. Even Laken couldn't help but laugh at that.

"Cherubs are not male or female," Heath said confidently.

"I would love to take your word for it, but I'm going to check with Autumn to make sure," Peyton said, much to the other boys' amusement.

"Qweezle," Baylor said softly.

"Qw..what?" Peyton said as the boys turned towards Baylor.

"Qweezle...Qweezle is his name." Baylor spoke u.

"How in the world do you know that?" Heath asked.

"I overheard some of the other cherubs talking," Baylor admitted proudly.

"Hey, Qweezle!" Peyton said as he chucked a half-eaten ear of corn towards the Cherub. Qweezle barely dodged the corn. It flew across the room, hitting a third-year boy in the back of the head. The very large boy stood up and whipped around, while rubbing the spot where the corn hit.

What happened next, no one could have predicted.

The much maligned third-year grabbed a handful of potatoes and whipped it at an unsuspecting second-year boy two tables over. The potatoes hit the boy square in the face, splattering all over the girls on either side of him. The three of them grabbed a handful of food, throwing it at the third-year, who ducked. Instead, the food hit three other kids behind him. At that point, an all-out food fight began.

Laken was hit in the back of the head with a handful of peach cobbler, while dumping his plate over the head of Cirque. Baylor's massive hands threw gallons of food at a time across the room. Peyton and Heath shapeshifted into a trampoline-looking object that, when hit with food, sent the food sailing back towards its thrower. Even the cherubs got in on the action.

Food zoomed back and forth from every direction. Kids were on the tables chucking hand after handful of whatever they could grab. Pitchers of drinks were being dumped over student's heads throughout the room.

Teachers ran around trying to stop the kids, only to be pelted by potatoes, pie, and corn. A large smile filled Laken's face as he watched Malgor get hit with a plate of potatoes. Laken's smile turned to puzzlement when he saw Malgor smile mischievously as he grabbed the potatoes off his neck and shoved them into the face of the fifth-year boy who had hit him.

Then, as quickly as the food fight started, the plates, drinks and edibles stopped in mid-air.

"Before the bell rings, the kitchen wants to know if everyone got enough to eat?" Gabriel's voice echoed through the hall. Heads all whipped towards the Portal, where the voice was coming from. Gabriel's lips looked like a smile was being held back. Laken moved to the left to see around the floating plate of potatoes and corn that blocked his view.

"Everyone full? Well, then, we should all get cleaned up for class," Gabriel said as he released the smile, allowing it to fill his face. Suddenly, all the food and plates disappeared with a pop. Gabriel turned and was gone through the Portal.

The kids stood searching their bodies and clothes for a sign of the food fight. But their clothes were dry and food free! Then the bell rang, and the commotion from all the students gathering their things echoed throughout the room, along with all the chatter about what had just happened.

"That was too cool!" Peyton insisted as they entered the Portal, each of their numas saying, "Study of the Chosen One."

As the boys exited out of the Portal, they each gave a startled jump to the large lion standing directly in front of them. "Please take a seat." The lion's deep, soothing voice responded to the boys' surprised expressions. The boys gave a nervous grin, and headed towards the left side of the room, trying to keep a safe distance between them and their unusual instructor.

"No matter how many times I see it, a lion up close freaks me out," Baylor whispered.

"A talking lion is even freakier," Peyton said as he sat down.

"No, a lion with a numa! Now that is freaky!" added Heath nervously.

Laken grabbed a seat next to Heath, and looked around the room—a large room that was well lit, with the six large fireballs floating effortlessly just below the ceiling. The walls were lined with large golden-framed portraits of men and women. Upon closer examination, Laken noticed that each portrait had a number above it, and they were arranged in numerical order, starting from the left front corner at one, continuing clockwise around the room until it ended at the middle of the left wall at 51. Just below each portrait was a golden plaque with a name engraved on it.

Based on the clothing in each picture, the portraits sat in chronological order. Laken couldn't help but notice the beautiful dark-haired woman in picture number one. She had a dark complexion and piercing brown eyes.

"Dinah must have been the first Chosen One," Dave guessed. Laken's eyes quickly went to number 51, which was blank. "Great picture of you. It really captures your true beauty," Dave chuckled.

"Yeah, they got my good side." Laken allowed a chuckle to escape. Laken's eyes glanced at number 50, and to his surprise, the picture did not show a hideous creature. Ricky was quite the opposite—tall, very skinny, and handsome in his own way. Shoulder length black hair bracketed blue eyes, and a very strong jaw. His skin was pale, and his cheeks were sunken in.

"That's the scary Brone? I think we can take him." Dave took a boxing stance.

"Class, if I can have your attention?" The lion's deep voice interrupted Laken's thoughts. Laken and the other students quickly turned to face the professor. "I am Professor Gideon. Welcome to the Study of the Chosen One." Gideon strolled up an aisle towards the front of the room, and the students shuffled backward to give him wide berth. "We will be studying each of the Chosen Ones. Why, what, and how will be the questions we will answer." Gideon gave a small smile as he paused and glanced over the room. Laken looked around. His classmates wore conflicted expressions; partly surprised, almost scared. Then his eye caught the eye of another student across the room, and the warm sensation stirred in his body sending goosebumps up his spine. She smiled at him and then turned her attention back to Gideon. Dave fainted. Laken felt as if his stomach had tried to escape through his mouth and got stuck in his throat instead. He tried to swallow, hard but his mouth was dry.

"Laken," Gideon's voice startled Laken.

"Aaagh, yes, sir!" Laken responded.

"No, no, boy, I wasn't calling you, I merely stated that you were the fifty-first Chosen One." Gideon gave Laken a warm smile. "It is a rarity to actually have a Chosen One in class, and this should make for a great year." As Gideon talked, Laken noticed Daeth lean over and say something to Grap and Scorpious, who gave out a snicker as they leered at him.

"His death should make for a great year," Laken heard Scorpious' numa say.

"Can anyone tell me how the Chosen One came about?" Gideon's gaze swept the room. Laken turned his attention toward Gideon and away from Scorpious. For the first time, Laken felt like he had the answer, and his hand shot up.

"This might impress Autumn," Dave said in Laken's ear. Gideon looked at Laken's hand, then Heath's, then over at Autumn's.

"Let's allow Laken a go at this one," Gideon gaze turned back to Laken. Laken couldn't help seeing Autumn's eyes turn towards him, and his stomach leapt back into his throat.

"Aaagh, caaa!" Laken attempted to clear his throat. "Jacob," came out very high-pitched screech. Laken shook his head and cleared his throat again. With all eyes on him, he took a deep breath then began. "Jacob wrestled with Gabriel until he gave him the blessing, which is this ring

I'm wearing." Laken paused as he held up his left hand purposefully pointing it towards Autumn. The class all let out a breath of excitement as they stared at the glowing ring.

"Very good. Now, within this statement Laken made, we will find some key elements that set the Chosen One apart from the rest of the Angels." Gideon paused, allowing the new-found excitement over Laken's ring to die down, and the class to turn their attention back to him.

"Can someone tell me why the mighty Gabriel could not defeat a mere human?" Gideon posed. Heath's and Autumn's hands both shot up as if they were each trying to catch a fly above their head. "Yes, Heath." Gabriel called, and Heath shot Autumn a glance.

"Angels cannot harm humans, as defined in our genetic makeup by the Creator." Heath's smirk overtook his expression.

"Very good. Yes, you were created to help humans, so in that, angels are unable to ever harm a human," Gideon's eyes narrowed. "This means that any one of you could take a sword out, swing it at Laken here, and the sword would simply disintegrate on contact. If you attempt to hit him, you, not he, would absorb the pain. If you attempt to grab him, meaning to do him harm, it would scorch your hand." As Gideon said this, Laken noticed Baylor rub the inside of his palm. "I, on the other hand, could eat him, and would feel nothing but a full stomach." Gideon smiled at Laken. The class let out a nervous laugh.

"Creatures in our world are not bound to the Angelic Law. Only *angels* are." When Gideon stressed the word "angels," he sounded discouraged. "So, it is not that Jacob defeated Gabriel, but that Jacob would not let go of his leg. The humans claim Jacob wrestled him, but the truth is he just held on, until Gabriel had no choice but give him the blessing—the blessing being that ring on Laken's left hand. Can anyone tell me what the ring does?" Gideon asked. Heath's and Autumn's hands shot up again. "Yes, Autumn." Gideon offered her a warm smile.

"It's what brings Laken to our dimension on his thirteenth birthday." She turned and smiled at Laken, and the look on her face nearly made Laken fall out of his chair. Laken felt like his face was going to melt. His heart thundered in his chest.

"She really has it for you. Must be that sweet talkin' of yours," Peyton whispered.

"Very good, Autumn. I now want to turn our attention to our previous Chosen One, Lord Pink Bunny," Gideon said with a smile as the class laughed; everyone except Daeth and his gang.

"What makes a Chosen One so dangerous in our world is that no Angel can defeat him. This is what led to Lord Brone's—" Instantly, all the students around Laken let out a horrifying scream.

Baylor fell to the floor crying, "Get the clown away. Get it away!" Others held their ears, banging their heads on their desks. Then, as quickly the panic began, the peace returned.

"Sorry, class, but that is a reminder of what Lord Pink Bunny brought to our world for nearly 50 years. He murdered, stole, and reigned over much of our world, all but Eden, for half a century. Until the day the ring was taken and passed to Laken some 12 years ago," Gideon added with an obvious heaviness in his voice. "Some of his Fallen were cast into Outer Darkness, while most of them blended right back into our world, biding their time, waiting for his return. They're holding onto the prophecy of Nostradamus, our forty-fifth chosen one, who wrote that number fifty would reign twice." Most of the class shivered at Gideon's discourse.

"Professor? What does Lord Pink Bunny want?" Heath's hand went up the same time he spoke.

"Aaagh, many people much smarter than I have tried to answer that question. There are many different opinions." Gideon began to pace, his head hung low. "I spent much time teaching Pink Bunny, and even more time trying to save him, from himself." His expression fell. Gideon stopped, and stared out towards the back of the room. You could hear a large beetle scurry across the floor. He began pacing again, his big paws padding along the floor. Gideon let out a small clearing of his throat, then continued. "I believe that deeply rooted in him was a fear of going back to the human world. He knew his time here was limited. He was an orphan who grew up in a horrible home. He was mistreated by the humans who were supposed to love him. I believe that it was this fear that produced a hatred for the world he was born into, and for the people there." Gideon's expression soured. "Lord Pink Bunny was mounting an army to destroy the human race. You see, if he is the only human, then the blessing has no heir to be passed to, giving him what he felt was immortality." All eyes were on Gideon as he stopped and bowed his large, maned head. "Finding Fallen Angels and dark creatures willing to do this was an easy task, and outside of Gabriel, no one would stand up to him. I believe that he was very close to launching an assault on the human race," Gideon finished, a rope of anger tightened within Laken.

"Isn't he there now? Why not do it now? There is not a human alive that could take him," Heath posited as his hand went up again.

"One human could not take him, nor could a hundred, but he knows that an army, coupled with human technology would easily destroy him. Yes, he is killing humans as we speak, but a few here, and few there, enough to feed the hatred in him, but not enough to draw attention." Gideon's voice trailed off as Heath asked another question.

"How could Fallen Angels help? They have no power against the humans." Heath sounded as if he had found a problem in Brone's plans.

"True, the Fallen cannot hurt a human, but they can protect Pink Bunny from the humans. That, and a few thousand Giants, Dark Elves, and Dragons, and then the human race has no chance." Gideon's lip tightened.

"But how would he get all of them to the human dimension?" Heath asked, but just then the bell rang.

"Think 1500 words on Lord Pink Bunny, due at next class," Gideon's voice echoed over the students' clatter as they headed to the Portal.

"This class is awesome," Heath announced as the boys entered the portal, each of their numas summoning them to "Wings."

"Today we fly!" Professor Cronus announced with bright white teeth shining through his exaggerated smile. Laken looked up to see all the wings attached to the walls, softly fluttering as if they were watching the students. Above them, rings floated in a symmetrical fashion throughout the arena.

"Obstacle course," Heath whispered to Laken.

"I knew that," Laken lied.

"I need everyone to spread out, so you can release your wings." As Cronus directed, his own wings expanded. A few of the girls gasped in awe. "I know, I know. They are beautiful, no matter how many times you see them." Cronus smiled around the room looking for agreement from the students, only finding it from a few girls scattered throughout. "Aagghh, anyway, everyone release your wings. This can be done by simply thinking *wings release*," Cronus said to the sound of many students releasing their wings before he even finished.

"Wings release," Dave said with anticipation, and with that, Laken felt a jerk in his back, and then his wings expanded outward from his body. "What a rush." Dave jumped up and down in excitement. Laken's wings gently moved up and down, as if they were balancing themselves.

"Everyone, watch out! Baylor is going to release his wings. We don't want them to knock anyone over!" Peyton called out to the giggles of the class. Baylor shot him a scowl, which quickly turned into a forced smile. Laken appreciated the effort he'd been making today. Baylor's tiny little wings popped out, to more giggles and snickers of the group.

"I don't care what you think, I love my wings!" Baylor announced proudly as his tiny wings fluttered vigorously, as if they were trying to prove a point.

"Now listen carefully!" Cronus interrupted, his expression narrowing. "There is a balance between you controlling the wings, your numa controlling the wings, and the wings controlling themselves. As you think it, your wings will respond to the voice of your numa. Remember, your wings are alive. Most of you probably have gone unicornback riding. I'm sure your parents or the scout explained to you that the unicorn can have a mind of its own, and will do so if the unicorn does not trust you. Your wings being alive are much like the unicorn. If your wings don't trust you, they can have a mind of their own."

Cronus continued talking while admiring his own wings. "Years ago, wings were forced into a slavery-type mentality, where it was, *Do all we say, when we say it*. This vastly limited what we could do in battle." Cronus paused as he offered his wings a smile. "Allowing your wings to move and act on their own frees you up to focus on the battle. This is the balance we will achieve." Cronus was now stroking his left wing with his hand, still admiring their beauty.

"Now, everyone attempt to fly a few feet off the ground. To do this, just think it," Cronus's attention still focused on his wings. Immediately Laken heard numas all over the arena calling out orders, and students wings began to flap. Dust from the all the wind produced from the wings billowed like smoke. To Laken's surprise, Baylor's tiny little wings seemed to effortlessly hold him up off the ground.

"What do you know? Elephants can fly," Peyton laughed, as his wings flapped him a few feet higher than everyone else.

"Laken, are you here to just watch?" Cronus' eyes were now off his own wings, gazing instead at Laken.

"Aagh, sorry," Laken bit his lip, his brow narrowed.

"Fly a few feet off the ground," Dave announced. Laken's wings immediately began to flap softly. Laken could feel a slight pressure in the center of his back where the weight of his body seemed to be lifting off the ground.

"We're flying. We are actually flying!" Laken shouted out in amazement. The students erupted into laughter at Laken's unbridled enthusiasm. Laken's head turned to the class, as he could feel his face turn a shade redder.

"Yes, Laken, you are flying," Cronus smiled. "Alright now, everyone, fly up 50 feet or so, straight up."

With the initial flap from most of the wings in the class, dust shot up from the ground like a huge cloud of smoke.

"Cckk, ccck!" Laken began to choke on the smoke, but as if intuitively sensing his discomfort, his wings gave a huge flap all on their own and Laken found himself shooting past everyone else, now some 70 feet in the air. Wind whistled all around him. The air seemed to get much cooler. Laken drew a huge breath of excitement. "Now this, this I can do," A grin stretched across Laken's face.

Cronus took them through drills—flying up, then down, then left then right. They did a complete lap around arena flying single file through six hoops that floated at different levels. They then did it again, but twice as fast.

The wind through Laken's hair, the exhilaration of flight—this, this he was good at, and he loved every minute of it.

"Alright, everyone, come back down," Cronus ordered as they finished the lap. Laken and the rest of the class floated back down to the ground. Wings rustled behind each student as they settled on firm ground

"Very good. No such thing as a great student, only a great teacher," Cronus assured them. "We only have a few minutes left in class. I need a volunteer to try the obstacle course."

At those words, Laken's wings gave a huge flap, sending him flying to the front, skidding face first into Cronus' feet.

"I like your eagerness. Looks like we got our volunteer," Cronus announced as Laken forced himself to his feet, clapping his hands to this cloak trying to get the dust off.

"What? No, I didn't voluntee—" Laken tried to get out, but Cronus was not paying attention.

"The record for first-year students is 58 seconds, which I would have broken, but there was a vicious head wind that day." Cronus shook his head. "The school record is 39 seconds, held for 6000 years by Gabriel, which I could beat, but that would hurt my relationship with the headmaster." Cronus now stood tall, like a statue posing.

"Alright, go stand on that line, and wait for me to say go, GO!" Cronus continued, as the students joined in polite applause.

Laken made his way over to the line, as some of the students cheered him on. He could hear a few rude comments thrown his way as he passed by.

"Haha, I'll bet he crashes."

"Good luck not dying."

"Hope your fallen wings don't get you killed"

"I hope you know what you're doing," Laken muttered to his wings

"They do!" Dave responded. Laken could feel butterflies fluttering in his stomach as he put his feet on the line. Laken looked up to see the first ring some 100 feet in the air. His heart felt like it was trying to escape his chest. Laken drew in a ragged breath and then, before he had a chance to think, he heard "GO!"

To this, Laken's wings gave out a huge flap, and Laken took off, dust exploding beneath his feet. With each flap, Laken's speed seemed to double. The wind screamed past him as Laken soared towards the first ring. Everything below him was nearly a blur. Laken looked back to see himself, still attached to his wings—thankfully—then he felt himself whish through the ring, only to feel his body jerked to the right almost at a right angle. His wings accelerated with each flap as they headed towards the next ring. In a blink of an eye the ring was upon them, and Laken's body shot through it, and then entered a dive nearly straight down towards the ring that was just 15 feet off the ground.

"We need to slow down or we will crash!" Laken's words were muffled by the wind.

"Wings say trust them." Dave's lips fluttered in the breeze. "Alright....Aaagh," Laken screamed with excitement as he closed his eyes. Laken could feel his stomach make its way into his throat as their speed kept increasing, and then he felt like he'd left his skin behind as he was jerked in an upward manner through the ring and sent skyrocketing upward towards the next ring. "I love my wings, I love my wings!" Laken could feel a warmth make its way down his back. Laken easily soared through the next ring and his body shot to the left towards the final ring. Laken could feel the wings power on each flap as their speed increased towards the end. Laken could tell his wings were fighting exhaustion to reach that final ring. The cheers of the students were faintly audible over the flapping. As Laken whished through the ring, his body twirled, performing barrel rolls like a military fighter pilot, and then his wings flapped backwards once and he was forced to a standup position, until he landed squarely on the ground. Students rushed over to him, as his wings slowly settled back into his back.

"Fifty-one seconds, fifty-one seconds! It's a new record!" Heath ran up to Laken. Students slammed into Laken nearly knocking him over.

"Holy crud, that was amazing!" Peyton hollered out over the cheers of the crowd.

"Finally, something I'm good at!" Laken's smile broke through his red expression.

"That, and talking to the ladies. Makes two things you're good at," Dave corrected with a big smile.

CHAPTER TWENTY-ONE
Den Championship Round 1

For the next few weeks, people cheered as Laken walked past them in the Great Hall and patted him on the back whenever he passed a group of people. He was hailed as Dogma's greatest flyer.

"Don't let it go to your head," Laken had to keep reminding Dave. Each student had a turn on the flying course, but no one's time came even close to Laken's performance. Daeth, after his third try, got his time to a minute, two seconds, while poor Baylor took nearly two minutes. Baylor didn't seem to mind all the remarks about his butterfly wings and how slow they were. He seemed to truly love his wings.

Laken's detentions weren't nearly as bad as he thought. Malgor simply had him think up 10,000 words on Malgor's life. Laken was sure it was supposed to scare and impress him; it did neither. Laken's mind was on Autumn, and this made it not only difficult for him to remember what he was thinking up, but he kept thinking words like: "She's so hot," and "I would give anything to kiss her," which would of course insert into his assignment. Thus, he had to keep deleting passages, hoping he didn't miss any.

When Malgor and Laken were alone, it was like Malgor almost tolerated him, but in the classroom, Laken knew he was hated. Because of Malgor, the Dragon's den was down to seven stars.

Laken still couldn't send messages from his numa and still couldn't make a rock fly. Once, he made it shake vigorously before he made it explode. Laken was becoming quite powerful with his exploding magic.

"I can't move something, but I can sure blow it up," Laken assured Dave one day after another disappointing Magic class.

Every night, Laken spent at the old basement next to Summer, and every morning he woke up somewhere in the room.

"Laken, you disappeared, actually disappeared. You were there, and then you were gone!" Baylor exclaimed the next morning to the awestruck boys.

"Laken, do you remember anything when you wake up?" Heath's expression narrowed.

"I go to my old house," Laken answered, purposefully leaving out the part about Summer. He took enough ribbing about Autumn. Another girl, even his sister, would be too much.

"Can you touch anything? Is there anyone around? Do they see you?" Heath rattled off as he attached his Hallow.

"I go right through anything in the world, and yes, sometimes there are people, and no, they can't see me, or hear me." Laken hurriedly grabbed his Rhema and stuffed it in his Hallow.

"Nothing in my Rhema has the answer. I have no clue, and no, we aren't going to ask Autumn." Heath cut off Peyton with a hand in his face.

Laken learned a lot about Eden as the weeks passed. Angelic History class still had not lasted the full hour before Professor Luvly released them. Professor Luvly continued to give Pete detention, and literally kicked him out of class one day for not answering the question, "What form did the first Fallen One take?" Baylor had to escort the plant out of the room.

The Chosen One class was one of Laken's favorites. Was it because it was interesting, or because he could stare at Autumn the whole hour? Laken learned that some heroes from his dimension were Chosen Ones. Samson, Hercules, and Merlin were all Chosen Ones who went on to do great things in his world.

There was another attempt on Laken's life just three weeks after Laken broke the flight record. Laken picked up a chicken leg off his plate and it burst into flames, turning into ash, as did the potatoes as Laken scooped them up with the spoon and put them to his lips.

"Probably that Qweezle! Little turd has taken it to the next level!" Laken muttered as Gabriel examined the plate.

"No, not a cherub. Cherubs are incapable of murdering a student. It was done by an Angel. Had anyone else eaten this food, it would have killed them instantly. Old Gnome poison used for centuries. Takes a trained magic eye to see," Gabriel's voice was heavy.

"Daeth! Daeth! Can I offer you some potatoes?" Peyton cried to the laughter of the boys and puzzled look from Daeth a couple of tables away. Gabriel shot Peyton a disapproving glance, and Peyton snapped to attention muttering, "Sorry, Headmaster."

"Why did it burst into flames?" Heath asked, changing the subject.

Gabriel's gaze slowly turned to Heath, as Peyton let out a sigh of relief. "Because an Angel cannot do Laken harm. The poison was intended for his harm, so when Laken picked up the poisoned meat, it simply burst into flames." Gabriel spoke as matter-of-factly as if Laken had dripped jelly on his pants.

After Gabriel left, the boys continued to try and figure out the conspiracy.

"Baylor and I saw Malgor talking to the cherub that delivered your food," Cirque mentioned.

"You know, Malgor goes out of Eden every night after lights out," Baylor whispered as he glanced behind to see if anyone was trying to listen.

"What? How do you know?" Peyton asked.

"Don't worry how, just know he does. What do you think he is doing?" Baylor continued.

"Probably getting poison and plotting Laken's death," Cirque said as the boys entered the portal each of their numas requesting, "Arena."

"Boys, are you ready for the D.C. tonight?" Argus's voice carried to the boys who had just entered the arena through the Portal.

"Yes, sir!" the boys said confidently, all except Laken, who looked down. Yes, he would win the flying portion, but unless the sword part was picking fruit, there was no way. For the last month, all he'd done every day was pick stupid cherries. Sure, he got good at it. Not even Argus was as fast as Laken.

"How in the world is that going to help us tonight?" Dave muttered as the boys stopped to look at the busy arena. The stadium chairs were full with cheering students and teachers. Laken was reminded of a football game he had seen on television once, when the neighbor lady had invited him and Summer in for some food. Students were dressed up in support of their den. There were large lion hats and full blown snake suits. One Angel had "Unicorns" painted in large purple letters on one wing and "Rock" painted in metallic gold on the other wing, both of which he had fully expanded in the stands.

"We are at a disadvantage because we only have one person to represent in each event, and we are all first-years." Peyton rubbed his hands together. "But if we all….Cirque, what are you doing? Peyton grabbed the arm Cirque was using to blow kisses to a group of screaming girls in the stands. "Can we leave the ladies alone for two minutes there, Romeo?"

"Yes, of course." Cirque gave one last wink towards the girls, who let out a scream.

"Like I was saying, if we all do our best." Peyton's roaming gaze became intense. "Now each event is worth ten points for a win, seven points for second, five points for third, three points for fourth, and one point for fifth," Peyton continued. "Heath, Baylor, and I should get ten points each for our events. Cirque, if you can get three points it would be a huge help. Cirque!" Peyton threw his arms up in desperation. Cirque, who was waving at some girls, quickly turned his attention back to Peyton.

"Of course, of course," Cirque smiled.

Peyton let out an exaggerated sigh. "Laken, you will get ten points on flying, and how many points do you think you can get on swords?" He raised his voice, as the five-minute warning horn was blowing.

"Aaagh, I hope I can get five, but probably only three," Laken shook his head.

"That's fine, it's fine. We're counting on your ten points in flying. Any other points you get us is gravy," Peyton looked off to the sky and started to mumble numbers. "So we have four tens, and if Cirque stinks it up, and we add three from Laken…"

"The total is 44 points," Heath interrupted.

"The total is 44 points. I figure if the Serpents win on the events we don't, and take second place the times we win, and lose the cloak—that Ravana couldn't hide a fly in an Ogre's back hair," Peyton paused again as he looked off in the distance.

"Forty-two points," Heath interrupted again, this time a little more annoyed.

"Yes, forty-two points, which gives us a good lead for—"

"Den Warriors please make your way to your Den master. The competition is about to begin." Argus'svoice boomed through the stadium.

"Let's hurry!" Peyton said as he took off towards Gabriel.

"This is a big deal for him." Laken gave Heath a smirk.

"You think?" Heath smiled back.

"Are we ready boys?" Gabriel asked as the boys trotted up to him.

"You bet! Well, you probably don't, but, yeah. I mean you don't bet, not that you don't. Well you might, but you…," Peyton excited voice finally trailed off.

Gabriel's puzzled look turned to a large smile. "Good. Remember there is no such thing as failure, only opportunities to learn, to grow, and to become better." Gabriel put a hand on Laken's shoulder.

Laken couldn't help but feel that warm unnatural feeling run down his spine. This time, something different happened, Laken felt his wings shudder. It felt good, and yet awkward.

"We have drawn the order of the events, and I need Archers to please report to the range," Argus announced.

"That's you Cirque! Cirque! Cirque!" Peyton screamed at Cirque, who was leaning on the stands talking to three girls.

"What? Oh yeah. I will see you ladies in the winner's circle," Cirque promised as he flashed his brilliant smile at them. Each of the girls' numas fainted.

"I'm starting to really hate him," grumbled Peyton as Cirque trotted off waving his hand at the crowd as if he were the center of a parade.

"I would like to welcome you to our 6010th D.C. A quick reminder, no Magic is allowed. Any use of Magic is grounds for immediate disqualification," Argus warned. "With that, let the Games begin!"

Serpent's Den was up first, and Laken now knew why they were champions. Three bull's eyes in a row, and then two arrows just outside the bull's eye.

"Lsarden scores 480 points," Argus announced over the invisible speakers. A large pink melon-looking fruit was shot into the air some fifty feet high. Lsarden put 5 arrows into it before it splatted on the ground. "With 5 hits, Lsarden scores 980 points, beating his old record of 960 points." Argus's voice was barely audible over the loud screams and cheers of the Serpent Den supporters in the crowd.

"Now we have Cirque from the Dragon's den," Argus said. The applause from the ladies in the crowd was louder than the combined cheers for Lsarden. "I love Cirque!" rang out from some girl in the top row, just as the crowd was quieting down. Peyton shook his head in disgust, mumbling something about giving Cirque some poisoned potatoes.

Cirque removed his first arrow from his sac. As he knocked it in the bow, he dropped the arrow to the ground. "Ooooooogh!" rang through all the girls in the crowd.

"It's all right, Cirque!" the girl from the top row screamed. Peyton had a handful of hair in each hand and was pulling strenuously. Cirque picked up the arrow and then gave a gleaming smile to the crowd. The girls let out a love-struck sigh in unison. Cirque then awkwardly knocked the arrow in the bow, pulled the string back, and sent the arrow soaring 20 feet over the target. The crowd let out another, "Ooooooh."

"That's alright, you can do it!" a group of girls screamed. Cirque grabbed another arrow, shot another cheesy smile to the crowd, knocked the arrow, pulled back and released. This arrow shot over the wall and out of the stadium.

"I hate him, I hate him!" Peyton said as Argus called out Cirque's final score of 100.

"At least he got a hundred points," Heath said reassuringly.

"A hundred points! He wouldn't have gotten those points if the Pink Chanderange hadn't landed on the arrow he shot into the ground," Peyton said in disgust as he kicked up some dirt.

"Come on, we expected this." Heath rested his hand on Peyton's shoulder.

"I know, but a hundred points? It's just embarrassing!" Peyton's voice was loud enough for Cirque to hear.

"Sorry, boys. Got some unlucky breaks on that one," Cirque offered with a big smile.

"Unlucky! Unlucky! I'll give you unlucky!" Peyton screamed as Laken and Heath tried to restrain him.

"Next event is the Great Sword. First off, we have Baylor from Dragon's den versus Salk, our undefeated champion from the Lion's den," Argus announced, and the boys released Peyton, who was still bright red and glaring at Cirque. Laken looked over to see a big fourth-year, who barely came up to Baylor's neck. Laken glanced up at the scoreboard. Serpent's Den 10, Lamb's Den 7, Unicorn Den 5, Owl's Den 3, Lion's Den 1, Dragons 0.

"Fight!" Argus announced, and the crowd let out a roar of excitement. Laken looked over at the battle. Salk went on the offensive, swinging the enormous great sword with a side cut at Baylor's waist. Baylor quickly jumped backwards, dodging the cutting blow by inches. The crowd gasped. Salk cut back the other way with his sword, but this time, Baylor blocked it with his own sword and then jabbed the hilt of his sword into Salk's face. Salk fell backwards with a look of surprise, blood gushing from his nose.

"SALK! SALK! SALK!" the crowd began to chant. Salk wiped his nose, saw the blood, and then went berserk. Swinging the blade with pure adrenalin, overhand, side hand, back, forth. But with each strike, Baylor effortlessly dodged or blocked each blow. Laken was utterly amazed at how fast and agile Baylor was for his enormous size.

"He could keep up with the best of us on daggers," Peyton admitted, in awe of Baylor's footwork. Salk, with two hands on the hilt of the sword, swung the great sword up over his head, and then downwards towards Baylor's head. With one hand, Baylor reached up, caught Salk's arm in his massive hand, and with the other hand gripping his massive great sword, swung and struck Salk in the ribs below his outstretched hands, knocking him ten feet, rolling and sputtering along the ground.

"Baylor is the winner!" the announcer informed the quiet and shocked crowd. Skar and Gorgos rushed over and helped Salk to his feet.

"Baylor! Baylor! Baylor!" a few students began to chant, and the crowd erupted with, "BAYLOR! BAYLOR! BAYLOR!"

"Quite a loyal crowd we have," Peyton smirked.

Baylor made even easier work of his next two opponents, defeating the last one in four seconds flat, winning the Great Sword competition with ease.

"The Great Sword competition ends in the following. Dragon taking first, Lion second, Serpent third, Owl fourth, Unicorn fifth, and Lamb last. Our next competition is cloaking," the now-familiar voice rang out. Laken looked up at the scoreboard as Heath headed towards the center of the arena. Serpents 15, Dragons 10, Lions 8, Lambs 7, Unicorns 6, Owls 6.

Laken glanced back to the center of the arena to see the five students from each den standing shoulder to shoulder.

"Go!" Argus'svoice bellowed. The five students began to move around in the open area like they were trying to hide. But there was nothing around them, just open space. One kid looked like he climbed an invisible pole and was hanging upside down floating in the air. Ravanah was lying flat on the ground, smack dab in the middle of arena for all to see.

Laken rubbed his eyes in disbelief, and then squinted to see something he missed. "I don't get it. What in the world are they doing?" Laken turned to Peyton.

"What? Oh, of course. If you get within twenty feet of the center, it is a forest. They can't hear us, or see us, so we can't help them cheat. In a second, they will release some Garmrs. Whoever is found last, wins," Peyton said as his attention turned back to the invisible forest.

"What's a Garmr…" but Laken cut himself off when three massive wolf-type beasts appeared. Each was the size of a horse, blood red, semi translucent, with huge sharp teeth. "Does the loser end up being eaten?" Laken grimaced as the Garmrs began to sniff the air, and move towards the invisible forest.

"No, no, they aren't real. RI's. Remember?" Peyton said out of the corner of his mouth.

"Ooghh, looks like one caught a scent." As if hearing Peyton's play-by-play, the biggest of the wolves took off running, and its large mouth wrapped around the Lamb's girl.

"Aaaagh!" sighed the crowd. Laken's eyes scanned the area, looking for Heath, but even in the open area, he could not see him. He could see the other four who were left. Just then a cheer erupted as Ravanah was caught. "Where is your brother?" Laken wondered in frustration.

"There! Look closely." Peyton pointed at a Garmr.

"That's a Garmr!" Laken responded even more annoyed.

"No, look down, under the Garmr." Peyton smiled. Laken squinted his eyes, and just barely visible, under the Garmr's feet, was Heath. Laken wasn't sure, but it looked like Heath was waving at him. There was another cheer as the girl from the Lion's den was found hanging from what must be a tree. Immediately thereafter, the girl from the Unicorn den was found, and a cheer erupted.

"Hey! Dragon's den is using magic!" a tall serpent boy cried.

"That's not magic you idgit!" Peyton's voice was strong. "Read a book on magic, why don't you! It's been proven numerous times not to be magic!" Peyton's voice continued to grow in volume.

"It's still cheating," rang out among the serpents.

"Whatever!" Peyton shot them a glare then turned his attention back to the event.

"Just two left," Peyton smiled as he pointed over to a girl who looked like she was hanging in midair, just feet from a Garmr. Laken looked closer, and his heart sank a bit. The girl was Autumn. Laken had to resist the urge to scream, "Watch out, Autumn," or, "I love you, Autumn." It wouldn't have mattered. The massive Garmr jumped up, and the event was over. The crowd erupted in cheers. Laken could hear, "Where is he? I still can't see him," as the amazed crowd looked for Heath.

Laken looked out towards Autumn, who hung her head for a moment, and then put a huge smile on, patting Heath on the back and making her way back to the stands.

"You have to cheer that. It is plain amazing to watch him," Peyton bragged. Laken looked up at the scoreboard. Dragons 20, Serpents 16, Owls 13, Unicorns 11, Lions 11, Lambs 7.

"We need the Dagger Class to please report to the Obstacle course," Argus'svoice rang out.

"See you in ten points!" Peyton said with a smile. Laken's eyes quickly shifted to the obstacle course he had seen that first day in the arena.

"That thing looks mean!" Dave's eyes widened.

"You're telling me," Laken agreed.

"How did I do?" Heath asked as he trotted over, an ear-to-ear smile stretched across his face.

"Unbelievable! That was awesome!" Laken exclaimed.

"I know, I know!" Heath smiled. "Not to the level of Cirque, but still good."

"Go!" Argus ordered, and Laken's eyes flew to the obstacle course.

A girl ran down the way, arrows being shot at her.

"Man, she is quick!" Dave cried out just as she lunged over a small wall and a group of arrows sunk into it behind her.

"Oooo," the crowd sighed. Ten large hanging axes swung back and forth, barely scraping the ground. The girl bounced in place in a rhythmic motion and then took off running. She ran past all the axes as they whizzed one after the other right behind her. She scaled a massive 30-foot wall like a spider. She jumped up, grabbing a long rope stretched twenty feet across and attached to a small wooden platform. She went hand over hand effortlessly, until her feet swung and she was standing on the platform. Then she leapt off the platform. Laken shook his head in amazement and terror, thinking she was going to plummet to her death. The girl grabbed a rope Laken hadn't seen and then swung from rope, to rope, to rope, finally releasing and doing a double flip to the ground and across the finish line.

"We have a new course record of one minute seven seconds!" Argus announced, and the stands erupted.

"Wow! Who is she?" Laken asked as he looked over first at Baylor and then at Heath.

"Don't know..."

Argus'svoice interrupted Heath. "Heldora from Serpent now holds the new Dogma record."

"Peyton will beat her!" Heath let out a nervous sigh.

"Go!" rang out, and Laken looked up to see Peyton moving like a blur.

"That little guy can move!" Baylor's brow raised. The arrows didn't even get close. He dove over the wall, and ran up to the axes. With barely a hesitation he dashed through the axes, as they whizzed by him, the last one catching his cloak. For a moment, he was being swung back and forth, the cloak stuck on the axe. With an insistent jerk, Peyton ripped the cloak off the axe and was once again running. He scaled the wall like Heldora, if not faster. Peyton leaped and caught the outstretched rope to the "oooohh" of the crowd. He went hand over hand along the outstretched rope effortlessly until his feet hit the platform. Laken looked up to see the timer at 58 seconds.

Peyton was on the ropes and it looked like he had it. Laken glanced again at the time, one minute and three seconds showed on the clock. Laken held his breath.

Peyton went from one rope, to the next rope, and then as he reached out for the last rope, it jiggled unnaturally away from his outstretched hands and he missed it, barely holding onto the rope he was on. Peyton released his grip, attempting to make it across the channel. His body slammed into the edge, and the crowd screamed out in pain as if they'd fallen themselves. Peyton grabbed a foothold and hoisted himself up, and then rolled past the finish line. The stadium was deathly quiet, waiting for the announcement.

"One minute nine seconds," Argus announced to the cheers and boos of the crowd.

"Cheat, I got cheated!" Peyton screamed as he ran towards Laken, Baylor, and Heath. "The rope was magically tampered with! I got robbed!" Peyton was still screaming when he slammed into Heath's and Laken's outstretched arms that were there to hold him back. "I got cheated! I got cheated!"

"Peyton, please calm down," Gabriel's gentle voice came from behind them. Peyton stopped, turned around, his face burning scarlet. "From what I saw, I have to agree, and we will look into it!" Gabriel offered a smile.

"So do I win?" Peyton's hand now waving in the air.

"As of now, you are in second place," Gabriel smiled.

"I won that! I won! I won..." Peyton screamed, and then his voice trailed off as he noticed Gabriel's hand motioning for him to calm himself. "I did win!" Peyton repeated, much more calmly this time.

"I believe it very possible you would have beat the new record. But we cannot change the past, only do better in the future. Well done, Peyton. I, for one, was quite impressed."

Gabriel turned and headed towards the Serpent's den. Gabriel leaned over, whispered something in Daeth's ear. Daeth looked shocked, tried to say something, but Gabriel's hand was already up signaling for him not to speak. Daeth lowered his head and slowly walked to the Portal.

The crowd let out a, "Woooooo, somebody's busted!" in unison, as Daeth entered the Portal and left the arena.

"Well that kind of makes up for it," Peyton said. Then a look of realization came across his face. "Serpent has no flyer with Daeth gone! That works out better than I thought," Peyton said with a renewed sense of excitement.

The other four den members each took a shot at the obstacle course. The Lambs girl got hit with an axe, knocking her some thirty feet out of the course, and the other three student's times weren't even close. Owl crossed the finish line in one minute thirty-three seconds, Unicorn came in at one minute thirty-eight seconds, and Lion came in at two minutes twelve seconds.

"I need those from swords to please report." Laken thought Argus'svoice sounded a little nervous on this announcement.

"Go get 'em!" Heath said as he patted him on the back.

"Just get us some points," Peyton said a little louder than Laken thought was necessary.

"Hope there are cherries over here," Dave joked.

"Me, too," Laken replied.

As Laken arrived with the others, he looked up to see the score board. Dragons 27, Serpents 26, Owls 18, Unicorns 14, Lions 12, Lambs 7.

"If we get seven points here, and ten points for flying, we have first no matter what," Laken reminded Dave.

"If you get even one point on sword fighting, I think everyone faints, and you are made supreme ruler of the world," Dave mocked.

"First up, we have Laken from Dragon's den versus Heidi from the Lamb's den." The crowd let out a mixed noise of cheers and boos.

"Laken, please get in the circle, and draw your sword." Laken grabbed the sword, held it up, and examined it. "For an RI it feels real." Dave said. As Laken entered the circle, the circle turned into a circular cage some ten feet high.

"I wonder why we didn't see this when Baylor fought?" Laken said to Dave.

"Probably like the forest, you can only see it if you are in it." Dave's eyes were wide.

"Laken, you might want to hold your sword up," Skar hinted as he walked thru the iron fence around them.

"Yep, it's imaginary!" Dave confirmed.

"Been so long since I had a sword in my hands!" Laken lifted his sword up, feeling it's weight.

"We have picked an orchard or two of cherries. Speaking of cherries, I could sure go for some cherry pie. Ohhh and maybe some of sowoo-doo's" "That tiny sac still freaks me out," Dave laughed.

"Concentrate, Dave!" Laken said firmly.

"Oh, yeah, battle time," Dave said as he made like he was focusing.

Laken looked over at Heidi, who flashed him a confident grin.

"This is going to be too easy," her bright blue numa said.

"Go!" Laken heard, and before he had time to raise his sword, Heidi's sword was coming straight down on his head.

"What the…?" is all Laken heard Dave say before everything went black. And then Laken was soaring through the air. Autumn was in his arms, and she was squeezing him tight.

"I got you. Don't worry," Laken said confidently.

"I know you do, Laken. I love you so much," Autumn said as she squeezed tighter.

"I love you, too, Autumn."

Then Laken heard Peyton screaming, "Laken! Laken, you alright?" Laken could hear the words, but it sounded like they were coming from the ground way down below.

"I love you," Laken said again.

"I love you, too," Laken heard Peyton say.

"Peyton? Why is Peyton here?" Laken asked Dave.

Then it felt like someone was shaking him, "Come on, lover boy. Wake up. Autumn is here to give you a big ol' kiss." Laken opened his eyes to see a collage of faces hovering over him. He shook his head trying to focus his eyes. Peyton's face was in the center of all the other faces.

"You alright?" Peyton asked again.

"What happened?" Laken asked.

"You got the mess beat out of you, in record time. Less than one second, an all-time record," Peyton said with a smile. "But at least you found true love." An eruption of student's laughter filled the air.

"You can be a real jerk sometimes!" Laken growled as he pushed everyone out of the way and got up. His head throbbed.

"Everyone back, get back. Are you alright, Laken?" a deep familiar voice said. Laken looked up to see Argus. Anger seem to boil inside of Laken. He could feel his face turning purple.

"Alright? Alright? I lost in record time because you have to be the worst trainer of all times. What is next? Planting carrots? Shining apples?" Argus looked at Laken until it felt like he was looking through Laken, turned around and strode back to his booth.

"Come on, Laken, just funning you," Peyton said as he put his hand on Laken. Laken ripped his shoulder away.

"Yeah, well, I'm done being your fun," Laken growled as he pressed through the crowd and went and sat down by himself.

Laken ended up losing the next two fights in similar fashion. He didn't get knocked out again, but he was done, and had lost in less than 10 seconds in each match.

Laken slammed his sword into his sac and stomped his way over to the stands, where he threw himself down. Disgusted and angry, he barely heard Argus announce the results.

"Owl takes first, with Unicorn coming in second, Lion coming in third, Serpent fourth, Lamb fifth, and Dragon…last." Argus's voice trailed off.

Laken whipped his head up to see the score board. The score was now Serpents 29, Owls 28, Dragons 27, Unicorns 21, Lions 17, Lambs 8.

"Come on, Laken, I was just messing around," Peyton smiled.

"I said, leave me alone!" Laken hissed. In the background, Laken could hear something being sung, something that was getting louder with each extra person who started singing.

"Laken and Autumn sitting in a tree k-i-s-s-i-n-g. First comes love then comes marriage then comes a couple of chosen ones in a baby carriage."

"Don't let it bother you. If you win this, we win. It is that simple. No one will remember how bad you stunk it up with the sword after they see you fly," Peyton encouraged.

"Alright, we need our flyers to please report," Argus's voice boomed out. Laken wrenched his body off the ground, pushed Peyton out of the way, and stormed over to the area the other flyers were waiting.

Laken could hear Peyton nervously screaming, "Bring it home. Bring that victory home!"

He could still hear the crowd singing, "…k-i-s-s-i-n-g." Cronus stood in front of the six flyers with his movie star smile lighting up the area.

"Laken, get your wings out, we are about to start," Cronus warned.

"WINGS OUT!" Laken demanded. Nothing happened. "WINGS, I SAID OUT!" Laken thundered. Still nothing.

"Go!" and all the other flyers took off.

"Please come out!" Laken said with controlled anger, and his wings came out flapping. Laken was instantly soaring and quickly gaining on the group. "COME ON, YOU SORRY SET OF WINGS! LET'S GO, FASTER!" Laken demanded, just as he was passing up the last place girl. And then, he began to just fall, down, and down. "FLAP, YOU STUPID BIRD!" Laken howled out over the whistling wind as he plummeted towards the ground. "YOU STUPID, DUMB, IDIOTIC, WI…!" Just before impact his wings gave one single flap, and Laken smashed into the ground. Hard.

"Aaaaggh!" Laken screamed out in pain. Dust filled his lungs, he began to cough. Then his wings were gone. "Yeah!" cough, cough. "You better go before I turn you into extra crispy, you dumb bird!" Laken let out another set of coughs. The dust from the collision still filled his lungs. At that, Laken's body gave a violent shudder and went still.

In the background Laken could hear, "Laken and Autumn sitting in a tree…"

CHAPTER TWENTY-TWO
Burning Squirrels and Laken Becomes Jack

October came and went. Early November meant midterms. Laken hadn't recovered from the games, nor had he said two words to anyone in the den.

"They can all stick it," Dave said as Laken waited for his private lesson with Gabriel.

Laken had been sick of the stupid "Laken and Autumn" song long before the other students lost interest in it. Autumn tried to tell Laken not to worry about it, that first week after the Den Championship. She approached him right after Creature Studies, but Laken snapped at her, and she ran off crying.

"Good! I'm glad she's gone. Her, my stupid wings, and my den. Glad they're all gone," Laken muttered as he stomped into the portal.

After the incident, Autumn wouldn't even glance at him. She pretended like he didn't exist. Once, as Laken walked toward her, she turned toward the wall and waited for him to walk by.

"Stupid jerk!" Laken heard Autumn's numa shout out as he walked by.

"Back at you!" Laken muttered, completely missing the surprised look on her face.

"Just apologize to her," Dave begged those first few weeks.

"Sure. That way everyone can get that stupid song going again!" Anger ripped thru Laken. "No thank you!"

During Art of War, Laken just sat off by himself. Argus hadn't said a word to him since the D.C.

"Fine, like I need to be trained on picking fruit," Laken pouted loud enough for Argus to hear.

Laken's ability to blow things up was rapidly improving. In the Great Hall during dinner one night, Laken had made an entire table explode into ash out from under Cirque who was calling out to Autumn. When Laken was alone, he would practice on bigger and bigger objects. A week earlier, Laken caused an entire oak tree to burst into smoldering cinders. Dave, too, was getting meaner and meaner, but Laken didn't mind. The darker Dave got, the more powerful Laken seemed to become. The more powerful he was, the fewer people picked on him.

Laken sent one third-year boy screaming to the hospital wing. The older boy started singing the "Laken and Autumn" song in the hall. Laken turned red, and then boom, a jolt of fire burst out of him. The boy was picked up into the air, and a blue light connected the boy to Laken. With each angry thought, a pulse of energy shot along the light, hit the boy, causing him to scream as his body convulsed. Malgor grabbed Laken by the neck, tossing him some fifteen feet across the hall. He smashed into a large statue of a Unicorn, breaking the blue light connection. Laken gave Malgor a smirk as he got up, dusted himself off and strutted into the Portal. After that, people got out of Laken's way when he walked by. Laken loved the new-found respect he seemed to have. Laken was now in charge, and in control. No one told him what to do. For once, he was the one barking orders.

His condition was far from perfect, however. Laken was now failing Wings because his Wings would not come out.

"Fine, stay in there and rot! Dumb bird!" Laken screamed in the middle of class. "What are you looking at?" Laken threatened a few kids who quickly turned around and made their way close to Cronus.

In recent weeks, Laken had turned his powers toward creatures in the garden. He had singed all the hair off a rabbit earlier in the week, and now he was tormenting a few squirrels.

"Burn, squirrel, burn!" Dave screamed as jets of light shot out of Laken's hand popping the squirrels in the backside, causing them to squeal out in pain.

"You can tell the character of a man by how he treats those less powerful than he." Gabriel's voice came from the distance. Laken stopped focusing on the squirrels, who quickly scurried into a hole.

"I think he saw that," Dave whispered.

"Good, I hope he did," Laken bellowed back.

Gabriel took a seat next to Laken and stared out towards the setting sun, barely visible through the blackened sky. The clouds were dark and seemed to hang low, as did the leaves on the trees, as if they echoed Gabriel's emotions. A herd of unicorns could be seen trotting by, their heads, too, hung low. Laken hadn't seen a single fairy in weeks. There was a long pause. Laken couldn't tell if it was a few minutes or a few hours. He felt so uncomfortable sitting there, listening to the noises of the Garden and the wind rustling through the trees.

"I have character," Laken squeaked through the silence.

"Do you?" Gabriel replied. His face held an expression of mock surprise.

"Yes, I do," Laken said as he tried to make eye contact with Gabriel, but Laken could only hold it for a few seconds before he looked down.

"So, what is character?" Gabriel inquired as Laken pretended to be interested in a purple beetle that was crawling up his leg.

"Character is respect," Laken answered as he knocked the beetle from his leg.

"Is it?" His tone held that perfect balance between sarcastic and Socratic. "And how does one gain respect?" Gabriel put his hands together.

"With power!" Laken squished the beetle beneath his sandals then shot Gabriel a glare.

"Hmmmm!" Gabriel's head slowly nodded, his lips curved downward. "So, power gives you respect?" Gabriel rubbed his hands together, Laken felt like Gabriel's gaze was burning into the top of his head.

"Power demands respect!" Laken returned the gaze. No sooner were the words out than Laken felt a tightness come over his body. It was squeezing and squeezing the air out of him. Laken gasped for air, but it was as if his lungs had no room. Laken fell to the ground, clawing the dirt, choking.

And as suddenly as it began, it was released.

"Do you respect me now?" Gabriel asked. Laken sputtered and coughed, finally drew a ragged breath. Laken hit the ground with his fist, and got to his feet. "Would you rather have people respect you out of fear, and hate you for it, or respect you out of faith and love you for it?"

Gabriel offered a weary smile. "Laken, character is what you are made of. Are you made of hate and anger, or love and kindness?" Gabriel's eyes narrowed as he leaned towards Laken. "Will you use your powers to torment and bring fear, or to help and bring hope? You are at the same crossroads Rick was at some time ago; I pray you choose a different direction." Gabriel's voice now sounded heavy. "I pray you choose good, faith, and love, not anger, hate and fear." Gabriel paused again as tears filled his intense blue eyes. "Know this: whatever thoughts you hold inside the longest will determine the road you travel. Will it be love or hate? Are they thoughts that build, or thoughts that destroy?" The pain in Gabriel's eyes reached into Laken's heart and squeezed. "Remember," Gabriel continued, "as you choose each thought, you are stepping in a direction. Just make sure it is headed towards where you want to go." There was another long pause as Gabriel used his long, crooked finger to wipe his eyes.

Laken quickly turned his head away, as if a blinding light had just caught his eye. Gabriel's tears were more than he could handle. Laken breathed a heavy sigh.

"I'm heading where I want to be heading!" Laken's jaw tensed.

"Laken, come sit down. I want to show you your future." Gabriel sat on a large boulder, leaving space for Laken.

"I'm fine over here. I don't need to see my future. Laken turned his back. Then something took control of Laken's legs, and he felt himself being walked over to Gabriel and then forced to sit down.

"Thank you for humoring an old man," Gabriel said, a smile tugging at his lips. Surprise flitted across Laken's face, and then anger once again set in. Gabriel pulled out his numanator, and then pulled out a second numanator.

"Dave, please spit into this one first," Gabriel said as he held the golden cylinder up to Dave. A look of anticipation covered Gabriel's face. Dave looked at Laken, who shrugged his shoulders. Dave spit, it was a scene in Laken's childhood—the time Laken had spilled some milk on the table. Jack was furious. His face was bright red as he bore down on Laken. Then the scene froze.

"Dave, please spit into this one," Gabriel said with a knowing smile. Dave spit yet again. This time it was Laken, red hot and angry as he bore down on the kid in the hall. Then both played simultaneously. Laken sat in horror as he saw the same mannerisms, the same hate, and anger in him that was in Jack.

"Turn it off! Turn it off!" Laken knocked the cylinders out of Gabriel's hands. "No! No! I won't be him! I won't be him!" Laken screamed through the tears as he buried his face in his hands. Laken felt a warm arm wrap around his shoulder and the tight embrace of a real hug.

"What do you say we don't become him? Ever," Gabriel's soft voice whispered in Laken's ear. Laken turned and buried his face into Gabriel's chest, crying like he had never done before.

"I won't. I won't. I promise. I promise!" Laken repeated between sobs.

Laken wiped his eyes, finally pulling away from Gabriel's gentle embrace. Laken had no idea how long he had been crying, but the sun had set, and the full moon was now casting long shadows over the garden, so he knew some time had passed. Laken looked boldly into Gabriel's eyes.

"What do I need to do? I hurt so many people. How do I make it right?" Laken asked as he wiped his eyes again with his sleeve. A slight breeze blew, and the sound of the garden became alive again. Laken's attention turned to the sky which was bright with moonlight, not a cloud in sight. Fairies were once again flitting through the trees, bushes, and flowers—almost a hypnotizing flurry of beauty. Animals played once again, running and jumping for as far as the eye could see. Gabriel cleared his throat, and Laken met Gabriel's gaze. Three colorful fairies buzzed between them for a moment and then darted off. Gabriel leaned over and picked up a dandelion and blew the white seeds into the wind. The seeds floated and flew out into the garden.

"Our actions are like this. A simple action of me blowing the seeds has changed where these flowers will grow. See those seeds on the rock?" Gabriel's crooked finger pointed a few feet away. "Those will never become a flower. My actions I can't take back. All I can do is go try and change the wrongs I have made." Gabriel illustrated his point by bending over and picking each of the seeds off the rock. Then, he blew them off into the garden. "I believe that your friends will welcome you back with open arms, and even your wings will be happy the real you is back. But it has to be you who makes the change. You have to fix the wrongs you've made!" At this Gabriel turned and disappeared into the Portal.

CHAPTER TWENTY-THREE
Laken Spanks Argus

"I'm sorry! Sorry, sorry, sorry, sorry. Come on! Two weeks of sorry, and you still won't come out and fly." Laken had made up with everyone except Autumn and his wings. Heath, Peyton, and Baylor were easy.

"Don't sweat it!" Heath said during dinner that night.

"We all get a little crazy. Women will do that to you." Peyton spit part of his crumb cake out of his mouth as he spoke. "I will never have that problem, because I steer clear of women."

"That, and the fact they steer clear of *you* should make you extra safe," Heath said, and the boys laughed.

"You were mad?" Cirque's eyes widened. The fact that he had to turn his head away from the two girls he was talking to just to join in the conversation made the boys laugh even harder.

Laken made a special effort to go out of his way for the boy he had sent to the nurse. The first day, the boy saw him and ran. The second day, he walked away fast. The third day, Laken caught up to him and apologized.

"Uugh, uugh, yeah, I forgive you," said the boy as he ran off.

"Of course I forgive you. Are you fast at anything?" Argus playfully shoved Laken, sending him toppling to the ground. "Took you how long to come to your senses? Let's stop wasting time. We've got some cherries to pick," Argus added, a grin tugging at his lips as he helped Laken up.

Maybe because Argus felt guilty, or because it was part of the plan, Argus scheduled half the practice with cherry picking, and half the practice with actual sword practice.

"Listen to your numa. He is your eyes and your ears." Argus motioned to each of these body parts. "To be a great warrior you have to let yourself be controlled by your numa," Argus repeated over and over to Dave's absolute delight.

"You work for me boy!" Dave screamed. This was good for Dave, because he still wanted to hurt people and blow things up. It had taken nearly two weeks before he had stopped yelling, "Burn them squirrels!" every time one of the little creatures scampered by.

Laken could finally see why the cherry picking was important. He had tremendous speed moving his sword from point "A" to point "B." The problem was that by the time he figured out where to move it, it was a little too late.

"Come on, you're not listening to your numa, boy!" Argus coached as he helped Laken up off the ground again. Laken was rubbing the spot on his shoulder that had been hit with Argus'ssword.

"I'm trying!" Laken's face flushed red.

"Boy, we don't *try. Try* gets you killed. Either you do, or you don't! And *you* don't, way too often!" Argus's face mottled into a darker shade of purple. "Will Gabriel be okay if you end up dead and I say, *Well, I tried?*" Come on!" Argus snapped as he lunged his sword at Laken.

"Sword coming," was the last thing Laken heard Dave say before being awakened by Argus…again.

"Wake up, you little sissy! Wake up! It's like I'm fighting my sister's kids out here! We are adding an extra hour of practice every day after dinner, and two hours extra on Saturday and Sunday! See you tonight at eight sharp!" Argus insisted as he stomped away.

After that class two weeks ago, Laken had done a full week of extra practices. Argus had tried blindfolding him, trying to force Laken to use Dave, with less than satisfactory results. Dave screamed, "I'm blind! I'm blind!" until Laken got hit with a sword. Argus tried switching stances, switching Laken's grip, even talked about changing Laken's hair style. Every morning Laken woke up stiff, sore, and bruised from head to toe.

Peyton snickered as Laken dressed. "Is Argus trying to make you the same color he is by bruising every square inch of you?"

"I love you, I love you, I love you!" Laken cried out again to his wings during wings class.

"Maybe we should ask if we can get another set of wings," Dave suggested.

"NO! I want my wings or no wings at all!" Laken blurted. At those words, Laken felt his body shudder. Laken looked at Dave with surprise. "Did you hear me? I will walk my Angel butt all over this world before I take another set of wings. You are my wings forever!" Laken shook his fist. At those words Laken's wings expanded out, and in an instant, Laken was flying. "Wooooooo!" Laken screamed as the air rushed through his hair, and his stomach was in his throat where it belonged. Laken could see Heath and Baylor clapping and screaming down below.

A group of students gathered to watch. "Let's give them a show!" Laken smiled, and his wings responded with a heart pounding jolt of speed as they rocketed skyward. They went through the first ring, dove and spun through the second. A huge crowd had gathered, screaming and cheering. Laken's stomach felt like it left his body as they lunged to the left through a ring, and then dove straight down towards another. Laken straightened out his body to allow for more speed. He passed through the ring and then ripped skyward giving him the feeling he left his skin behind. They went through the last ring to the screams of the crowd.

"Forty-one seconds! Forty-one seconds!" Laken could hear Peyton screaming.

"Forty-one seconds! You crushed the school record! Watch out Gabriel, here comes Laken!" Peyton screamed as the crowd chanted, "Laken! Laken!"

"Class, class, calm down. Calm down!" Cronus yelled. "THRRRRR!" a loud whistle from Cronus quieted everyone down. "Thank you. That was an unofficial time of forty-one seconds, because we didn't start timing him until he was already flying," Cronus said, much to the dismay of the students. Just then, the bell rang, and students began to scatter to gather their belongings and enter the Portal.

"I need 2000 words thought about the type of wing you have, its benefits, and some famous angels who have had similar wings," Cronus' voice called out as the boys entered the Portal.

"Art of War," each of their numas said.

"Get up! Get up, you little sissy!" Argus said as he hoisted Laken up off the ground again. "Come on! Listen to your numa!" Argus growled as he stared at Laken.

"I do, but by the time he says something I'm on the ground," Laken winced as a shot of pain in his shoulder vibrated down his arm.

"Let me try it slower this time." Argus rolled his eyes. "Tell me when you hear Dave!" Argus didn't really try to hide how annoyed he was.

Argus raised his sword, and at that moment, Laken heard something new. A shot of exhilaration shot through him. He had the answer.

Argus's numa said, "Downward strike, go slow for the sissy!" Laken didn't have to listen to Dave, who was no help. He could do what no one else could do. *He could tell what they were going to do before they did it.*

Laken's sword shot up in the air and blocked Argus's sword before it had even started a full downward strike. Argus stepped back, eyed Laken for a moment out of the corner of his eyes.

"Do that again, boy!"

"Sideswipe right!" Argus's numa said. Laken's sword shot up, but missed everything all together because it went to Laken's right, as Argus's sword connected with Laken sending him soaring to the ground.

"A little dyslexic there boy, but you were fast!" Argus said as he jerked Laken up by his collar.

"Right means left, right means left," Laken said to himself as he shook the cobwebs out of his head. "Do it again!" Laken demanded as he held his sword up in defensive position.

"Downward blow," Argus'snuma said, and Laken's sword was up blocking it before it had barely moved. "Side swipe left," Argus's numa screamed, and Laken had blocked that one almost before it had begun. "Step right! Sword right, slice across shoulder," Argus's numa yelled. Laken jumped to his own left, ducked under the coming sword and hit Argus in the ribs with his sword, barely moving the massive elf.

"I got you! I got you!" Laken screamed as Argus stood there in utter surprise.

"So you suck for months now, and I slow down one time, and now you are the sword master? Let's go again, pretty boy!" Argus said, a smile curling the corners of his mouth.

Before Laken had his sword up and was ready he heard Argus numa say, "Attack now, upward right." Laken dove to the right the blade sweeping across his cloak.

"Aagh, you have to cheat now, do you?" Laken mocked.

"Just teaching you that in battle there are no rules." Argus laughed.

"Lunge, over hand right!" Argus's numa boomed. Laken jumped to his right allowing Argus's forward motion to carry him past Laken, providing Laken the rare opportunity to strike him across the butt with his sword.

"You have been officially spanked!" Laken laughed, as Argus turned around with an expression of sheer disbelief, which quickly turned to a smile and then a hearty laugh.

For the next hour, Laken got the best of Argus all but one time, when Laken got confused on the left-means-right rule.

"Today you have improved a little." Argus's massive hand rested on Laken's shoulder, giving him a hearty shake.

"Thank you, Argus." Lakenwrapped his arms around the massive Elf's waist and gave him a hug. Laken had no idea why he did it, and he quickly backed away, embarrassed. The Elf's eyes looked like they had something in them, and Argus blinked rapidly. He turned and walked away and called out, "You're still a sissy."

Laken's heart was soaring as he walked into the Portal, Dave said, "Discipleship."

For the first hour of discipleship, Laken went on and on about his new-found secret. Gabriel just sat and smiled proudly, saying things like, "I'm proud of you" and "That is impressive." Finally, when Laken paused to gather a breath, Gabriel said, "Let's see if we can have the same success in Magic." Laken looked up as if his ice cream had just fallen off his cone.

"Gabriel, I, I, I'm not good at it." Laken stared down at his feet.

"You can be good at anything you work at. Didn't we find that out in swordsmanship?" Gabriel reminded him with a crooked smile.

"That is different. I'm good because I can hear numas, not because I practiced," Laken argued.

"I would disagree. Had you not developed the speed from picking cherries, even if you had known what was coming, you would be much too slow to stop it." Gabriel paused and regarded Laken. "We need to find that same type of secret for you to use in Magic."

Laken looked up at Gabriel, wondering if he could ask the question.

"No, better not!" Dave said.

"Why can't I ask him about my ability to make things burn and explode?" Laken argued.

"Because that is Fallen Magic! He will probably kick you out of the school."

"Laken? You have a question for me," Gabriel began to massage his hands together.

Laken hesitated. "Well, I don't want you to think less of me."

"Do you think I am that shallow? I cannot disciple you if you can't trust me with what is going on inside of you." He eyed Laken with curiosity.

"I… can make things explode, and make them burn up. I am really good at it." Laken finally let out.

Gabriel paused, still massaging his hands together. "That is Fallen Magic. You know this, I assume?"

"Yes, of course, but I don't understand why I can't use it." Laken's gaze fell to the ground.

"Fallen magic's power comes from anger and hate, and is used to generate fear. Our power comes from faith, and is used to produce hope." Gabriel raised his right hand and gently stroked his beard. Laken looked out across the meadow at some gophers chasing a rabbit then turned back to Gabriel.

"But isn't it written, *be angry and sin not*? If I use my anger against evil, how is that wrong?" Laken leveled his gaze. "Isn't it written we should hate evil, so how is me using my hate to destroy evil wrong?"

Gabriel took a long moment rhythmically stroking his beard. "You bring up some good points. I just worry that this path leads you to destruction. You cannot give a foothold to evil. If you give it an inch, it will want a yard. If you give it a yard, it will want all of you." Gabriel looked at Laken with alarm.

"I won't give it an inch. I will take that which is used for evil and use it for good. How can that be wrong?"

Gabriel thought for a moment. "We will slowly try this as long as you promise that the second I say no more, you stop using it forever." Gabriel eyed him concern.

Laken looked up at Gabriel. "I promise, I promise." Laken was more excited about Magic than he had ever been.

"The second your anger starts to control you, we will stop. You control your anger." Gabriel held his hand up.

"Yes, of course," Laken promised, a huge smile spreading across his face.

"That rock over there. If you want to destroy it, what do you have to think?" Gabriel pointed.

"I just think about something that makes me mad." Laken shot a smirk at Gabriel.

"Now, *there* is where the danger lies," Gabriel shook his head. "You cannot hold onto things in your past. You have to forgive, get over them, and move on. It is also written, *don't let the sun go down on your anger.* Meaning that when you wake up in the morning whatever, or whoever, made you mad yesterday is no longer something you think about. You forgive, forget, and move on."

"So how do I blow up the rock if I can't get mad?" Laken asked.

"I don't know the Fallen Arts, but I can guess," Gabriel put his finger to the side of his mouth. "What if the rock was attacking you, trying to do you harm? Anger in that circumstance would be understandable," Gabriel was now tapping his lips. "But once again, you have to control the anger. If the anger controls you, you will lose control." Gabriel gave another warning look at Laken. "I want you to concentrate on the rock, picture the rock attacking you, and unleash your power."

Laken looked at the rock and began to get mad at the rock. "Laken." The sing-song voice of Summer called his name from far off in the distance. Laken shook his head free from the thought and concentrated on the rock. He started to feel the anger rise up. "Laken!" Laken could hear his voice being called from a little closer now. Laken pushed the thought aside and refocused on the rock. "Laken! Help!" It was Summer's voice. Laken looked around frantically. He saw a blank and surprised expression cross Gabriel's face.

"What's wrong?" Gabriel asked.

"Summer. Summer is in trouble!" Laken said as he whipped his head left and right searching for the voice.

"No! I didn't do it! NOOOO!" Laken heard Summer scream, and then everything went into a blur as he felt himself in that all too familiar fashion being sucked out of the Garden and into the old shack. But this time, he wasn't in the basement. Laken was upstairs in Jack and Carla's shack. Laken blinked a few times to get his eyes to focus.

"You stupid girl! How many times have I told you not to touch my stuff!" Jack snarled. Laken's head spun to the sound to see Jack had his hands on Summer.

"You let me go!" Summer screamed. Laken felt the monster in him rise up, the anger and hate boiled in him. SMACK, Jack hit her across the face.

"NOOOOO!" Laken screamed, and the beast in him was released. Jack was sent flying with such force that he crashed completely through the wall, smashing into the refrigerator in the kitchen.

"Laken, no!" Summer screamed. Laken looked over to see Jack moving and moaning as his body lay sprawled out on the kitchen floor. "Laken, please don't!" Summer softly pleaded, tears splashing her cheeks.

"What the—" Carla's voice rang out as she pushed Summer out of the way and darted to Jack. Summer turned and quickly made her way down the stairs, throwing herself onto the make shift bed. Laken was on her heels the whole way.

Summer's sobs were now soft as she picked her head up and whispered, "Thank you, Laken. I know you mean well, and I love you!" Laken's eyes welled with tears as he went to hug her and then Laken felt himself being sucked out of the basement and back to Eden.

"Laken, you're back!" Gabriel's frantic voice rang in Laken's ear, as Laken fought to refocus his eyes. Laken shook his head and started to get up, but was immediately and forcefully shoved back down. "Stay down!" Gabriel's tone told Laken this was serious.

The ground began to swirl with wind. Laken looked up to see an army of wings coming down around them. Laken saw Gabriel say something to his numa, and then his numa split and dashed off. With a massive thud, a large group of Angels landed on the ground surrounding them.

"Must be over a hundred of them," Dave mumbled in astonishment. Each of the Angels' wings folded up, but did not disappear. They remained out, like soldiers standing at the ready.

"Gabriel! We are here for the boy!" a dark voice echoed from the back of the group.

"We both know I can't allow that!" Gabriel's voice was soft, yet serous.

"Gabriel, I do not wish to see you hurt. Just give us the boy!" The dark voice threatened, and Laken saw a tall skinny Angel wearing a Golden Cloak step out from behind what looked like a wall. No, not a wall, that was a qwerub. The qwerub was even bigger than Zog. His massive golden sword was on fire swaying left and right. The light from the sword lit up the skinny Angel's blackened face. The Angel's hair was white and pulled into a single ponytail. A large scar ran across his entire face diagonally, as if someone had started to slash an X across his face and only finished half way. He wore a crooked sneer, and his red teeth looked like they had been sharpened.

"Hurt me?" Gabriel gave a small laugh, and then his gaze became serious. "Broxst, I am getting old, but I do believe I still have it in me to take on twice as many as you have brought here tonight." Gabriel's eyes radiated a bright blue light that lit up the area they stood. Broxst paused. Laken saw fear flitter across his expression, and then it disappeared.

"Gabriel, we just need to take the boy in for questioning," Broxst's voice cracked.

"Questioning for what?" Gabriel's gaze was sharp and dangerous.

"Question him about the harming of a Human. You know this is against our laws. He has a hearing in front of the High Judge Vulgate tomorrow morning," Broxst sounded more confident. Gabriel looked down at Laken, who nodded his head in admission.

"Then I will bring him myself in the morning," Gabriel smiled.

"My orders are to take him now! You may come in the morning to the trial," Broxst warned. A few Angels took a half step forward.

"I will say this one last time." Gabriel's eyes glowed brighter than ever. The sky turned black, lightning cracked across the sky. "Laken will not be going with you!" Gabriel's voice shook the trees around them.

"Then you leave us no choice!" Broxst's voice echoed as he drew his sword from his hallow.

CHAPTER TWENTY-FOUR
Attack of the Squirrels

Gabriel's wings shot out his back, and his massive sword was drawn in a blink of an eye. Each of the other Angels had drawn their swords, bows, and daggers, and were slowly closing the surrounding circle. Laken attempted to stand up, but an invisible force shoved him back down and held him to the ground. A light green glow seemed to cover him in a bubble.

"Must be some sort of protective thing?" Dave wondered as Laken's gaze went back to the events outside the bubble.

"Don't move!" Gabriel warned, never looking in Laken's direction, his glowing blue eyes sweeping the area. A wave of nervousness washed over his skin.

The sky became even darker, as if it were angry. Thunder roared and lighting flashed across the horizon, shaking the ground. Before Laken could warn him, a dozen Angels behind Gabriel made a sudden move just as four massive oak trees smashed from overhead into the ground between Gabriel, Laken and the Angels. Leaves, dust, and debris filled the air like a smoke. The center tree swung a massive branch into the angels, sending them flying some 40 feet into the pond.

Laken noticed that the entire Garden was alive, and it was in protection mode. A large group of Angels was completely engulfed in shrubs and bushes. Screaming, they tried helplessly to fight their way out of thorny shrubs that had wrapped around them. Hundreds of large flowers had charged in and bound Angels up, toppling them to the ground, holding them so rabbits, squirrels, and gnomes could jump on their faces. An army of a hundred squirrels had three dozen other Angels rolling on the ground screaming, "Get them off!"

The huge squid in the lake was hitting unsuspecting Angels with massive boulders, thrown hundreds of yards across the garden. Positioned like snipers fifty yards away, Centaurs released their arrows with military precision. When those arrows found their mark, DAS agents collapsed where they stood. Unicorns thundered in, knocking Angels to the ground as they stampeded through the battle. Thousands of Fairies engulfed large groups of angels like a hive of angry bees, the angels swatting, and screaming as the fairies bit, scratched, and kicked. Laken thought he saw some spitting at the DAS agents.

The massive qwerub battled three oak trees, each of which were smaller than him. Limbs flew to the ground with each sweeping motion of the qwerub's sword. Broxst was not attacking, not even fighting. Instead, he seemed to be hiding behind the qwerub, sword drawn, hands shaking. A half dozen bears and a pride of lions charged into the middle, forming a protective circle around Laken and Gabriel. Overhead, three dragons circled, raining fire down upon the unsuspecting DAS Angels. Laken smiled, recognizing Peaches as the dragon leading the charge.

Just then, the enormous qwerub slashed the last tree down and charged toward them, knocking bears out of the way like they were flies. The qwerub was just ten feet away, fiery sword raised, when a deafening noise rocked the garden, as if a thousand wings were clambering down on them. The giant qwerub paused. He and Laken both looked up to see thousands of cherubs flying overhead. The lighting-filled sky was blocked by an insane number of cherubs, each with a tiny little bow and pencil sized arrows. The whoosh of a thousand tiny bowstrings rivaled the thunder as the cherubs released a volley.

"Don't think those little pin-sized arrows will do much," Dave remarked.

The arrows hit with thousands of pricking sounds. The qwerub screamed out in agony. Laken looked over to see the qwerub slashing his colossal arm through the air, trying to block the next barrage of arrows.

"He looks like a giant porcupine," Dave smirked. Another volley of arrows set in, dropping him to one knee. The qwerub looked over at Laken and Gabriel and an explosion of anger filled his face. The giant raised its sword and swung down on them.

As the sword crashed downward, Laken felt the heat from the sword, Laken closed his eyes iin anticipation of the blow. Moments passed, and no impact, Laken looked up to see the sword stopped just ten feet above them, the fire igniting the fury in Gabriel's face. Laken shook at the sight of Gabriel, as a storm of emotions swept thru him. He had a hand slightly raised, and Laken watched in amazement as he moved the sword like a puppet master moves a puppet. The sword was forced back. Then, in a blink of an eye, the sword and the Qwerub were sucked backwards and up. To Laken's total astonishment, the Qwerub was being held in the air by Grog, who had the qwerub up over his head. The indignant qwerub kicked like a trapped pig. Grog, with a large grunt, tossed the qwerub some hundred yards into the lake, where the squid wrapped itself around the qwerub, the two of them disappearing beneath the lake's surface.

"Sorry it took me so long!" Grog said with a smile the size of an elephant.

Grog's gaze shot to Broxst, who in an instant soared through the air, and with a massive thud, was in Grog's grasp. Grog's hands were a little bit bigger than Broxst's body, so all Laken could see were his arms flailing from the top.

"Grog, don't hurt the captain," Gabriel said softly.

"I suggest you all go home. I will see some of you at court tomorrow!" Gabriel's voice boomed through the clearing.

One by one the DAS officers caught a glimpse of their leader in Zog's massive hands and stopped fighting. It took only a few moments until everyone had stopped fighting, except for a few squirrels who were still kicking an Angel in the ear.

"Come on, all of you stop. Derek, Sam, Artie!" Gabriel smiled. One squirrel gave a final kick and then the creatures and trees all let up. "Grog, please put Broxst down!" Gabriel brow narrowed. Grog looked disappointed as he slowly lowered Broxst to the ground. Broxst's face was white as a sheet.

"You, you will be hearing from my superiors about this! This is cause to be cast into Outer Darkness!" As Broxst backed away, he tripped over a group of squirrels who had made a mini squirrel wall behind his legs. Broxst sprawled on the ground, rolled over and got up, shaking his clinched fist at the garden.

"Guys, come on. Leave him alone!" A smile tugged at Gabriel's lips. There was a slight pause as Gabriel regarded Broxst. Then Gabriel's eyes narrowed, his gaze locked to Broxst. Even more color drained from the captain's face.

"Broxst, we both know I will not be going into Outer Darkness. The Garden is my domain, and you have no rule over it. I will see you tomorrow at the courthouse. Good day,"

Broxst and the twenty or so DAS angels who were not too badly injured took off in flight towards the gate. The squirrels let out a high-pitched scream. The lions and bears roared. Fairies flitted wild about, screaming cheers of triumph. The trees jumped up and down in a ground-shaking victory dance, filling the air with dust, leaves, and debris.

Laken looked around at all the Angels injured on the ground. There must have been 75 of them. Some were attempting to get up. Most just lay still, moaning. They had arrows stuck in them, torn cloaks, cuts, scrapes, blood all around. A few held severed wings in their hands, while others were attempting to put their limbs back in place.

Gabriel held up a hand and there was a flash of bright light. Laken blinked hard a couple of times to see if it was real. The arrows had all disappeared, the blood was gone, and garments looked like new. It was just like the food fight. The angels all got up to their feet and took off in flight.

"Gabriel, are you all right?" Argus's voice snapped Laken out of his daze. Argus, Skar, Malgor, Gorgus, Jez, Gideon, and Zeetle were all running up to them.

"We are fine, we are fine. We had a slight disagreement with DAS, but in the end, they saw my side of the argument," Gabriel greeted his arriving staff with a smile. Gabriel leaned over and helped Laken up, the bubble dissipating with a small pop.

"I know how your disagreements usually go. You should have waited for us," panted Argus.

"I forgot to politely ask them not to attack until you arrived. For that I am sorry."

"What did they want?" Skar growled.

"Not to worry. Laken and I have a little trip tomorrow to clear the whole matter up. I will be explaining the details to you in just a moment."

Laken looked over at Malgor who was staring at him with disdain.

"They will kill the boy!" Malgor's numa screeched.

"Malgor, go talk to…" Gabriel paused. "You know what needs to be done." Gabriel's voice startled Malgor who quickly turned to Gabriel.

"Right away!" Malgor took off in flight.

"Grog, thank you," Gabriel said with a smile.

"Any time," Grog had that same elephant sized grin on his face.

"How did they get in?" Gabriel questioned, his expression became serious.

"They appeared out of the emergency portal, showed Zog their orders. I argued, but Zog said rules are rules." Grog said, anger in his voice. "When I saw what was happening, I left the gate to help." Grog paused as he lowered his head, "I might be relieved of my guard for that."

"No Grog, I would never let you be punished for doing what needed to be done." Gabriel smiled as Grog lifted his head with a hopeful smile across his face. "Let Zog know that I am the Lord of Eden and I am act-ing on behalf of the Almighty. No one enters Eden who is not a student, or staff member, unless I give you specific permission. I don't care if it is Eljen the Angelic Lord. He does not even enter without my say so. Do you understand?"

"Yes, my lord." Grog turned and disappeared, reappearing way off in the distance at the gate.

"If you will all excuse me, I need a word with Laken alone," Gabriel said as his staff members headed back towards the Portal. "You, too!" Gabriel addressed a group of squirrels peaking around a large rock. They scurried off.

"Come sit, Laken." Gabriel sat on a large rock and patted the spot next to him. Laken made his way over to Gabriel trying to figure out what he was going to say. How would he explain what happened? But how did they know? Does Gabriel know?

"Maybe I'm going crazy," Laken said to Dave.

"*Going* crazy, I thought you *were* crazy," Dave made a loco motion with his finger.

Laken sat down and looked out across the water.

"Laken, you were here, then you said something about Summer, and you disappeared. Then you reappeared, flushed and distraught. Then the officers showed up." Gabriel looked at Laken. "I need you to tell me what happened while you were away. Give me all the details. Please do not leave anything out, even if you think it will upset me. It is very important I get all the information."

Laken thought for a moment, and then told Gabriel everything. He talked about how he had gone to the basement every night since he had gotten to this world. How he had scared the bullies away from Summer. Why he wasn't in his bed when it caught on fire. Finally, he told what had happened just before DAS arrived. Laken paused when he got to the part with Jack.

"Laken, I won't get mad unless you don't give me all the information," Gabriel said softly. Bolstered by Gabriel's unconditional support, Laken told him what Jack did, how mad he had gotten, and what he had done to Jack.

"Not good, not good at all," Gabriel shook his head dismayed. Gabriel looked with his bold blue eyes into Laken's. "Remember the promise," Gabriel said.

"The promise?" Laken asked.

"You said that when I said no more Fallen Magic, you would stop," Gabriel said an outstretched finger pointing at Laken. "Yes… but that…but…it like… it just happened. We haven't given it time…" Laken tripped all over himself.

"You promised, and I am saying no more fallen magic." Gabriel interrupted Laken. "Do you see how you lose control? How anger took over, and the destruction it brought?"

"Yes, but I did something good. I stopped him from hurting Summer," Laken pleaded.

"Laken, I am sorry. I got caught up in the possibilities of you using Fallen Magic against them. I, the great, wise Gabriel, was duped by the enticement of power. Don't you see? Doing evil, even to stop evil, is wrong. Had you used faith with Jack, had some furniture move into harm's way, restrained him. Don't you see the difference? You would have been in control," Gabriel put a hand on Laken's shoulder. "Anger, hurt, and hate make Fallen Magic much easier. Oh, you can become powerful very fast. But it always leads to destruction, and it brings hurt and it brings pain." Gabriel's gaze held affection.

"Let me ask you this. Which Magic would Summer have wanted you to use tonight? Anger or Faith?" Gabriel said with a warm smile as he tilted his head slightly. Laken thought for a moment. He remembered that night when he was first brought to Eden and what it did to her, and then what it did to her this time.

"I'm doing it for my sister," Laken said to Dave. Then he turned back to Gabriel. "You're right."

Gabriel gave Laken a proud smile as he placed his hand on Laken's shoulder, the unnatural warmth sent a tingle down Laken's spine. "Hey!" Laken let out playfully. "I thought qwerubs were the most powerful beings here in the angelic world," Laken's eyes widened.

"Yeah, that is what I thought, too," Gabriel shrugged. "Well, enough fun for tonight. Now go get a good night's sleep. We have to keep you from being thrown into hell tomorrow." Gabriel rose and disappeared into the Portal.

CHAPTER TWENTY-FIVE
Laken is Sentenced to Death

"Laken, Laken, get up!" Laken heard a voice in the distance as someone shook him. Laken rubbed his eyes and looked up at Malgor.

"What, what are you doing?" Laken snapped as he whipped himself to his feet.

"I might ask you what you are doing, lying in the middle of the floor!" Malgor's cold voice echoed in the den.

"I was, well, my back bothered me so I slept on the floor." Laken's face flushed red.

"Whatever. Get dressed now. We need to get you to the courthouse," Malgor threw a cloak into Laken's face.

"Who's taking me?" Laken gave him a sharp look, then pulled the cloak off his face. Even though he already knew the answer, he was hoping he was wrong.

"I wish I had time to play the game *Answer the Boy's Foolish Questions*, but I don't. Now, get your cloak on. Let's go."

Laken unbunched the cloak he had subconsciously bundled up tightly while Malgor spoke, and then got dressed.

"I hate him, I hate him, I hate him. I wish he was a squirrel. Burn squirrel burn!" Dave went on.

"Really? I'm facing hell, and they send the devil to take me there," Laken interrupted Dave's tirade.

"Maybe you will luck out and Malgor will kill you first," Dave suggested as he pretended to be stabbed through.

"Very funny, very funny."

"I don't have all day to babysit you. Can we hurry?" Malgor said as he examined his fingernails.

"I'm ready. Let's go," Laken's jaw clenched.

Laken and Malgor exited the Portal out into the Garden and headed for the gate.

"Where are we going?" Laken panted as he attempted to keep up with Malgor's brisk pace. Malgor seemed to ignore the question while picking up his pace even more. The gates to Outer Eden swung open as Laken and Malgor approached them.

Grog gave Laken a half-smile and murmured, "Good luck."

"Shhhh!" Zog growled between clinched teeth.

"What took you so long?" Laken heard Argus snap. Laken looked over to see Argus and Gorgus casting a massive shadow on the courtyard.

"Everyone hold on, especially those of you who can't appearate," Malgor said coldly as he shot Argus a snide look, ignoring Argus'squestion.

"I will *appearate* your head from your…" but Argus was cut off with the jolt of air being sucked from their lungs. Light raced past and around them until their feet connected with ground and they could breathe again.

"I never get used to that!" Gorgus muttered as he shook his head, exhaling a huge breath.

Laken's eyes focused to see a sight of beauty and grandness unlike any other. In front of them were gates twice the size of Eden's, walls of gold and embedded jewels that stretched for as far as the eye could see. Laken had to squint because the glow of the city was so bright. The city was at least a hundred times bigger and more beautiful than Eden.

"Where in the heaven are we?" Laken gasped.

"Welcome to Shiloh! Capitol of the World," Argus's massive hand landed on Laken's shoulder. Laken exhaled a ragged breath at the impact.

"Can I get you tourists some postcards, or can we get moving?" Malgor turned and headed towards the gate. Once again, there were two qwerubs at the gate, who said nothing, but opened the gates to Malgor's request.

"Wow!" was all Laken could get out as they stepped into the city. The sheer business and hustle and bustle of the people, creatures, and animals was overwhelming. Shops lined the streets, fronted by carts and peddlers selling everything imaginable.

"We got dragon eggs for sale. Get Razor backs, Hellnins, Nochshires. You name it we got it," a small Dwarf with an orange hat was yelling out to the passersby.

"Nirbs, get your Nirbs; three shekels," a plump man shouted to the crowd.

"I thought everything was free?" Laken asked as he nudged Argus.

"Only in Eden." Argus shook his head. "That thinking went away thousands of years ago out here in the real world. Greed and lust fuels this place," Argus pushed past a couple of Ogres arguing about the price of a qwizzdidler.

"Real world?" Laken was confused. "Is this another dimension?"

"No, no. Eden and Shiloh are both cities in our–"

"Dimension," Laken finished his sentence.

"Yes. My point was just that Eden still preserves that perfect balance of all that is good and trustworthy, and Shiloh, well, Shiloh is like the rest of the world."

The words were barely out of Argus's mouth when something grabbed Laken's ring and took off. It wrenched Laken's arm, dragging him along the ground. Laken looked up to see a small Elf wearing only a red loin cloth wrapped around his waist pulling at the ring. Gorgus grabbed the Elf and lifted him off the ground causing him to release the ring—and Laken's arm, still attached.

"Looks like we've got a thief on our hands," Gorgus said shaking the elf vigorously.

"Put… me… down! Put… me… down!" the high-pitched voice squeaked in rhythm with each shake. "I… wasn't… stealing…, I…, I…" the elf paused as Gorgus held him dangling right in front of his face, staring eye to eye with him. "I, I, I thought it was mine!" the high-pitched voice rang out.

"Stop playing around. We need to get to the courthouse!" Malgor snapped and began to shove his way through the crowd, knocking vendors and pedestrians aside.

"Don't let me catch you again!" Gorgus warned as he tossed the Elf to the side. The elf let out a scream of agony as it smashed into a cart of Nirbs. Gorgus grabbed Laken's arm and pulled him through the crowd.

"It's the Chosen One, the Chosen One! I saw his ring!" the Elf's high pitched voice rang out from under the pile of Nirbs. Everyone's attention focused on Laken and the group. And then the rush of excitement hit, and everyone pushed and shoved to get a look at Laken. Argus and Gorgus placed Laken between them and began to push away anyone who got to close. But the crowd kept shoving, and pressing until Laken felt like he was being suffocated. Gorgus flung bodies up over the crowd, but the pressure kept coming. Then, a blinding green light made Laken wince, and then the intense light began to herd the crowd back until there was no one within ten feet of them.

"Hey, it's like the bubble from yesterday," Dave reminded.

"Good morning," Gabriel's bright voice rang out as he entered the lighted area. "I am so glad you decided to bring Laken in discretely."

"Gorgus here might as well be carrying a massive sign that says, *I'm with the Chosen One.*" Malgor's dark tone filled the bubble. Gorgus took a step toward Malgor, when Gabriel stepped between them.

"Let us go and do what we came to do. Follow me," Gabriel directed as he turned and headed the other direction. The green light followed them, keeping everyone else at bay. When they got to the end of the block, they turned left toward the massive capitol. The building sat well above the surrounding structures. There had to be over a hundred steps leading up to the building. Laken thought it looked like one of those castles from Aladdin, with the huge tower, and the big dome in the middle that reminded him of the White House in his old world.

"Huhhh, huhhh!" panted Argus and Gorgus as they reached the top of the steps. "Holy heaven, don't want to do that again." Argus could barely speak between breaths. They walked under the 50-foot-high roof, to the qwerubs standing at the door.

"Gabriel, Argus, Gorgus, Malgor, and Laken, here on appointment," Gabriel announced. The massive doors swung open, and they entered.

Laken's eyes swept the room and took in its business. Numas were flying all around the room. Blue ones, black ones, gray ones. Hundreds and hundreds of numas scurrying up down, around. The noise was deafening to Laken.

"I need your word that you will pass this law!"

"No he doesn't know, and he won't find out!"

"That's blackmail!"

These ear-piercing numas were hard to block out. Laken held his hands to his ears and began to look around at the Angels. This place had the feel of the main entrance, but the people were different. Their cloaks were quite a bit brighter, and here, probably a lot more expensive. Everyone's hair was perfectly coiffed. These Angels walked around with a sense of pride; even arrogance.

"Cronus! We found out where Cronus' relatives are all at!" Dave's eyes wide with curiosity.

"You are absolutely correct!" Laken laughed.

Just then, a cherub flew down from the ceiling and greeted them. "Gabriel, they are waiting for you in courtroom six. Please follow me," his little voice rang out, and the cherub headed left towards a long corridor.

The further down the corridor they progressed, the less the numa noise assaulted Laken's ears. They passed the first five courtrooms, until they reached the large open doors at the end that had two large Angels with the words DAS on their cloaks guarding the doors.

"Your associates will have to wait outside," one of the Angels insisted firmly. Argus and Gorgus gave the Angel a threatening glare, and then looked at Gabriel for direction. Gabriel gave them a nod, and they reluctantly backed out of the doorway. Gabriel took a step forward.

"That, that, that means you. Only the defendant is allowed," the guard stuttered timidly. Gabriel paused, grabbed Laken by the shoulder, and began to walk Laken in.

"I said you can't come in!" the guard repeated and reached to grab Gabriel's arm. The guard's arms snapped instantly to his side, and the doors slammed behind Gabriel and Laken.

"This hearing is for Laken only." Broxst sounded nervous as his voice echoed in the courtroom. Out of the shadows stepped Broxst and six of the DAS officers from the previous night. Each one had battle wounds resulting from the scuffle.

"Must have left before the healing," Dave whispered to Laken.

One Angel looked like he had bite marks the size of a squirrel's mouth lined around his ear. If it weren't for the gravity of the situation, Laken might have allowed himself a smile.

"We both know that our laws allow the defendant legal counsel, and if he is a juvenile, then a guardian also can be present. Either will do for me," Gabriel continued to usher Laken towards the front of the courtroom, dismissing Broxst's demand.

Laken and Gabriel stopped at the table positioned at the front of the room and sat down. In front of the table sat a substantial golden ornate judge's bench that rested some six feet above them. A large emblem the size of a tractor tire was centered under the bench. The words, *Our Court's Justice Determines Our Society's Morality* ran along the outside of the emblem. The center motto blazed, "In the Almighty we trust." The emblem glowed brighter than the material it was on.

DAS officers lined the courtroom walls. Laken counted 27 in all. Most had marks and scratches that revealed their presence in the garden last night.

"Please rise for the honorable Judge Volgate," a small, heavy-set angel standing next to the emblem said with a crackled voice. Laken and Gabriel stood as a door behind the bench swung open, and a short, very pale-skinned Angel in pure white robes emerged. To say the Angel was skinny was an understatement. His cheeks were sunken in so far, his face looked like a skeleton. His eye balls protruded from his face, while his nose looked like it wasn't there. Where his nose should have been, two slits moved with the rhythm of his breathing. His eyes made Laken shiver, as there was only white, no pupil, no iris color.

"I think this dude is dead!" Dave whispered in Laken's ear.

"What is this Angel doing in my courtroom?" Volgate's lifeless, cold, voice echoed as he pointed at Gabriel. Gabriel examined a small mark on his finger as if it were the only thing of importance in his life.

"Can someone answer me?" Volgate demanded.

"Aagh, he is the boy's counsel and guardian, my lord." Broxst's jumpy voice cracked and was two octaves higher than normal. Gabriel rubbed the small mark, smiling as if he were at the beach. There was a long pause while Laken looked nervously to Gabriel for some sort of response.

"He is not the boy's guardian, and he does not have the qualifications to be Legal Counsel. Remove him," Volgate growled. Laken looked around to see who would come remove Gabriel, but no one moved. The Angels all looked around anxiously to see who else would do it.

"Volgate," Gabriel began, but the bailiff interrupted.

"He will be addressed as 'Your Honor'!"

Gabriel's gaze slowly moved from his hand to Volgate, a bright blue light emanating from his eyes., "Volgate, let me state that I received my Order of Law Practice in 1987 B.C., I have defended and won seven hundred, thirty-two cases. I have been nominated thirty-seven times to the Supreme Angelic Court. Currently, I am the presiding Lord of The Angelic Judicial Committee, and there are two things I am sure of." Gabriel paused for a moment as the blue light intensified. "One, I do belong in here. Two, if these presiding are not conducted in a fair manner, your time as judge will be very short lived."

There was a long pause, as Volgate looked from officer to officer. "Fine. He may stay...For now!" Laken saw the DAS officers breathe a collective sigh of relief.

"You may be seated," the bailiff rang out. Laken looked over at Gabriel who nodded, and the two of them took their seats.

"Bailiff, read the charges!" Volgate's gaze shifted to the small man in front of the bench.

"Laken, a.k.a. the Chosen One, has been charged with one count of intention to harm a human, and seven counts of bringing harm to a human," the clerk read from his Rhema.

"Bailiff, collect the testimony from the defendant," Volgate ordered. The bailiff grabbed the numanator from his sac, walked over and had Dave spit in it. Behind the judge a large picture of what had happened with Jack and Summer began to play. "Laken, no!" Summer screamed and then the recording stopped.

"What do you say to this witness?" Volgate asked with confidence.

"Volgate, the problem is, there are no laws that states Angels cannot hurt humans." Gabriel's voice was like thunder booming throughout the courtroom. "Since we are unable to hurt humans, encoded into our DNA, there has never been the necessity of a law. Secondly, even if there were a law stating Angels can't hurt humans, Laken is a human and the law would not apply. Humans hurt humans all the time."

Gabriel continued his argument. "According to Laken's own witness, he intended to harm and he did harm a human. Laken is guilty and is thus to be sent back to his dimension." As Volgate raised his gavel and moved to strike it down, it stopped an inch from impact. Volgate's knuckles turned even whiter as he pushed with all he had, trying to get it down.

Gabriel drew himself to his full height, and the sound of 30 DAS officers taking a nervous breath filled the room. "Volgate, you mean to send an innocent boy to his death?" Gabriel's voice accelerated towards rage. Volgate now had two hands pressing down on the gavel in attempts to push it down. "All so your master, Brone, can return?" At that name, half the DAS officers let out a scream of pain and fell to the floor. Vulgate, Broxst, and half the officers were unaffected. "You have dishonored your position long enough," Gabriel declared, enunciating each word as he came around the table and began to walk slowly and purposefully toward Volgate.

Three officers drew their swords and were instantly hoisted into the air and smashed into the ceiling. Gorgus and Argus crashed through the doors, knocking the two Guards across the floor. Gabriel walked around the bench to where Volgate sat and grabbed him by the robes.

"As Supreme Head of these Lands as granted to me by the Almighty, I remove you from your judicial seat." Gabriel threw Volgate across the room into the chair next to Laken. Chains sprung from the chair around his hands and feet. Instantly another chair appeared, and Broxst's body floated through the air, landing in the chair. Chains once again popped out of the chair, wrapping around his feet and hands.

Gabriel's eyes had that blue glow of rage as he scanned the room. "These two are charged with treason against the Almighty, and for conspiring for the death of the Chosen One! Are there any objections?" Gabriel's voice thundered in the room. Not one guard moved a single muscle.

"I find you *guilty*. You will be sent to Dante's Hold, where you will await final judgment from the Almighty!" The gavel struck the plate. Volgate and Broxst let out a blood curdling scream as their bodies simply disappeared.

"This court is adjourned!" Gabriel boomed as the gavel struck again.

CHAPTER TWENTY-SIX
Baylor Falls in Love with a Squirrel

"Gabriel just sent two Angels to hell!" Laken whispered to Heath, Baylor, Peyton, and Cirque in the Great Hall.

"You have to be joking. Sent them to hell!" Peyton cried out, drawing attention to their group.

"Shh!" Laken said as he pulled the group in. "Well, maybe not hell, exactly, but Dante's Hold." He went through the whole story of the night before, Shiloh, and the courtroom.

"So where was Malgor?" Cirque asked.

"Someone has to be sent to hell for you to listen? Don't you have some girls to talk to?" Peyton murmured.

"Probably afraid he would be next!" Laken interrupted.

"Last night we followed Malgor to the gate, "The boys' heads whipped towards Baylor.

"What? You followed Malgor?" Laken couldn't believe it.

"Yes. We came down to see what had happened in the Garden, but you were gone. Then we saw Malgor skulking around all suspicious like, heading out of the gate," Baylor paused for effect.

"And…?" Laken prodded.

"Well, Cirque reminded me that Zog wouldn't let us out, so I watched from the Gate while he was a look-out. Some creepy looking guy's numa spit into his numanator. Real evil looking guy. I think he had small horns." Baylor continued, the boys' full attention on him.

"And?"

"And what? He headed to the Gate, and we ran back to the Portal, got back to the room and you were already in Summer Lan.," Baylor finished, looking like he just won the lottery.

"I want to know what's in his numanator!" Laken said to the surprised expressions of the boys.

"You thinking about breaking into his quarters and getting it?" Peyton rubbed his hands together.

"No! No!" Heath said. "That will get us kicked out of the school, and Mom will send us off with Volgate for sure."

"Stop it. This might be what we need to prove Malgor is evil, and save Laken's life. Plus, we are the Dragons, and we have to stick together." Peyton finished with a smile. "Come on, big brother. Dragons!" Peyton put his hand in the middle.

"'Dragons' is the best you could come up with?" Heath shook his head.

"Off the top of my head? Yes. Come on…Dragons." The boys looked at each other.

"Dragons!" Laken, Baylor, and Cirque all said as their hands reached in.

"Fine, but if we go to hell, I refuse to speak to you ever again." Heath put his hand in the middle.

"1-2-3 DRAGONS!"

"It's the day before Christmas and still nothing!" Heath complained to Laken, Baylor, Peyton, and Cirque, who were just waking up.

"Some call it Christmas Eve." Peyton slid his cloak over his head.

"Seriously, Malgor doesn't sleep. The Angel is a Narcolept Dragon. I don't think he has even been to his sleeping quarters," Heath said as he put on his sandals.

"Did he go out again last night?" Baylor asked.

"Yep, left right after lights out, and, according to Cirque, he hasn't come back yet," Heath said. Cirque nodded in agreement. "Seven plus weeks, and nothing. Who knows if the witness is even in the numanator anymore."

"Maybe he's a vampire?" Peyton suggested.

"Yeah, I thought that too, but then I realized if he were a vampire, he could kill Laken, which we know he can't," Heath said as he tied his sac around his waist.

"Even as a vampire, he couldn't kill me because of that teachers' oath thingy, right?" Laken argued.

"No, the oath doesn't work on vampires since they are dead, and it's because of that Gabriel would never hire one." Heath tossed his shoulders in confidence.

"But wait, the night he grabbed me, his hand didn't burn, so maybe he is a vampire. Maybe Gabriel doesn't know. I mean if Malgor is an Angel, he can't grab me!"

"Yeah, I walked myself through that. Malgor wasn't trying to hurt you the night when he grabbed you. That's why he didn't get burned. Vampire or not, it doesn't change the fact that we need to get that numanator," Heath added as he entered the Portal and disappeared.

Laken continued getting ready for the day, trying to go over the night's events. Gabriel had wanted Laken to really try and remember what happens as he is sucked into his old world.

"If you can go from our world to yours, it will make you a very powerful adversary for anyone who tries to kill you," Gabriel said that first discipleship session after the court date.

"Why do I go there? And where is it? Since it really isn't in their world," Laken added in puzzlement.

"That, I think I have figured out," Gabriel smiled. "I spoke with Bacchaus, the DAA. He informed me that they have not been able to assign a Guardian Angel for Summer."

"What do you mean, assign a guardian?"

"The DAA is in charge of humans' Guardian Angels. When you arrived, her guardian was replaced."

"Who was the replacement?" Laken asked.

"That they have not been able to figure out. Bacchaus said it was not any Angel of this world. And that was the clue I needed."

"Clue? What clue? Who is Summer's Guardian? Laken said.

"*You*, Laken. You are her Guardian."

"Me? How me?" Laken asked as he slowly shook his head.

"How? I don't know, but there is a connection between you two. I believe that connection is the love you have for her. Love allows us to do things that are impossible. It was love that allowed your mother to do the impossible." Gabriel paused for a moment, staring off into the distance. He then shifted his gaze back to Laken. "You are her Guardian. That is why when she is in trouble, you are sucked out of our world and into hers. At night, you told me she calls for you. That is why you spend your nights in the basement!" Gabriel smiled as if he had solved world hunger.

"So, Guardians live a life of being sucked away at any given time?" Laken asked.

"No, no. A Guardian lives his or her entire existence in the middle world, the world between ours and theirs. You are one of a kind. You can enter that world, which is a mystery in and of itself. For any other angel to do so, they must go through the Guardian Portal." Gabriel began stroking his beard. "The bigger mystery is that you can come back to our world." Gabriel looked at Laken as if he were a scientist studying a rare specimen.

"I believe you have the ability to enter the middle world any time you choose, making you invisible to both worlds, and thus a very powerful

Angel. This could be what helps you defeat Rick. For now, we will hold off on Magic, and focus on you moving into the middle world."

"I have no clue what happened last night. I fell asleep and woke up next to Summer," Laken muttered to Dave, snapping out of the memory of Gabriel's conversation. "There is no secret to it. It just happens. I have no control."

"You can control whatever you believe you have the power to control." Dave did a really good imitation of Gabriel.

"Knock it off," Laken laughed as he entered the Portal.

"Great Hall," Dave said.

Laken exited the Portal and headed towards the den's table. Laken looked around the Great Hall again, fascinated by what was around him. No matter how many times he saw the Christmas decorations, they left him in a state of awe. Gabriel-sized Christmas bulbs of every color floated overhead. Mixed with them were life-sized candy canes also floating.

"Must be hundreds of bulbs and canes," Dave sounded amazed.

In the center of the Hall stood a fifty-foot Christmas tree, covered in lights, bulbs, decorations and a life-sized Angel on top that seemed to be alive with movement. The ground was covered in snow, but not like the snow from home. This snow wasn't cold, didn't melt, but made awesome snowmen and snowwomen. The students had made over twenty of them and displayed them around the room. The snow also made for some intense snowball fights. A warm feeling filled Laken as he took it all in. He then looked around at the students to see an unusual amount of commotion.

"Why does everyone have their Rhemas out?" Laken asked as he sat down, looking at his den members with their heads in their Rhemas.

"Straight Arch Angels for me. Seven big ol' AA's." Heath put his Rhema down.

"Like that is a surprise," Peyton said, just a little annoyed. "Come on, little brother, how did you do?" Heath grabbed Peyton's Rhema.

"Give it back!" Peyton cried as Heath turned his back to him.

"One Arch Angel, three Angels, and three Humans. Not that bad, little brother. At least you didn't get any Cherubs, or worse, a Squirrel." Heath handed Peyton his book back.

"Hold on here. What in the world are you talking about?" Laken asked.

"Your grades are out, in your Rhema. Check it out." Heath nudged him with a big old smile on his face.

Laken reached into his sac, ruffled around and finally grabbed his Rhema and pulled it out. Laken's hand trembled as he set it on the table.

"I know I stunk up those mid-terms!" Laken muttered to Dave.

"Those were weird," Dave responded. The mid-terms had simply consisted of Laken walking into each class, Dave spitting in the cylinder, and that was the mid-term. The problem was that with the trial, and the angry Laken period, he knew he hadn't studied like he should have.

Plus, there was that third attempt on his life the morning of the exams. Someone put a baby Basilisk snake in his sac as he was sleeping.

When Laken reached into his sac to get out his Rhema, he felt a lurch, then a jerk, then smoke issued from his sac. Laken felt through the bag and felt a huge slimy thing he had not felt before. It took Laken, Baylor and Cirque to get the massive snake out.

"That's a baby!" Peyton said as Gabriel was examining it.

"Yes, just under a day old," Gabriel responded.

"A day. A day? And it's that big?" Peyton gasped.

"They are more poisonous the younger they are," Gabriel said as he flipped the snake over. "One drop of venom could kill every one of us in this room."

"How in the world did someone carry that in here and sneak it into Laken's bag without anyone noticing?" Peyton posed the question as his eyes swept up and down the length of the snake.

"My guess would be it was put in there some time ago as an egg. The Basilisk takes up to three months to hatch," Gabriel poked the snake with his foot.

"But I would have felt an egg!"

"Placed towards the bottom, and with all the other stuff in there, you wouldn't know it was in there unless you were looking for it," Gabriel said. "And where is the head?" he asked, looking at Laken.

"Don't ask me, I stopped at snakezilla there," Laken said as he put his hands up.

"Must still be in your sac," Gabriel said as he walked towards Laken. "No! Don't put your hand in." Gabriel's intensity startled Laken who yanked his hand from his sac. "The teeth can still emit the poison if touched," Gabriel explained as the color came back to his face. Gabriel leaned over, put his head and then both arms into the bag, so only the bottom half of him was outside the bag. Laken looked around at the other boys in the room, as Gabriel rustled through his bag.

"Slap his back side," Peyton mouthed and made a hand motion to Laken.

"Stop!" Laken whispered back.

"Hrfdtlis," Gabriel's muffled voice came from the bag, and out he popped, a head the size of Peyton's body in his hands. Gabriel tossed it to the floor next the snake's body. "Hold on," he said as he reached back into the bag, this time pulling out Laken's blood soaked sword. "Here is our savior," Gabriel announced as he held up the sword. "Must have sliced the head off. Quite a sword you have there, Laken," Gabriel smiled. The boys looked on in astonishment. "Okay, boys, get cleaned up. We have mid-terms today," Gabriel said as he disappeared into the Portal, the snake and blood disappearing.

"I was way too frazzled to take those," Laken reminded Dave as he opened his Rhema.

"Grades," Dave said as the book opened.

"What you get?" Peyton asked from across the table.

"Not bad," Dave answered.

Discipleship: Arch Angel

Art of War: Arch Angel (hits like an old woman)

Intro to Wings: Angel (lack of participation)

Study of the Chosen One: Arch Angel

Angelic History I: Purple

Introduction to Magic: Human

Numa Training Year I: Cherub

"Cherub, Cherub! That rotten no good..." Laken went on as they headed to the Portal. "Gabriel gives me a human?" Laken complained.

"You are a human. Don't complain," Peyton said.

"And what in the world is a Purple?"

"Don't sweat Miss Luvly's grades. I got a triangle from her," Peyton confessed, and the boys all let out a laugh as they entered the Portal.

"Let's go. Sit down! That means you, Chosen Boy!" Malgor spit out as the boys exited the Portal into Numa studies.

"Christmas must be the reason he is in such a good mood," Peyton said as he grabbed his seat.

"Yes, Peyton, what do you say you and I have a Christmas detention Saturday. You can help me decorate for the holidays," Malgor said in a slow tone. "Now, open your Rhemas to 'Nineteen Indispensable Traits of Great Numa' and read chapters twelve through sixteen."

"Ughh," issued from the students as the sound of Rhemas slamming on the students' desks echoed through the classroom.

"Somebody peed in his eggnog," Peyton whispered.

Laken opened his Rhema and pretended to read, while he focused on the conversation between Malgor and his numa.

"Stupid Christmas Ball," Malgor's numa grumbled. "We have better things to do than get our dress robes on and chaperone a bunch of giddy students."

"Laken, how is it that you can read by looking to the corner of the room?" Malgor's voice made Laken jump.

"Sorry, I, I was daydreaming," Laken said as he put his nose in his book.

"How about daydreaming about doing what you are told! Students, keep reading. I will be next door in my study." Malgor disappeared into the next room.

"He is one unhappy evil dude," Peyton whispered.

"Peyton, make it next Saturday detention also. Now get back to reading," Malgor said, his voice oozing from the next room.

"Tonight is the night!" Laken said as the boys sat down in the Great Hall for lunch. Plates with hamburgers and fries were being dropped off by cherubs. "The chrmstmsss blllth," Laken added, his mouth full of hamburger.

"Say it, don't spray it." Peyton wiped burger droppings off his robe.

"The Christmas Ball." Laken took a big swallow.

"I have no idea what you are talking about." Heath shoved a handful of fries in his mouth.

"Malgor is chaperoning tonight at the ball. He will have his dress robes on, which means no sac." Laken had an ear-to-ear smile spread across on his face.

"One, how do you know this? And, two, how do you know this?" Heath asked as he shoved another handful of fries in his mouth.

"One, don't worry about it, and two, it's an amazing plan. None of us have dates anyway, so we sneak to his quarters, get the numanator, prove he is evil, send him to Outer Darkness, and then open our presents tomorrow morning. It's the perfect plan." Laken took a large bite from his burger. He paused to look at each of his den members.

"Sounds good to me." Baylor said in agreement.

"How do you know I don't have a date?" Peyton asked with a stern expression.

"Because Mom couldn't make it," Heath quipped, and laughter erupted.

"Good one, bro, good one. You're getting faster," Peyton admitted as the laughter died down.

"Gentlemen, I will have to pass. I have five ladies counting on me for the ball tonight." Cirque's pearly white teeth shone from his huge smile.

"Who would have guessed? Only five?" Peyton snapped.

"No, it's fine. We will need someone at the dance keeping an eye on Malgor, so that will be your job," Laken said.

For the rest of the day, the boys spent every non-school minute inventing the plan, revising the plan, and going over the plan.

"Now, how do we get into his quarters? I'm sure the Portal won't just let us in," Cirque asked as he put on his dress robes.

"For the fifth time, I have already been in his room months ago. I grabbed his cloak as he entered the portal and followed him in. Of course, it was after thirteen other attempts, the most disturbing being when we shared a few moments in the bathroom together, me blending into the wall as he released some bears from the cave," Heath recalled while the boys let out an, "Oooooh, gross," followed by laughter.

"I'm off, ladies," Cirque announced as he flashed a smile and disappeared into the Portal.

"Keep your eyes on Malgor, not the ladies, you big dumb idget," Peyton called out after Cirque was already gone.

Ten minutes later, Cirque's numa arrived letting Heath know Malgor was at the ball and confirmed that his sac was not with him.

"Let's go," Heath said, and as they entered the Portal his numa said "Malgor's quarters."

"Ow, watch what you're doing."

"Hey, you stepped on my foot."

"Shhhh," Heath interrupted. "Let me get some light in here." Four small blue fireballs erupted from Heaths fingers and went to each corner of the room, giving off a slim frisson of light. As Laken's eyes adjusted to the low light he began notice how much junk was all over the room. Swords, shields, and axes were in a pile in one corner. Robes and cloaks were thrown all over the floor.

"What is that smell?" Peyton plugged his nose. "Smells like a turd having babies."

"No wonder he doesn't sleep here," Baylor said as he gagged. Laken noticed his bed no sheets on it, just Malgor's professor cloak draped across it.

"This isn't take-a-tour of Malgor's room. Come on, we need to find the numanator quickly," Heath barked as he headed over to the dresser.

Baylor got down and looked under the bed, Peyton searched the wall behind the portal, and Laken found his way over to the far wall. Newspaper clippings that had been torn out carelessly were stuck to the wall.

"I didn't know you got the newspaper here," Laken said.

"We don't. Our news comes through our Rhema, why?" Heath asked and then grimaced as he held up what looked like a big pair of underwear. Laken took a closer look at the headline on each clipping. *Seven Bodies Found Burned Beyond Recognition, No Suspects, Five Bodies Found Burned Beyond Recognition, No Suspects....* Then Twelve, then Three, then Seven again. Winter *Wisconsin Daily Press: Cabin Destroyed, Woman's Body Found, Child Still Missing.* Laken read the caption then looked at the picture of the lady. Long black hair, dark complexion, striking brown eyes. She was beautiful. Laken's eyes went to the next clipping. Laken recognized this small-town paper. It was the *Vineyard Gazette.* Carla got it every Sunday for coupons. The clipping was from the classifieds circled under Lost and Found: "Two babies found the night of the comet. If you have any information, please call..." Laken's heart felt like it was going to pop out of his chest. His eyes looked back to the woman. The dates were two days apart. Was this his mom? She definitely had his eyes. Laken looked below the picture. DANIELLE. That was the name Gabriel used. It was *her*. Laken's heart was racing. He ripped the picture of the wall, and was putting it into his sac when a hand stopped him.

"What in the world are you doing? We can't take that. He will know," Heath warned, as Laken tore his hand away.

"This is the only picture of my mom, and I'm taking it."

"Shhh! Shut up," Baylor's voice came from underneath the bed.

"Let me have your Rhema," Heath demanded.

"What? No! Get away," Laken said.

"Trust me," Heath insisted. There were a few moments pause, and finally Laken shook his head, reached into his sac, pulled out the Rhema and handed it to Heath.

"Copy," Heath said as he opened the Rhema. "Put the picture in here." Heath smiled. Laken hesitated, then carefully placed the picture in the book. Heath closed the Rhema, then opened it handing Laken the picture. "Now go put it back," Heath ordered as he held up the perfect copy of Laken's mom now in his Rhema. Laken looked at Heath, then the picture, then went back to the wall and put the clipping back. "Now, let's get back to looking."

Each the boys went back to work searching everywhere for the numanator. Laken dug through some clothes that seemed to be blood-soaked. He found some stacks of newspapers from his world. Baylor flung all sorts of stuff out from underneath the bed.

"I found it!" Heath said. The boys all rushed to his side. "Bottom drawer." Heath reached into the sac and fumbled around. He first pulled out an old hat, then a flask of some sort of green bubbling potion. "What is this?" Heath asked as he pulled out a red glowing stick. "Looks like we found some Goblin fire!" Heath smiled as he put the stick back. "Aaagh, here it is, I think." Heath pulled out a dingy old numanator.

The boys looked at each other in excited anticipation. "Play last!" Heath ordered. The numanator showed Laken watching Malgor earlier in the day. "Back!" The scene showed Laken the day prior. "Back." Laken again. "Back." Laken, then Laken, then Laken sleeping.

"That proves it. He comes in our room when you're sleeping," Peyton cried.

"Back," Heath said, and the numanator showed Laken training with Argus while Malgor looked on from a distance.

"You've got a serious stalker there!" Peyton shook his head.

"Yeah, looking for the perfect time to kill me," Laken murmured.

"Back, shhh, listen," Heath said, as very dark man appeared on the screen.

"Malgor, our Lord is getting very impatient. Three tries and the boy still lives!"

Then Heath jammed the numanator back into the sac, and closed it back in the bottom drawer.

"What the heck are you…" Laken started, but Heath grabbed him.

"He's coming. Stupid Cirque didn't notice he was gone till now! We have to go!" The boys rushed to the Portal, but just as they got to it a dark figure walked out of it. Baylor knocked it out of the way as the boys holding hands rushed into the portal, leaving the shouts and curses of an outraged Malgor behind.

Out of the Portal, the boys fell to the ground.

"Holy heavens, that was close," Peyton said.

"Close? He *has* to know it was me," Baylor gasped in frustration.

"Where in the world are we?" Laken asked as he looked around the room that was bright white, with millions of red hearts painted all over it. The boys stood up, looking around.

"Over there!" Peyton said, pointing. Way off in the distance of the gigantic heart room were a hundred cherubs.

"Hey, they are kind of cute," Peyton admitted as the cherubs slowly flew closer. They each had a little white diaper-looking cloth wrapped around their bottoms and little hearts for wings.

"Hey, little buddies, where are we?" Peyton asked. Each of the cherubs reached back and whipped their bows around to the front. "Hey, what you guys doing?" In the flash of an eye, each bow had a tiny arrow with a little heart at the tip, drawn back. "They are attacking! Run!" Peyton screamed as a hundred arrows flew towards them. The boys dove into the Portal, rolling out of the Portal into a room full of squirrel statues. Big statues, little statues, fat statues, all statues of squirrels.

"Anyone get hit with an arrow?" Heath asked.

"Not me," came a relieved answer from Laken.

"Me neither," said Peyton.

"I love you, squirrel, yes I do. I love you so much." The boys looked over at Baylor, who was kissing a small squirrel statue. "You are my princess, and I am your prince. I love you. I love you. I love you,"

Laken, Heath and Peyton all looked at each other and fell to the floor laughing. Each time they stopped, gasping for air, Baylor would say something to his squirrel that would start the giggle fits all over. Finally, when the boys' sides hurt so bad, their eyes were cried nearly shut, Heath made his way over to Baylor and pulled the five tiny heart arrows out of Baylor's behind. As the last one was pulled out, Baylor shook his head then looked around in total surprise.

"Where in the world are we? Why am I holding this squirrel?" Baylor asked dumbfounded as the boys fell over in laughter again.

As the boys entered the Portal, Peyton called out," Bye, snookems, I love you!" And each of their numas said, "Dragon's den." Shock and guilt flicked across each of their faces as they stood in front of Gabriel and a bright red (nearly purple) faced Malgor.

"They were in my private quarters!" Malgor shouted.

"Well, you have been trying to kill me!" Laken shouted back.

"Had I caught you in my room, I might have!"

"Laken, Heath, Baylor, and Peyton, I am very disappointed in you," Gabriel said.

"He has Goblin fire in his sac!" Laken blurted.

"Liar and a thief. Check my sac," Malgor snapped.

"I'm sure you removed it. Probably removed the guy telling you to kill me on your numanator also." Laken's face was beet red with anger. The monster in him was growing. "You killed my mom!" Laken took a step towards Malgor. He could feel the beast in him, ready to be released.

"Malgor, go, now! We will talk more of this later," Gabriel said with an air of haste, his gaze on Laken's red expression. Malgor shot Laken a glare and then disappeared into the Portal.

"Laken! Laken! Look at me!" Gabriel gave Laken a tug on the shoulders so he was looking at Gabriel. "Let it go!"

Laken released a large breath, shook his head and felt some of the anger release. Gabriel looked into Laken's eyes, "Laken trust me. The truth will come out very soon. But I need you to trust me," Gabriel implored softly. He then turned his gaze to the other boys. "Garden duty with Professor Zeetle for the next month of Saturdays should be punishment enough for all of you."

Gabriel turned abruptly and whisked his way into the Portal.

CHAPTER TWENTY-SEVEN
Laken Gets a Christmas Present From?

"Merry Christmas! Merry Christmas! Come on, Laken, get up!" Peyton's voice echoed in his dream.

"Let me sleep!" Laken argued as multiple hands shook him.

"Come on! Let's open presents!" a chorus of voices rang out. Laken opened his eyes to see the whole den staring down on him. Laken rolled over, got to his knees and stood up in the middle of the den.

"We should put a mattress on the floor right there, since that is where you end up most nights," Baylor joked.

"Whatever. Let's open gifts," Peyton began to pull presents out from under the Christmas tree and pass them out. They had put the tree up weeks ago, but Laken still couldn't get over how beautiful it was. Taking up an entire corner of the common room, it stretched from the floor to the ceiling. The bows were perfectly formed and the needles had a dark glossy sheen. They had spent any free time they had adding ornaments and lights and tinsel. It was a far cry from the pitiful tree at the end of the Charlie Brown special Summer forced him to sneak upstairs and watch every year.

"This one is for me, and this one's for me. Oooh, here is one for *Smoochems* Baylor, from a certain squirrel," Peyton got his dig in and they all laughed.

"Give me that. It's from my mom," Baylor snatched the gift from Peyton.

Laken thought of the picture in his Rhema. He must have looked at it fifty times last night. Why his mom? Why him?

"Malgor will pay!" Dave hissed.

"Laken, here is one for you," Peyton interrupted Laken's thoughts.

"Thank you." A thin smile played on Laken's lips as he took the gift. "Our first gift ever that wasn't from Summer." Dave whispered.

"We always got a rap on the back of the head followed by, *Merry Christmas, brat!* from Jack." Dave reminded Laken.

"Hahaha, good point."

Laken turned the gift over in his hands, staring at it as if it was a precious gem. The gift was the size of a shoe box, wrapped in golden paper with a huge satin red bow with loops and curlicues all gathered on top.

"Who in the world could this be from?" Dave watched carefully.

"Don't know. It can't be from anyone in the den." They had opened those gifts last night after being caught.

"Hey it's after midnight, let's have a little fun tonight!" Peytontossed the gifts to each of the den members. Peyton had whittled each of them a statue out some sort of glowing wood. Laken got a Chosen One ring, Heath got a brain, Cirque got a mirror, and Baylor got a large squirrel with the phrase 'I love Baylor' written on its chest. Heath had given each of them a coupon for three homework answers, redeemable at any time. Cirque had given them each a large picture of himself.

"This is the best Christmas ever!" Peyton screamed as he opened Cirque's gift, and the boys did a great job of hiding their laughter as Cirque proudly nodded his head saying, "Yes, it is, yes it is."

Laken had a hard time coming up with anything, until finally Dave suggested getting some 'nirple' from Soowoodoo's.

"Great idea," Laken thought. He then asked Gabriel, and during their session they went to Soowoodoo's.

"Convincing Gabriel to go to Soowoodoo's was a little too easy," laughed Dave. Each of the other den members seemed to love Laken's gift.

Laken's thoughts came back to what was going on in the room as he shook the new found present. Something heavy rattled in there. A storm of emotions galloped thru him.

"Open it up!" Peyton said excitedly. Laken looked over and saw Peyton had already opened up his half dozen gifts. His twelve-inch high Gorgus action figure was fighting three other warrior figures.

"It looks alive," Dave said in amazement. He watched as Gorgus hit one figure with the hilt of his sword and was now lifting another warrior off the ground, and threw it into the third warrior.

"That's pretty life-like," Laken said puzzled.

"Yeah, they're second generation AI's—Angelic Intelligence," Peyton explained as he pushed a switch on the back of Gorgus and Gorgus shouted, "Gorgus Smash!" and then stopped moving. Peyton switched the other warriors off and turned back to Laken's gift. Laken looked at the tag which said, *You will know who this is from…* Laken shrugged his shoulders and opened up the gift very carefully, not tearing the wrapping paper.

"Rip it open!" Peyton screamed. But to Laken this was his first Christmas, and every present was special to him. He wanted to savor the moment, and he wanted to hold onto the paper and present forever.

"Wow!" Dave screamed as Laken looked down in amazement. It was a box of Nirbs.

"Gabriel," Laken said softly.

"Hey, Laken, there is another one here for you. This one isn't labeled," Heath eyed him with curiosity. Laken looked over at smaller box that was wrapped in what looked like an old red cloth and then tied at the top with some green worn rope.

"Based on the wrap job, I would say there is a turd in there," Peyton joked. Laken drew a ragged breath as he reached over and took it from Heath. He felt it, weighing it. Then he shook it.

"I have no idea," Dave said. Laken grabbed the rope at the top untied it and the red cloth fell away from the gift. Laken looked down at a numanator.

"Wow! You don't get one of those until you pass fifth-year Numalistics!" Heath gave him an expression of sheer disbelief. Laken picked it up and held it out. As he did so, a holographic picture popped up.

The scenery was out in the woods, by a small cabin. "I love you, Jason," spoke a beautiful voice that sent an unprecedented warmth through Laken's body. Then the picture changed to a newborn baby in the grass. "I'm going to get you," the beautiful voice called, as the woman picked the baby up and spun the baby around in her arms. The woman! It was the woman from the picture. It was his mother. Laken held the numanator closer to his face and watched as she hugged and kissed the baby.

"That must be you!" Dave said, "Jason, huh? What a weird name," he joked.

"I love you, Jason, and I love you," Laken's mother moved close to a point off screen—would that be the numa whose memories these were? And then the holograph disappeared.

"HOW DO WE TURN IT BACK ON?" Laken hollered in desperation.

"Easy, killer. Just think what you want it to do," Heath made a calming motion with his hands.

"Replay," Dave cried out, and the scene played again, stopping again at the same point.

"Why does it stop? How do we get the rest?" Laken demanded.

"Let me take a look at it," Heath offered as he took the numanator and looked it over.

"Nope, that is all that is on there. Whoever did it knows what they were doing. They erased the information that tells you whose numa is the witness," Heath said thru tight lips. "Love to know who that was. Bet it was your father."

December turned to January, January to February, and February to March. Laken had watched the witness of his mother thousands of times, trying to get a glimpse or clue of his father. Anytime he felt down, all he needed to do was turn it on and she cheered him up. He knew the hologram was a memory, not a person, but to Laken, she was as close to a mother as he had ever had.

There hadn't been another attempt on Laken's life since the Basilisk.

"I think they are afraid of me!" Peyton said one day as they were mulling the question over in the den.

"I think they are planning something big," Heath suggested, ignoring Peyton.

"Good, that will help me sleep at night," a smile curling the corners of Laken's mouth.

"You don't have to worry. You are never here when you sleep," Cirque said as he studied himself in the mirror.

Gabriel and Laken had been working tirelessly the whole month of January, but with no success on getting Laken to the middle world.

"I can't do it!" Laken cried out one day in frustration.

"That is the problem, you think you can't," Gabrie said with a weary smile.

"Gabrielisms!" Laken said under his breath.

"So much of your mom is in you, Laken. Have I told you about the time she saved your life doing the impossible?" A fresh smile now played across his expression.

"Yes, like a thousand times…but tell me again," Laken sighed with a fake irritation. Laken loved the story, and could hear it all day long. He just didn't want Gabriel to know it.

The second Monday in February, Gabriel began to have Dave spit in the numanator, and then they studied the moment Laken went to the middle world.

"Summer is the reason," Gabriel said one day. "Laken, I will be right back." With that, he disappeared.

Laken looked around at all the animals playing; beautiful trees full of flowers, and fruit of all colors. He had been so busy training he'd forgotten how gorgeous and peaceful the garden was.

"Laken, help!" a voice called in the distance. Laken whipped around to see where the voice was coming from. Summer, and she was a couple hundred yards away.

"What is she doing here?" Dave couldn't comprehend it.

There was no time for that, though. A dragon was just feet behind her, his razor teeth shown mouth collapsing on her. Laken had to help her. He didn't have time to get there, but he *had* to. Laken saw himself between her and the dragon, and in an instant, he was sucked from his spot and was between Summer and the dragon. The dragon and Summer instantly disappeared.

"That confirms my suspicions." Gabriel's voice came from behind Laken. Laken whirled around confused and annoyed by what had just happened.

"Where are Summer and the dragon?" Laken said as he frantically looked around.

"Sorry for putting you through that. It was just an illusion to test my theory."

"A test? You scared me half to death for a test?" Laken threw his hands in the air in frustration.

"I do apologize, but it proves that the connection of love you have for Summer allows you to do things impossible even for me," Gabriel said as he stared off in the distance.

"What? You can move across the field in an instant," Laken said puzzled.

"Oh, of course I can, but I can't go to the middle world, and it is the connection for Summer that allows you to. This is a connection that supersedes even the processes of our world. We can't even assign her a guardian, because of your connection, Because of *love*," Gabriel said dreamily, as if appreciating fine art. They stood there for a moment, as Gabriel stared off towards the lake.

"Now, rather than focusing on getting to the basement, I want you to focus on getting to Summer," Gabriel said, breaking the silence.

Laken thought hard about Summer.

"Go to Summer, go to Summer," Dave repeated over and over.

"Nothing!" Laken said five minutes into it as he released a heavy sigh. "It doesn't work."

"No, it works. You just have to make it work," Gabriel said. "I want you to picture her needing you. Go back in your mind when she desperately needed you and focus on that."

Laken thought about the time when they were kids and the cops came, and the time Jack found them counting the money, but, no. The strongest one was the last time when he hit her. Laken pictured this, replaying it in his mind. The beast in him was growing strong. Laken had to get there, He had to save her. Then Laken felt the air being sucked out of his lungs and him being taken from this world, and then it all stopped and he was standing next to Gabriel.

"You were gone for a second," Gabriel's lips peeled back from his white teeth.

"I almost did it. What went wrong?" Laken's eyes widened.

"You probably stopped focusing on Summer too early. Let's try it again. This time, focus until you get there."

Laken focused again, until he felt himself ripped from the world, and found himself in the basement. Summer was there counting her money.

"Two dollars and sixty two cents, two dollars and sixty three cents… Laken, is that you?" Summer called out as she looked around the room. Laken walked over and put his arms around her trying not to let them pass through her. "I miss you," she whispered as she gave herself a hug and shook herself.

"Laken, can you see me?" Gabriel's voice was audible but distant. Laken for the first time ever looked up. Above him was Eden.

"Why haven't we ever looked up?" Dave shook his head.

"This really *is* the middle world," Laken said to Dave. Laken walked underneath a group of squirrels playing what looked like football with an acorn. He then found himself staring up at the stream.

"Cool, check out the fish." Dave could barely contain his excitement.

"Alright, Laken, come back." Gabriel said.

"I wonder how we do that?" Dave asked.

"Don't know, never had to," Laken said. Laken focused on leaving, and focused on leaving some more.

"Nothing! Great we are stuck here till morning," Dave complained.

"Laken, close your eyes and see Summer safe," Gabriel called out. Laken closed his eyes and pictured Summer giving him the hug, and all was fine. Immediately, his body was released from the middle world, but he began to sputter and cough. He was wet and couldn't get air. Then he was lifted out of the water and put on dry land.

"An important lesson is to look above you and see where you will be coming out. A stream might not be your best bet." Gabriel laughed as Laken got up, still sputtering water.

For the next month, Laken worked solely on going to and from the middle world. He got quite good at it, and had used it a number of times to scare the den members. Once, he even used his new skill to spy on Malgor and Gabriel's conversation, though Gabriel kept looking down at him as if he knew he was there. Gabriel whispered into Malgor's ear, and the two parted ways.

It was now the second week in March, and the big buzz among the students was the DC coming up the first Saturday in April.

"The score is Owl 31, Serpent 30, Unicorn 28, we are tied with Lion at 27. Poor Lamb is at 13. We are sitting pretty," Peyton rattled off excitedly as they all sat down in the Great Hall. "If we get first in our four," as he pointed to everyone but Cirque, "and of course zero with Robin Hood here, and seven points on swords with Laken, we would have--"

"Seventy-four, and if Serpent did their best on every event, except cloak, which would be last for them, they would score 71," Heath interrupted.

"Yes, and make us DC champions and we would live happily ever after!" Peyton exclaimed with that five-year-old–at-a-candy-store smile.

"Hey, Cirque and I were talking, and we think we should try and follow Malgor one of these nights." Baylor's change of subject caught the boys by surprise.

"You mean past the gate?" Laken asked.

"Yeah, I think we need to find out what he is up to," Baylor offered a crooked grin.

"You know we can't go out. Zog will never allow that," Laken lips tightened.

"Well, I was thinking. What if Laken goes to his secret place while holding our hands? We then walk by unnoticed," Baylor said as he looked at Cirque who gave Baylor a nod of approval.

Heath thought for a moment. "I assume you are correct. Makes sense, otherwise you would end up naked in the middle world. You must take anything connected to you."

"Can't hurt to try!" Peyton added.

"Let's do it tonight then," Cirque suggested as he winked at a couple of girls walking by.

"Tonight is the night we take Malgor down!" Peyton could barely contain his excitement.

CHAPTER TWENTY-EIGHT
The Night Malgor Went Down

"Shh!" Peyton's face flushed in frustration as a loud *snap* came from the branch Baylor had just stepped on. "You're like a dragon in a mirror shop. Watch where you are walking, you big ox."

"I'm trying. You walk with these feet and see how quiet you can be," Baylor hissed back.

Laken looked at Baylor's feet under the full moonlight.

"He has a point," Dave said, thinking that Baylor's feet looked like two big dogs.

"Alright, let's wait here," Peyton held his hand up. *Crack, crumble, snap!* Baylor stepped on an entire bush.

"Sorry, sorry," Baylor whispered as he yanked his foot out of the bush with another barrage of noises escaping out into the night.

"How about we put out a big neon sign that says, *Malgor, we are watching you?*" Peyton threw his arms up in mock defeat.

"I'm sorry," Baylor grimaced under his breath as he hid behind a tree. Laken looked over and smiled. Baylor's massive frame stuck out at least two feet on both sides.

"You big Ogre. I could see you from heaven. You will have to lie down behind those bushes," Peyton said, his cheeks flushed red. Baylor walked over to the bushes, stepping on every single branch along the way. "Should have brought Peaches instead. That big dragon would be much easier to hide," Peyton whispered.

The night air was cool, with a light breeze brushing through their cloaks. The soft sounds of small animals scurrying through the leaves on the ground complimented the calls of bullfrogs echoing from the lake.

Laken looked up to see a sky that went on forever, splattered with stars. Big stars, little stars, clusters of stars throughout.

"We just don't look up that often, do we?" Dave observed with a smile.

"Shh! Someone is coming!" Laken looked towards the Portal to see a figure dressed in black skulking through the shadows. Laken held his breath as the figure stopped some ten yards from where they were. The moonlight lit up Malgor's face under the hooded cloak as he turned towards them. Laken held his breath. His heart felt like it was going to give him away, pounding through his chest.

"Run! Run! He sees us!" Dave screamed.

"No! Heath said never move, even when you think they see you."

Malgor's eyes scanned the tree line pausing with his line of sight directly on Laken, and then continuing on. Malgor turned and headed towards the Gate.

"Whew!" Laken released his breath. "That was close."

"Well done. You did just as I taught you." A smile played on Heath's face.

"I think I pee'd my pants," Peyton joked, as the boys covered their mouths to muffle their giggles.

"We better get moving if we are going to keep up," Heath said, and the boys began to move through the forest. Malgor reached Grog and Zog, and the gates opened up and then shut behind him.

"This is far enough. We better do it here," Cirque's voice cracked as he held up his hand.

"Kind of far, don't you think?" Heath argued.

"Yeah, we must be fifty yards out," Peyton's brow narrowed.

"No, why take a chance?" Cirque met their gaze.

Heath and Peyton looked at each other, and then in unison, nodded their heads and said, "Okay."

There was a pause, and then Peyton took charge. "Everyone hold hands. Laken, you in the front." Peyton grabbed Heath's hand and then Baylor's hand. Baylor grabbed Cirque's hand who then grabbed Laken's. "Let's go."

Laken had gotten quite good at this over the last few weeks. He could go in and out of the middle world without much thought at all. There was a jerk, air sucked from his lungs, and then they were in the basement. Laken could see amazement in his friends' eyes as they looked around. They got an even bigger shock when they looked up.

"Holy heavens. That is the garden up there," Baylor said as he yanked Cirque off the ground holding his hand up.

"Put me down!" Cirque gasped as he dangled four feet off the ground.

"Sorry," Baylor apologized as he lowered his hand.

"Look at this dive!" Peyton said as the boy's gaze swept the dim, small, cluttered basement. "Is that your bed?" he asked, pointing his and Heath's hand towards a piece of plywood up on some blocks.

"Yep. Nothing but the best here at Jack's."

"Shhh. Someone is coming!" Peyton whispered as he tried to pull the others down. "Relax. No one can hear us or see us,"

Laken smiled. The old steps cracked and moaned as a pair of legs became visible coming down the stairs. Out of the shadows stepped Summer, her long blonde hair pulled back, blue eyes gleaming, and a small smile on her face.

"Laken, you're here. I can feel it." Her eyes widened.

"Man, she is *hot!*" Peyton said. Laken gave him a heated glance. "Sorry!" Peyton ammended quickly

Summer turned to the right and headed right for Peyton and Baylor. Baylor panicked and let go of Peyton's hand.

"Nooo," the voices of Peyton and Heath trailed off as they were sucked away. The other boys looked up to see them throwing their fists up in disgust.

"Sorry!" yelled Baylor.

"Go ahead without us. Get a move on!" Heath shouted back down towards the ground.

"Yeah, we better catch up before we lose him," Cirque announced as he tugged on Laken and Baylor. Cirque walked right through Summer and a surge of emotion shot through Laken.

"Hey!" Laken's jaw tensed as a rope of frustration tightened within him.

"Hey what?" Cirque expression blank.

"Hey, let's get going," Laken said as he took the lead.

Laken wasn't used to trying and move in the Angelic world through the middle world. It was too hard to see up. When they walked into the cellar wall, they decided to head upstairs and then outside where there wasn't as much in the way.

"Number Seven Hank Drive?" Cirque asked curiously as they passed the front of the house.

"Aaagh, yeah," Laken said, paying little attention to the question. He looked up, trying to figure out where they were. They walked down the street, went through a couple houses.

"Wish we never saw Miss Nerbit in her sleeping attire. I may never close my eyes again," gagged Dave.

The boys passed right under Grog and Zog.

"Owww!" Laken gasped, shaking the hand holding Cirque.

"Sorry," apologized Cirque. Laken's muscles tightened as he awaited Grog's hands, sucking him towards him and then evaporating him, but it never happened. The group sped up to catch up to Malgor, who was now walking at a brisk pace towards the outer gates. The boys ended up going through two more houses and a pizzeria as they kept pace. The main gates swung open, and Malgor exited, heading towards the lake. Laken jumped as a hooded man appeared out of nowhere. Malgor jumped slightly, too, but Laken could tell the visit was expected. They began to talk.

"We need to get to the real world if we are going to hear them," Cirque pointed up as Laken and Baylor cupped their hand to their ear, trying to hear the muffled conversation. Laken walked the other boys twenty feet further, behind a large tree, and then transferred them to the Angelic world. The boys all sucked in a breath of air that had been forced out of them, and then peered out from behind the tree.

Malgor was talking about some sort of plan, when the hooded man held up his hand to quiet him.

"The plan worked! Tonight, the Chosen One dies!" a dark voice rang out, and the hooded turned and faced the three boys.

"I don't care what Heath says, run!" Dave screamed. Everything happened so fast, wind from an army of wings was being forced on them from above, as a group of Angels thudded to the ground around them. Laken looked up to see a massive sword crash down upon his head, and then disintegrate. Baylor already had his massive sword out and was countering the attack of three Angels that were half his size. His speed and quickness had the Angels confused. A hand gripped Laken's arm followed by the sound of burning, and an agonizing scream. Laken reached into his sac and pulled out his sword, and slashed across the face of the man holding his charred hand.

"Elves. Lots of them, with bows," Dave called out. Out of the corner of Laken's eye he saw Elves with huge bows appear out of nowhere. There was a sharp 'twang' from a multitude of bows, followed by as many arrows whistling through the wind. With a snap from his back, Laken's massive wings had formed a protective shield around the three boys, knocking several Angels back. Laken felt the wings shudder as if in pain as the thuds from twenty plus arrows embedded into them. Laken's wings shot back outward sending four more Angels soaring into the lake. Laken looked to see Cirque lying on the ground in a fetal position.

"You have to be kidding me!" Dave hissed, his expression changing quickly. "Watch out!"

Laken looked up just in time to dive out of the way of a massive club covered in spikes. The club shook the ground as it struck. Laken rolled to his feet and faced the huge Ogre.

"That thing is bigger than Baylor!" Dave said in shock.

"Hit hard!" the Ogre's numa said.

"That doesn't help," Dave said as the Ogre raised the club over his head and slammed it back down at Laken. Laken dove out of the way again, the club catching his cloak, and pinning him to the ground, like a dog who reaches the end of his chain. Laken yanked at his cloak, desperately trying to free it from the club.

"Grab him and kill him!" the Ogre's numa said. Laken looked up in horror as the Ogre leaned down with his massive hands. *Bam*, Laken's right wing crashed into the Ogre and the lodged club, sending both sailing to the ground. Laken heard another volley of arrows being released, and Laken's wings performed as a shield again, shaking one more time at impact. The wings returned to outstretched position, sending the Ogre sailing yet again.

From above, Laken felt an incredible thrust of heat bearing down on him. He looked up to see a house-sized Dragon with fire shooting from its mouth some hundred feet above, diving straight for him. Laken's right wing flipped upward blocking the blast of fire, the inner part of the wing turning bright red.

The wing retracted and Dave screamed, "Watch out! Malgor!"

Laken looked at Malgor, hand was now up, and a force shot from him that hit the three boys, sending them flying thirty yards and splashing into the lake. Laken looked up to see the Dragon smash into the ground they had just been standing on, Angels being crushed beneath its massive feet. In a saddle, attached around the dragon's neck, was a small Goblin controlling the Dragon's movements and actions with reins made out of chains wrapped around the Dragon's head. The Goblin slapped the reins and sent the Dragon charging, fire spitting from its mouth burning everything in its path.

Cirque was gurgling water and screaming like a sissy. Baylor stood up in the lake, though Laken's feet couldn't touch the bottom. Baylor thrust his sword out in a battle position, looking as if he were ready to die if need be.

"Wow," Dave gasped. The Dragon reached the water's edge, reared its head back and whipped forward, shooting flames toward the three boys. With a pop, the boys were back in Summer's basement, Cirque still screaming, Baylor's sword still out in front, and Laken holding onto both of them. Each of their cloaks were blackened and singed.

"Well, I'd say that went fairly well," Laken said with a black, soot-covered grin.

CHAPTER TWENTY-NINE
Laken vs Lord Brone

As Laken, Baylor, and Cirque exited the Portal into the Dragon's den, they noticed Heath and Peyton sitting somberly on their bed.

"You will not believe…" but Laken's words were cut off as Gabriel stepped into view, his blues eyes glaring in rage. There was a long, uncomfortable pause as Laken looked over at Peyton, then Heath, who just stared down at the floor.

"Gabriel, we have proof…" but Laken was cut short again as Malgor stepped out from behind Gabriel. A snide look covered his face.

"Him! He tried to kill us!" Laken cried out as he shook his finger vigorously at him.

Malgor gave a crooked smile. Then, in a calm cold voice, denied it. "Kill you? I saved your life."

"Saved my life? Saved my life! You had Elves, Dragons, little Goblins attack me, and you saved my life?" Laken's face turned scarlet.

"Who saved you from that Dragon?" A hateful smile snaked across Malgor's face.

"Not you. You shot me a hundred feet with some evil power. It was just your bad luck that you didn't wait and let the Dragon stomp me out." Laken's voice was rising.

"YOU LEFT EDEN!" Gabriel's angry voice brought instant silence to the room. Laken tried to look up at Gabriel, but he couldn't meet his gaze.

"We, we, we trying…"

"TRYING TO GET YOURSELF KILLED!" Gabriel's voice trembled with anger.

"Malgor is a murderer. He had us ambushed!" Laken's head shot back up in defiance.

Gabriel took in a deep breath, then slowly exhaled. "Malgor saved your life!"

"You weren't there! He tried to kill us!" Frustration welled inside him, swirling like lava. "Malgor is a teacher at Dogma, he has an oath that does not allow him to ever harm a student!" Gabriel's voice echoed through the room.

"Secondly, Malgor is an Angel. His Magic, if trying to harm you, would have no effect on you. Since it was meant to save you, it threw you out of harm's way." Gabriel's pained expression eased. "Laken, I said to trust me! Trust means you don't go following Malgor out of the Garden in the middle of the night, where there is no protection."

Laken looked back down at his foot as it scraped the floor.

"I expected much more from this den!" Gabriel's gaze swept to each boy. Laken's heart felt like it dropped into his stomach. "As punishment, this den will not be allowed to compete in the Den Championship."

"Come on..." Peyton said, but stopped as Gabriel's glowing blue eyes turned to him.

"Furthermore, you are confined to this den for the rest of the semester. You may only leave to eat and go to class!" At that Gabriel and Malgor whisked past Laken, Baylor, and Cirque and disappeared into the Portal.

Laken's tale of what happened seemed to brighten the mood a little among the den members. Cirque's recollection had him saving Laken's life with three well-placed arrows into the Ogre's back, and defeating two Angels single-handedly.

"Hey, let's watch it on the numanator!" Heath suggested eagerly as they finished up the story.

Laken pulled the numanator out of his sac, Dave spit in it, and the events unfolded on the holographic picture.

"Defeated two Angels? You're lying on the ground sucking your thumb!" Peyton cried out with laughter. "What, did they trip over you?" he quipped as all the boys except Cirque began to laugh.

"It *does* look like Malgor saved your life." Heath's lips twisted. "He could have attacked you a dozen times before that," he pointed out as they watched Malgor in the distance. "He seems to just be watching you. Actually, he looks concerned."

"He knows his Magic won't work on me. That's why he isn't wasting his time. Probably thought he could drown me in the lake!" Laken argued.

It took Laken a few hours to fall asleep that night. He kept playing back the events of the night, trying to come up with something, anything, that proved Malgor was trying to kill him. Finally, he found himself lying next to Summer, and everything seemed safe again.

A shudder from Laken's back woke him suddenly.

"Aaaaagh!" came a woman's scream from above.

"What the – ? Get out of my house!" a rough man's voice hollered from the same place. Laken's head shot up off the plywood bed. Summer's body sprang up, her head shifting left and right as she tried to find where the screams were coming from. There was a bright red glow that came down the stairwell. Then an explosion, and a blood curdling scream that sounded like Carla.

"Jack! Jack! What did you do, you monster?"

Then another red light, another crash, and then silence.

Laken jumped in front of Summer as she made her way behind the furnace. Laken could feel his heart pumping like it was trying to break free from his chest. A black cloak hovered above each step as it descended the rickety stair case. The cloak glided down until a hooded figure appeared in the dimly lit basement. Burnt and blackened hands extended from the sleeves of the cloak. The figure paused, and Laken could tell Summer was holding her breath, trying to be invisible. The dark figure turned, and the basement's dim light illuminated the cloaked face. Summer let out a whimper of fear. The figure slowly glided towards Summer while removing the hood.

"That is one ugly dude!" Dave's voice caught in a whisper. The figure's skin looked burnt, and there were large cracks in the skin where a red burning light showed through. His eyes looked like they were on fire, except for the deep black centers.

"He has horns! The freak has horns," Dave cried out. Where his nose should have been, were two slits like a serpent would have, moving in rhythm to the beast's breathing.

"Hello, Summer!" the cold, empty voice said. Summer let out a scream like Laken had never heard before. The monster in Laken was alive; it clawed to get out. Laken shot a force unlike any he'd ever used towards the creature. There were sparks, fire, and a connection between the two of them. The figure just stood there. No pain. Then a deathly smile filled his blackened face. The ember glow under his skin glowed hotter as if the fire was being stoked.

"Summer, I believe Laken has arrived!" the cold voice echoed in the basement. Laken's chest tightened. "Aaagh, Dark Magic. I didn't expect this from Gabriel's pupil." His words pinned Laken in place. "Gabriel, who does not know the power of Dark Magic, has never taught you that the Arts of the Fallen need fear to connect to." A smile slithered across his face. "I have no fear, so...." He paused. "It does not affect me. Let me demonstrate." The figure raised its bloodless hand towards Summer, and fire connected her to his hand. As she was thrown backwards into the wall, she cried out in pain.

"Noooooo!" Laken screamed, and the figure freed Summer from the fiery grasp. Laken dropped his hands to his side, releasing his magical connection to Brone.

"Good! You are teachable." His expression recoiled like a snake that just struck. "Now, I cannot hear you, but I believe I know your response to my demands." The cold voice sounded confident. "You have twenty-four hours to return to this house, in this dimension. Failure to do so will result in the painful death of Summer, here. If you tell anyone, I will know, and I will kill her!" He shot another small burst of fire causing Summer's body to gyrate in pain.

"No, Laken, don't. Please. Don't…Aaaghh!" a blast of fire interrupted her plea. Laken hurled his body into the flames, but they went right through him. He then jumped on the creature, hit, kicked, but it was like a shadow trying to hit a tree.

"You will need to locate the Portal of Emere! Hurry along. You have less than twenty-four hours to go!"

Laken forced himself to exit the middle world, and sprang from the floor in the center of the den.

His mind raced.

"How in the world do we find the Portal of Emere?" Dave asked. Laken ran over to his bed, grabbed his sac and thrust his hands into it, desperately rummaging around.

"See you guys down at breakfast!" Baylor called from somewhere in the distance.

"There it is!" Laken yanked his hand out of the sac holding the Rhema.

"Portal of Emere, Portal of Emere!" Dave screamed out. Laken thrust the book open.

Restricted in bold red ink covered both pages.

"What the heaven!" Laken screamed as he slammed the Rhema closed.

"Portal of Emere!" Dave shouted

Laken forced the Rhema open again. *Restricted* it read again. Laken threw the Rhema up against the wall knocking one of the hanging flames out.

Laken looked over at Heath who was getting dressed for the day.

"Hey, you look like you just saw a human!" Heath said as Laken ran over, grabbing him by the shoulders.

"Where is the Portal of Emere?" Laken pleaded, while he shook Heath's shoulders.

"Calm down!" Heath said as he pried himself free of Laken's grasp. "Why do you want to know?" curiosity played across his expression.

"I, I, I can't tell you! As a friend, I need your help, no questions asked." Laken's hands shook Heath's shoulders again.

"Alright, Alright. The Portal of Emere is used for Angels to go into your world. It's used mainly to go over and give messages, warnings, to humans." Heath eyed him with concern.

"No, where is it?" Laken pleaded, trying to grab Heath again, but he slipped out of his grasp.

"Well, I don't know. Let's look it up in the Rhema," Heath reached into his sac.

"No, it's not in there!" Laken cried, searching around the room as if there might be an answer somewhere.

"If I wanted to know something, I wouldn't waste my time on Heath. Go right to Autumn," Peyton said as he put his sandals on.

"Great idea!" Laken rushed to the Portal.

"Thanks a lot, friend," Heath yelled back as Laken felt his body leave his den and enter the Great Hall.

Laken's eyes frantically searched the room for Autumn.

"There!" Dave cried out. Autumn sat with three other girls from her den. Laken rushed to where she was, bumping into a number of students, knocking a plate of food out of a cherub's hands.

"Autumn!"

Autumn looked over at him, shot him a dirty look, and then went back to talking to her girlfriends.

"Autumn, hghghgh!" Laken panted, trying to catch his breath as he put a hand on her shoulder.

She yanked it free. "What do you want?"

"Autumn, it's an emergency. I'm sorry I was a jerk, but I need your help."

"You *were* a jerk!" Autumn turned her back on him again.

"Come on! Please, I'm begging you!"

Maybe it was the tone of his voice, maybe she was in a forgiving mood. He didn't care. Autumn paused, stood up facing him and said, "Fine, but make it quick."

"Thank you. Thank you. I need to know where the Portal of Emere is located!"

"Why?" She regarded him for a moment.

"I…can't…tell…you." Laken said enunciating each syllable slowly, panting in between each word.

"Well, if you are going to be rude…" Autumn turned around again. Laken grabbed her shoulder.

"Please, it is very important," Laken said softly, his big brown eyes seem to radiate his plea for help. Autumn turned around slowly, looking like she was in deep thought.

"I don't know where, but I can look in my Rhema."

"No, it is restricted," Laken murmured. "Is there anyone at Dogma smarter than you or Heath…"

But just as Laken spoke, the Portal came into view.

"I have it!" Laken said, grabbing Autumn's hand. "Follow me," he said, pulling her to the Portal. Autumn nearly tripped several times trying to keep up.

"Riddle room, or big brain room, no, no room of questions and answers, no ROOM OF CONUNDRUM," Dave finally shouted out as they entered the portal.

The bright light made them both squint and look down.

A riddle I have to give,
A riddle I have for you,

Answer me correctly
And two answers I have for you.
Go you won't, stay you will,
Portal you will see,
When an answer is given to me…"

"Hey where did the Portal go?" Autumn asked turning around in place.

"It is greater than the Almighty and more evil than the Fallen. The poor have it, the rich need it and if you eat it you'll die. What is it?"

The high-pitched sing-songy voice rang the riddle out.

"Laken, what is going on?" Autumn demanded.

"The way the room works is, if we answer the riddle, then we get to ask the big brain over there two questions." Laken pointed at the massive brain in the middle of the room.

"That's creepy," Autumn whispered in Laken's ear.

"I brought you, because if I came in here alone, I would spend an eternity with riddle boy over there," Laken said, his eyes wide.

"Ok, so one more time with the riddle," Autumn shouted, as if the brain had no ears.

"It is greater than the Almighty and more evil than the fallen. The poor have it, the rich need it and if you eat it you'll die. What is it?"

"Greater than the Almighty?" Autumn was speaking to herself. "More evil than the Fallen? Hmm! Well there is nothing greater than the Almighty, nothing more evil than the Fallen, the poor have nothing, and the rich need nothing," she concluded. "Nothing, the Answer is *Nothing!*" Autumn hollered.

"Right you are, right you be, ask two questions and correct answers you will get from me." As the voice said this the Portal appeared.

"Who asks the question?" Autumn asked.

"Answer to question one of two is either of you." The high voice responded.

"Oh my Almighty! You wasted a question!" Laken snapped.

"Sorry!" Autumn's expression tightened.

"Oh, mighty brain, where is the Portal of Emere?" Laken said loudly and slowly.

"Answer to question two of two is South of the plains of Gilboah, past the sands of Gath, before the waters of Gilgad, and it is in the heart of Death's Triangle of the Three G's." Chills ran up Laken's spine as the voice finished.

"Where in the world is that?" Dave cried out.

"It would be cool if I had an extra question right now," Laken snapped at Autumn with a look of desperation.

"Gilboah, Gath, Gilgad? The three G's? How in the world do I find that?" Laken threw his hands up. At that, Laken felt a massive shake came from his back.

"The wings say they know," Dave said with a grin.

Laken grabbed Autumn's hand and pulled her into the Portal.

"Garden," Dave intoned, and Laken and Autumn stepped out into the cool garden. The sun was just rising over the horizon, the wind whipped through their hair.

"Gotta go. Thanks," Laken said without hesitation.

"Wait," Autumn said as she grabbed his arm. "You're not really going to the Portal are you?" Laken caught her worried look. Laken looked into her eyes not realizing how close their faces were.

"I'll be back. I promise." Laken smiled, and then without thinking, he leaned in and kissed her. Though it was just a moment, it felt like the connection had been birthed in eternity. Dave screamed, did back flips, while Laken's heart was trying to come out his mouth. Their lips separated, and Laken's eyes opened to see a look of utter surprise flicker across Autumn's face. To Laken's relief, it was replaced with a big beautiful smile.

Laken turned and ran towards the gate, Dave screaming, "If we die today, this is the way I want to go!"

CHAPTER THIRTY
Dagon's Wings

Laken unfolded out of the middle world outside of the gates, and instantly, his wings were out and he was soaring through the air. Laken was surprised at how the wings understood the urgency. They beat against the air vigorously, unlike they ever had.

"Bet we would beat Gabriel's record for sure if they flapped like this at the obstacle course," Dave shouted over the deafening wind rushing past them.

They flew over forests, deserts, and rivers. The wings climbed out of sight when they approached a city.

"Probably for safety reasons?" Dave suggested. The air was cool, and the speed felt exhilarating.

"What's the plan?" Dave asked over and over again.

"Don't know." Laken's mind was having trouble figuring out how to take care of the one he assumed was Brone.

"I say we go in, kill Rick, rescue Summer, go home and kiss Autumn," Dave said.

"Seems like a good plan," Laken agreed with a grin.

"Wings say, 'Almost there'," Dave hollered as they dove below the clouds, and the sandy desert below presented itself. "That's a lot of sand," he added, as they looked left, right and saw nothing but sand.

With a thud, Laken's feet sank ankle deep into the sand as they landed. Laken's wings sent sand into the air as they beat to keep Laken's balance. Laken felt the pop in his back that meant the wings were put away.

"Get down," Dave said abruptly. Laken fell to his stomach.

"Over there." He pointed at a light shooting up into the air some 50 feet.

"That must be the Portal," Dave said cautiously. Laken got up to walk towards the Portal, when his wings sprung to life forcing him back down. Then with a thud they were gone again.

"I guess I should stay down," Laken said with some sarcasm. Then he saw it. Like a desert mirage. There were three qwerub angels, semi-translucent, like they had a camouflage to them.

"The inability to see them was the least of our problems." Dave said with awe. "They must be twice the size of Zog!"

"Their flaming swords alone are the size of Zog!" Laken whispered. "I guess they don't let just anyone travel through the Portal."

"You think?" Dave shook his head.

"So what, or how, do we get through?

"I got it. Middle world," Dave said with excitement.

"Great idea," Laken answered as he forced them into the basement of the middle world.

Laken was glad Brone and Summer weren't in the basement. From the sound of the muffled cry, they were upstairs. It took everything in him to stay focused on getting through to the Portal. He walked through the basement walls until he was sure he was well past the house. When he was under the first qwerub, Dave tried lightening the mood.

"Check out the qwerub underpants."

"Stop!" Laken muttered as he kept walking. "Alright, we are under the Portal, where do you think we come out?"

"My guess is it works like the one at the school," Dave shrugged.

"Sounds good to me."

With a pop, they returned from the middle world, jumped into the Portal, Dave screaming, "Jack's house!"

Laken felt himself being sucked from the world, air gone, everything a shadow; and then the tiny living room appeared. Brone was sitting at the table, Summer huddled in the corner, and Jack's and Carla's bodies under rubble next to her. Laken's feet felt the floor connect, and then his legs collapsed. Something went wrong. He felt lifeless. He wanted to get up, fight, do something, but nothing would move.

"At least open your eyes," Dave screamed, but he couldn't.

Was he dead already?

"That seemed quick, but painless," Laken grimaced.

"Oh, the journey through the Portal of Emere. I, too, learned the hard way that it was made for Angels, not humans," a cold voice said from so very far away.

Laken heard a scream that sounded like Summer. Laken was able to pry his eyes half open to see that everything was a blur. He could feel a foreboding presence. Somewhere in the blur, he could see something dark coming towards him.

"Takes a minute or so for the lag to wear off. *So* sorry you won't be around to witness it." The words seem to slither out. Laken felt his body thrust into the air and smashed into what must have been the ceiling. Pain shot through Laken's body, as dust and debris filled his lungs. He attempted to scream through the coughing and hacking from his lungs. Something wet was soaking into the back of his cloak.

"Do wish I had time for a fair fight, but I have to kill Summer and then take over the world. I've got a lot on my plate."

As the name 'Summer' was uttered, Laken felt a pop from his back, and with a cold scream of pain, Laken's body hit the floor. Laken's eyes began to focus, and he could see his massive wings beating the air, the force pinning Brone against the wall. Laken shook his head and with a rush of adrenaline, his body felt alive. Laken reached into his sac, and his sword seemed to jump into his hand. Laken yanked the sword out of the sac, holding it out in front of him. Laken was surprised to see the sword had a slight red glow to the blade that had never been there before. There was a rhythm to it that pulsated in time with Brone's breathing.

"What do you say we do this thing fair, little Ricky," Laken said, sounding out of breath as his wings settled into an outstretched position.

Brone let out a soft, eerie cackle. "I wouldn't say it will be fair," he said softly as he raised his right hand and electricity shot out, hitting Laken square in the chest. Laken felt a slight tickle that made him smile. The electricity stopped as Brone let his hand fall to his side. "No fear? Interesting," Brone eyed him with varying of expressions. "You would be valuable to the Fallen. Wish I didn't have to kill you for the ring." He sounded as droll, as if he were telling Laken about the weather.

Laken looked over at the blue light floating in the corner. "Why don't you just leave us alone and go through the Portal back to the angelic world?" Laken said pointing at the blue light.

"Oh, silly fool. Only the one who entered the Portal can go back through. I do wish it were that easy." Brone's gaze shifted to Summer who had finished crying and had replaced her tears with a look of angry determination.

"Well, if you have no fear, I guess I will have to produce some," Brone laughed as his hand outstretched towards Summer, a jet of light shooting into her.

"AAAAAGH!" her screams pierced the air. Laken's back shook, then popped, and Laken's wings were on their own, soaring through the air, colliding into Brone, smashing him through the living room wall and out into the yard. The wings were off Brone in a second, back through the newly formed hole and, to Laken's amazement, attached to Summer.

"Traitor!" Dave said

"No, it's better that she's safe," Laken nodded.

"Watch out!" Dave screamed, just in time for Laken to see a table flying towards him. He dove and rolled as the table smashed into the wall where he had been just seconds earlier. Laken's eyes flitted to where Brone was, and then Brone was gone, and a pain struck Laken in the back, sending him skidding through the kitchen door, his sword flying out of his hand. Laken was up in an instant.

"Duck!" Dave screamed, and Laken rolled under a flying refrigerator which crashed into the sink, sending water shooting into the air. Laken frantically searched for his sword, and then, as if his sword had a mind of its own, it flew into his hand. Laken looked over at Brone who was smiling.

"Impressive!" he said. Brone slowly reached into his sac and pulled out a sword engulfed in, but not destroyed by, black flames.

"His numa!" Dave reminded. Laken quickly changed his focus to the dark numa sitting on Brone's shoulder.

"Pipe!" it screamed. Laken knew instantly it was the one behind him. Diving to the left, the pipe missed him by inches and imbedded itself in the wall.

"Downward strike!" Brone's numa screamed, and Laken dodged left as Brone instantly appeared in front of him, sword crashing down where he was a millisecond earlier. Laken slashed, cutting into Brone's ribs. The sword emitted a blinding red flash at the point of impact. Brone instantly disappeared with a howl of pain, reappearing in the next room. Brone looked down where his cloak was ripped, a small stain of blood forming.

"Very impressive!" Brone said, tapping the flame-engulfed blade with his black finger.

"Refrigerator, downward strike, side strike, table!" Brone's numa yelled.

"Holy overload!" Dave screamed out as a refrigerator crashed into Laken and a sword came slicing down toward him. Laken's sword forced his arm up, blocking the downward plunge, and he felt a snap in his arm. A searing pain shot through it. Then his arm went limp, the sword crashing to the ground. Something then struck him from the side and the sound of flesh tearing was followed by intense pain careening across his chest. Then, he felt what must be the table crash into his face and pin him between the wall and the table. Water cascaded down on him, making it hard to catch a breath as he coughed and sputtered.

Laken heard what sounded like sirens in the distance.

"Come out and put your hands up," a voice called out.

"Of course," Brone's voice rang out with sardonically, and then Laken heard screams, that were quickly drowned out by a series of explosions.

Laken felt the sword find his left hand. "Destroy the table!" Dave screamed out. Laken allowed the beast in him to shatter the table.

"Why didn't we use that earlier?" Dave complained. Laken scanned the empty room, and then with a pop, Brone appeared, his lifeless lip curling. Laken could feel his heart pumping blood out of his chest with each beat. He began to feel like he was going to faint. Everything was going in and out of focus. Brone began to glide slowly towards him.

"Downward strike for the kill!" the blackened numa droned.

Laken blinked slowly as he felt his consciousness wane, and when his eyes opened he saw his wings expanding from Summer, and with a great force, knock Brone back through the wall out into the yard. Then something had him.

"This is it!" Dave sighed. Laken forced his eyes open for what he thought would be his last look at life. "What?" Dave whimpered.

Laken used all his strength to blink, and when he opened his eyes again he saw that Summer had him in her grasp.

"Portal!" Laken gasped. His eyes closed, and then he forced them back open.

A scream. Was it his? Was it Summer's? Then a bright light, and he felt nothing.

He was nothing.

He was dead.

When he opened his eyes, a flaming sword flashed before his face, the heat from it grazing his face. The sound of flapping wings pounded in his ears. Laken blinked and opened his eyes again. Summer seemed to be moving backwards with him.

"That's weird," Dave said, barely audible.

Laken looked out at the wings going up and down faster than he had ever seen.

"COME ON!" Laken heard Summer scream. Laken slowly turned his head to look behind only to see the qwerub's massive outstretched hand pulling them towards it. They were just feet from its grasp.

"That stupid qwerub is going to crush us like Sithius!" Dave moaned with what sounded like his last bit of energy. Then, with a lunge backwards, Laken felt the group collide with a massive hand. He opened his eyes to see the hand closing around them, and then everything went dark.

"Middle! Wo—" Dave was cut off with a pop, and everything went dark and silent.

CHAPTER THIRTY-ONE
Baylor, Why Would You?

L aken felt a heat go through his entire body. His right arm and chest burned like they were on fire, and then a tingle vibrated rapidly from his head to his toes. Laken felt a surge of energy, and he could hear voices. He slowly opened his eyes. There was an intense light overhead, and everything was white.

"Well, at least we made it to heaven," Dave said slowly.

"You had us worried!" Laken heard a calm, mothering voice say. Laken turned to see two Angels in all white looking down on him.

"Am I in heaven?" Laken moaned, and then heard a small laugh.

"No, you are in the healing ward at Dogma," the kind Angel said. Laken felt a warmth in his left hand, and looked over to see that it was Summer holding his hand. She looked at him with tears flowing down her face.

"My hero," she paused. "When you promised that you would get me out of that house, this wasn't how I imagined it," Summer leaned over and gave him a soft kiss on the forehead. Laken's face mimicked the heat from the healing.

"Alright, you are in perfect health," one of the attending Angels said helping Laken sit up.

"What? I don't know if I'm read—" Laken started to say as she forced him up. To his surprise, everything felt as good as new.

"How long have I been here?" Laken asked as he looked at the tall thin woman in all white, her gray hair pulled in a tight bun.

"Argus brought you in a couple of minutes ago. Took a little longer than we thought. You were close to dying there."

"Laken, you brave, brave young man," Gabriel's calm voice came from the corner of the room. Laken turned his head towards the voice. There was Gabriel, a big proud smile on his face. "Teressa, Mary, you mind sending the others in and giving us a few moments?"

"Of course," the two women said as they exited the room.

Laken stood up, turned towards Summer and wrapped her in a huge embrace. As the doors swung open, Laken released the hug and let his hand fall down and grab his sister's hand as his den members came running towards him.

"You crazy nut!" Baylor screamed as he shook the floor with each step.

"Taking on the Pink Bunny! Well done," Peyton yelled right behind Baylor.

"Good job, Laken!" Cirque joined in. The boys surrounded Laken, hugging, and patting him on the back. Laken looked over at Malgor slowly walking in, the door closing on its own behind him.

The boys all stepped back from Laken, turned and stared at Malgor.

"What is he doing here!" Laken growled as he looked over at Gabriel. "He's the one responsible for all this!" Laken accused. "He told Brone where Summer was!" All the boys let out a scream. Baylor's hands shot up to each ear as he shook his head, and then it became silent again.

"Don't say his name!" Peyton whined.

"That is why we are here!" Gabriel said as he glanced over each person in the room. "To find out who is responsible."

Everyone looked from person to person as if they were trying to discover who it was.

"I must say, they had me fooled all year long. But something gave it away… Malgor!" Gabriel said as his gaze fell on Malgor.

"I told you!" Laken cried out.

Gabriel turned and gave Laken a weak smile. "I had my suspicions, and then Malgor gave me the final clue," he said calmly as his gaze settled again on Malgor. "Pink Bunny," Gabriel paused and looked at Peyton,

"Pink bunny could not find Summer until…" he looked over at Laken. "Until the night you followed Malgor."

"Malgor told him where she was!" Laken said as he threw a hot glance at Malgor. Malgor shot a smirk back at him.

"So, when did Malgor find out where she was?" Gabriel asked with a hint of mocked puzzlement.

Laken thought for a moment and then it hit him. "His newspaper articles…The ones in his room. One of them said they found two babies, and had the information on where we were." Laken said looking triumphant.

"Think, Laken. *Why wait so long to tell the Pink Bunny?* Why not take care of you years ago?" Gabriel gave Laken a curious glance. "Who was there the night you went outside the garden and found out where Summer was?" Gabriel smiled as he saw surprise turn into revelation on Laken's face.

"Baylor?" Laken asked softly, as ropes appeared and wrapped around Baylor. Baylor began to scream but with a flash of Gabriel's hand was silenced.

"All along! Acting like my friend!" Laken scolded as the animal in him rose. "You almost killed Summer!"

"Laken, stop. Justice will be done." And with that Laken felt his body sucked from its spot and he was standing in front of the bridge leading up to Grog and Zog at the entrance gates. Laken looked around at Gabriel, Heath, Peyton, Summer, Cirque, Malgor and the bound Baylor.

"As we get close to the gates, Zog will sense Baylor is not Baylor, and that he does not belong. We all know what happens then," Gabriel said somberly. Laken instinctively grabbed Summer's hand and she looked at him wide-eyed, wondering what would happen.

Gabriel, who was behind the group, began to usher them towards the front gate.

"Uh, hey, why not just let Baylor go up by himself?" Cirque suggested nervously.

"I think it is perfect justice for us as a den to be there with him," Gabriel said as he gave Cirque a nudge from the back.

"No, no, I don't want to see it," Cirque stammered as he whipped around behind Gabriel.

Laken couldn't believe his eyes as ropes wrapped around Cirque, and disappeared from Baylor. Baylor stood in surprise as he rubbed his skin where the ropes had been.

"What?" Laken cried out. Gabriel smiled at Laken then looked over at Cirque. "I had to watch my numanator to see how you passed Zog on that first day. Genius, I must say. Poor Sithius made quite a sacrifice.

"Your total lack of skill at the bow should have given you away. I, like the rest of us, thought you were so girl crazy that you didn't practice. That's not true, Garakus, your weapon is actually a sword if I remember correctly."

Gabriel waved his hand and Cirque's beautiful blonde hair turned black. His perfect features became jagged and oversized. He transformed into the total opposite of Cirque – dark, putrid gray skin, crooked teeth, large red goat-sized horns on his head, silver beady eyes, and a scar across his neck.

"Very good. Slow, my old friend, but good!" Garakus' voice was much deeper than Cirque's.

"You! It was you!" Laken cried.

"You stupid, idiot! Losing the D.C. for us!" Peyton said as he kicked Garakus in the shin.

"Easy, Peyton," Gabriel said as Garakus danced in place trying to avoid the next shot from Peyton. Peyton turned, gave one more kick and then stepped back.

Just then Argus and Gorgus showed up sounding out of breath. "Came as quick as possible, haaa, haaa." Argus said leaning over grabbing his side.

"You are getting old there Argus," Gorgus said with a smile.

"Thank you, Argus and Gorgus" Gabriel said as his eyes became intense on Garakus.

"The clue? What clue?" Laken suddenly remembered.

"Oh, yes. Malgor told me the night of the attack that Baylor fought valiantly while Cirque had lain on the ground doing nothing. Then when Laken and Summer showed up at the gates, it all made sense," Gabriel said with a sense of satisfaction.

"Garakus, the fire and the poison would be easy to get into Eden. The snake egg, as large as it is, puzzles me." Gabriel looked over towards Garakus, who threw back a sneer.

"Gabriel, Gabriel," Garakus said slowly and with an air of pride. "Always underestimating the Fallen." He let out a small evil laugh. "You think I work alone? That I'm the only one who has breached your safe haven?" He cast a sideways glance at Malgor, then his gaze flitted across the garden. "We have a small army in here, waiting, waiting for the true Chosen One. I did do the fire, but I didn't do the poison, and I wish I had come up with the egg." Garakus paused to look at Laken. "Oh, you have many enemies here. You will die, and so will all your friends." He finished with his lip curling in profane manner.

Gabriel stared at Garakus for a moment, then looked over to the gate. Grog, will you please come down here?" Gabriel's summons echoed through the garden.

"Right away, sir." A deep rustled voice sounded back.

"The Dark Lord will return. He will return!" Garakus began to shriek. The tremors of the ground moving from each of Grog's steps stopped twenty feet up the bridge. Laken looked over at Grog where a look of anger flitted across his face. Grog's arm shot out, and with a whoosh, "He will returrrrn!" ended with a thud into Grog's hand. Then a 'pop' and Garakus was gone.

"He will not be returning today, Cirque boy!" Peyton said as the group let out a chuckle.

"Where did he go? What happened?" Summer said looking at Laken then to Gabriel.

"To Dante's Hold, awaiting judgment," Gabriel answered with that fatherly smile.

"Cirque was trying to do you in all along!" Peyton cried out.

"I guess so, and it sounds like he had some help," Laken said. "How did he know where Sumer lived?" he started to ask, but then answered his own question almost immediately. "Summer's address. He was very interested in Number Seven Hank Drive the night we followed Malgor."

"What about the Oath of Furies?" Laken's gaze turned back to Gabriel.

Gabriel's expression turned from puzzlement to pain. "I forgot about the Oath," he said shaking his head. "I can only make a guess, but I'm quite sure I am right." Gabriel paused as a look of pain settled across his face. "Garakus's soul was already so torn, so rotted and destroyed, that the Oath could not do any more harm to it." His eyes grew moist and he looked away.

There was another long pause as the birds chirped overhead, and a herd of Centaurs came galloping past.

"But, Malgor, I heard your numa say you must kill me," Laken said. Reading everyone's reactions he caught himself, but it was too late.

"You heard his numa?"

"What do you mean you heard his numa?" The barrage of questions was thrown out like darts from all around.

"Laken is a *whisperer*," Gabriel announced and deafening silence hit the group.

"A whisper what?" Peyton said.

"A whisperer, one who can hear other people's numas. There have only been two other documented whisperers in 6000 years," Heath explained matter-of-factly.

"Whatever. That doesn't matter. The point is I heard your numa!" Laken exclaimed to Malgor.

"When?" Malgor snapped, a look of awkwardness settled on his face.

Simultaneously Gabriel intervened, "I'm sure what you heard isn't what he meant."

"The night you were introduced as a professor. The first night at Dogma," Laken insisted. Malgor thought for a moment, took out his numanator from his sac, and then replayed the event. At the time the numa spoke, Malgor was looking at Cirque who was standing close to Laken.

"I suspected him all along. I had overheard that the Fallen had a spy here, but they would not trust me to the identity," Malgor said calmly. "I thought it was Cirque or Baylor. After the fire, I spent many nights in your room watching over you, and trying to find any clue. But Garakus was good, and he was onto me. He made me the suspect, and kept the attention off himself. The night of the fire he was in the room planting the fire."

At this, Laken felt Summer squeeze his hand, and his thoughts turned to his sister who was with them.

"Can Summer stay?" Laken turned to Gabriel and asked warmly.

"Since I don't know how to get her back without going through the Portal of Emere, I would say so." He welcomed Summer with a huge smile.

"Now, Laken I do have one question for you," Gabriel said as he walked towards Summer and Laken. Gabriel stopped right in front of the two them. Laken and Summer were still holding hands. "Dave did not pick Cirque from the Unicorn den, did he?"

"I told you to listen to me," Dave said heatedly.

"No, I picked him," Laken said as he looked down.

"Ask Dave who is to be in the Dragons den," Gabriel said kindly.

Laken turned to Dave. "So, who is it? Say Autumn. Say Autumn!" Laken pleaded in his head.

Dave looked around, then back to Laken. "Summer."

Laken looked in utter surprise, then turned to Gabriel and said, "My sister?"

Gabriel flashed him a knowing smile, the garden gave off an unusual warmth, and a drizzle of rain began to fall. "Your sister she is not, because that would make you my grandson, and we know that isn't true." He smiled again. Everyone looked around in amazement. "Yes, Summer, you are my granddaughter, and I have gone to great lengths to protect you, and your identity."

Gabriel looked warmly at Summer who looked over at Laken, then to Gabriel.

"What...how...who? We're not brother and sister?" Summer's gaze settled on Laken.

"Not our sister?" Dave said puzzled. Laken's hand that had held Summer's for hundreds of hours before, now felt hot and sweaty. He looked at Summer and noticed her hair, her eyes, her smile in a different way than ever before. The monster in him stirred.

"She is hot!" Dave said loudly.

Summer looked over at Dave and said, "Dave? That is rude!"

"What?" Laken blurted out.

Summer smiled broadly at Laken. "Oh, Laken. I could hear your little monster all along. I just wanted you to feel special."

CHAPTER THIRTY-TWO
Goodbye Hot Mom

Laken felt faint. It felt like an eternity passed since he'd been able to take a breath.

"Need….air….can't…..breathe!" Dave gasped.

"Mbbtththtblkk!" was all Laken could say, his face forced into a large cloak. Finally, there was a release, and Laken fell to the ground, landing on Peyton and Heath. Baylor had finally released his bear hug.

"I don't know how I am going to make it over the summer without you guys!" Baylor said over the hacking and coughing noises made by the three other den members sprawled out on the ground like a game of Twister gone bad.

"That's one of us, you big dumb oaf! I almost passed out!" Peyton gasped out as he got up.

"A few more seconds of that hug and you would be missing us for a lot longer," Heath stood to his feet straightening out his cloak.

"We are actually going to miss him," Dave said as Laken took in one last big breath of fresh air and got to his feet.

Another perfect day in Eden. A cool breeze brushed across Laken's face, bringing in the smell of flowers blossoming. Laken shook the kinks out of his body as he glanced over at Grog, then Zog, then to the huge open gate leading to Outer Eden. Kids were exiting the gate on this last day of school. Many with their arms around each other, talking and laughing. Shout outs were exchanged left and right by the students.

"See you next semester!"

"Numa me!"

"Have a great summer!"

Parents wrapped their kids up in their arms, some swinging them around, others tossing them in the air. One way or another they all ended up in a warm embrace. Then for some it was: "Mom, stop, your embarrassing me!" or "Dad! Everyone is looking!"

Part of Laken felt like an empty hole. He didn't have anyone waiting, no loved ones that missed him.

"At least we have Summer back!" Dave reminded Laken. This filled the empty hole with a warmth. Even though Laken hadn't seen her since the day Cirque was exposed, the fact that she was in the same place as him made him happy.

Actually. Laken hadn't seen her or Gabriel since that day. Argus told Laken that Gabriel was making up for lost time with his granddaughter. Laken missed his time with Gabriel, but he understood. He desperately missed Summer, but he knew that time with a loving relative would mean the world to Summer, and for this reason he chose to be happy for her.

Laken looked up and let out a small smile as his eye caught Baylor's. "Yeah, I guess things will be kind of quiet around here, I mean with you not trying to kill me anymore and all." The boys let out a laugh, that quickly faded.

Laken's gaze was suddenly arrested. Something so, so indescribable. A beauty that was too beautiful, if that were possible. So unbelievably beautiful that it hurt. Laken felt a sharp pain inside of him. The slight breeze was brushing her golden hair off her perfect face. Every feature, every detail was perfection. She let out a smile toward the boys, and Laken felt faint, felt like he did in Baylor's embrace. Then in a voice that seemed so distant, yet was actually right next to him, he heard Baylor.

"Mom!"

Laken shook his head as if trying to rattle something back into place. "Mom?" Laken, Heath, and Peyton chorused in astonishment.

"Yeah, that's my mom!" Baylor said, as he pointed to the gorgeous woman who continued towards them.

"Baylor, I hate to inform you but I'm going to ask your mom out!" Peyton straightened his cloak.

"Stop!" Baylor argued as he gave Peyton a slight, playful shove.

"No, seriously. You may want to get used to calling me *Daddy.*'"

Baylor's face flushed red. "Stop it!" Baylor's tone sounded threatening.

"Hey! That's no way to talk to you father!" Peyton joked as Baylor's massive hand shot around his throat.

"Bay—" Peyton struggled to squeeze the word out.

"Put the boy down!" came a voice that sounded so smooth, it was as if she sang the words. Baylor's eyes turned to his mom. Then his face flushed shame rather than anger, as he released Peyton, who began to hack again. Baylor's mom opened her arms up and embraced her giant son. She barely came up to his navel.

"I missed my little Bay, Bay" she sang out. Baylor's redness took to a shade darker.

"Mom, stop!" Baylor whispered.

"I think we will all miss Bay Bay." Peyton coughed, massaging his red throat. Laken and Heath let out a controlled snicker as Baylor shot an icy glare at Peyton.

"Introduce me to your friends." Baylor's mom smiled warmly at each. Laken felt his heart pounding through his chest.

"Mom, these are my friends Laken and Heath, and this is Peyton," Baylor intoned as pointed to each.

Very nice to meet you. Gabriel has been bragging on each of you." She offered another heart-melting smile. "He told me how you got him away from those bad…" Her voice trailed off as Daeth and his gang strode by, each of them shooting Baylor a cold stare. "…bad influences," she finished. She looked to each of them. "I am truly grateful." And at that she leaned over and gave each of them a small kiss on the cheek.

All of their numas screamed, flipping, spinning, running around in circles on their shoulders.

"See you boys later. Let's go, Baylor." She smiled as she grabbed Baylor's hand and they slowly excited the gate.

"See you guys!" Baylor's voice boomed, snapping them out of the trance.

"Whose your Daddy!" Peyton called out. The boys let out a big belly laugh.

"Mermaid. That has to be it," Heath concluded as Laken and Peyton snapped their heads toward him.

"What? What are you babbling about?" Peyton said.

"Baylor's mom," Heath paused to take in the boys reaction. "Baylor's mom has to be a Mermaid," Heath said.

"How in the world would you even know that?" Peyton sounded disturbed. "Plus, owl boy, let's not forget the obvious. She has no fin."

"Of course she doesn't have a fin. She must have fallen in love with an Angel and left the Merworld. Very rare, and very dangerous." Heath's tone became serious.

"Dangerous how?" Laken's expression turned curious.

"Mer-people are very proud, and look down on Angels. They feel that to leave their world is dishonorable, and punishable by death. If Baylor's mom ever gets too close to water, well..." Heath stopped. "If they ever found out that Baylor was half-mere, it wouldn't turn out good for him either," Heath leaned in and whispered as he cautiously looked towards the Lake and then back to them. The boys stood there bug-eyed for a moment until Heath broke the silence. "That would explain Baylor's size and abilities. He is half-mere."

"And now, I have all summer to figure out how to tease him about it," Peyton added gleefully.

"No, let's wait for him to tell us." Heath said. "Plus he might not even know."

"Fine," Peyton conceded, "but when he does, I will be ready for him," Peyton smiled as he rubbed his hands together.

Laken found himself smiling, enjoying the moment with his friends. His real friends. The first friends he'd d ever had. Laken was going to miss Peyton and Heath. It hurt to think about not seeing them over the summer break. They had invited Laken to come with them, but Argus said it was forbidden and way too dangerous. Plus, he had training every day. Six hours of weapon training and two hours of flight training with his new wings. Laken missed his wings of Dagon, but he was happy that they were with Summer. He would rather she be protected anyway. Plus, he was matched with the wings he had originally wanted. They were big, beautiful, and white. But as Argus said, they were almost a whole year behind working together. "I love our wings," Dave sighed, as a warm shake hit the middle of Laken's back.

"There's mom! Gotta go!" Peyton blurted as he took off running past the gate.

"See you, Laken!" Heath gave Laken a quick hug, turned and started toward his mom. Peyton had turned into an octopus and had all eight tentacles wrapped around his mom in a hug as she kissed the bald head over and over. Heath transformed into an exact image of Peyton.

Peyton transformed back to himself whining, "No, we said no doing each other!"

"No, we said no doing each other," Heath repeated mockingly.

"Mom!"

"Mom!" Heath copied again.

"Boy's, stop. Let's get home," their mom said as she put her arms around each and led them away.

"Fine! I'm Heath, look at me, I'm soooo smart…" Laken could hear Peyton faintly say.

"Their mom is a candidate for sainthood," Dave quipped.

Laken let out a smile as he took another big breath of the fresh air. A group of fairies flittered by, flicking wisps of Laken's hair. Laken looked over and saw the squid waving to the remaining students. The whole Garden seem to be saying goodbye in its own way. Dragons overhead, spurting fire, thousands of cherubs flying about waving, Centaurs somberly looking on. Gnomes looking as if they were showing off for anyone who would look at them.

Laken thought of his den and how he would miss them. The Dragons Den had won the Lord of Dens honor. It was the first time a den had lost every month and still won. Laken's escape from Brone had garnered him 100 points for his den, and with Heath earning 50 points for perfect scores of 100 percent on every assignment and test that year, they beat out the Lambs den by 7 points.

"Still doesn't make up for losing the Den Championship!" Peyton had groaned out at the awards ceremony. "Stupid Serpents!" he said as Daeth and the others went up for their award.

"It's back to just you and me," Dave tried to sound casual.

"I guess so," Laken said as he turned to the gate for one last look. But something stopped him from turning back. Walking toward him was frail-looking woman. She couldn't have been any older than Peyton's mom, yet the years had not been kind to her. Her cheeks were sunken, and her skin was chalk white. There was no color to her skin. Her eyes were gray and cold, her numa was dark and withered. Her black hair looked sparse, and fashioned as if she were trying to use too little hair to cover too much head. Laken could see past her. Daeth waited at the gate.

"Daeth's mom," Dave whispered. She stopped a few feet from Laken and glared at him. Laken gave her a mocking smile of triumph. Then a sinister smile rose on her face.

"Yes, boy, yes… Smile now, your death will come all so soon. Lord Brone is Back! Lord Brone is Back!" The black numa cackled.

One more slice of his sword, and the ring would be his. "Downward strike for the kill!" his numa screamed out. BAM! Something hit him hard. He felt his head spin as he felt his body fly through the air. With a crash, he rolled along the grass, smashing into a large, smoldering vehicle. He raised himself up, but his head felt like it was spinning.

"Gather your senses! You are Lord Brone, Most Powerful Being in the Universe!" his numa shouted. With a shake of his head he regained his focus. "Stop playing with him, just kill him!" Then, "NOOOOOO!" his numa screamed as realization struck him. The girl and Dagon's wings had grabbed Laken, and he knew where they were headed.

"The Portal!" Brone whispered to himself. In an instant Brone was back in the house, his head turning towards where the boy had entered the room through the Portal. Just a leg was now sticking out of the Portal. Brone saw himself there, and was there in an instant. He grabbed the foot that was now disappearing into the Portal. Brone's body was squeezed from space and time. The air was gone, and that lifeless sense he remembered from so many trips into the Portal came back to him. He knew what he had to do now. He knew he had to reserve just enough energy to get far enough away from the Qwerubs.

"But the boy... The boy won't make it," Brone chuckled as he felt himself hit the sand.